*The Summer Without You*

Karen Swan was previously a fashion
editor and lives in East Sussex with her
husband and three children.

Visit Karen's website at
www.karenswan.com or you can find
Karen Swan's author page on Facebook or
follow her on Twitter @KarenSwan1.

Also by Karen Swan

*Players*
*Prima Donna*
*Christmas at Tiffany's*
*The Perfect Present*
*Christmas at Claridge's*

# *The* SUMMER WITHOUT YOU

## KAREN SWAN

PAN BOOKS

First published 2014 by Pan Books
an imprint of Pan Macmillan, a division of Macmillan Publishers Limited
Pan Macmillan, 20 New Wharf Road, London N1 9RR
Basingstoke and Oxford
Associated companies throughout the world
www.panmacmillan.com

ISBN 978-1-4472-5520-8

Copyright © Karen Swan, 2014

The right of Karen Swan to be identified as the
author of this work has been asserted by her in accordance
with the Copyright, Designs and Patents Act 1988.

3 5 7 9 8 6 4 2

A CIP catalogue record for this book is available from the British Library.

Typeset by Ellipsis Digital Limited, Glasgow
Printed and bound by CPI Group (UK) Ltd, Croydon, CR0 4YY

Visit **www.panmacmillan.com** to read more about all our books
and to buy them. You will also find features, author interviews and
news of any author events, and you can sign up for e-newsletters
so that you're always first to hear about our new releases.

*For Ollie.*

*You're golden. My son and my sun.*

# Chapter One

'We are not breaking up.'

'No? What else do you call disappearing halfway round the world for half a year without the person you've spent nearly half your life with?' Rowena Tipton did her best not to let the tears drop from her lashes, but her voice sliding up to soprano was just as telling.

'Not a half-measure?' Matt tried joking, before seeing the look he knew all too well that told him now wasn't the time. He rubbed her hands which always felt so small in his. 'I call it a new beginning.'

'But why do we need a *new* beginning? We had one eleven years ago. I like our middle.' She hiccupped, letting her hair blow in front of her face as she stared back at him with her soulful dark brown eyes – 'doe eyes', he'd always said – willing him to see reason. But the omens weren't good. It would be so much easier to talk him out of this notion under a whimsical blue sky, clouds frolicking in the wind above them and daisy chains round their wrists – it would mean her cleavage was out for a start. He could never get his way against that. But she was wrapped and swaddled, and the weather was as bleak as his words, the sky as grey as an old towel, the ancient oaks that stood around them like elders still bare and budless. Everything seemed lifeless and spent. She strained to hear the first birds of spring on their return migration, scanned the clodded ground for flowers, but the daffodils had made a poor showing this year, the bluebells not yet pushing their sharp green tips above the earth. It was mid March but nature seemed suspended. The dormancy had a scattering effect every bit as effective as a gunshot and the park was deserted, driving families inside to huddle round the last of the winter fires and leaving the unseen sun to slip from the sky for another day.

Matt tucked her hair behind her ear, his hand cupping her head so that she could rest her cheek against his palm. His tone, when he spoke, was calming, his eyes steady upon hers. 'Because our middle is flabby. We're in a rut, baby. We need to freshen things up.'

'Which is code for "see other people", you mean?'

'No, that is not what I mean. This is not a break-up, Ro.'

'What *is* it, then? You have to call it something. It's not something without a name. Nothing's anything without a name. I mean, how will I explain to peo—'

'It's a pause.'

She blinked at him, her lashes dewy with poised tears. 'A pause?'

'Before we commit to each other for the rest of our lives, it's a pause, an opportunity for us both to be selfish for the last time.'

'But I like being unselfish!' she wailed.

Matt nodded, as though he'd predicted every one of her responses. 'I know you do; it's one of the things I'll miss about you. But I also *want* to miss you, Ro. I want to feel that –' he shrugged, reaching for the word '– I don't know, that yearning for you again, and I can't if we're lying

2

together in the same bed every night and sitting on the same park bench in the same park every Sunday morning.'

'So you *have* got tired of me.' The wail was replaced with a wobble.

'No!' he laughed, exasperated. His hand dropped from her cheek and he sat back, draping his arms over the bench and looking out over the Ham corner of Windsor Great Park. The wind blew Ro's tangled not-brown, not-blonde hair across her face again as she studied his profile; it was a face she knew almost better than her own, the one that had excited her when she'd seen it for the first time among the university library stacks, the one that had soothed her when she hadn't got the 2.1 she'd craved (and needed) to win a scholarship on the post-graduate photography course that was otherwise financially out of reach, the one that made her laugh with its impressive eyebrow flexibility . . . How could she not see this face – those blue eyes with the halo of fire round the pupils, the crooked smile that veered left, the cleft chin she could almost rest her thumb in, and that thatch of almost-black hair – for six months?

He looked back at her and for the first time what she saw in that familiar face frightened her: certainty. He was going to do this. He was going to go.

'I could never tire of you. I've just tired of our routine. We've been doing this for too long already and we're only just thirty. We've been together since uni and I don't really know life without you. I don't know who I am without you. You're the love of my life, Ro, but we met too young.' He stroked her cheek tenderly. 'I need to do this. I want to be away from you specifically so that I get to come back to you. I want us to fall in love *all over again* – do you see?' His eyes searched hers, trying to see if she did, but it was hard to see anything behind the tears. Panic was overriding everything.

'No, I don't see! I don't understand why you want to go back to the "getting there" phase when I already love you.'

He shook his head. 'You're not hearing me, baby. I want us to fall again, get back that feeling of running off a cliff and realizing we can fly! I fell in love with you eleven years ago, and I am deeply *in* love with you now, but everything's too . . . cosy. I want us to shake everything up, refresh the page, come back to each other with passion. I mean, who said you can only fall in love with someone once?'

'Because that's how it works. Nobody falls in love twice.'

He dropped his dimpled chin. 'Is there a law against it?'

She knew he was taking the mickey out of her, puncturing her earnest words with a faintly mocking, bemused smile. 'There'll be some law of chemistry or something that says once a chemical reaction has occurred, it can't be repeated. It either mutates into something else or just . . . dies.'

They stared at each other. Neither one of them had taken chemistry beyond GCSE.

'And what if you meet someone else?' Her voice sounded hollow and small, scarcely up to the task of articulating such an apocalyptic thought.

'That's not going to happen. The whole point of this, Ro, is that I'm wanting to rediscover *you* again.'

'But what if you change while we're apart? Or I do? Or we both do?'

'We've been together our entire adult lives already. You really think that much can happen in six months?'

'Famous last words,' she muttered, watching a red deer graze nearby. She felt Matt take her hands in his again. She looked back at him.

'Ro, I don't want that to happen, and I don't think it will – on my life I don't – but if we're meant to spend our lives together, we'll pull through this.'

'So you're saying it *will* be difficult.'

He rewarded her with a crooked smile. He'd never won an argument against her yet. 'I'm saying it's not going to be easy. The reality is, I'm not going to be able to call regularly, maybe sometimes for a few weeks at a time.'

'A few weeks?' she spluttered.

'I don't think mobile reception is all that great in Cambodia. Anyway, that could be a good thing! We speak probably twenty times a day, but when did you last feel excited to see that it was me on the line? Or actually not hear what I was saying because you were listening to the sound of my voice? You always used to do that, but now we just talk about cleaning the fish tank or covering the bay trees before the frost. I want you to be desperate to get my call, like you used to be. I want you to blush when I see you naked, just like you did first time round.' She saw a small light ignite in his eyes at the memory. 'We can get all that back, Ro. This six months is just an adventure that's going to bring it all back.' He winked at her. 'It's sexy, I reckon.'

Ro blinked at him in disbelief. 'Six months' enforced chastity is sexy? Are you mad?'

'Just think how mad for it you're going to be when I get back.' He smiled. 'You'll be ripping my clothes off.'

She pouted, but her eyes were dancing. 'You could just play a little harder to get. You don't actually need to fly all the way to Cambodia to force me into making the first move.'

'You know I can never turn you down,' he said, his finger tracing down her nose to the tip. His eyes locked on hers. 'I want you disoriented and desperate without me.' She saw the smile twitching on his lips, the look of conspiracy in his eyes. He was joking and yet she could see that the idea of her unsated lust appealed to him.

'I already am.'

'Now multiply it by six months.'

She swallowed. The thought of even a weekend without him was unbearable.

'And then when I'm back . . . straight to Happy Ever After.'

Ro looked away. His words hurt to hear – he knew the weight they carried. He knew he was all she had – her family, her love, her best friend. But he was going anyway. He cupped her cheek with his palm again and made her look back at him.

'That's a promise, Ro. This isn't just about six months off from the rat race. I'm going to take this time and think of a way of asking you that shows you exactly what you mean to me. You deserve more than just a bended knee.'

'A bended knee would do me fine.' After eleven years, frankly a plastic ring and a train ticket to Gretna Green would pass muster.

He shook his head. 'Think bigger. Let's not settle for this.' He gestured to the park around them, distant cars stopping for the occupants to take photographs of the herds of deer grazing by the road, the tower blocks of Roehampton peeping through the tumbling grey clouds. 'I've got grand plans for us, Ro. I don't want there to be anything humdrum about our lives. Let's take this six months to stretch and really wake up. You've got that wedding in New York in a few weeks, anyway. It's your first overseas commission. You never know – it could be the start of you taking the company international! Or transatlantic at least. Why not? Think big.'

Ro rolled her eyes and huffed crossly. He wouldn't be saying this if he'd met the bride. He'd never leave SW14 again if he met *her*.

He hooked his finger under her chin and made her look back at him. 'I know that look. Stop being so stubborn. You need to set up the company properly. The website's too slow, for a start. This is your chance to really focus on getting everything just the way you want it. By the time I come back, you could have the company in a completely different place. I'll be refreshed, and we'll both have our eyes wide open again. We'll be unstoppable.'

Ro had lost. She knew she couldn't talk him out of this. He had played his trump card – promising to propose – and what was she going to do, anyway? *Not* wait for him? As if.

Slowly she gave a small shrug. What else could she do? 'Well, it doesn't look like I've got much choice, does it?'

He swooped down and kissed her gratefully, his fingers winding through her hair as jubilation slowly began to give way to lust.

'Let's go home,' he said in a low voice.

'Already? But I thought we were having brunch at—'

'I fly out on Tuesday, Ro.'

Ro felt her stomach lurch. *This* Tuesday?

'Shh, shh. I didn't want to upset you even a week longer than I had to. But six months off from this body is going to

KAREN SWAN

drive me almost out of my mind,' he murmured, running his hands up her waist. It was true. What she lacked in height or athletic prowess, she made up for with a naturally curvy, soft pin-up figure. It was camouflaged in her signature boyfriend jeans, but gave a knockout punch in dresses at the almost constant stream of friends' weddings. Even now, after over a decade together, when their sex life had cooled to several degrees below simmering and could justifiably be called 'regular', Matt couldn't walk past her in just her underwear. Could he really do without her for all that time?

She saw the same doubt in his eyes as his hands traced the contours he knew so well. Muscle memory alone led him around her, knowing exactly where to skim and where to pause and explore.

He grabbed her hand and pulled her up to standing, kissing her more passionately now. When he pulled back, Ro felt her stomach flip to see his eyes so clouded with desire. 'Home. Now. I've got forty-eight hours to stock up on six months' worth of you.'

Ro giggled delightedly as he suddenly pulled her into a fast run back towards the shiny red Polo parked at the bottom of the hill. Maybe he was right. Maybe it was working already. If they were missing each other before they were even apart, this could be the making of them after all. Six months from now, she'd be Mrs Rowena Martin and they'd both have what they wanted: Matt his bright new beginning, her the happy ending.

# Chapter Two

'Look at me, please . . . And just one more,' Ro said from behind the camera, her right hand making tiny micro-adjustments on the lens until she found the pin-sharp focus she was looking for on the bride's face. Not that this bride lacked focus. This was a million-dollar wedding if it was a cent, and Ro had several times glimpsed the veins of steel that had bagged this bride her groom – most recently, dressing down her own father through gritted, whitened teeth for standing on the hem of her dress.

Outwardly, everything was as perfect as a Martha Stewart set: the twelve bridesmaids were all dressed in blue-sky silk columns and pearl chokers, with buffed shoulders and upswept hair; the huge potted blossom trees were in full bloom, the aisle densely carpeted with pink petals; and the guests had, thankfully, all honoured the cream dress code. Ro had been grateful to have the camera to hide behind as she'd snapped away in the bridal suite before the cere-mony, shocked and embarrassed by the no-knickers (full Hollywood) look the bride was working under her modest tiered silk mousseline dress by Vera Wang. Personally, Ro gave them eight months. She didn't see this couple getting to a year, not judging by the way the groom kept looking over at the maid of honour.

She walked slowly round the Waldorf Astoria ballroom, her camera dropped by her side as she watched the guests; some were still seated at their tables, but most were beginning to get up and mingle again, and the room was starting to throng. She guessed they were mostly around her age, possibly slightly younger – late twenties, rather than early thirties. There wasn't a baby to be seen anywhere, though they may have been banned – probably had been: this bride didn't do 'messy' or 'unscheduled' – but she had clocked a few bumps. They were likely all still in the throes of wedding fever, that time in their lives when they went to five or six weddings a year as friends and acquaintances jumped on the merry-go-round and life seemed like one long party lived out in a marquee and pretty dresses.

It was interesting seeing the differences to the British weddings she usually covered. She'd never photographed an American wedding before. The commission for this had come through the bride's sister, who'd been a bridesmaid at a wedding Ro had covered in Dorset ten months earlier. She'd taken Ro's card after seeing her signature colour-saturated filters, which lent each image a dreamy, nostalgic vibe. The most obvious difference between the Atlantic cousins was the men all wearing dinner suits rather than morning suits – the strong black and white stamping effect looked great through the lens – and the bridesmaids all looked a lot more sorted, professional even, than their British counterparts. None of them was drunk yet, for a start. The speeches had been a lot more corporate too, and obviously the couple had written their own vows – something that hadn't really taken flight back home, where it was considered more proper to go along with the traditional King James version and have a reading of 'The Owl and the Pussycat'.

Yes, it was interesting, all this – but not diverting. It didn't matter that she was in the ballroom of the famous Waldorf Astoria in Manhattan, 3,500 miles from home. That only told her that she was even further away from where Matt was, now nearly 9,000 miles away in fact. The distance between them had never been greater, and they'd spoken only three times in the three weeks since he'd gone (and one of those had been as he'd boarded the plane).

'Not going to be easy' – his phrase – wasn't even close to covering it. 'Devastating' was closer to the truth. It had been one thing accepting the sentiment behind his grand plans in theory, but returning home from the airport to a house full of his absence – his clothes strewn across the floor, his electric toothbrush wet next to hers ('There won't be any electrical points where I'm going'), his pillow still indented with the shape of his head – had poleaxed her. She'd barely told anyone he'd left, and she wasn't sure the milkman counted, anyway. Matt had kept his plans a secret from everyone, not just her – knowing they'd try to talk him out of it, question why he was really leaving her behind – so the phone had sat quietly on its cradle, no offers of rallying drinks at the pub or Indian takeaways or shopping trips to boost her spirits. She'd spent the first week dressed almost entirely in his clothes and spraying herself with his deodorant, and the house was so quiet that one evening in the kitchen, she'd actually convinced herself she could hear Shady, their long-crested goldfish, moving through the cloudy water of the fish tank.

But extending her trip here by a few days had been a mistake. Just because the days were dragging by in London didn't mean they would actually be any shorter over here. Going to bed early only made the nights longer instead of the days, taking the boat out to Staten Island didn't make the minutes tick past any quicker than cycling over to Barnes Common, and walking through Central Park may as well have been Richmond Park. The only concession she could make was that spring seemed more forthright here. It was early April and already the trees were fully in bud; the grass was speckled with daisies basking in the sun; joggers were wrapped in lighter layers . . .

Ro watched as the bride – bored, now, of her veil – wandered off to a cloakroom to touch up her make-up, her shoulder blades swishing like scythes above the top of her dress, while the groom made a dash for the bar. She rested against the back of a chair for a moment, exhausted and parched, and wondering whether to run to the kitchens to beg a plate of food. She'd been on her feet all day and no one had had the presence of mind even to offer her a glass of water, much less a sandwich. Everyone had eaten but her, and the reception was segueing into the 'party' section of the night, with drinks being drunk at twice the speed and the band tuning up by the dance floor.

She turned quickly, too quickly, the rubber tip of one shoe catching the other, and she tripped, almost colliding with a waiter who was walking towards her with a tray carefully balanced with drinks.

'Whoa!' he laughed, his arm swaying above her like a tree branch. 'Easy, tiger.'

'Easy, *tiger*?' Ro echoed, mortified and grasping for dignity. 'You – you can't speak like that to the guests, you know.'

His eyes swept over her black trouser suit and red Converses. 'But you're not a guest,' he replied. 'I've been watching you. You haven't stopped all day.' He grinned and held the tray out to her. 'Want one of these?'

She eyed the champagne regretfully. 'Well, like you say, I'm not a guest.' Her voice sounded peevish even to her.

'I won't tell,' the waiter replied.

'No. Thanks, but I never drink when I'm working. There's a direct correlation between a blurry head and blurry pictures,' she said, automatically raising her camera to her eye as she saw a line-up of groomsmen behind him lifting one of the bridesmaids in a replay of the shots she'd taken of them all outside the church earlier. Clearly, beer was hitting bloodstreams.

'I bet you haven't eaten either, huh?'

'What? Oh, uh . . . no,' she replied politely, her finger rapidly depressing the shutter button.

'Tch. They never cease to amaze me, these people. They'll spend thirty grand on flowers, but not . . . Come on, follow me.' He put his hand over the lens and she pulled away, annoyed.

'Hey!' She pointedly grabbed a microfibre cloth from her pocket and began cleaning the glass. 'If I end up with your fingerprints overlaid on the photos . . .'

'What, it might distract everyone from the bride's mother's Botox addiction?' he laughed.

Ro laughed back. It was true – the bride's mother had an expression every bit as frozen as a ventriloquist's dummy and Ro had been struggling to get a 'natural' shot of her all day. In every frame she looked like she'd just hiccupped.

Ro looked at him properly, this irreverent waiter. He was tall and easy on the eye, his light brown hair closely cropped in not quite a buzz cut but only a grade above, and he was sporting week-old stubble. 'Come on, I'm offering you a once-in-a-daytime opportunity here. Dinner on the house while the bride's preoccupied with her own reflection. What time are you on till tonight? Midnight?'

Ro bit her lip. She was ravenous. She didn't cope well without food. Matt always said her appetite was one of the things he loved most about her. 'Well—'

'Just follow me.'

He set off at a rapid pace, expertly balancing the tray above people's heads – one advantage of his extra height – as they wove through the crowd. Several people tried to stop him for drinks, but he smiled and told them he was on his way back to the kitchen for refills, even though the glasses on his tray were blatantly full and untouched.

Ro followed, jogging lightly behind, her camera swinging round her neck.

'Uh-uh, keep right here,' the waiter said, as he kicked open a right double door just as the left one swung open in the opposite direction. 'See what I mean?' He grinned as another waiter sped past with an overloaded tray.

She only just jumped out of the way in time.

'Lethal,' Ro breathed.

'Yo, José!' he called out, sliding the tray onto an empty counter. 'We got any food for the photographer here? We're not the only ones being worked like dogs.'

A minute later, a medium-rare filet steak with a red wine jus and vegetables was passed through to the serving station. Ro was so hungry she wanted to fall into it face first.

'Over here,' the waiter said, carrying it over to a small chef's table in the corner and grabbing some red-hot cutlery from the still-steaming dishwasher. Someone placed a glass of water in front of her too.

'Thanks,' Ro marvelled, sitting down quickly and tucking in without delay. She only had a few minutes before the bride would be back.

'So, you're English?' the waiter enquired, watching her follow every hot mouthful with a gulp of water.

'Yup.'

'First time to New York?'

'Second, technically,' she mumbled, her mouth full.

'Technically?'

She chewed quickly, not sure she had time to eat *and* chat. 'I was born here. My parents moved to England when I was eight months,' she said quickly, spearing a broccoli floret.

'Oh, right. So then you're American.'

She shrugged. 'Well, technically, but I don't have any sense of it. I feel as British as pie.'

'What – key lime?' He grinned.

'Steak and kidney.' She chuckled.

'You're lucky you belong to both. I've always wanted to go to London. Stay for a bit.'

'Mm.' She glanced at him suspiciously, hoping this wasn't some warm-up for an invitation to stay.

'You here alone?'

'Yup.' The video cameraman back in the ballroom was a local freelancer she'd hired on recommendation from a photographer friend but only met for the first time yesterday morning: he didn't count as company. 'My boyfriend's travelling,' she added, just in case this was also a warm-up for a chat-up line.

'Well now, that's a shame,' he said, but with such a hapless grin she found herself grinning back again before she caught herself and abruptly stopped – she didn't want it to be confused for flirting. 'So do you like it here?'

'Mm.' She made a so-so movement with her head.

He nodded. 'Yeah. New York can be a tough place to be on your own.'

'Yo, dude! What you doing sittin' there, man?' They both looked up to see a man in a white jacket marching towards them. 'You can't be chatting up the chicks! I got people with a thirst on out there! Don't you need the money or nothin'?'

The waiter stood up with a heavy sigh. 'Guess I'd better shoot. Nice chatting to you.'

'Yeah, you too,' Ro nodded, having to place a hand in front of her mouth for politeness's sake. 'And thanks . . . For the meal, I mean.'

He winked and jogged off. 'All right, I'm coming, I'm coming!'

Ro watched him go, bemused to notice a flash of lurid Hawaiian-print boxer shorts peeking out between his shirt and trousers.

She finished her meal quickly, wiping her mouth with the napkin that had also been – thoughtfully – provided and marching quickly back through the kitchen, remembering to stay to the right on her way back out through the double doors.

The bride was on the dance floor – veil shed like a snake's skin – and had changed into a strapless miniskirted version of her wedding dress, the groom nowhere to be seen. She was standing with her hands on her hips, a gaggle of nervous ushers variously trying to persuade her to dance/drink/take a seat. But the more solicitous they became, the more her eyes narrowed.

Ro's gaze quickly skirted the room for the groom too. She couldn't see the maid of honour anywhere either, and from what she'd glimpsed earlier . . . Oh dear, this wasn't good, not good at all.

She walked quickly round the perimeter of the ballroom. Everyone was waiting for the first dance so that they could get on with hitting the dance floor themselves, and the absence of the groom and maid of honour was becoming more conspicuous by the minute.

Ro reached the doors and looked out into the hallway. Some smaller rooms had also been reserved for the wedding – cloakrooms, bathrooms – including a modest, quiet conference room that had been set up specifically for interviewing the bride and groom's friends and families for the video that Ro would splice and edit back in the UK.

She padded silently across the hallway in her rubber-soled shoes. A few of the older guests were already collecting their coats, some men checking their texts on the way back from the toilets.

She was passing a mobile photo booth when a sprinkle of flirtatious laughter stopped her in her tracks. The curtain was drawn, the light popping as shots were taken. Just in sight – though she'd almost walked straight past them – she saw a white shirt and a pair of black trousers had been stuffed round the back of the booth.

Ro hesitated. Kicking out below the curtain was the distinctive blue silk hem of a bridesmaid dress. Oh no. No, no, no. This wasn't happening. No way was this marriage imploding on its very first day. There could be no break-up until *after* she'd been paid.

Looking around her quickly to check that no one was watching, she bent double, searching for the pair of legs that must be, now, trouserless, and in the booth too.

They were.

She heard more laughter from behind the curtain, a low buzz of muted voices. 'No!' a female voice screeched delightedly, clearly meaning 'yes', as the light popped again.

Ro rolled her eyes and reached down for the discarded clothes – how reckless? – just as she heard the furious rat-a-tat-tat of stilettos on the marble floor behind her.

She looked down at the clothes balled in her hand and turned in the same instant she switched them behind her back, a frozen smile on her face.

'Have you seen my husband?' the bride demanded, her eyes scanning the empty spaces of the corridors like a sparrowhawk hunting mice.

Without visibly moving, Ro threw the clothes behind her, hearing just a soft, muffled *thwump* as they fell to the floor of the booth. 'Uh, no . . . now you mention it, I haven't seen him recently. I was just in the loos and he wasn't there.' The bride scowled. 'In the bathroom, I mean . . . obviously.'

The booth began to hum, vibrating softly, and the bride looked behind Ro, her attention diverted. She looked at the drawn curtain. 'Who's in there?'

'In there?' Ro echoed, her voice an octave higher than usual. 'Um, no one.'

'The drape is drawn.' She bent to the side. 'And I can see legs. Someone's in there.'

Ro looked down. At least the legs she could see were encased in black trousers again. 'Oh yes, of course. And, uh . . . you're right. Obviously someone's in there. It's just not . . . your husband.'

The bride's eyes narrowed suspiciously again.

A sudden whirring started up and they both looked down as a strip of photos slid out. The bride reached for them, but Ro got there first, whipping them away before either of them could set eyes on the images. 'Uh . . . I can't let you see those.'

'Why not?' the bride demanded furiously.

'Because—'

But the bride wasn't hanging around to hear Ro's story and in the next instant she had flashed open the curtain. Her jaw dropped at the sight of her maid of honour and the waiter who had fed Ro only twenty minutes earlier smiling back at her, a sign hanging from the bridesmaid's neck.

'What the . . . ?' the bride stormed.

The waiter locked eyes with Ro, who was looking on, open-mouthed with shock. They both knew he was going to get fired for this.

'It's not what you think,' Ro said, hurriedly closing the curtain again, much to everyone's astonishment.

'Why is . . . why is my maid of honour standing in that booth with a *waiter* and wearing a sign that reads—'

'It's a surprise!' Ro blurted out. 'For the video.'

The bride blinked at her.

'Yes, uh . . . I mean, it may not work, but . . . we thought we'd give it a go and . . . if it doesn't work, I'll leave it out. It's just good to have options, that's all.'

She nodded frantically, smiled manically, her fingers threading through the strap of the camera round her neck.

'But what—' At that moment, the groom appeared from the men's bathroom, fiddling with his cuffs.

'Where have you been?' the bride shrieked as he walked over, taking in the testy scene. 'Everyone's waiting for our first dance.'

'Well, I'm ready when you are, baby,' the groom

shrugged, as his bride grabbed him by the elbow and steered him back to the ballroom.

'Hayley!' the bride snapped over her shoulder. 'Are you *coming*?'

The maid of honour peeped out through the curtain, giggling nervously and mouthing 'thanks' to Ro as she skittered past.

A moment later, the waiter peered round the curtain. 'Is it safe to come out?'

'Just about.' Ro turned back to him.

'I don't know how to thank you. You saved my ass for sure,' he said, buttoning up his shirt and hurriedly tucking it back into his trousers. He reached over and picked up the tray she hadn't noticed sitting on a side table just a short distance away. 'You don't know how badly I need this money.'

She shrugged. 'Well, I figure one good turn deserves another.'

'Here. By way of thanks,' he said, pulling something from his back pocket.

'What's this?' she asked as he handed her a small card. She noticed a smudge of dark pink lipstick near his ear.

'A friend's having a party tomorrow night. Just tell 'em, "Shaddywack".'

'Huh?'

But he was already back on duty, walking towards a group of guests with his tray.

She looked down at the card he'd handed her:

### Hamptons summer weekends house share

4-bed, 2.5-bath cottage on Egypt Green, East Hampton. 2-acre lot.
MD–LD $25,000 ¼ share. Responsible professionals only.

To make the cut, bring a gift that defines you and come to
the Pink Room, Penthouse Level, 53rd Street and Broadway,
April 10, 7 p.m. to 11 p.m.

Contact h.slater@googlemail.com to register
for entry password on the night.

She shook her head, slightly baffled, before remembering the photos still in her other hand. She looked at them
and squinted in disbelief: the maid of honour was variously pouting and laughing at the camera, her hands in her
hair, the waiter bare-chested with a buttonhole rose behind
his ear, nuzzling her neck. Ro looked at the hand-painted
sign round the bridesmaid's neck and sighed: 'Get Humped
this summer.' What did it even mean? And, more to the
point, how the hell was she going to work it into a wedding film?

# Chapter Three

Eight p.m. and the city was out for the night. Ro leaned against the wall, pretending to text, as the clique in Brooks Brothers suits stopped at the door ten metres further up and spoke in lowered tones to the doorman. Rowena followed them with her eyes, her gaze fixed on the magnums in their hands. They were the sixth group to pass her so far brandishing premier cru by way of identity. She thought of the ridged glass jar in her pocket. How, in all seriousness, could she hand that over by way of hers?

Ro sighed and looked away. She'd been standing here for twenty minutes now trying to work up the courage to go in, but she'd seen enough to convince her there was little point. She pushed herself back to standing and stared down the long avenue. Tail lights glowed red into the distance even though the traffic lights were green. The milky sky she could only glimpse in fragments was leaching into a shadowy dusk, and everyone clearly had somewhere to be, except her.

She turned a circle on the spot, not sure which way to go. She couldn't go back to the hotel room, not without losing her sanity. She'd spent eight hours in there already today, downloading yesterday's wedding images onto her laptop and whittling out a first edit, but she couldn't really scrutinize them until she got them under the magnifying loupe back home. There was a gym in the hotel basement, but she had long taken the view that being a DD cup was God's way of saying she shouldn't exercise. And she felt too conspicuously alone to sit at a restaurant table reading a book and pretending that it was fine, that it was her choice.

A couple of women, deep in animated conversation, were walking towards her, or rather the door just past her – gold foil bottle-tops clearly visible through their closed fists – and she turned in the opposite direction, not wanting to come face to face with what she wasn't. She wasn't slick and metropolitan, the kind of woman to walk alone into a party. She wasn't like Matt, bold and adventurous, somewhere in the Cambodian mountains, living his dream and trekking in the Elephant Mountains for fun.

No. She was standing outside a skyscraper that had a party at the top and she was too scared to go in and chat, even to pretty much the only person who'd talked to her in the three weeks since Matt had left. She hated that she couldn't make herself go in, hated that she was even contemplating it in the first place. Was she really that desperate? How could she be this pathetic without him? Since when had she blurred into his shadow, losing her own angles and borders, merging into him and becoming subsumed?

A cab pulled to the kerb ahead of her and she saw the woman inside handing over notes from the back seat as she continued a seemingly intense conversation she was having on the phone, head bobbing frantically in profile. Ro ran over and waited patiently for the busy girl to get out. She didn't care where she went; she just had to get out of here.

The door opened and one lean, toned leg swung out with a stiletto heel at one end and a sharp pencil skirt at the other. Ro looked down at her own boyfriend jeans and jade-green hi-tops. Was she actually the only woman in New York not wearing heels?

'No, no, that's not working for me. The pitch is already maxed as it is.' The girl glanced disinterestedly at Ro as she got out, reaching back for a large A1-sized portfolio with her free hand as she kept her other hand – and the phone in it – clamped to her ear. 'Well, if they can't go up, they'll have to go down. There's no other way. They certainly can't go out.'

The portfolio behind her jammed between the door frames, pulling her back towards the cab, and she tugged at it, the rigid leather sides bowing slightly. Ro leaned forward to nudge it free at one side, seeing – to her astonishment – the far door open on the other side of the bench seat and a pair of dark grey flannel legs bending in.

'Hey!' she shouted, straightening up to make furious eye contact with the legs' owner above the cab, but he was already sliding in. She quickly bent down again, just as the pointed, metal-capped corner of the portfolio suddenly came unstuck and jabbed her hard in the eye.

She gasped and reeled backwards, tripping over the kerb and banging her head against a lamp post as she went down. Just for good measure.

'Oh what? Goddammit!' she heard the girl mutter. 'Jerry, I'll have to call you back . . . Yeah, yeah . . . Hey! You OK?'

Ro, her hand clamped like a patch over one eye, shook her head, trying not to cry. She was seeing flashes of red behind the shut lid as her eye began to stream. It was her 'working' eye, the one she used to peer through the lens.

'What were you *doing*? Couldn't you see I hadn't gotten out?' the girl demanded in a tone that suggested this was Ro's fault.

'I was helping you,' Rowena spluttered. It was impossible to open even the 'good' eye: that one was streaming too.

'Helping? You were *helping* a stranger in Manhattan? What are you, crazy?'

'English, actually,' Ro replied petulantly.

'That figures.'

They fell into silence, but even with her eyes shut, Ro could tell the girl was still there, crouched by her. Horns were hooting in frustration at the hold-ups further down the street, and Ro could hear people muttering as they had to dodge her on the pavement. How inconvenient of her to hold them up like this . . .

'I suppose the cab's gone,' Ro said, trying to scramble to her feet with both her eyes scrunched shut. She felt the girl's hand on her elbow, lightly guiding her back up.

'Yeah. Shall I get you another? Least I could do.' The girl's tone was slightly more friendly as Ro's enduring distress became more evident.

'Thanks,' Ro mumbled, turning her face down and removing her hand from her eye, but the moment she opened it, it was like being lasered by a sharp white light and she winced in pain. She reached out for the lamp post for support, swinging wildly for it and still missing.

The girl placed a hand on her arm. 'Dammit, you can't get in a cab if you can't see where you're going. Not in this city. And definitely not with you being *English*,' she muttered under her breath, making Ro's Englishness sound like an impediment. Ro heard her whistling through her teeth, trying to work out what to do. 'Look, I'm headed just over there anyway. Why don't you come with me and we'll take a better look inside? You can get some warm water on it, do a salt bath . . .'

Ro thought she might be pointing the way, but with both eyes weeping copiously, she couldn't be certain. She nodded silently, letting the girl take her arm and lead her towards wherever 'there' was. It wasn't like she had a lot of choice.

'Shaddywack,' the girl said.

What?

'Second elevator,' she heard a man reply, and then the acoustics changed and they were inside, Ro's trainers squeaking adolescently beside the pin-sharp tap of the girl's heels on a marble floor. They stopped again and she heard the soft ping of lift doors opening, felt carpet underfoot as they stepped in.

'I'm Bobbi, by the way,' the girl said, as they started moving skywards.

'Rowena.'

'How long you in New York for, Rowena?'

'Going back tomorrow night.' She thought she could hear the faint swish of hair and imagined the girl, Bobbi, was nodding – or checking her reflection. She kept her head down; she felt awkward having a conversation with a complete stranger with her eyes clamped shut.

'Your first time here?'

'Pretty much.'

'You like it?'

Rowena shrugged, wiping her 'patch' hand, which was wet, on her jeans. 'It does what it says on the tin, I guess. Bright lights, big city.'

'You're not much of a city girl, huh?'

'Actually, I live in London.'

'Yeah? I love London. Whereabouts?'

'A place called Barnes.'

There was a pause. 'Down by the river, right? Got a duck pond and a cute little green?'

'That's the one,' Ro said in surprise, her mind perfectly conjuring the little whitewashed Victorian cottage with shiny red door that she called home. The orange blossom had been on the verge of blooming as she'd left and she wondered whether Matt had noticed before he left her and their life together behind him. It had been the seal on the deal when they'd first viewed the house three summers ago.

'Well, no wonder you don't like Manhattan, then,' Bobbi said, and from the direction of her voice, Ro could tell that she was indeed now checking her reflection in the mirror.

'I didn't say I didn't l—'

But the doors had opened and she felt Bobbi's hand on her elbow again, guiding her along a corridor. Ahead of them, she could hear the muffled beat of music and raucous conversation. Ro slowed her feet as they got closer.

'To be honest, I think I'm fine now. I really don't need to go in there with you.' She tried to open the uninjured eye a little and she had just enough time to take in a charcoal-grey carpet and pale grey-striped wallpaper before it watered up again.

'But your eye – you look like Rocky! We should try to ice it for sure.' And before Ro could protest further, a door was opened and they were swamped by the din inside. She felt Bobbi hesitate at . . . What? The noise? The wall of champagne that had been built in the past half-hour as everyone

27

arrived with identical gifts? 'Oh *Jeez*! You have got to be freakin' kiddin' me . . .' There was a long pause and Ro tried to imagine what on earth had made the girl stop in her tracks. 'Just keep hold of my hand, OK?' she shouted eventually.

Ro could only nod, one hand still clamped protectively over her eye, as she felt Bobbi's hand close over her free one, their connected arms outstretched and taut like a mooring rope as Bobbi made holes for them in the dense, heaving crowd – seemingly knocking people's knees with her portfolio, if the number of 'Hey!'s was anything to go by. Ro yelped as someone trod on her foot; someone else splashed her with a drink as their arm was jogged; she could hear people shrieking a lot. The smell of cigars burning wafted past her and Ro knew she had been right to follow her impulse to walk away from this. She didn't need to open her eyes to know she'd be the only person in the room wearing jeans – at least, wearing jeans with rips in them and that hadn't cost $400 – or the only woman not in make-up. (Although thank God for that: she'd look like Frankenstein's bride if she was wearing mascara right now.)

'Watch yourself here – it's slippy,' Bobbi warned her.

Ro frowned – slippy? – but stepped with care, still almost slipping. Against her better judgement, she instinctively opened both eyes and in the second before pain shut them again, she saw foam. Bikinis. Waxed, muscled chests. A ball. Then red-pulsing blackness.

The crowd was less dense over here and she could actually feel space around her now as Bobbi continued towing her through the apartment. And then suddenly the noise was behind them and a door closed again.

'Jeez-us,' Bobbi muttered. 'Didn't I just know it would be like this?'

Ro said nothing: she wasn't sure Bobbi was actually directing the question at her. And anyway, her own thoughts were racing. A foam party? She thought of Barnes again – the duck pond, the orange blossom, the pretty red door – and calculated how many hours it would be till she was back there, safe in the silence of her own home, sniffing Matt's pillow.

She heard the sound of water running.

'Here.' Bobbi placed a warm, wettened corner of a towel in her hands. 'Press that against your eye while I get a dish and some salt. Lock the door behind me, OK? Don't let anyone else in.'

Ro nodded, pressing the towel to her eye and finding the lock with her hands. She slumped in relief at the momentary solitude. She wet the towel again and patted it against her eye over and over, grateful for the comfort it brought. The good eye had just about stopped watering altogether now and she could at least take in her surroundings without feeling like she was doped.

The bathroom she was standing in was tiled with dark green slate, the washbasin she was using seemingly carved by hand from a slab of limestone. Cubbyholes made from iroko wood housed grey folded towels, and glass bottles of colour-tinted toiletries had been coded to the rainbow. She clocked a generous-headed shaving brush next to a lime-stickered wooden box of Geo Trumper's shaving soap.

There was a knock at the door and Ro unlocked it, but it wasn't Bobbi on the other side.

'Hey, you made it!' beamed the waiter from the wedding

with the disarmingly easy smile. He had a beer in his hand and was today wearing chinos with flip-flops.

'You can't come in here,' she said abruptly. 'Medical emergency.'

'I can see that,' the waiter said again, still smiling. 'I saw you coming in. Maybe I can help.'

'*Not* likely.' She could guess his game. Bikini-clad women frolicking in foam? Hooking up with a bridesmaid at the wedding he was waitering at, minutes after he'd hit on her? It was pretty obvious why he'd invited her to this, and now that she'd gone and shown up, he probably thought he was in with a chance, in spite of – or maybe even because of – the travelling boyfriend.

'I'm a doctor.'

'No, you're not! You're a waiter. I saw you last night, remember?' Oh God, had he forgotten already? 'I'm the photographer? We met at the wedding at—'

Just then Bobbi reappeared, carrying a bowl that looked like it had recently held peanuts. Was that what she meant by salt bath?

'Who's this? What did I say about keeping the door locked?' she demanded bossily, throwing the guy a dirty look as she barged past. 'You're English. You don't know what these frat boys can be like.'

'I think we're too old to qualify as frat boys,' the waiter replied.

'Yeah, well, you'd *think*,' Bobbi muttered. 'But try telling that to the flesh mob out there. Come on, fella – move it. This ain't no pickup. The girl needs some first aid.'

'Listen, I'm a doctor.' The waiter gave a goofy grin. '*Was* a doctor, strictly speaking. Can I see? It looks sore.'

Ro shrugged, in too much discomfort to argue the toss.

He came further into the bathroom. 'You happy for me to lock the door?' he asked them both.

'So long as you're only coming in here to do some doctoring,' Bobbi said in a steely tone of voice.

'We're all safe, then,' he grinned, locking the door and turning towards Ro. 'So what happened?'

'Her eye picked a fight with the corner of my portfolio,' Bobbi said quickly.

'Really? Feisty eye,' he murmured. 'Do you mind if I try to look at it?'

Ro shook her head, watching warily from her good eye as he angled her face in the direction of the mirror lights, but not directly at them. 'Can you open it for me?'

Slowly, hesitantly, she opened the eye, feeling it fill with tears as the light streamed in like water in a bath. The waiter peered closer at her, his face just inches from hers so that she could smell his cologne. She pulled away quickly. The smile left his eyes, if not his mouth, as he registered her evident distrust.

'Well, from what I could *briefly* see, it looks like there's a scratch on the retina. You're going to need to keep it covered for a day or two. It must hurt like hell,' he added.

Ro nodded.

'I can patch it for you if you like.'

'With what? Your shirt?' Bobbi asked dubiously, watching the two of them.

The smiling guy looked behind her and nodded. 'Well, I'd rather not, given there's a first-aid kit right there.'

Bobbi turned. Sure enough a green plastic case with a red cross was stowed in the bottom cubbyhole. She retrieved it and watched as the waiter pulled out a crêpe bandage, an antiseptic gauze pad and safety pins.

'So, you having fun?' he asked, making small talk to fill the silence.

'Not really,' Bobbi said, folding her arms.

Ro stood quietly at the basin, watching her assailant/ good Samaritan through her now-dry eye. Bobbi was tall and lean, with narrow calves, and judging from her shoes, she clearly had the indigenous ability to balance on the balls of her feet for hours at a time. Her shoulder-length hair was top-flight brunette: low lit with plum shades and cut in layers around her oval face, which was beautiful rather than pretty. She had gently rounded cheekbones, a pronounced jaw and large, dark, steady eyes that Ro guessed missed nothing.

'No?'

'It's a complete waste of a cab fare. I mean, a foam party? Seriously? I thought this house share was supposed to be for people who *didn't* want to live in an animal house? The ad clearly said "responsible professionals" were wanted.'

The waiter nodded. 'I guess you have a point.'

Bobbi stared at his flip-flops suspiciously. It didn't look like the foam party was such a surprise to *him*.

'And anyway, what's with the one-hundred-strong crowd?' Bobbi continued, warming to her theme. 'There's only four bedrooms, right? I reckon this guy's looking to capitalize on his power while he's got it, if you get what I'm sayin'.'

'I think I do.'

Ro didn't, but she didn't ask for clarification. Bobbi was clearly on a rant.

'I mean, everyone wants a summer spot in the Hamptons and they'll do anything, *anything* to get it: inside-trading tips and football tickets from the guys; and as for the girls . . . Ugh!' Bobbi batted a hand disgustedly. 'It's not bad enough that it costs nearly half my salary just to get a room there for the summer *weekends* or that we have to compete against each other for them like performing monkeys? I bet he hosts one of these a week. Why wouldn't he? It's a sure thing, right? He probably filled the rooms months ago.'

'What do you think?' the waiter asked Rowena. He had placed the patch over her eye and was beginning to wind the crêpe bandage round her head.

She just shrugged. 'I wouldn't know. I'm English. Our seaside scene is somewhat different to yours – there's no guarantee the sun will turn up, for a start. And Cornwall's lovely, but we don't have to audition for it. We certainly don't have to go through –' she waved towards the door vaguely '– that.'

They all three fell quiet again, listening to the party rocketing along without them. Ro wondered how it was that she could be at the party and still not actually be part of it. *How* pathetic exactly?

'I don't know your names,' he said, breaking the silence. 'I'm Hump.'

Of course he was! Ro saw Bobbi roll her eyes.

'Bobbi. Winkleman.'

'Rowena Tipton. But everyone calls me Ro,' Ro added.

'So what did you bring? You know, the gift that defines you?' Hump asked, still unwinding the bandage ball asymmetrically round Ro's head. 'No, wait, let me guess – a magnum of champagne, right?'

'Ha! It doesn't matter now. I'm not staying,' Bobbi interjected. 'I've seen enough.'

'So? I'm curious – indulge me.' Hump smiled. 'What else have we got to do in here?'

Before he could come up with an alternative scenario, Bobbi immediately reached for the portfolio she'd propped against the wall, pulling out a huge black and white sketch on thick artist's paper of a low clapboarded house with three shuttered dormer windows and a covered stepped-up porch that wrapped round two sides.

Hump stopped what he was doing. 'Did *you* draw that?' he asked, impressed.

Bobbi shrugged.

'But how did you even know what it looked like?'

'I Google Earthed it.'

'It's awesome.'

'It's a waste of time is what it is,' Bobbi refuted. 'I'm not handing it over after this. He couldn't *pay* me to stay in his house, not if even one of those people out there is going to be my housemate.'

Hump grinned, clearly amused by her outspoken feisti-ness. 'But I don't get it. That's someone else's house. How does it define *you*?'

Bobbi blinked at him, as if astonished by the stupidity of the question. 'I'm an architect. This is what I do. It's who I am. Know me, know my career.'

Hump looked back at Ro, finishing winding the bandage and securing it in place with the safety pins. 'What about you?'

Ro folded her arms. 'Oh no,' she replied defensively. 'I don't think so. I wasn't even going to come in.'

Bobbi looked surprised. 'You were coming here too?'

'Not once I saw the cliques walking in. It was pretty

obvious I wasn't going to fit. And I was right – funnily enough, I *don't* wear a bikini underneath my suit,' she said with impressive sarcasm.

'You gotta show me what you brought,' Bobbi said, her almost-black eyes shining with interest. 'I showed you mine.'

Ro hesitated – she sensed nobody said 'no' to Bobbi – then reached into her coat pocket. Sheepishly, she held up the jar of marmalade.

'Is that . . . ? What *is* that?' Hump frowned.

'Marmalade.'

'What?' Bobbi asked, looking dubious.

'It's a big thing back home. You have it on toast.'

'With a cup of tea?' Hump suggested in a bad posh English accent.

'Exactly.'

'It looks home-made,' Hump said, his eyes on the hand-written sticker on the octagonal jar as Bobbi took it from her.

'People have been known to befriend me just to get on my annual list. My social diary goes mad in the run-up to navel-oranges season. I have to limit friends and family to just three jars each,' Ro replied.

'Power!' Hump grinned.

'It was all I could think of to bring. I always travel with a jar. I bring my own teabags too,' she mumbled.

'It's cute,' Bobbi proclaimed – if a little patronizingly – handing back the jar of marmalade. 'You're a nester, right?'

Ro didn't reply as she pocketed it again. A nester. It wasn't the first time she'd been told that. Her friends at school had laughed as she'd hosted dinner parties at fifteen when all they'd wanted to do was try to get into the pub.

Making a home took on an urgency those with families couldn't ever understand.

'So what about you? What did you bring?' Bobbi asked, turning the tables on Hump.

'Actually, I didn't,' he replied.

'Well, that's not fair!' Bobbi said, instantly indignant. 'Why should you—' Then the penny dropped as her eyes fell back down to his flip-flops. The foam party really hadn't been a surprise to him. 'Oh. Oh, I get it. He's a friend of yours. You just come here for the *social* element.'

'Who? Who's my friend?' Hump asked, smiling even more broadly.

Was he ever not amused? Ro wondered.

'The guy behind all this, the one with the house! Humphrey Slater.'

Another penny dropped. A bigger one.

'You!' Ro exclaimed.

Hump shrugged. 'Busted.'

Ro watched Bobbi's mouth opening and closing repeatedly as she trawled back over the insults she'd unwittingly hurled at their host in the past five minutes. She couldn't have done a better job of doing herself out of the house share if she'd tried.

'Well, I stand by everything I said,' she said finally.

'And I agree with all of it,' Hump replied, making both girls frown. 'That's exactly why I do this.'

Ro looked between the two of them. 'Sorry, you've lost me. I'm English – we're divided by a common language, remember,' she said.

Hump leaned back against the basin. 'The house in East Hampton was my grandfather's. I need the money the summer season generates for my new start-up—'

'I thought you said you were a doctor?' Bobbi interrupted.

He pulled a grimace. 'I *was* a doctor. It wasn't for me. I gave it up last year.'

'You're saying you just walked away from all that schooling?' Bobbi scowled, disbelieving. 'Listen, buddy, I'm an architect and I've spent as long in school as you, give or take a few years. No one just walks away from that. What really happened? You failed, right? Got thrown out?'

There was a slight pause. 'I need to be my own boss.'

Bobbi stared at him like he'd said he needed to be an amoeba.

'So what do you do now, then?' Ro interjected, saving him.

'I'm an entrepreneur. Like you.'

'Is that your way of saying "unemployed"?' Bobbi demanded, and both Hump and Ro shot her annoyed looks. Ro had had comments like that too.

Hump looked a little hurt. 'I have some irons in the fire.'

They all stared at each other suspiciously – three strangers locked in a bathroom, one with a patch, another with an attitude, another with no job.

'So that's your interview process,' Bobbi said finally, jerking a thumb towards the party happening on the other side of the door.

Hump shrugged. 'Actually, *this* is.'

Both girls looked back at him blankly. He sighed. 'This is my fifth year of renting out the rooms. Initially, I needed the money for med school, so it seemed like the obvious thing to do, but I didn't want the place wrecked, y'know? It's my grandfather's house, but it didn't matter how much I tried to vet people, they'd ace the interviews and then turn into animals the second they got off the Jitney. That's the local coach,' he explained for Ro's benefit. He frowned. 'Finally, I figured the best thing to do was good old-fashioned reverse psychology – put people in the kind of environment they were telling me they didn't want and then see who went for it – and who didn't. And you didn't.'

Bobbi narrowed her eyes suspiciously. 'Are you saying . . . ?'

Hump shrugged. 'I can't *pay* you to stay there,' he grinned, quoting her own words back to her. 'I do need the capital for my next venture, but there are two rooms still free. They're yours if you want them.'

Bobbi didn't hesitate. 'We'd need to negotiate on the price. I work like a bitch and can't guarantee I can get away every Friday.' She folded her arms across her chest, unrepentant. 'I don't want to pay for something I can't use. Every other weekend would suit me better.'

Hump pulled a face. 'I don't know. That would mean half-rent and I do need to bring in a full season's income.' He shrugged. 'It's a shame. It would have been nice to have you both, given that you're already friends.'

'Hang on a sec!' Ro said hurriedly. 'There's been a misunderstanding. *I'm* not looking for a room.'

'Are you kidding me?' Hump laughed in genuine astonishment. '*Both* of you are turning me down? Do you know what those guys out there would do to be in your shoes?'

'I think we've already established that,' Bobbi said, not budging from her tough stance. 'And I haven't turned you down flat. We're negotiating terms.'

Hump looked across at Ro. 'Why did you come to the party if you didn't want a room?'

Ro felt her cheeks flame. How could she admit she

couldn't bear to go another day without speaking to someone? 'To give you these,' she said, reaching into her pocket and handing him the photo-booth snapshots. 'And because you invited me.'

He glanced at the photo strip with a quick smile. 'But you brought a gift that defined you,' he said, looking back up.

'To be polite.'

'I don't believe this. Who knew the Hamptons would be such a hard sell?' Hump said to neither of them in particular, pocketing the photos. 'Thanks for these, by the way. I was wondering how I could get hold of them.'

Ro shrugged. 'I don't really get all this, to be honest. What are the Hamptons, anyway?' she asked. 'I mean, I'm getting that it's a nice beachside resort, but seriously? Auditions? Reverse psychology?'

Both Bobbi and Hump's jaws dropped.

'Are you shitting me?' Bobbi whispered.

'Where exactly is it?' Ro continued.

'*It* is a series of villages on Long Island.'

'Long Island . . .' Ro echoed sceptically.

'Go over Brooklyn Bridge, hook a right and keep going for ninety miles till you drive into the Atlantic. It's pretty much the single most exclusive enclave of beach villages in the whole of the entire US of A.'

'Oh, right, I see.'

'No. No, I really don't think you do,' Hump said, shaking his head. 'Everyone who's anyone holidays out there. Even the West Coasters – Steven Spielberg comes over, Puff Daddy, Martha Stewart, Gwyneth Paltrow, SJP . . . pretty much anyone who's an aire.'

Aire? As in millionaire? Billionaire? 'Do you mean rich?'

'I do.'

Ro shrugged. 'Well, I don't get why you'd think *I* would want to come here for the summer. You already knew I was English.'

'Yeah! With US citizenship!' Hump laughed, holding his hands out in disbelief. 'Why wouldn't you use that? It's like you won the jackpot and you don't even know it.'

'My jackpot's coming in just over five months,' she mumbled.

'Huh?' Bobbi asked, leaning in.

'Nothing.'

Hump stared at her. 'Give me one good reason why you couldn't spend the summer here.'

'What?' Ro laughed. 'You mean beyond the fact that my entire life is across the Pond?'

'Yeah. Beyond that. Why couldn't you spend time here? You're self-employed, right?'

'Well, yes, but—'

'You got sick parents that need you to stay there?'

'Dead ones, actually. Car crash. When I was twelve. I lived with my aunt and uncle.'

There was a stunned silence and she knew she'd said it too harshly, the words abrupt and cold as she rushed to get them out, knowing they'd come out sooner or later and wanting to control the situation. 'Sorry,' she mumbled. 'Didn't mean to . . . throw that at you.'

Bobbi was frowning at her – Ro wasn't sure whether that was her version of sympathy. Hump rubbed her arm.

'Well, you're not married, I can see that,' he said more gently, his eyes on her ringless finger.

'Not yet, but—'

'Or engaged,' Bobbi said quickly.

'Not yet, but—'

'You said your boyfriend's travelling,' Hump smiled.

'Yeah? Where?' Bobbi interrupted.

'Far East.'

Bobbi's eyebrows shot up. 'For work?'

'Pleasure.' The word was out of her mouth before she could stop it. The sound of it stunned her momentarily, the simple truth of it a hard smack. He was out there for pleasure. He was having a great time. Without her. Because he wanted to.

'When is he coming back?' Hump's expression had changed. Was that . . . *pity* she could see in his eyes now?

'September. Listen, I can see where you're going with this, but really I don't have time to spend a summer gallivanting on American beaches. I'm in the middle of expanding my business.'

'What d'you do, Ro?' Bobbi asked, hoisting herself up onto the basin unit and crossing her ankles.

'She's a wedding photographer,' Hump replied for her.

'Family media, actually. I do weddings but as part of a bigger, longer-term project where I reconnect with the clients every year. Plus, I edit and organize digital videos into short films and photos into albums and books. People have literally thousands of pictures stored on their hard drives that they never even see – and more often than not, aren't backed up. An entire life story can be lost with one spilt glass of water.'

'Spilt water?' Bobbi echoed, lost.

'I'm just illustrating a disaster scenario.'

'Oh. What's your company called? I'll look it up.'

'Well, I'm in the middle of changing it, actually. I was

thinking something like Tipton Family Media?' She may as well road-test the name on them as anyone.

'Too dull,' Bobbi said decisively, shaking her head and crossing her arms.

'Pedestrian, I was going to say,' Hump agreed. 'You can do better.'

'Oh.'

'But isn't it a great idea?' Hump asked Bobbi, clocking Ro's disappointment. 'I bet you have tons of photos you never look at, right?'

'Oh God, like you wouldn't believe. You don't even *wanna* go there.' Bobbi rolled her eyes.

'Ro's right, though. There's no way a business like that would translate over here. I mean, all those cash-rich, time-poor New York families – they totally wouldn't be your target market.' Hump's voice was heavy with sarcasm, almost moronic. 'And I mean, *who* would want to capitalize upon them all being in one place for the summer?'

Bobbi guffawed next to him and Ro wondered when *they'd* suddenly become allies.

'My life is in England.'

'Your boyfriend isn't.'

Ro glared at him with her one eye.

'You could have an adventure of your own too, you know. You've got a summer without him. Why should he have all the fun?'

'It's not like that.'

No one said anything and Ro knew they thought it clearly was. She studied her trainers. It wasn't that the idea was a bad one. If this place really was the summer play-ground for Manhattan's elite, it could indeed be the perfect launch pad for her business. Why *not* start it here? Her US citizenship meant she could work in the States, and she'd already forecast to grow the business through franchises. Once she'd set it up here, she could sell it to a licensee and then concentrate on the UK market back home. It was back to front maybe, but—

She stopped the thoughts abruptly. It was ridiculous even to think it.

'It won't work. If nothing else because it's a weekend share you're renting out. Where am I supposed to go during the week? I don't have a place in New York.'

Hump's face fell. 'Oh. Yeah.' He sighed, looking towards the closed door. He was going to have to go back out there.

Bobbi smacked him on the arm. 'Unless . . . unless Ro stays at the Hamptons house full-time! That way, she can pay you extra and I can pay you less. Everyone's a winner.'

Ro narrowed her eyes, convinced only Bobbi would be the winner in this. She had that victorious sheen about her.

'It's the perfect solution: you get your full season's income, I get the flexibility to do every other weekend, and Ro has a full-time base here.'

'Wait,' Ro protested again, trying to hold back this train of thought that was fast gathering momentum. 'There's no way I could afford to live there full-time. I have a mortgage back home.'

'Couldn't you rent it out?' Bobbi asked simply.

Ro was quiet. She could – easily: people regularly posted notes through their letterbox asking whether she and Matt would ever lease.

She looked across at Hump. He was taking in her unruly neither-blonde-nor-brown curls and scruffy tomboy clothes . . . a socialite she wasn't. In fact, she realized with a bit of a shock, she could have passed as his sister.

He smiled broadly. 'It seems to me the only barrier to this working is whether Ro thinks she could put up with *me* all day long . . . I'm out there for the summer too.'

'Well, of course I could,' Ro said politely.

'So then, we're agreed?' Bobbi said quickly.

Ro looked at Hump and Bobbi in panic. She hadn't meant to imply she would, only that she theoretically *could*. This whole conversation was pie in the sky. She couldn't just drop her life in London on a whim and hop over the Atlantic for the summer. That was madness. That was . . . That was exactly what Matt was doing.

'I'm in!'

The words were as much a surprise to her as the vehemence in them.

'Great!' Hump said, punching the air. 'Wait here. I'll get us some beers and we can celebrate.'

'And you can tell those guys out there that they're frolicking in foam for no good reason,' Bobbi added.

'What? And break up a perfectly good party?' Hump grinned. 'I may not want those guys living in my house, but your assessment of me wasn't entirely wide of the mark.' He winked and disappeared down the hall.

Ro felt the butterflies take wing in her stomach. Oh God, what had she done? What had started as a desperate need to talk to someone, even to strangers, had become an agreement to *live* with them? A fizz of nerves surged up inside her as her mind began to process the news: she'd beaten off the sharp suits and champagne-bearing socialites to win a much-coveted summer share in the Hamptons! She wasn't sure whether to laugh or cry. She wanted to tell Matt. She could already imagine his grin, the light in his eyes as he took in that she was doing this for him. She wouldn't just wait; she'd be part of the adventure too. She'd be showing him that she was also capable of change, that she wasn't stuck in a rut or old before her time. This was what he *wanted* her to do: live, explore, find adventure.

'Well, I guess this means I'm going to get to try your famous jelly,' Bobbi said.

Jelly? Ro realized she meant the marmalade and her fingers found the jar in her pocket. 'I'll bring a box over. I'm a regular Paddington Bear.'

'A who?'

'Oh.' Ro pulled a face, embarrassed again. 'He's a character from my childhood. It's an English thing – a bear who travels from deepest, darkest Peru and ends up at Paddington Station with a note round his neck saying, "Please look after this bear."'

'"Please look after this bear"?' Bobbi shook her head apologetically. 'We had *Sesame Street.*'

'Well, Paddington loves marmalade too,' Ro added lamely. 'That's why I . . .' Her voice trailed away. Why was she talking about Paddington Bear at a party in a penthouse with a girl who looked like she sprinkled gold dust on her cornflakes?

They were quiet for a moment, the silence between them growing more awkward as they considered their new relationship: they'd gone from being strangers – hell, combatants – on the street to housemates in twenty minutes.

'But the similarities end there, right?' Bobbi asked. 'With the bear, I mean. No . . . excess body hair issues I should know about? 'Cause if we're sharing a bathroom . . .'

Ro laughed. 'No, it's all good,' she grinned, as Hump burst back in, a beer bottle wedged between each finger.

But that wasn't strictly true. There were distinct similarities between her and the famous bear – lots of them, in fact: she was on an adventure now too, relying on the kindness of strangers and with a jar of marmalade in her pocket. And if she had had a tag round her neck, it would have read almost identically: 'Please look after this girl.'

# Chapter Four

'Right. Just stay right,' Ro muttered between gritted teeth, gripping the wheel a little harder as she drove beneath another green road sign that she was, again, past before she could understand. Oh God. Was 44E the junction or the road? she panicked, her eyes flicking down to the sheet of paper printed with map directions on the seat beside her, before the sharp hoot of the car to her right told her she was drifting across the lanes again. Dammit. Navigation really wasn't her thing. It had already taken her four circuits of JFK Airport before she'd found her way out to the highway – she'd visited the DHL depot twice, much to the security guard's chagrin – and she had no idea if she was heading towards Manhattan, Montauk or, frankly, the moon.

So much for just hooking a right and keeping going till she drove into the Atlantic. It had looked so easy on the map – Long Island a long, skinny arm that shot out of America's mainland and straight into the Atlantic Ocean, Montauk sitting at the fingertips, East Hampton – where she was headed – more in the wrist.

But then, all of this had seemed easy before she had actually had to go and do it. It had been one thing sharing her news when she'd flown home in early April, revelling in the shocked expressions and envious eyes as she'd casually dropped the bombshell that she – *she*, who needed moral support getting in a round at the Pig & Whistle – was moving to America for the summer. She hadn't been left behind after all, see? Brenda, her cleaner, had agreed to 'adopt' Shady in her absence – it had been depressing to realize that the humble goldfish was pretty much her only responsibility tying her there – so that she could have her own adventure too. She'd delighted in recounting how she'd 'won' a coveted bedroom in Hump's house from the bathroom, boasting about Bobbi's sharp ambition and slim ankles, showing off the photos of the white-sand beaches and the sunny forecasts that she brought up on the internet. It had been so good being the one with the surprise for once, when she'd spent years listening to everyone else's of secret weekends away, long-awaited pregnancy joys, big promotions, intricate marriage proposals . . . And it had restored a little of her pride. She'd seen the way everyone had looked pityingly at her as news got out about Matt's tour of Asia – alone – for six months. They hadn't heard her when she'd reassured them that they weren't actually breaking up; they were simply pausing, taking a breather. They'd just nodded politely when she'd said Matt had told her he was going to spend the entire trip dreaming up an original and romantic marriage proposal for his return. They hadn't known that she had repeated his words with a beatific calm she didn't feel: 'It's not the end. He just wants us to have a new beginning.'

So yes, she had enjoyed talking about this 'adventure'. It had given her a glamour and an edge that had caught her friends unawares. But now, wedged between two monster trucks on an expressway in rush hour and unable to remember the laws about overtaking, she wasn't feeling so confident. The New York suburbs had given way to dense woodland that bracketed the highway, occasional dead raccoons in the road reminding her that it wasn't just the cars and accents that were different over here. Even the roadkill had an American flavour.

After a while, a sign for '27E Montauk' directed her to take the right-hand slip road and she relaxed her grip on the wheel, grateful for this karmic mercy. She knew the 27 Highway ran like a bone down the length of Long Island's skinny arm, and that she only had to drive in a straight line now, right into East Hampton's high street – or rather, Main Street.

Still, Hump had promised to keep his phone near him, in case she got lost. He was already at the house. It was the end of May; the summer season officially started this weekend and Greg – a lawyer friend of Hump's brother who was in the fourth bedroom – and Bobbi would be over tomorrow. Ro was looking forward to seeing her again: as the only other person she vaguely knew in the whole of America, Ro felt an artificial closeness to the architect – like a gosling imprinting on a panther – that paid no heed to the bolts of terror that flashed through her every time she read Bobbi's tweets: 'Five a.m. kettlebells. #hellyeah'; 'To M.I.T. 4 talk on Spatial Strategies of Resistance #bringit'.

Ro was looking forward to seeing Hump again too. They had communicated with increasing frequency via Facebook for the past six weeks, their messages becoming more relaxed by the day as their updates and photo posts educated them remotely about each other's lives. For instance, Ro already knew Hump could surf (a little bit – the photos mainly showed him wiping out), that he changed girls like he changed underpants (every three days), and he considered the lime that came with his vodka to be one of his five a day. He knew that she, on the other hand, was partial to 'box-set weekends', drank only wine in pubs and bought fish food in bulk (Brenda wasn't going to have to spend a penny on Shady, even if she didn't come back for a year). Greg was technically their Facebook friend too, but his page didn't even have a photo of him, and he hadn't posted anything at all in the six weeks since they'd paid their deposits.

'It's all going to be great. Just great,' Ro whispered to herself as she drove through Southampton and then Bridgehampton, where preppy-looking men and nautical-chic women were clustered round cafe tables, sipping soy lattes and reading the local papers as the Manhattan commuters looked on enviously in their scramble to join them.

The road had become narrower now, having segued from a dual carriageway to a single-lane road a while back, and was flanked on either side with standalone units housing antiques and contemporary furniture shops; long, low, painted wooden deli huts with the shutters pushed up and fresh fruits and vegetables arranged on trays; enormous, grand redbrick schools with pretty white windows, flags in flagpoles and yellow buses parked out the front. The houses she could glimpse through the trees were set back from the road, clapboarded and rustic, with no fences or walls to delineate their garden boundaries, and she didn't see any cats, but plenty of deer.

The road came to a T-junction and Ro followed the traffic round to the left. She knew she was close now. She had just passed the sign for East Hampton Tennis Club and there was a marked shift in tone as she rounded the corner – everything tightened suddenly, raised its game.

A sweeping, daffodil-fringed green (only the leaves left now) with a pond and a windmill on it sat to her right, a ribbon of bucolic, wainscoted and cedar-shingled houses streaming down a straight and widened road that was shaded by giant horse chestnut trees. Ro put her foot on the brake, gliding more slowly down the street with an almost reverential wonder. Everything was so neat and pretty – the colour palette like a watercolour painting, all misty greys and heathery greens, gardens bracketed with the famous white picket fences as stationary swing seats hung on covered porches and carved shutters were pressed flush to the walls.

Her eyes grew even wider as the homes gave way to shops and she counted Tiffany & Co., Ralph Lauren (not one store but three!), Juicy Couture, Tory Burch . . . Her eyes wandered to the people milling around – most of them looking like they were heading to a yoga class or a tennis match – and all shrunken to 30 per cent thinner than the average population.

She stopped at another set of lights and hurriedly reread the directions. Hump had said to take the next right turn after the cinema, which she could see out of her passenger side window. Then it was next right onto Egypt Lane and his house was a quarter of a mile on the left, just by the green.

The trees grew in girth and height as she moved a block away from the town centre, their canopies interlacing like fingers above her, tunnelling the road, and she could tell from the dazzling glare at the end that the ocean lay directly ahead of her. Ro pushed her sunglasses onto the top of her head, her chin almost resting on the wheel as the car idled slowly past houses that were rapidly swelling in size and stature.

She'd never seen anything like it – set back from the wide streets, with no pavement but a wide cycle lane, every single house sat amid a large, manicured plot. Some had barn-style hipped roofs, others multiple pretty dormers; some had covered verandas that ran round the perimeter of the house, others stepped porches, loggias and balconies. They all had pools. They all had Mexican gardeners riding on sit-on mowers or adjusting sprinkler systems. And every, but every estate was pristine and immaculate. There were no wild brambles winding round the picket fences, no flaking paint at the windows or missing shingle tiles, no cars that hadn't been hand-polished – heck, no cars, it seemed, that were more than two years old. How was it possible for an entire community to share the same sense of aesthetic perfection? Did they have neighbourhood meetings where they chose their house colours from a coordinating palette so that none clashed? Maybe it was somebody's job to make sure that newcomers to the area kept to the scheme. This wasn't a simple case of 'keeping up with the Joneses'. Out here, even the Joneses were keeping up – with the Spielbergs and Martins and Parkers, if Hump was to be believed.

She saw the triangular green Hump had told her to watch out for, passed it and indicated left as she spotted the red water hydrant. Ten metres on, she pulled into the drive signposted, 'Sea Spray,' and switched off the ignition with a muffled shriek. She had done it! She was alive!

She peered through the windscreen at Sea Spray Cottage – her home for the summer. The house was far smaller than those she'd passed further up the street – it was indeed only a cottage with three dormers upstairs, a small porch with steps – and there was almost no garden at the front, just a short patch of lawn behind a low, undulating hedge. Why had there been such a clamour for a room in this house? There had been at least a hundred people at the party that night, but this cottage was nothing compared to its neighbours (even though she personally preferred old-world charm to grandeur). Clad in cedar shingle that had weathered to a dove grey, plain shutters flanked the downstairs windows, and it had a wisteria growing along the porch roof that was in full flower.

Ro stepped out of the hire car and leaned against the door. She could hear the sound of the Atlantic pounding the beach in the distance.

'Hey! I didn't expect you so soon,' Hump said, coming round the porch. He was wearing board shorts and carrying a box in his arms. He dropped it on the Adirondack chair beside him and vaulted over the wooden railings, landing lightly in front of her, his arms out wide.

Ro wasn't sure whether to hug him or shake his hand. She knew him better online than in the flesh, and right now, shirtless, there was a lot of flesh to deal with. She decided to err on the side of caution, opting for the hand-shake – only she caught her own foot as she stepped towards him, and ended up in the next instant with her cheek pressed flat against his warm (seemingly waxed) chest.

Hump grinned as she jumped back in horror and tried to restore composure by thrusting out her hand like a toy soldier.

'You Brits, so *formal*.' He laughed, folding her back into a bear hug.

'Sorry,' she mumbled against his chest.

'And apologetic.'

'Sorry.'

He laughed again, thinking she was joking. 'Are your bags in the trunk?'

'Mmm-hmm,' she nodded, as he opened the boot and pulled out her giant, battered canvas holdall. He peered back round the car at her. 'That's *it*?'

'I travel light.'

'Yeah, but . . . you're gonna be living here for four months. There's hobos with more on their backs than this.'

Ro smiled. 'Did my stuff arrive?' She had sent her photographic and computer equipment ahead by air freight several weeks earlier.

'It's all in the studio, ready for you to unpack.'

'Oh God, I'm so excited – I can't wait to see it,' Ro said, biting her fingers.

'Well, you don't have to. I was just going to stop by the unit before you got here. I've got to drop off the ads.' He pulled a poster from the box on the chair and unrolled it. Hayley, the maid of honour, pouted back at her, looking sexy and vibrant and enticing in her glamorously dishevelled get-up with the provocative sign 'Get Humped this summer' round her neck. 'Remember her?'

Ro laughed in astonishment, a hand clapped over her mouth as she took in, at the bottom, what appeared to be a timetable of shuttle runs from Main Street to the beaches. He'd been doing ads for his business?

'We could do the tour when we get back.'

'Totally . . . You did get her permission, right?'

'Yeah. And her number,' he winked. A phone inside the house rang. 'Listen, I gotta take that call – I've been waiting the past half-hour for it. Why don't you check out the beach and I'll come pick you up in ten minutes?'

Ro looked down the street towards the band of bright sky. 'That way?'

Hump was already barging through the door, racing for the phone. 'That's it. Left fork, first right onto Old Beach Lane,' he called. 'Three-minute walk.'

Ro started walking, waking her body up again. It felt good to stretch after so many hours sitting cramped on the plane and then hunched, rictus-like with tension, as she negotiated the traffic. A couple of girls cycled past her in the opposite direction, wearing swirled, brightly coloured minidresses and chatting away in high-pitched voices, cars driving past at a leisurely pace, everyone relaxed from a day at the beach.

To her right was a panoramic golfing green, and at its fringe, a sprawling building that Ro could tell was grand from the roof alone. As she passed the car park, she clocked a line-up of top-of-the-range Range Rovers, Mercedes SLs, Jaguars and Aston Martins.

The beach car park just beyond it had cars with a lower spec – SUVs, a couple of saloons and vans. A group of bare-chested teenage boys in baggies were laughing with some girls in cut-off jeans and bikini tops sitting on the tailgate of a Chevy, low music pulsing from the dash. Ro walked past them towards the wooden railings that delineated the beach, pulling off her Converses without bothering to undo the laces, her eyes fixed on the huge heave of the ocean, which broke and smashed upon the shore, the wind pick-ing sand off the set-back dunes and combing it up into the sky, while bending the bleached grasses almost flat to the ground. Either side, left and right, stretched miles of unending blond beach chopped up with footprints, distant dog-walkers and joggers silhouetted by the low sun that cast angled rays across the water, making it gleam like cut glass.

The light was incredible, strong and blinding, and her hand instinctively reached for the camera hanging round her neck. It was always there, like a favourite necklace, ready to point and click – not just to capture the moment but make it real. For Ro, ever since her parents had given her a camera for her eleventh birthday – the last one before they died – life was only real through the lens: she only felt a moment in the fraction after the 'click'; she only remembered it when she saw it on film – even her last image of Matt before he'd disappeared through airport security had to be confirmed on the display screen before she could actually believe and process that he'd gone.

She walked down to the shore, camera poised at her eye as she framed the landscape, making sense of it in neat circles, adjusting the focus by single degrees as it pinned on the plovers that wheeled in the sky, the dot-dot-dash of the wind over the water. The zoom lens found a dog chasing a frisbee into the surf, and as she tracked its leap through the air, droplets from its coat shining like crystal in the blue sky, she picked up on something else beyond: two young children standing by the shore, throwing something into the water.

They looked like ebony cameos from her vantage point, but Ro could see one was a girl from her dress billowing behind her in the wind. Their chins were tucked down, their hair lifted off the backs of their necks as they watched something floating in the water in front of them.

Ro started clicking automatically, loving the way their silhouettes were picked out in such high definition against the sparkling water behind, tiny ambassadors of childhood with their duck curls and plump limbs. The shutter came down repeatedly like a fluttering eyelid – black, image, black, image – the children oblivious to her presence or the way the camera tracked their movements.

But Ro was as lost as they were; she didn't see the man racing towards her, his fists clenched, the sand kicked up in plumes behind him, and when, in the next moment, everything went black, Ro jumped back in alarm.

The man had clamped his hand across the camera lens and was staring at her with a trembling, pinched fury.

'Who the *hell*,' he said quietly and ominously slowly, 'do you think you are?'

Ro stared back at him, open-mouthed and too shocked to reply. Who was he? Where had he come from?

'Why are you photographing my children?'

She blinked at him.

'You think it's OK to intrude with your goddam camera? A *pretty* scene, is it?'

Ro literally couldn't find her voice. The anger in his eyes was terrifying. He looked wild and barely restrained, his dark brown hair blown forward like a nimbus around his face, which was angular and planed, his blue-shock eyes red-rimmed and unblinking.

'Give me the camera.' His hand was still on the lens and his grip tightened round it, no longer merely obscuring the view but trying to pull the camera away from her.

That was enough to bring back her voice. 'What? No!'

'You are not keeping those images. Give me the camera.'

'I bloody well won't!' Ro cried, trying to step back, but with the strap still round her neck and a full-grown man attached to the camera lens, she was stuck. Her neck bent forward from the jolt and she winced. The man released the camera at once and she stepped back, out of reach immediately, rubbing her neck with her free hand to make a point.

'This is a £3,000 piece of equipment. Over my dead body am I handing it over to some bully boy like you,' she said fiercely, adrenalin beginning to surge through her now.

'Bu-*bully* boy?' the man demanded incredulously. 'You take photographs of my kids without consent and I'm the bully boy?'

'I couldn't see your damned kids. They were just silhouetted. They could have been cardboard cut-outs for all I could see. And what's so bloody special about your kids, anyway, that people need to sign some kind of consent form to photograph them on a public beach?'

He stared at her contemptuously, as though he didn't believe she could possibly understand. 'Is it digital?' His forefinger pointed to the camera.

'What?' Ro brought both hands to it. 'Of course it is.'

'Delete the images. I want to see you do it. Right now. In front of me.'

'Or what?'

'Or I'll destroy the photographs another way.' His eyes flickered to the thundering surf behind them. Ro got the point quickly.

'That would be criminal damage!' she shouted, taking another step away from him, her knuckles white as she grasped the camera strap in a death grip.

'And *this* is an invasion of privacy,' the man shouted back. 'Do it now!' He took a step towards her.

'All right! All right!' Ro cried, holding up her hand. 'Jeez! I'll delete the bloody pictures.'

'All of them.'

'Yes, fine. God! All of them.'

'Now.' He took another step closer, but his voice was fractionally calmer again, his body language marginally less threatening.

She stared at him for a moment, then looked down to do as he asked, but the sun was so bright she couldn't see the images playing on the screen. She turned her back to the sun and bent her head down, brushing her hair forward to shade the screen. She started, disturbed as the man came and stood right by her, actually moving her hair on one side so that he could see the screen too.

'I said I'd do it,' Ro snapped, but unable to turn her head without her face being centimetres from his.

'And I'm just making sure you do,' he said, his voice a low growl over her shoulder.

He smelt of limes and salt, this stranger, his hair tickling her neck as they stood side by side, and she rubbed her neck ostentatiously, tutting and showing her revulsion at his proximity.

She scrolled back through the images, which were clearly visible now in the shade the two of them were creating. Her heart almost broke as she saw her own work – the photographs were beautiful: the children standing in profile, truly anonymous, as she'd said, perfectly backlit by the early evening sun, their snub noses and rounded tummies, even their long lashes picked out against the glittering bleached water behind them, the dunes rising like mountains in the distance. Ro felt her breath hitch – there was a poignancy to them that was almost tangible. Ambassadors of childhood they certainly were. Little did this fool know he'd ordinarily have to pay £2,500 for the privilege of getting her to photograph his beloved children.

'Delete them,' the man said beside her ear.

There were eighteen images and she reluctantly pressed 'delete' as she scrolled back through each one. It was such a waste. Even in this light she could tell these photographs were some of her best work – that happy collision of finding the perfect subjects in perfect shooting conditions. But he wasn't a photographer; he had no idea how difficult it was to marry those two things together, she thought resentfully as each one disappeared into the ether, and all because he was some overprotective parent who didn't know any better.

She came to the last image, her finger hovering above the button. The children were holding hands in this picture, the little girl's dress caught like a sail by the wind. It was the best one of the bunch: she didn't want to delete it. It was almost unbearably beautiful, and a flash of defiance streaked through her as her finger hovered in mid-air. Could he make her delete it? What legal right did he have to control what she photographed on a public beach? Would he *really* throw her camera in the water if she refused? She hesitated, quickly assessing her chances against him. He was only a bit older than her – maybe mid-thirties – tall at over six feet, but of slim build, certainly lighter than Matt anyway, and she was used to wrestling him (well, after a fashion). And that was if he caught her. He wouldn't be expecting her to run, and if she could get a head start, he couldn't very well chase her down the beach and abandon his kids . . .

'Do it,' he said more forcefully, as though reading her mind.

'No!' Ro snapped, her temper quicker than she was – but not quicker than him. In a flash he had grabbed her, scooping her off her feet and cradling her in his arms as he headed furiously towards the water.

'Stop it! Put me down!' she screamed, shocked and kicking her legs uselessly as he began to wade in, splashing them both. 'You're a bloody maniac! You can't do this!'

'I was very clear,' he said through gritted teeth as he stepped in deeper, moving towards the waves breaking forcefully just a few metres away.

Ro threw her arms round his neck, holding on to him like grim death. 'All right! OK!' she shrieked, forced to turn her body into his to protect the camera still hanging round her neck from the water frothing around them.

He stopped walking. 'Do it,' he said, his unfamiliar voice reverberating in her ear.

She pulled away, disgusted to be so close to him, to be held by him like this. 'I said I would, didn't I?' she said furiously, her cheeks red with anger and humiliation.

'You said it before too. I don't trust you. Do it now before I drop you on your ass right here.' He was thigh-deep in the water, his navy linen shorts well and truly soaked. If he dropped her here, the camera would be a write-off. His face was just inches from hers, and she could see from the look in his eyes that this was no bluff: he absolutely would do it. With a furious huff, she let go of his neck and opened up the screen again.

'There!' she said, as the bin icon popped up on the screen, tears stinging her eyes. She'd never felt such rage before – to have a total stranger accost her on the beach like this and threaten to destroy her camera, throw her in the water . . .

'Thank you.' His voice had changed again. He sounded calm, almost polite, and as though it was normal to wade into the ocean with unwitting passers-by.

He turned and walked them both back out of the water, setting her down on the sand gently as though he'd just rescued her. Several people had stopped to watch, and the children had come over and were standing in front of them now.

Ro was trembling and not just from the chill of the water. What the hell had just happened? Was this assault?

'What you doing, Daddy?' the little girl asked. She looked to be maybe three, four? Blonde bobbed hair, wide blue eyes and wearing a navy and white striped pinafore dress that looked more expensive than anything Ro was wearing – or owned.

'Just playing,' the man said, his hand smoothing the little girl's hair. 'Did it look funny?'

The girl nodded.

'Me now!' said the little boy. He was smaller, probably not long out of nappies, his hair dark brown like his father's.

'Uh-uh. Not in those clothes.'

Ro felt another surge of anger. Oh! But it was fine to get her soaked, was it? She shook out her khaki cargoes and pulled away Matt's grey T-shirt, which was now clinging to her skin.

She looked up to find the man watching her. At least he

was even wetter than she was. 'Well,' he said quickly, nodding at her, 'thanks for being a sport.'

Ro's jaw dropped. *A sport?* A bloody sp— She realized he was covering in front of the children and bit her lip, certain she would draw blood. What could she say, anyway? It was done. He'd got what he wanted, even if it had humiliated her in the process. Without a word, she turned and stomped away, back towards the car park, her breath coming in short, angry hiccups. Her Converses were where she had left them in the sand and she sat on the wooden railing to pull them on. In the distance, she could see the man walking away after the children as they ran ahead of him. She saw him turn after a while and look back, and she fell still, hoping he couldn't make her out at this distance. She was completely shaken up by what had just passed, trying to rewind the events and make sense of them.

A car horn beeped behind her and she saw Hump leaning out of a bright yellow, long wheel-based Defender with a canvas ragtop. 'The Hamptons Humper,' was emblazoned in navy lettering along the sides.

'Holy shit! What happened to you?' he laughed, as she trudged over, hands clamped to the camera, her clothes clinging to her. 'I leave you alone for ten minutes . . .'

'Don't ask,' Ro muttered, wiping the bitter tears away with the back of her hand as he leaned over to open the door, and she slid in beside him. 'It's a long story.'

# Chapter Five

'So whaddya think?' Hump asked, his eyes resting on her as Ro turned another circle on the spot, her eyes recording every last detail of the studio. 'You like?'

'Like? I love!' she gasped, clasping her hands above her heart. 'I never dreamed it would be so . . . so adorable!'

'Amagansett is pretty cute, period, but the Square is totally prime. I can't tell you how lucky I was to get this for a summer let. Right place, right time. Right housemate,' he added, acknowledging that this opportunity was only theirs because they were sharing the costs together. Ro was just about able to stretch to it after her colossal rent by dipping into what was supposed to be the contingency fund for the cottage back home and crossing her fingers, hoping that the boiler didn't break down.

Ro ran to the window and stared out again at the little green. It was set back from the road – the Montauk Highway, which she'd already travelled on and which was the official in-out to the Hamptons – and bordered on three sides by low-lying white clapboarded units. Neat paths connected them all, criss-crossing the spotless grass and mature trees, and there was a tiny bandstand in the middle. Ro and Hump had one of the smallest units, with a smart beach store on their right and a yoga studio on their left as you faced them. Just beyond it was an ice-cream parlour with low-slung shell-backed wooden Adirondack chairs – ubiquitous out here, it seemed – outside, and further round, a vinyl record store and a spa, and finally, opposite, an interiors boutique.

Ro wrapped her arms around herself happily. It was a shopping destination within a proper community. How could her business do anything *but* thrive here? There was plenty of free parking on the road and round the back, and the demographic of the users – if the other retailers were anything to go by – would be AB1s, her target customer.

Hump was opening up one of the many boxes stacked inside the studio. 'Tada!' he sang, pulling out a yellow vinyl banner inscribed with 'The Hamptons Humper' in navy lettering. She laughed again at the name. Very few people could get away with something quite so outré, but Hump had both semantics and a guileless, winning smile on his side.

'So talk me through this,' she said, walking back across the room and sitting on one of the boxes, watching as he lovingly unfurled the banner and began threading laces through the eyelets. 'What's so entrepreneurial about being a taxi driver?'

'The fact that I'm running for free, for starters.' He pointed to the edge of the banner near to her foot. 'Step on that corner, will you, to stop it rolling.'

Ro did as she was told. 'I know you're being deliberately oblique. How can a taxi service be free?'

He sat back on his heels and looked up at her. 'As of tomorrow – Memorial Day weekend and the official start of the Hamptons season – only residents can get permits to park at the beach parking lots. Everyone else either has to walk several miles with all their beach stuff or get a mortgage to pay for cabs.'

'It can't be that bad, surely,' Ro scoffed.

'How's sixty dollars to Montauk sound to you?'

'From *here*, or do you mean New York?'

'Exactly. People have had enough. So this is my idea – I do runs from the Indian Wells, Wiborg, Egypt and Main beaches to and from Main Street every ten minutes. All free.'

'But where's the profit? For goodness' sake, where's the income?'

'Advertising. I've had mounts put in for posters in the back of the car. Local businesses get to bid against each other to have their ads and special promotions inside the Humpers. I've got a fleet of four Landys – with an option on another two if I decide to expand into the Amagansett beaches – which can take eight passengers at a time, and you can bet your teeth that they'll all be between eighteen and thirty-five and wondering where to go that night. I've estimated for each car to do six runs an hour for ten hours a day, so sixty runs per car with eight passengers each time. That's four hundred and eighty people per vehicle. Multiply by four of them and you're looking at nearly two thousand *target* customers a day. The ads have to change on a daily basis, so the riders get something new to look at. Plus all riders get free entry or a drink voucher or some sort of discount from the winning advertiser, depending on the type of business they've got.' He finished lacing the runner and fastened it with a reef knot. 'Auctions close at midnight the day before, and I've got a deal with the local printer to do short runs for us between six and eight in the morning, getting the posters printed before nine a.m. for the first run that day.'

'Wow.' Ro nodded, impressed. 'That really is entrepreneurial thinking.'

'I've been coming here my whole life. I know how pissed people get at having to fork out crazy money just to get to and from the beach. This way, we keep visitors happy and they use the local businesses.'

He shrugged and picked up the banner, carrying it outside. Ro followed after.

'Can you attach that corner to the hook there?' he asked, doing the same at his end.

They both stepped back and admired the vivid banner hanging to the left above the door. The colours looked great – nautical, sporty, chic – against the pristine white woodwork.

'Shouldn't it be centred?' Ro asked, suppressing a yawn as she pointed to the remaining area. Her long day was catching up with her, the adrenalin from her unpleasant encounter on the beach now all but ebbed away and leaving her with a throbbing fatigue.

'Aha!' Hump said mysteriously, ducking indoors again and returning with a small box. 'For you. A welcome present.'

Ro looked at him quizzically as she took it. Inside was another banner – same dimensions, same font; even the colourway was identical – just reversed – with yellow writing on a navy background: 'Marmalade Family Media.'

'You wouldn't give me a name!' he said, watching as her hands flew to her mouth. 'I kept asking you.'

'Because I didn't know. I couldn't decide!' she laughed. 'I can't believe you did that! That was why you were asking?'

He caught her eye and she saw he looked nervous. 'Do you like it?'

'I love it!' she trilled, jumping on her toes and clapping her hands excitedly.

'Yeah? 'Cos you don't need to keep it. Far be it for me to be interfering with your business plans. I just thought . . . well, you needed something. Everyone has a sign out here.'

'Hump, it's great. I could never have thought of such a good name. Come on, help me hang it up.'

Together, they unfurled it, threading the eyelets with the cord and hanging it from the hooks beside the yellow banner.

'We look good together,' Hump said, crossing his arms, casting a sly look in her direction.

Ro laughed, knowing his flirtation was half-hearted and more for appearance's sake than anything. 'No. We really don't.'

'Really, though?'

'Really,' she grinned, slapping him lightly on the arm.

'Ah well, at least I can say I tried,' he said, bouncing up the steps. Ro followed after, catching her foot on the top step and tummy-surfing in through the door.

Hump turned with surprise and burst out laughing at the sight of her, arms outstretched.

'Hey! What is it with you?' he asked, helping her up. 'You OK? You are *always* tripping up.'

She dusted herself down, her pride bruised again. 'My left foot is a size bigger than my right, meaning I always catch it.'

'You mean I got a real-life Big Foot lodging with me?' he laughed, throwing an arm round her shoulders and squeezing affectionately.

'Yeah, yeah, never heard that one before,' Ro quipped, but with a smile. She doubted anyone could get cross with Hump.

The studio was sparsely furnished inside with only a small battered desk, a chair and a laptop in Hump's 'corner'. (He had generously given Ro two-thirds of the space, even though they were splitting the rent fifty-fifty. 'I only need a place to make calls,' he'd insisted.) There was a long, painted wooden counter and a tall tripod stool in hers.

'I guess I should make a start on these boxes,' Ro sighed, eyeing the stack wearily. It was only half past seven, but her body was telling her it was past midnight, and she'd been up at dawn for her flight. She'd been on the go for nineteen hours straight, and frankly, those boxes were beginning to look like beds to her.

'You look . . .' Hump took in her salt-dried clothes and wild hair. 'You look like you could do with a coffee.'

Ro's shoulders slumped. 'Kill for one.'

'How d'you take it?'

'Just normal.'

Hump looked at her, baffled. 'You mean filter, full caff, dash of fat, double-shot espresso?'

Ro furrowed her brow in return. 'I think I do.'

'OK. Well, I'm going over to Mary's Marvellous – thataway.' He jerked his thumb towards the highway behind him so she could see where he was going. 'Back in five.'

Ro took a deep, galvanizing breath – caffeine was coming! – and tore open the first box. Inside was her edit of the best family portraits she'd photographed in London – some in Richmond Park, others Barnes Common, some in a studio she rented, others at people's homes – and had framed. She had packed twenty-two, unable to be any more ruthless than that.

She looked around at the long, bare walls – they were certainly big enough to take them all, but she'd need to get some nails and a hammer first thing. She bit her lip excitedly as she saw her favourite one. It was significantly larger than the rest, taken of two young brothers, aged three and eighteen months. Their heads were tilted together and she'd come in so tight on the shot their faces couldn't be deciphered in isolation but became a composite of everything that babies are: rosy blushed cheeks, gappy milk teeth, shining eyes and lustrous, long lashes. What rendered the image so captivating, though, was the mistake in it – they had been shooting outside and the wind had blown one of her own hairs in front of the lens the very moment she clicked. It was too blurred to be identifiable in itself but lent a dreamy haze to the feeling of the picture. The mother had actually wept when she'd seen it for the first time. (And Ro had learned to tie her hair back in a ponytail. She'd been lucky that time, but . . .)

Ro smiled as she decided, mercilessly, to hang it immediately opposite the front door. She propped it against the skirting board, ready to hang, and arranged the others at spaced intervals. With these images on the walls – and this one in particular – she could show customers exactly what she could do and win them over before she even opened her mouth – much less told them her fees.

She moved on to the next box. It was the heaviest, rammed with fully bound photobooks – the digital generation's photo albums – which were tall, glossy and printed on thick non-fade photographic paper. The ones she had brought with her – again, a tight edit of her entire collection – showed the gamut of her clients' experiences: one depicted the life story of an eighty-year-old university lecturer (and had taken over a hundred hours to edit), another a baby's first year (almost as long, given the obsessive amount of photos taken of the precious child), a gap yah in South America, a country wedding in Somerset, a 'leavers' book for a group of public-school girls . . . Ro decided to leave them in the box for safe keeping until she could buy a large table to arrange them on and position in the centre of the studio for easy browsing.

The third box held some of her hardware: three small flat screens that could be wall mounted and rigged with headphones, playing the short films she'd made of the subjects on loop. She almost wept at the sight of her Apple Mac sitting at the bottom. It had been shockingly hard coping without it for three long weeks as it was air-freighted over, and she dusted it off lovingly, arranging it on the corner of the long counter, where it booted up without a hitch, thanks to the Square's upgraded Wi-Fi and broadband connections.

Hump wandered back in, a cardboard tray of coffees and giant cookies in his hand. 'I thought sugar too. You look like you need it.'

'Charming,' Ro quipped, accepting both her caffeine and sugar hits gratefully.

'Whoa!' Hump exclaimed, catching sight of the prints lined against the skirting board. 'You did these?'

'Indeed,' Ro sighed, sliding her arms out on the counter and resting her head for a moment.

'These are awesome. I had no idea you were so good! I mean, when I saw you at the wedding, you were so engrossed, so in the moment, you know? I thought it was cool, but . . .' He turned back to her. 'No, you can't sleep! Not yet or you'll be awake at four!' Hump ordered, jogging over and pulling her hair back from her face. Her eyes were closed, her breathing already slowing down. 'Drink up. Now.'

Ro groaned and reluctantly did as she was told.

'Do you ever take that thing off?' he asked, clocking the camera still hanging round her neck. 'I don't think I've ever seen you without it. You even drove with it on.'

Her hands automatically wandered to it, stroking it like a pacifier. 'I've got to be ready. You can't imagine how awful it would be for me to miss the moment because I didn't have my camera with me.'

'Huh.'

'I know, it's weird,' she said, embarrassed. 'It's my thing. Matt doesn't get it either.'

'Matt's this famous boyfriend of yours?'

Ro nodded, digging her teeth into the side of the paper cup as she wondered where Matt was right at this instant. Trekking through a jungle? Sleeping in a mountain-top monastery? What time was it even, over there? She was going to have to recalibrate now that she was another five hours behind him. They hadn't spoken since Sunday, four days ago, and even that had been only their fourth call since his departure. She'd need to give him her numbers out here – both for the house and the studio. She couldn't afford to miss his calls. They were rare enough.

Hump took her silence as a cue not to probe further. 'So did you take any photos on the beach?'

'What?' She looked back at him, fuggy with tiredness.

'Earlier, when you went to the beach. Did you take any photos?'

'I—' The humiliation rained down on her again. 'No.' She shook her head. 'No, I didn't.'

'You *must* be picky. It was a killing sunset tonight.'

'I know,' Ro mumbled. The light had been so perfect when she'd been photographing the children, before their maniac father had assaulted her and—

With a small gasp, she grabbed her camera from round her neck, ejected the memory card and booted it into the computer.

'What's up?' Hump asked, taking in her intense expression. He wandered round the counter to stand by her and see what she was doing. '"System Recovery,"' he read aloud, watching the screen as she typed quickly. Obscure code was tracking along the bottom of the monitor. 'So what's all this?'

'I'm recovering some photos I deleted earlier,' she murmured, her brow deeply furrowed.

Hump looked astonished. 'You can do that? I thought when they were gone, they were gone?'

Ro shook her head. 'Not necessarily. When you press "delete", all you actually lose is the pathfinder to the photo in the system, not the file itself. I've got data-recovery software that I bought for precisely this reason. It's my insurance policy. I can't afford to lose images from a shoot,' she said, never moving her eyes from the screen. 'As long as you don't take any new photos, you should be able to recover them; if you do, the new ones will write over the old ones and then they are gone for good.'

An image of the two silhouetted children standing by the water popped up on the screen. 'Aha!' she cried, clapping her hands together delightedly. 'Gotcha! You can't bully me, mister!'

'Who's bullying you?' Hump asked, looking around the room as though to check whether he was missing anyone.

Ro turned to face him, rubbing his bare arm with her hand. 'I'd love to tell you,' she said, beaming, 'but . . . it's a long story.'

# Chapter Six

She was awake at four. It wasn't the sound of a sparrow pecking on the windowpane that did it, or even the distant cymbal crash of the waves on the beach, but the vast, spreading emptiness of Matt's side of the bed that blew over her like a cold breeze. Her right hand had habitually reached behind her, her right foot exploring the space for his legs, but only the smooth expanse of uncrumpled cotton had met her touch – she could still only sleep on her side of the bed – and the realization he was gone had shattered her sleep for the night.

Ro groaned and blinked blearily, her face half smothered by the deep, feathered peach pillow, her left arm dangling over the side of the bed to the floor. Without moving her head, she swivelled her eyes slowly, taking in her surroundings and trying to remember how the rooms in the house joined together, but she couldn't. Last night's tour had been brief to say the least – they had stayed at the studio longer than expected, Hump intrigued to see more of her work and insisting she show him her back catalogue, and she was so tired on their return (3 a.m. London time), she'd felt almost punch-drunk. Hump's plans for supper on the porch had had to be drastically revised. That cookie had been her dinner, the coffee her nightcap, and Hump had no sooner shown her her room – the largest guest room on account of her living there full-time – than she had started untying her shoelaces, drawn to the bed as though hypnotized. Hump had only just managed to bolt from the room before she'd pulled her T-shirt over her head, too tired even to care whether her new housemate saw her in her underwear.

She saw now the floor was wooden with wide, glossy boards the colour of treacle and had a pale green cotton rug atop it. Her bedstead was brass – creaky when she turned over – and the old, tumbled linen sheets were covered with what seemed to be a hand-stitched eiderdown decorated with faded yellow, green and blue diamonds arranged in a star. Both Bobbi and Greg had to bring their own bedding and towels, but Hump had agreed she could use his linens and save on the hefty cost of transporting her own over from the UK or having to buy new here. She noticed a thick bundle of forest-green towels folded neatly on a rattan chair by the window, her own cargoes, T-shirt and bra strewn across the floor like a breadcrumb trail.

She swept a leg across the fitted sheet beneath her – it was so old it had a silken feel to it now – and turned over with another groan, the pillow billowing either side of her face like an airbag. The ceiling was boarded white, with a plain brass pendant light and peach shade, and a pair of unlined curtains hung from a metal pole, not quite meeting in the middle so that a column of strengthening light was drawn along the floor and up the opposite wall, beside her head. There was a narrow pine wardrobe in the far left corner, with a matching chest of drawers with heart-shaped handles and two bedside tables.

Strictly speaking, the decor wasn't Ro's thing. She liked

twenty shades of taupe and reindeer-hide rugs – at least, that was what she'd been planning for the sitting room before Matt had interrupted her with his 'pause' – but even so, the room had warmth and a personality to it that she liked. Hump had said this was his grandfather's house, but she was pretty sure this room had a woman's touch.

Ro had slept with the windows open – more by accident than design – and she swung her legs out of bed, crossing the floor in a curious jog as every floorboard she touched creaked. She pulled the curtains back – which rattled like cargo trains on a track – and leaned on the sill. The sky looked as bleary as she felt – pasty white with just a hint of colour – still shrouded by a thick sea mist that wasn't yet on the retreat; the grass on Egypt Green opposite was beaded with dewdrops and glistened like it had been threaded with crystals in the night; small brown-tummied birds she couldn't identify pecked at the ground for worms; a battered white pickup truck drove slowly past with a posse of Hispanic labourers wedged inside, all wearing baseball caps, their brown arms hanging out of the cab. She watched as they hooked a left and then a right past the junction and motored towards the standalone grand building she'd passed yesterday. Through the trees on the opposite side of the street, she could just make out the form of the vast neighbouring house – grey-cedared, white-windowed, a turquoise pool unwrinkled by the breeze.

Looking left and right at her own house, she saw that her room was in the middle of the row of three dormers, the other guest rooms presumably either side of hers. She vaguely wondered at what time Bobbi and Greg were arriving and how it would be seeing Bobbi again. Things had felt so easy with Hump last night, but Bobbi was more intense, demanding. More New York. Ro yawned and stretched. Right now, she was feeling very Barnes.

She turned away from the window with a shiver. It was chilly at this hour and she was in just her knickers: she had been too sleepy last night even to think of bringing her bag upstairs. She eyed yesterday's clothes with disdain – they had dried stiff with salt, and the cargoes had tide marks on them from the seawater. Every time she looked at them she was reminded of the horror on the beach. She had to get some fresh clothes from her bag.

Pulling the eiderdown from the bed, Ro wrapped it around her shoulders, opened her door tentatively and peered out. The landing area was square, with the staircase rising from a void in the centre, and was framed with balustrading all the way round. Again the floor was wooden, with a couple of lamps standing on small tables and various stippled oil paintings on the walls – all of them seascapes, clearly worked by the same hand. It was apparent no designer had ever been let near the place, yet it had a look of substance about it, that the person who'd arranged it last may not have known about trends, but had known their own mind.

On the far side of the staircase, a door opposite – Hump's room, she assumed – was closed, as was a door to the right; she vaguely recalled Hump saying his room was ensuite. To the left, she could see through the gap, was a bathroom. Ro tiptoed across, tripping on the corner of the eiderdown as she approached and falling forwards with her arms outstretched so that the door banged loudly against the bathroom wall.

'Dammit,' she muttered, using the facilities as quietly as she could, even putting a flannel beneath the water from the tap so that it didn't make a noise hitting the porcelain bowl. The last thing Hump needed was to be disturbed by his jet-lagged lodger.

She crept down the stairs, her body hunched beneath the quilt, grimacing every time a floorboard groaned beneath her weight. She frowned as her feet touched the downstairs floor and she took in the hall, as though seeing it for the first time. She had clearly passed through here last night, but she had no recollection of it at all. Had she sleepwalked up the stairs?

The cottage was far roomier than it appeared from the street, with as much depth as it had width, and downstairs shared the same square layout as upstairs, with rooms flanking off from the central hall. The front door – to her left – was half glazed behind a porch screen, the walls a dark olive green and hung with a few sepia-tinted photographs of a sailing yacht. In the corner to her right, beneath the turn of the staircase, stood an old writing desk, a stack of papers on it gathered into a messy pile and secured by a large McDonald's Coke cup, the straw bent at a jaunty angle.

Ro walked into the room immediately opposite the bottom of the stairs. Three small sofas covered with a faded blue and pink floral print were arranged in a U-shape, a round, glass-topped coffee table between them ringed by coffee mugs. A bowl of potpourri – *potpourri?* – was gathering dust on the mantelpiece of a brick-front chimney, and curling copies of crossword magazines were slotted into a magazine rack.

Next to the sitting room, at the back of the house, was a small dining room. It boasted the same wooden floor and subtle cream wallpaper of the sitting room, but was dominated by a long mahogany table with eight spoon-back chairs. A pair of silver candelabras still held the stubs of cherry-red candles – wax tears dripping down their sides and puddling in soft pools below – and elaborately swagged curtains were held in place by brass scroll tie-backs.

The dining room led into the kitchen – a blue vinyl and veneer 1950s job that seemed not to have been touched on the last redux thirty years earlier. On the plus side, it looked spotlessly clean and had a certain retro cool to it. Ro made a beeline for the kettle. She realized she had left her 'morning box' of teabags and marmalade at the studio with the other items she'd had air-freighted over. She rummaged the overhead cupboard, trying to find something that would pass as tea. Green tea didn't cut it, nor did camomile in her opinion. She had no idea what 'rooibos' even was. She filled the kettle, but the water clattered through the pipes like children down slides and with an accompanying whistle as the pressure was released. Bloody hell, was nothing in this house quiet?

'Yo,' a voice behind her said, and Ro turned to find Hump yawning, wandering into the kitchen as he stretched his long, bare – really very defined – torso, like a big cat.

'Oh my God, Hump!' Ro cried, sagging against the worktop, her hands clapped over her hammering heart. 'You nearly gave me a heart attack! What are you doing out of bed at this hour?' she whispered furiously.

He raised a bemused eyebrow. 'Why are you whispering? We're the only people in the house and we're both up.'

She narrowed her eyes in a 'ha, ha' response. '*Why* are you up? I was being so quiet.'

'Yeah? I've heard quieter bulldozers,' he said, scratching

his head. 'What are *you* doing up? I thought that was the point of you staying up till the point of delirium last night. I was beginning to think you were on drugs.'

'I was *trying* to find my bag.'

'Well, it's not in there,' Hump wise-cracked, looking at the open cupboard behind her.

'*And* I also thought I would make a cup of tea,' she added. 'Not that I can find any tea with tea in it.'

He grinned. 'Your bag's in the hall, by the desk.'

'Oh. I must have missed it.' She realized she was standing before him wearing just the quilt, and pulled it tighter around her shoulders. It was still odd, this sudden intimacy between them – they had become friends online, but were scarcely past 'strangers' in real life, living together after just two fleeting meetings when it had taken her seven years to live with the man she loved. She briefly wondered what Matt would say if he could see her right now, standing in just a quilt opposite a man wearing only a pair of cut-off trackie-bums.

Hump clearly had no such reservations. 'So, what do you think, then?' he asked, spreading his arms wide and gesturing to the house.

'Love it. So charming.'

He looked pleased. 'Thanks. Yeah. I love it too. I mean, I know it needs doing up . . . updating, but—' He shrugged and she knew he meant money he didn't have. 'Besides, I kinda like having it how they had it.'

'They? I thought you said it was your grandfather's?'

'Yeah, he left it to me. My grandmother died a few years before him.'

Ro nodded. 'Did she make this?' she asked, looking down at the quilt.

'For their twentieth wedding anniversary apparently.'

'Cool!' She twisted her head to get a better look at the pattern down her back. 'I can see why you didn't want a load of reprobates trashing the place. It feels like a home.' The kettle began whistling even more insistently. 'Fancy a cuppa?'

'"Fancy a cuppa?" That's tea, right?' Hump echoed with a big grin, mimicking her accent but sounding more like Lord Grantham instead. 'No, thanks. I'm strictly a Joe guy.'

'Ha! Backatcha! That means coffee. I know that – you can't fool me,' Ro said, pointing a finger at him. She reluctantly took a camomile teabag from the box – the least of all evils on offer – and dropped it in her cup. 'By the way, where can I buy some hammers and nails and things? I need to get some stuff before my car's picked up by the hire company later.'

'There's a hardware store on Newton Lane. Guaranteed to sell anything you need.'

'Newton Lane. Now where's that?' The aroma of camomile drifted to her nose and she tried not to gag. She moved the spoon lethargically through the infusion. Tea that looked like wee was no way to start the day.

'From here? Back up to Main Street, straight over the lights, on the right.'

'Great. I'll head over there now, then.' She poured the untouched cup of camomile straight down the sink.

Hump raised an eyebrow. 'Not yet you won't.' His eyes rose to the clock. 'There ain't nowhere open at half four in the morning round here.'

'Oh yeah,' Ro remembered. She felt so awake already. 'Bummer.'

'They open at eight.'

Ro grunted. What was she going to do for three and a half hours? 'You should go back to bed, Hump,' she said miserably. 'You've got a busy day ahead of you. I should probably wash my hair. It looks like someone's tried to knit it.'

He watched her for a moment – disgruntled and out of sorts with her new home and time zone. He ducked low to look at the pale sky through the window. 'You've brought a swimsuit, right?'

Ro looked across at him suspiciously. 'Why?'

'Go put it on. We're going out.'

'Not in the ocean we're not!' She'd had more than enough exposure to the Atlantic temperatures yesterday.

'Did I say that?'

'So what are we doing, then?'

'You're so demanding!' he chortled. 'Just trust me and go put it on, will you?'

Ro exited the kitchen with narrowed eyes but did as he asked. She was never going to get back to sleep now, and there was nothing else to do. She picked up her bag as she passed the desk, doubling back for the cup of Coke. It was half drunk and completely flat, but it was still better than camomile tea.

'Now *this* is how to wake up,' Ro sighed, letting her paddle drop on her thighs as the orange kayak continued to cut through the water without her assistance.

'Don't worry about me! I'm fine! I'll just carry on, shall I?' Hump called mockingly over her shoulder, his paddle a syncopated blur as alternate ends cut through the water.

'My arms are killing me. *And* I've drenched myself,' Ro half laughed, half wailed as she looked down at her T-shirt, which, for the second time in twelve hours, was soaked and now also clinging to her swimsuit beneath.

'That's because you're putting the paddle in flat. You've got to twist your wrist.'

'Yeah, yeah. I bet you say that to all the girls,' Ro quipped, making Hump splutter with laughter behind her.

'I could get used to this.' She sighed happily again as they drifted past long reeds. They were the only ones out on the 'pond' – a large saltwater lake that was set back behind Georgica Beach, where the ocean had breached the sandy banks to create a spit. All the inhabitants of the shoreline houses were still tucked up in bed, making this expedition feel even more secretive and special as a result. It felt so wild and natural here, unlike the groomed perfection of the streets and beach, with its whiter-than-white sand and picture-postcard bars. She watched a couple of swans gliding on the green water on the far side of the lake – or pond, as Hump kept calling it, although it was pretty damn big to be called a pond in her estimation. If something was halfway between a puddle and a lake, then that was a pond.

'Do you do this a lot, then?' she asked, turning her head slightly so that he could hear.

'Much as I can.'

'I expect your party lifestyle gets in the way, doesn't it?' she asked. His Facebook page had been gruelling to read at times.

'Actually, those are the mornings when I like coming here most. Reminds me of what really matters when I've travelled too far down the path of hedonism.' He paddled on one side for a few strokes, turning the craft slowly away from the reeds. 'Sunset's a good time to come out too, although it's busier. Hey, you ever tried stand-up paddle-boarding?'

'No, and I'm not sure I should. My centre of gravity is all in my chest. I'd be permanently face first in the water.' She heard Hump chuckling behind her. 'What?'

'Well, between that and your crazy feet . . .'

'Hey, it's not funny. It was mortifying when I was younger. I was always convinced someone would notice during swimming lessons. It was like having a third nipple or something.' It was true she had lived with a fear of being noticed for most of her life, and the inhibitive worry about her feet had transferred to her curves when puberty hit. Strangely, though, she didn't feel as self-conscious around Hump. He was so unthreatening, non-judgemental. He was easier company to be around than many of her girl-friends, and they hadn't stopped talking, laughing and joking since she'd arrived. The only thing they hadn't done enough was eat, and her tummy grumbled loudly as if to make the point.

'Urgh, I'm starved,' she said, slapping her hand over her stomach and almost losing her paddle to the water. Hump caught it and handed it back.

'Yeah? Me too.' He checked his watch. 'Hmm, it's gone seven. I know a great place does early-bird breakfasts.'

'Perfect.'

'Wanna head back?'

'Totally. But then I must get home to wash my hair before we go to the studio and greet Joe Public. I can't keep getting all this seawater in it and not rinsing it. It looks like it was styled by crabs on crack.'

'You're a riot, you know that?' Hump chuckled behind her as he started paddling again.

Ro began paddling too. 'Actually, I think I'm pretty good at this,' she said, as they picked up speed rapidly. 'I don't usually do any exercise, but any sport that involves sitting down, I just seem to be a natural,' she said, just as her paddle hit the water flat, with a smack, and lifted half a cubic ton of water with it as she pulled it back up. It landed on Hump like an upturned bucket and he jumped out of his seat from the shock, landing so hard that the kayak wobbled precariously beneath them, pushing out waves in the water that raced for the reeds.

'Hump!' Ro called worriedly, letting go of her oar to hold on to the sides for balance.

'No – don't let go!' Hump cried, just as the paddle drifted past him. He reached – she could feel his weight shifting as he extended his arm for it, but the kayak was still rocking violently and gallons of cold water slopped into the seats.

'Hump!' she cried again, trying to counterbalance by leaning the other way, but Hump was too heavy, his limbs too long as he made one last effort for the paddle, and in another second, they had overturned.

Ro surfaced with a splutter. The water was so cold she was too shocked to speak.

'You OK?' Hump asked calmly, running his hands over his face and hair like he was in the shower.

Ro reached her arm out for the capsized kayak and leaned on it. 'Yeah. Think so,' she gasped, shocked by the cold for the second time in twenty-four hours.

'Pst, look casual,' he whispered as a family of curious ducks floated past them treading water, and he began whistling nonchalantly. She giggled helplessly as the ducks did a glide-by before drifting off.

Hump swam over to her, effortlessly turning the boat the right side up. 'Anyway, sorry,' he grinned. 'You were saying you're a natural . . .'

'Do your thing. I'll be in here ordering breakfast,' Hump said, jerking his thumb towards a cafe called the Golden Pear. 'What do you want?'

'Uh. Tea and toast, maybe? I don't mind. Surprise me!' Ro said, pushing open the door of the hardware store.

She paused in the entrance, wondering where to start and wishing she'd written a list. If they'd had time to go back home, she could have done that *and* changed into dry clothes. Instead, because they were passing anyway, Hump had insisted it made sense to drop by on the way past. It made sense to him maybe: *he* was practically dry, his hair was so short it was dry before they'd even got back to the car, and he'd only been wearing a pair of surf baggies. She, on the other hand, now had hair like a swan's nest and a still-wet T-shirt that clung to her like she was Pamela Anderson on a modelling shoot.

'Right, think, Ro, think,' she muttered, her eyes scanning the floor-to-ceiling shelves housing plastic sweeping brushes, metal bins, pots of paint and coils of rope. 'You need a hammer, picture hooks . . . um, some wall brackets for the TV screens, Rawlplugs, screws . . . picture wire, a spirit level . . . um . . .'

'Can I help you, ma'am?' a man asked her. He was in his fifties and wearing grey overalls.

'No, I think I'm OK, thanks,' Ro said, standing to attention and smoothing her hair self-consciously, but her watch strap caught in it and she had to disentangle herself in front of him, awkward, embarrassed smiles on both their faces. 'Oh . . . Oh. There we go. I'm fine.'

He nodded, hearing her accent, and handed her a blue plastic basket. 'Maybe this would be useful, then.'

'Thanks.'

She wandered down the dark, crowded aisles, finding herself tempted by the gardening trowels and fireplace grates. She always spent far too much in places like this, coming away with new kettles or willow screens when she'd just popped in for some turps; B&Q held the same fascination for her as the Selfridges shoe department did to most other women.

She found what she needed – and what she didn't, but no way was she walking away from that ceramic Chinese runner duck; it would look adorable outside the studio door – and brought it to the counter, just as the bell above the door jangled and some more customers came in, their voices tumbling over one another like wrestling puppies.

'You just visiting?' the man in the grey overalls asked, as he scanned the barcodes into the till.

'Actually, I'm staying for the summer,' Ro nodded. 'I'm a photographer. I've got a studio in Amagansett Square.'

'Yeah? You can put an ad in our window if you like. Five bucks a week. Lots of passing trade.'

'Maybe I'll do that,' Ro said politely. She'd need to think about how she advertised here. People wouldn't just wander past the studio on foot like they did back home. Everyone drove everywhere. She couldn't just wait for people to stumble across her.

'That's forty-six dollars eighty-four,' the man said, and she handed over her Visa card. She had yet to get some cash out and knew that was another job for this morning. 'I'm Bob, by the way.'

'Ro.'

'Pleased to meet you, Ro.' He offered his hand to her and she shook it with a smile. Her eyes fell to the display by the till as she waited to sign: LED torches, gum, copper travel-sickness bangles, waterproof cases . . .

She picked up one. It was large with double zips, a hanging cord and a belt clip – ideal for keeping her camera dry should she dare to venture out on a kayak again. 'Do these *really* work?' she asked sceptically, examining the seams.

'Best I ever found. I use mine all the time. I keep a boat out in Shelter Island and it's saved my cell more times than I can count.'

Ro deliberated. Phones weren't cheap, but her camera was a whole other level at £3,000 new. 'You're sure, though? They don't leak even a little bit?'

The shopkeeper shrugged, looking up at someone behind her. 'Ted, how you found that waterproof case I sold you?'

'Fine, Bob. Not let me down yet,' the man replied.

Ro turned politely – and froze.

Him! From the beach!

His face, when he saw her, echoed hers – mouth agape, eyes wide with horror. In front of him, his two children were pulling twine off a coil and watching as it looped over his feet on the floor. He looked down at the sudden distraction and Ro quickly turned and grabbed the duck and brown bag full of miscellanea from the counter. Bowing her head low, she darted past him. He caught her by the elbow, but she yanked it away angrily. No way was he going to accost her again.

'Get your bloody hands off me!' she spat, and he recoiled immediately, holding his hands up in the air like she was pointing a gun at him.

'I—'

'Hey, wait!' she heard the shopkeeper call, but Ro didn't turn back. She wasn't going back there for a stupid waterproof case when that maniac was around. She pushed the door open so it hard it almost flung back in her face, and ran down the street to the Golden Pear.

Hump was waiting for her, two enormous steaming cups of coffee sitting in front of him. He looked up from reading the local paper as she burst in, breathless and agitated, turning back to make sure she hadn't been followed.

'Hey, what's up?' he asked, frowning as he saw her expression. 'Now what's happened?'

Ro shook her head, too upset to talk. How could she have run into him – *him* of all people – twice in under twenty-four hours? She pulled her chair back and it scraped jarringly across the floor, but she didn't register; she caught sight of her reflection in the mirror as she sat down: Matt's unflatteringly oversized grey T-shirt clung to her in some places, billowed in others – giving her the shoulders of a prop forward – and her red and turquoise striped swimsuit had soaked through her beige shorts, giving her the bottom of a toddler. 'Nothing.'

'Doesn't look like nothing.'

She shrugged and took a gulp of coffee.

He leaned forward on his elbows. 'Why is it that whenever I leave you alone for ten minutes, you come back looking like your dog just died?'

'I don't have a dog.'

'Matt have this much trouble with you?'

'No!' She rolled her eyes. 'It's really nothing.'

'It's a long story, I bet.' She met his eyes at her own refrain, just as the waitress came over with their plates. '*It is?* Jeez, I think you'd better tell me this long story. What else we got to talk about?' he said, gesturing to their over-stacked piles of wholegrain pancakes with fruit that seemingly came as the sidebar to tea and toast. 'Trust me, we're gonna be here a while.'

# Chapter Seven

Ro sat on the porch, an untouched beer in her hand and an ache in her bones, her hair finally washed and wrapped in a wobbly towel turban. She hadn't stopped all day. Hump had been out doing his beach runs since 9 a.m., giving her time alone in the studio to finish setting up. All the portraits were hanging now, and she had finally managed to get the brackets up for the small TV screens – although not without quarrying a few holes in the walls first, which meant they were hanging slightly lower than she'd originally intended. She'd also found a good-sized square table at an antiques store further up the road that Hump had sweetly collected for her – making a small diversion via the studio on one of his runs to Indian Wells Beach and strapping it to the roof bars – and which now stood centrally in the room, stacked with the oversized album books and a potted blue hydrangea.

After all that activity in the morning, things had been rather quieter after lunch – no one had stopped by, although she'd seen a few women darting into the spa – but she was grateful for that today. As if the 4 a.m. start wasn't bad enough, her body was still lingering in Greenwich Mean Time and since 5 p.m. had been ordering her to go to bed.

She'd closed up on the dot of five and Hump had given her a ride home, where she'd wallowed in the bath for an hour while he'd caught up with the latest bids for tomorrow's advertising board, before sitting cross-legged on the bed and trying to Skype Matt. She'd calculated the time difference between here and Cambodia was twelve hours, which in a way was almost an easier, cleaner time-cut to navigate than back in London, where the seven-hour lag was more inconvenient and meant he was always out by the time she woke up and in bed by the time she got back.

She looked up, hearing the agricultural rumble of the Landy long before she could see it – Hump had gone to collect Bobbi from the Jitney stop on Main Street – and Ro unfurled her legs from beneath her, taking a nervous breath as she waited to see Bobbi again.

She couldn't help but smile as the cheery yellow car rounded the corner, up the drive, and she saw Hump talking away as Bobbi looked about her dubiously in the basic cab. A Merc it wasn't. The passenger door opened and Bobbi slid out – sliding was all she could do from that height, in such a tight skirt.

Ro stood up. 'Hi!'

'Hey! How are ya?' Bobbi called back, striding towards her and leaving Hump to get her bags from the back. She enveloped Ro in a fierce hug, pulling back to study her face, and Ro wondered whether Bobbi had forgotten what she looked like during the six-week gap between their two meetings.

'Weird seeing you without a patch,' Bobbi said. 'Your eye OK now?'

'Oh yes, totally. I'd forgotten all about it,' Ro said,

waving away her concerns with the beer bottle. 'Want one?'

'Sure,' Bobbi replied. 'Only, let me just change quickly. I can't bear wearing black out here.' She gestured to her skin-pinching black skirt suit, which Ro thought would fit her right leg. 'You gonna give me the tour, Hump?'

Ro sat back in the chair as the two of them disappeared inside, occasional words floating out to her: '*Ercol?* Hump, are you serious . . . ?'

They emerged several minutes later, Bobbi looking refreshed and unnaturally colourful in an almost-neon-peach skinny-knit top, thong sandals and white shorts. Her legs were even better than her pencil skirts had let on – slim, toned, brown – and Ro felt instantly dowdy in her rolled-up navy chinos and Matt's ancient school rugby shirt. (She was beginning to wonder if she'd gone over-board packing half his clothes to wear over here. The view in the mirror at the Golden Pear hadn't been pretty.)

'I mean, I *heard* people used to have avocado baths, but . . . I thought they were suburban myths, you know?' Bobbi was saying as they stepped back onto the porch. She clasped his arm intently. 'Hey, listen, I say this with love, OK? All I'm saying is I've got contacts. Use 'em.'

Hump nodded obediently. 'Will do, Mom.' His eyes met Ro's and she swallowed down the giggle tickling at her throat. 'Now have a beer.'

'Cheers!' Ro said brightly, and all three clinked their bottles together. Ro took a tiny sip, hoping no one would notice. She'd never acquired a taste for beer. 'Here's to summer.'

'So when's Mystery Greg getting here?' Bobbi asked, settling herself on the other end of the swing love seat to

Ro, her long legs folded like a flamingo's. 'Did anyone else manage to get a response from him? He didn't respond to any of my pokes.'

Ro shook her head.

'He'll be here soon, I'm hoping. But you never can tell – he can work pretty crazy hours,' Hump said.

'Not as crazy as me, I'll bet,' Bobbi replied competitively.

'He passed the foam-party test too, then?' Ro asked.

Hump laughed out loud at that. 'Ha! He's so not the foam type. I'm helping him out, actually. He needed a place to stay and he's a friend of my brother, Sam. They were at Penn together.'

'Yeah? I was at Penn. What did he do?' Bobbi asked, interested.

'Law.'

Bobbi wrinkled her nose, losing interest again. Clearly if he wasn't in architecture . . .

'So, what about you? Who do you work for?' Ro asked, even though she didn't know the name of a single architect in New York, but as she well remembered Bobbi saying that night in the bathroom, 'Know me, know my career.' If they were going to get off on the right foot . . .

'Brew Eastman Schwarz Associates, Seventh Avenue.'

Ro nodded as though the name meant something to her. 'Oh yeah, right . . . Enjoying it there?'

Bobbi looked surprised by the question. *Enjoying* it is irrelevant. They're a name you've got to have on your résumé if you want to work in an inter-disciplinary consultancy which I do because that's the future, I'll tell ya that for free. Once I make partner –' She whistled and Ro could only surmise that she was suggesting she'd be home free.

'Of course, yeah. Totally . . .' Ro trailed off.

'How about you? Hump said you and he are sharing a studio.'

'Yes, it's great. So pretty and such a great location. I think we're going to do really well there.'

'Busy today?'

'Today? Uh, no, not so much, but I expect most people were travelling down after work this afternoon, like you. I'm bracing myself for a rush tomorrow. It'll have to be early to bed for me tonight.' The thought of bed reminded her body how tired it was and an entirely unsuppressable yawn bubbled up.

Bobbi nodded. 'And how's your boyfriend? Still gone?'

Ro felt a flash of annoyance at Bobbi's choice of words. She made it sound like he was gone and not coming back, which was categorically not the case. Why didn't anyone believe they were just on a pause? 'Matt? Yes, yes, he's on an expedition to some lost city they just found outside Angkor Wat last year. They found it from laser-mapping or something and he wanted to see it for himself. There's twelve of them doing it. He's having a ball,' she said carelessly. In truth, she didn't know exactly where Matt was. He had told her but all the names were so long and unintelligible that his itinerary had long since slipped from her mind and she didn't want to admit to Bobbi that all she really knew – right here, right now – was that her beloved boyfriend was somewhere in Cambodia.

Bobbi watched her for a beat and Ro felt herself grow even more agitated in her studied silence than her careless words. 'Well, at least you're out here now and having your own fun back. You can show him what he's missing . . .' Bobbi drawled. 'Hey, there's an idea! Quick, snuggle up to me,' Bobbi said, grabbing Hump and Ro each by the wrist and pulling them in to her on the swing seat. 'Now look seductive,' she ordered, angling her phone to face them all and clicking the button before Ro could pull her features into any considered expression at all. 'That'll do,' she murmured, before nodding and pressing 'send'.

'Where did you send that to?' Ro asked, aghast to see she'd been caught mid-blink beside candy-coloured Bobbi, who was pouting up a storm.

'Facebook. I'll tag you. He's friends with you, right?'

'Of course.' Oh God, how many people would see that photo of her?

'So now you can show him just how much fun you're having. We'll take a shot a day. You never know, he might get so jealous he comes back early.' Bobbi winked.

Not with her looking like that he wouldn't, Ro thought miserably as the towel on her head finally collapsed like a soufflé and wet hair dripped on her shoulders. He might never come back if he kept seeing her looking like that!

She checked her watch. Half eight. That meant it was half past eight in the morning over there. Her earlier calls had rung off, but surely now would be a good time? Another yawn caught her unawares and she covered her mouth with her hand. 'Mmmghm. Guys, I'm so sorry, but I think I'm going to have to hit the hay.'

'But I only just got here!' Bobbi protested. 'I thought we had reservations at Nick & Toni's tonight?'

'We do.' Hump shrugged.

'I know, and I'm so sorry to flake, but I've still got evil jet lag.'

'You shouldn't go to bed so early. You know what'll happen,' Hump said, watching her as she stood up.

'Given what happened this morning after a *late* night, I think I'll take my chances, thanks.'

Hump grinned. 'You can't wait up to meet Greg?'

Ro shook her head. 'I really can't. I consider it a personal achievement to have managed to greet Bobbi. I promise I'll be more sociable tomorrow.'

Hump shrugged. 'You want me to drop you at the studio in the morning? I'll be leaving at ten to nine.'

'Thanks, but I can't keep relying on you for lifts all summer. Is there a bus? I should learn to be independent out here.'

'What you need is a bike,' Bobbi said. 'Everyone has them here. I get one every summer. Amazing. So easy. I'm getting mine in the morning if you want to come along.'

Ro considered for a moment. She'd seen the wide cycle lanes here; they looked safe enough. 'OK, yeah, perhaps I should do that. Thanks.'

'Tell you what, you can come with me to my yoga class beforehand.'

'Uh, no . . .'

'Yes! Don't give up, there's still time for you to get toned.'

Ro frowned. What? 'No, I mean, I've never done yoga before.'

Bobbi waved a nonchalant hand at her. 'You'll pick it up, no problem – my girl's the best. Everyone does yoga in the Hamptons – seven o'clock tomorrow morning, the entire East End will be chanting to "Om Na Shivaya" salutations.' She looked across at Hump, who shrugged and nodded obediently. 'Besides, I've got a guest pass for tomorrow as it's the first class of the season. I'll wake you in the morning,' Bobbi continued magnanimously.

'Oh . . . OK,' Ro replied nervously. She supposed bonding with Bobbi was never going to be a stress-free affair.

'Sleep well,' Hump grinned. 'You'd better rest while you can.'

Ro walked away, puzzled. What did that mean? Yoga was just heavy breathing and stretching. Right?

Ro tried again. It was her seventh attempt at getting into a headstand and she wasn't going to give up. Or rather, the teacher wasn't going to let her. Everyone was watching now.

'Just think about creating a triangle with your head and your arms,' the teacher intoned, as though her request was perfectly reasonable. But since when did people start creating geometry with their bodies? That was what Ro wanted to know. She'd never been triangular in her life. Round, maybe.

She put her head back down to the ground and kicked her right leg into the air, closely followed by the left, both legs vaguely assuming an upright position just long enough for Matt's khaki gym T-shirt to come untucked from her waistband and the whole heavy thing tumbled around her upside-down ears. A collective intake of breath swept round the room like a wind as everyone took in her bosom resting on her chin.

'Well . . . I think we can say that was a . . . good start,' the teacher nodded, clearly equally as startled by the vision and eager not to repeat the process.

Bobbi, sitting cross-legged beside Ro in honeycomb-blond leggings and a white vest, reached over and patted her on the shoulder. 'Just try to engage your core. That's what I always focus on when I'm kicking up.'

Engage your *what*? Ro nodded, mute with shame as she tucked the T-shirt back into her tracksuit bottoms. Everything about this was wrong. The fact that the room temperature was 110 degrees – on purpose! – was wrong. The fact that the class had started at 7 a.m. was wrong. The fact that no one else in here was wearing – or needed to wear – a bra was wrong. The fact that they were all wearing second-skin kit and had the tight, sinewy bodies of lizards was wrong, and as for wearing a tracksuit in here . . . well, she wouldn't have looked any less incongruous had she come dressed as Buzz Lightyear.

Thankfully, everyone was sitting cross-legged on the ground now, doing lots of breathing. This, at least, she could do, she told herself, as she settled into the cross-legged pose she'd last assumed, aged fourteen, in class assembly. As she'd told Hump yesterday, she excelled at any exercise done sitting down (or rather, lying down, wink, wink, as Matt always said), and she had actually been breathing all her life. She'd be a natural at this bit.

Beside her, Bobbi – eyes closed – was exhaling incredibly quickly through her nose, like a dog panting on a hot day, only with its mouth closed. It looked easy enough. Ro copied her, managing to keep up for at least ten seconds before she was left behind as her body – becoming gradually more keen on the idea of a really big inhale instead – became confused and she actually forgot how to breathe properly.

'Unbelievable,' Ro muttered to herself, opening one eye and looking quickly around the room. Everyone was still exhaling away in unison, the collective huffing beginning to get louder from the effort of sustaining the rapid breathing, so that it sounded more like a steam engine than a yoga class.

She closed her eye and tried again, but goddammit! – her nose just wouldn't play ball. Within fifteen seconds, reflex won out over control and she found herself inhaling and gulping down air rapidly, instead of expelling it. Seconds later, she hiccupped loudly.

She opened one again and saw the instructor frowning at her, as though she was being disruptive on purpose.

She tried again. Breathe out, out, out, she told herself, trying to keep up with Bobbi's frankly spectacular breath sprints. She was doing it! She was doing it! At least half a minute had passed and she was still breathing out, out, out— Oh!

'Was that . . . ?' Bobbi asked.

'No,' Ro replied quickly, her hands cupped over most of her face in absolute horror – too horrified to sniff – both women's eyes locked on each other. Ro blinked, wishing time travel was real, wishing she had never gone to that stupid party, wishing she'd never tried to match Matt on his thirst for adventure and knowing she couldn't keep her hands up for much longer. She couldn't even get up to standing without putting one hand on the floor, so she couldn't make an escape that way. Bobbi looked away, more scared than revolted, and Ro quickly, inevitably gave the giant sniff that immediately confirmed her housemate's fear that actually, yes, she had heard what she'd thought she'd heard.

Ro closed her eyes – even she was disgusted with herself – and, as best she could, got up and tiptoed out of the room. As she closed the door, she saw a look of relief cross the teacher's face and everyone began to chant in fluent Om.

She leaned against the wall of the corridor, tears of humiliation pricking her eyes. Tomorrow, she didn't care what anybody said, she was damned well sleeping in.

'And how was that?' Hump asked, as she walked into the studio an hour later, only slightly less apple-cheeked, thanks to the cold shower she'd stood beneath for half an hour. 'Feeling zen?'

'Hump, I could not even *breathe*.'

Hump laughed, thinking she was joking.

'No. Seriously,' she said. What would he do if he heard she'd blown her nose over her own face? No one would hear about it from her lips, that was for sure, but what about Bobbi? Was it going to be turned into a house-share anecdote, wheeled out over every breakfast? Or worse, a Hamptons myth talked about at smart Manhattan cocktail parties, thirty storeys high in the sky? Why had she even gone along with it? From the moment she'd fallen out of the hire car, dressed in Matt's clothes, it had been abundantly clear she would never be like these glossy spa people who all seemed so in control of their lives when she couldn't even control her own hair. 'What are you doing here anyway?' she asked. 'Aren't you supposed to be driving?'

Hump checked his watch quickly, before resuming rifling through the papers on his desk. 'I've still got ten minutes.'

Ro dumped her bag down despondently on the counter and logged on to the computer.

'Hey, you OK?'

She looked across at her languid landlord and gave a shrug. 'Sure.'

There was a pause. 'It's Matt, right? You're missing him.'

Her heart pounded at the very sound of his name. 'A little, maybe,' she replied, her voice tremulous suddenly.

'Did you speak to him last night?'

She shook her head. 'He's out of contact almost all the time at the moment. He did warn me we wouldn't be able to talk much, but . . . when you've spent eleven years talking to someone twenty times a day, it's a bit of a shock to go down to once a fortnight.'

Hump frowned. 'You're a very tolerant girlfriend, I'll give you that. I don't think I know any woman who'd give her man permission to just take off round the world for a year.'

'Half a year,' she corrected him, slightly too sharply. 'And I don't see why everyone makes it out to be such a big deal. We trust each other. Why shouldn't he have a few months to himself before we settle down? We've been together a long time.'

'I just don't get why he didn't ask you to go with him, that's all.'

She looked down, stung by the brittle simplicity in his words. 'He knows temples and sleeping bags aren't my thing.'

They lapsed into silence, her tapping away primly on the keyboard, Hump sipping a takeaway coffee, his feet on his desk, intermittently reading incoming emails and watching her. Ro opened up her email inbox – it was depressingly empty, with more spam than personal correspondence, and nothing at all from Matt. A client she'd done a wedding film for, back in Richmond, wanted her to do a life-story film of her grandfather who'd flown as part of the Fighter Command of the RAF during the Battle of Britain. He'd been presented with a Distinguished Flying Cross, and was due to celebrate his ninety-sixth birthday in November. Ro chewed her lip. November? Still six months away. Who was it who'd said he wouldn't be buying green bananas at his age?

'Oh! I got something that'll cheer you up,' Hump said suddenly, swinging his legs off the desk and crossing the room in a couple of strides. He produced a small plastic card with a flourish from his back pocket. 'Been missing this?'

Ro took it from him. 'My Visa? But where—'

'Long Story brought it in,' Hump grinned.

'Excuse me?'

'Your beach assailant.'

Ro shot him a sharp look for giving the man such a flippant nickname, although she shouldn't have been surprised. Hump had been delighted by her story as she'd recounted it to him over breakfast in the Golden Pear yesterday morning, seemingly understanding none of the horror and shame that had accompanied it.

'He's surprisingly good-looking – if you go for preppy.' He shrugged. 'Funny you never mentioned that. It puts an entirely different slant on the story.'

Ro scowled at him. 'How? How does it? The man *assaulted* me. Are you saying what he did doesn't matter because he's good-looking?'

Hump put up his hands. 'Whoa! No! I'm just saying some women might have found it exciting to have a tall, dark, handsome stranger wade into the ocean with them.'

Ro's mouth moved several times, but nothing would come out – at first. 'Have you lost your bloody mind?' she cried eventually. 'He was going to throw me in and destroy my camera, my livelihood, Hump! The man is a sociopath. It is completely irrelevant that he's a good-looking sociopath.'

'Ah, so you did *notice*, then?'

'What? No!' Ro stared down at the plastic card in his hand. 'How did he even get hold of this, anyway? I didn't know I'd even lost it.'

'He said you left it behind in the hardware store yesterday morning.'

Ro looked up at him in alarm. 'And how did he know where to find me?'

'Apparently, you told Bob you had the studio here for the summer.'

Ro thought back to her conversation with the hardware-store owner and relaxed a little. She had told him that, and he had suggested she advertised in his window.

'Oh. Right. Thanks,' she said, taking it from him.

'Hey, don't thank me,' Hump said, stuffing his hands into his shorts. 'Long Story's the one who went out of his way to return it to you.' He wandered back to his corner of the studio. 'He was here for quite a while, actually. He really liked that photo of those two kids there,' he said, jerking his chin towards the portrait of the two small brothers. 'I kinda got the feeling he was hoping you'd turn up. Who knows . . . maybe he wanted to apologize?'

'I sincerely doubt that,' Ro sniffed, remembering with a new burst of fury how he'd called her 'a sport'.

'Yeah? Well, it's a good thing he brought it back. We're

all going out to Navy Beach tonight and my card's already in overdraft.'

'Hump, how can you be overdrawn? I, alone, am paying you a small fortune!'

'You know as well as I do that being an entrepreneur basically means being broke until you hit the jackpot.'

'I guess so,' Ro agreed. She'd been overdrawn since university and didn't see a time she would ever climb her way out. Maintaining her current level of debt was the best she could seem to manage. She sat down on the stool and replaced the credit card in her purse. 'So, did you all go out for dinner last night? I'm sorry I couldn't wait up to meet Greg. I was beyond shattered.'

'It was as well you didn't. Something came up at the last minute and he had to stay in the office. He's coming out this afternoon instead.'

'Really? Is it worth coming all that way just for a day?'

'I guess it is to him,' Hump replied. 'Did you get the bikes sorted?' Hump had started reading from his screen, his eyes moving side to side rapidly.

'Yes, they're brilliant. Real old boneshakers, but so pretty! Bobbi's is green. Mine's yellow – like the Humper!'

He looked up at her and winked. 'Careful, I might brand you. You've got that beachy vibe going on already.'

I do? Ro thought to herself, smiling and looking out through the open doors. Sharp sunlight cast crisp shadows on the grass and she could see some shoppers sipping on frappés and browsing in the expensive interiors boutique on the opposite side of the square. 'Please come over. Oh, please come over,' a voice in her head pleaded as she watched them examine some cushions and switch on a lamp.

'What's Bobbi up to today?'

'She said something about hooking up with some friends on Main Beach. Red umbrella, if you need her.'

'Uh-huh.' Hump looked over at her, his eyes taking in her (well, Matt's) navy chinos, tightly belted and bunched at the waist, her ankles peeping beneath the roll-ups, her white linen shirt pushed up her forearms and her hair pulled into a scruffy topknot. 'You going to the beach later?'

'No. I've got to work. I must start as I mean to go on. I can't spend my summer on the beach, tempting though it is,' she mumbled, her heart sinking as she saw the customers in the homewares store wander back out onto the pavement. Damn.

Bobbi's yoga class on the other side of town had been heaving this morning, and it had taken her and Bobbi almost twenty minutes to be served their coffees after getting the bikes, yet the studio was empty.

She filled the small watering can in the bathroom off the back of the unit and watered the hydrangea on her new table, before going outside and doing the same to the flower boxes on the deck. Next door, in the yoga studio, she heard soporific chanting and she wandered over, peering through the windows at the still but seemingly alert bodies lying in the dark room. Unlike the almost ecstatic shouts in Bobbi's class, this had a different quality to it altogether – it sounded almost monastic, Asiatic somehow – and she closed her eyes for a moment, letting the sound wrap round her like a shroud and take her to a different place, somewhere far away from here, the land of big trucks and good teeth. In the darkness of her own head – these sounds – she could let go of her sensory anchors and she felt herself transported to somewhere dark and ancient, the place where Matt was hidden from her view for the first time in over a decade, and she sensed somehow – though it was elusive as an angel's kiss – his presence, as if he was right behind her.

But he wasn't. It was Hump, on another coffee run.

'Filter?' he called out, running across the grass before his next shift.

She nodded and wandered back into the studio, replacing the watering can on the table. And taking a seat at her high stool, she waited for the customers to come.

# Chapter Eight

Ro scuffed the surf lightly, watching it fly and dissipate before her eyes as she walked through the shallows. The sun was so low the sand seemed to glow pink, and Ro had lost track of time trying to capture it on film, before moving on to lying on her belly and training the camera on a hermit crab that was making its way down to the water, its pinprick footprints barely making an impression on the soft beach.

She was supposed to have been back at the house forty minutes ago – Greg was due in on the 5 p.m. Jitney, and Hump was keen for them all to have drinks together on the porch before they headed out to Navy Beach for the night – but she couldn't quite bring herself to make the journey home. The light on the water was too enticing for one thing, but that was just her alibi for being late. In truth, she just wasn't looking forward to seeing Bobbi after the yoga horrors this morning, or to telling her frighteningly driven housemate that, yet again, not one person had stepped foot in the studio and she'd spent the afternoon – once Hump had left – playing solitaire on the computer. Throw in the thought of being jolly to another stranger she had to share a bathroom with and it was all slightly more than she could bear.

She knew she was lucky to be somewhere like this – watching dancing water skitter upon sunset sands and feeling the breeze that had blown all the way from home across the Atlantic to her here – only, she hadn't asked for it. Coming here hadn't been her ambition in the way that Cambodia had been Matt's. It had just been a proposition, a whim, a chance meeting with a twist, an opportunity for her to save face while her boyfriend freeze-framed her life for six months. She knew it could have been worse, as these things went. She could have found herself somewhere where the weather was bad or there was a language barrier, but just because it wasn't terrible in any definition here didn't mean it was a source of happiness for her either. The naivety of what she'd done was hitting home. She had uprooted her business, left behind her friends and planted herself in the midst of strangers, all so that she could say, 'Me too,' in the years to come, when she and Matt would tell their children about their half-year out and the adventures they'd each had.

Grudgingly, Ro put the cap on her camera lens and turned her back to the ocean, walking up the dry sand in a wobbly gait. It was hard to get anywhere fast, and it was beyond her how all these fit New Yorkers – looking so vital as they jogged in the last of the sun's rays – could get up any pace. Ahead, a woman in a straw hat was walking slowly with her dog, sporadically throwing things into the dunes, which were cordoned off by double-rowed wooden fences. Ro squinted as she began to catch her up. Was she littering?

The woman was carrying a basket on one arm and Ro couldn't help but stare in as she passed. Inside were hundreds of tiny chocolate truffles. What on earth . . . ?

Ro stopped in astonishment at the sight, and the woman turned, as if sensing her.

'Well, hello,' she smiled, her grey eyes crinkling at the corners. 'Did Nathan send you? Have you come to help?'

'I-I . . .' Ro stammered. 'No, I was just passing, actually. I couldn't help but notice that you were . . . throwing things.'

'Indeed I am. Would you like to try one?' She held the basket out and Ro hesitantly took one. They were heavier in her hand than she expected, and she put it to her mouth.

'I wouldn't!' The woman smiled, and Ro's hand paused – poised mid-air, her mouth open. 'They're not for eating. They're seed bombs.'

Ro's hand dropped. 'Excuse me?'

'They're a combination of sand, clay, soil and dune-plant seeds: so, beach rose, golden rod, Atlantic panic grass, things like that . . . I make them myself.'

'But why?' Ro rolled the seed bomb in her hand.

'Sandy.' The woman paused, seeing Ro's bewilderment. 'You're not from here, are you?'

Ro shook her head.

'Hurricane Sandy all but wiped out the beaches here last year. I'm trying to get an initiative going to revegetate the coastline.'

'Oh. The hurricane, yes,' Ro nodded. She'd seen the coverage of last winter's super-storm on the news back home, although it had mainly focused on the damage to downtown Manhattan and the fact that Wall Street had had to be closed. Long Island's destruction hadn't made the headlines in the UK. 'But . . . you're not doing all that on your own, surely?' Ro's eyes tracked the unending miles of beach-fronted coastline.

'Well, sometimes it feels a little like that,' the woman

sighed with a smile. 'But no. I distribute the seed bombs at food fairs, and I've done some workshops in the city. Volunteers take them to distribute along coastline they're passing either on foot or by bike. There's quite a few of us now. We call it guerrilla gardening.' She raised an eyebrow at Ro. 'Go on, just throw it, anywhere you like in the dune. It's quite therapeutic, although I think I may have overdone it today. It's bringing on my tennis elbow.'

Ro threw the small ball into the protected area, watching as it disappeared among the grasses.

'And it'll take root, just like that? They don't need to be dug in?' Ro asked. 'Don't the birds go for them?'

'Uh-uh. The clay creates a pod for the seeds till they're strong enough to sprout; then they penetrate the sand.'

'Cool,' Ro murmured.

'It is, isn't it?' The woman smiled, holding out the basket again for Ro to help herself.

Ro threw a few more and they fell naturally into step, walking side by side.

'I'm Florence, by the way. And that's Maisie, my daughter's dog, there. I'm dog-sitting this week while she's on vacation.'

'Pleased to meet you. I'm Rowena. Everyone calls me Ro.'

'Ro and Flo, how funny,' Florence laughed. Ro guessed she must be in her early sixties, but she was a tall, handsome woman, with grey – almost white – hair and deeply tanned skin that retained a rosy blush. She wasn't dissimilarly dressed to Ro, wearing rolled-up cornflower-blue utility trousers and a white striped cotton blouse.

'Would you care to throw a few more?' Florence asked, holding out the basket.

'I'd love to,' Ro replied, carefully throwing the bombs into the bald patches of dune. Florence was right – it felt surprisingly good.

'So, where are you from if not from here?' Florence asked, her eyes on Maisie.

'London. I'm just here for the summer.' She threw some more bombs, watching as they skidded down the sandy slopes before juddering to a stop.

'You have friends here?'

'Kind of . . .' Ro gave a shy laugh. 'Actually, not really. Or . . . not yet, anyway.'

Florence gave her an interested look. 'So what brings you here?'

Ro paused. 'Showing my boyfriend he's not the only one who can be unpredictable?' She looked out to sea and took a deep breath – telling this story always required one, she'd found. 'We've been together eleven years. Then, just over two months ago, he threw it on me that he'd decided to take a six-month sabbatical to go backpacking around Cambodia. I think he thinks he's Jason Bourne or someone.' She swallowed, trying to smile. 'Anyway, he went two days later.'

'Oh!'

'Mm.' She shrugged her eyebrows, recognizing the pity that characterized everyone's reaction when they heard this tale. 'He wants to travel, feed orphans, commune with orang-utans, that kind of thing.'

Florence chuckled.

'So when I got an offer to spend the summer here, I just thought, well . . . Why not?' She threw a few more bombs, harder this time.

Florence held out the basket again and Ro took the entire

thing, smiling gratefully and scattering the balls with abandon.

'That's rather brave – relocating yourself across the Atlantic when none of it was even your idea.'

'I know. And now I'm slightly wondering if I haven't . . . made a mistake.' Her shoulders slumped. 'My housemates are . . . They're lovely, but a little terrifying. We don't know each other well yet, and work isn't taking off the way I'd hoped. I'm a photographer,' she added. 'At least back home, I had a full diary and complete control of the Sky remote.'

They had reached the car park now and Ro looked down at the empty basket, suddenly embarrassed at having talked so openly to a stranger. Throwing the seed bombs had distracted her from the weight in her words. 'Tch, listen to me prattling on. I'm sorry. I don't usually burden complete strangers with my problems.' She gave another embarrassed laugh before handing back the basket. 'It was nice meeting you.'

Florence regarded Ro carefully. 'You know, I may just have a proposition for you.'

Ro blinked, surprised.

'I'm the town officer for the East Hampton Town Board. We need some photography for a regeneration programme we're trying to initiate. How would you feel about doing it for us?'

'Oh! Uh . . .' Ro hesitated. 'To be honest, I'm not really that sort of photographer. I mean, thank you for thinking of me, but I wouldn't want to let you down.'

'You wouldn't.' Florence watched her through keen, bright grey eyes and Ro was surprised – and flattered – by her certainty. 'Let's at least discuss it further. Why don't you drop by my house tomorrow morning and we can talk about what it is we need? Mine's the second house in on Middle Lane. Grey Mists.' She gestured to the road leading off to the right.

'OK,' Ro nodded.

'Shall we say eleven o'clock?'

'OK. I'll look forward to it.'

'Good. Me too. Come along, Maisie,' Florence said, flicking her lead and setting a brisk pace across the car park, the dog trotting at her heels.

Guerrilla gardening . . . Ro mused as she unlocked her bike and began pedalling up the lane to home. She liked the sound of that.

Bobbi and Hump were swinging on the love seat on the porch as she wheeled into sight of Sea Spray Cottage, a vast jug of Long Island iced tea on the table in front of them.

'Well, there's one housemate at least,' Bobbi grumbled, as Ro glided towards them slowly till her front wheel nudged the bottom step. Bobbi was dressed in a slinky black dress that was split up the side, and looked ready for cocktails.

'I was beginning to think you'd been abducted,' Hump said, the word 'again' hovering, teasingly unspoken, at the end of the sentence.

Ro narrowed her eyes at him in her signature 'ha, ha', unable to meet Bobbi's gaze at all. Her morning humiliation felt as fresh as milk, and it didn't help to be standing in front of her in baggy off-the-hip chinos while Bobbi looked ready to walk a runway. 'I'm sorry. I lost track of time.'

Hump's eyes fell knowingly to the camera about her neck. 'Well, it doesn't matter anyway. Greg's not here yet.'

'What, *still*?'

'I don't get why we're all hanging around waiting for him. If he can't be bothered to get here on time . . .' Bobbi said sulkily.

'Trust me, you're gonna love Greg. He looks like that guy from *Grey's*, with manners like Gatsby. He's a lady-killer, but he don't even know it.'

Bobbi made a 'whatever' sign with her fingers before looking back at Ro again. 'Are you going to get changed?' she asked, her eyes clearly making out the wide straps of Ro's masonry bra through the linen shirt.

'Why? I thought we were going to Navy Beach?'

'So did I.' Hump shrugged. 'But Bobbi says there's an LBD party at Cappelletti.'

Ro wrinkled her nose. 'It sounds like a cricketing convention.'

Hump guffawed. 'Little black dress party? Wear a little black dress and you get in for free.'

'Oh.' It sounded hellish. 'Looks like I'm paying, then,' Ro shrugged.

'What? You don't have one?' Bobbi looked stunned. Ro may as well have said she had no lungs. Or broadband.

'Well, I mean, I do have one. Just not *here*.'

'You came all the way to the Hamptons without a party dress? Where did you think you were coming to, a kibbutz?'

Ro opened her mouth to defend herself, but just then an engine rumbled round the corner and she turned to see a cab pulling over to the kerb.

'Ah! The maestro,' Hump grinned, draining his glass, getting up and leaning against the frame of the porch.

They all watched as the taxi door opened and a man in a dark grey suit and red tie stepped out, carrying a briefcase and brown leather holdall. He was tall – at least six foot three – with the bearing of a soldier, his shoulders pressed back as he strode up the path to the house.

'Yo, dude,' Hump called, sounding more like a Harlem rapper than a one-time doctor with a pile in the Hamptons. Why was it that when men hung out together, they had to sound 'street'? Matt did the same thing on the phone with his mates. 'Thought you were gonna leave us hangin'.'

'Sorry about that,' Greg replied, having the grace to look sheepish, his bright brown eyes scanning their group quickly, the first traces of five-o'clock shadow on his cheeks. Ladykiller was right. He was gorgeous. 'I just couldn't get away from the office.'

'Yeah? That's why you need to meet your new house-mate. Bobbi here is about the only person I ever met as focused on her career as you.'

'Is that so?' Greg looked across at Bobbi – even standing on the top step, she was only barely higher than him. 'Well then, I'm pleased to meet you, Bobbi,' Greg said, dropping his bags by his feet and holding out a hand.

'Hey,' Bobbi smiled, leaning against the pillar and some-how managing to make it look as provocative as a dancing pole.

'And this Brit chick here is Ro – as in "yo",' Hump grinned.

'Short for Yowena?' Greg asked, fixing his eyes upon her, amused already.

'Yes, exactly!' she laughed, determined not to move. Moving usually meant falling over for her.

Picking up his bags again in one hand, Greg climbed the steps and fell into some sort of mason's handshake – all thumb grips and shoulder bumps – with Hump.

'It's been too long, my man,' Hump said, gripping Greg's shoulder hard, and they exchanged stares that seemed weightier than their words.

'You've been much missed.'

Hump laughed. 'Well, you'll be glad to hear yours is the only room in the house that's *not* covered in girls' clothes,' Hump said, sliding his eyes over to Bobbi, who already had hand-washed cashmere jumpers draped over every radiator in the house and tiny workout kit strewn on chair-backs and stair banisters.

'Hey!' Ro protested. She could hardly be accused of having shoes and dresses lying all about the place.

'No, actually you're right,' Hump acknowledged. 'Ro's room is covered in her boyfriend's clothes. Some sort of he-she thang going on there.' He wrinkled his nose. Bobbi laughed, but Ro felt cloddish suddenly in her oversized gear. 'Now go change out of that monkey suit and we can get this party started once and for all.'

'Why wait?' Greg asked, pulling off his tie and indicating to the cab that was sitting in idle still by the kerb. 'I'm ready if you are. Summer's begun, right?'

'Hell, yeah! Ladies,' Hump beamed, motioning for them to lead the way, 'we are game on.'

Ro sat in the booth, her finger idly skimming the rim of the glass, occasionally falling off. She was staring at it when

Hump came back with the drinks, his fingers splayed wide as he held as many as was possible.

'Hump! I think even my fingers are drunk,' she half shouted, half slurred as he slunk in beside her.

'Not drunk enough!' Hump hollered back over the music, pushing a hi-ball towards her. 'Try that.'

'Uh-uh. That would break my drinking rules.'

'Drinking rules? What are they?' Hump asked, picking up the glass and angling the straw towards her lips. She sipped it greedily.

'Well,' she said, smacking her lips, 'Matt did them for me because I'm, like, really rubbish: I should never mix wine and beer because it makes me sick; I should never drink tequila because it makes me sad; I should never drink beer because it makes me fat; and I should never drink anything with an umbrella in it because it's déclassé.'

Hump slapped his hand over his tummy and laughed, because he was really drunk too. 'Well, what *does* he let you drink? OJ?'

'Cava, because we can't afford champagne, and gin and tonics – although they give me headaches, but don't tell him that.'

'I won't,' Hump agreed, shaking his head sombrely. He took the umbrella out of the glass. 'There? How's that, now? Classy enough?'

Ro beamed. 'Totally upper middle!' And she sipped the cocktail through the straw happily, her eyes on Greg and Bobbi talking at the bar.

They had spent most of the night so far head to head, talking intently. Early on, they had established they'd both been at Penn University at the same time and from that moment on neither Hump nor Ro had been able to get a word in edgeways as they reminisced over old bars and friends of friends they knew and how come they'd never met. Almost an hour ago now, they had gone to the bar to get refills, but on finding two stools there, they had sat down and basically not come back.

'*You* don't think I look like a man, do you?' Ro pouted unhappily. What had happened at the door had been among the most embarrassing moments of her life.

'Ro, the guy was a douchebag! First off, he clearly needs new glasses. You couldn't look *less* like a guy. So what if you wear men's clothes? You're a gorgeous woman, absolutely gorgeous. Like . . .' He looked up at the ceiling, trying to find inspiration in the colours and shapes thrown out by the lasers and glitter balls. 'You're like a bundle of pillows all stitched together.'

'Hump!' she shrieked. 'That is not a compliment!'

'What?' he asked, open-mouthed with surprise. 'It totally is! That's what every guy wants – softness and comfort.' He pulled a face. 'These skinny girls, they just don't get it,' he said, swiping his hand through the air, just as a girl in a size-zero, very little black dress sashayed past, drawing his stare like it was magnetized.

'Oh, *really*?' Ro said crossly, sipping her drink harder. 'Well, Greg obviously doesn't think so.'

They both watched as he leaned in to hear something Bobbi was saying.

'Hump, look at his hand! Look! It's resting on her bare thigh!' Ro shrieked again, properly scandalized.

'Oh no, I don't like this. I don't like this at all,' Hump said, watching them with exaggeratedly slitted eyes, although it could just have been the dry ice. 'If they hook up now and then break up . . .' He clicked his tongue against the roof of his mouth. 'That wouldn't make for a pretty summer.'

'Well, it'd be fine as long as Bobbi got to do the dumping.'

'Yeah, true. Greg's a gent. He'd take it on the chin.'

They watched as Greg and Bobbi stood up, making their way over to the dance floor, Bobbi looking sinuous as she shimmied gently like a quivering flower in front of Greg.

'Come on, let's join them. Can you dance to this?'

'Can I dance?' she laughed, sliding along the booth and standing up just as Eminem screamed his angry lyrics over a bass beat. 'Can *I* dance? Hump, nobody does the mashed potato like me. Watch and learn, fella. Watch and learn.'

# Chapter Nine

Bonding came at a price, Ro remembered, as she struggled to identify the alien sound that was pulling her from the comforting fug of her bed. She hadn't drunk so much since university. The Long Island iced teas had segued into mojitos and dirty martinis (a filthy combination) before finally ending, lethally, with tequilas. Bad dancing had been involved – she was vaguely recalling a pole. *A pole?* Some bad singing too. She couldn't exactly remember how they'd made their way home, but she was now on top of her bed, still in yesterday's clothes.

Her hands found her phone on the bedside table and she – in a misjudged, too-violent move – slapped it to her ear. 'Ow! Yes?' she groaned.

There was no reply. It wasn't on. The alien ringing was coming from somewhere else.

She groaned again. There was nothing for it. She was going to have to open her eyes.

She tried and light blasted at her like a cosmic glare, forcing her to shield her eyes with an arm. The room appeared to have grown its own centre of gravity overnight, spinning round her as she gripped the bed for balance.

Ro sat up, groaning yet more. Why wouldn't it stop? The spinning, the ringing . . .

And then she realized!

'Uuuh, uuuh,' she grunted, clambering out of bed and trying to make her way to the laptop sitting on the chest of drawers.

She pressed 'answer' and just like that Matt was in front of her, like a genie from a lamp, bid at her command, drawn from her dreams.

His face fell as she materialized in front of him too. 'What the hell's happened to you?' he asked, sounding genuinely worried.

Ro pushed a tangle of hair back from her face. It moved as one solid form – and felt sticky.

'Oh God, you look *amazing*,' Ro wailed as she took in his tan, bright eyes and stubble, which was on the right side of sexy. She was vaguely aware that her mouth was hanging open, but keeping it closed was a reflex too far just now; her body had more than enough to deal with. 'Where are you?'

'In Tuol Sleng.'

Was . . . was he grimacing at her?

'Tuol what?'

'The genocide museum.'

'I'm a bad person,' she wailed again. 'You're . . . you're off being noble and human and healthy, and I'm . . . I'm hung-over.'

She ran her hands over her face, wanting to hide but wanting to see him too, to drink him in.

'You're having a good time, then?'

'I got here *three days ago*. Why haven't you called?' she whined, her hands falling petulantly to her sides. Why was he all the way over there and not here, warm in bed and gently combing out her hair while she slept through this on his tummy?

'Because we've been trekking for five days to get here and there was no Wi-Fi in the middle of the jungle.' His features softened. 'You know you're green, right?'

'And you're so brown. *Why* do you have to look that good and be so far away?' she whimpered. Her mouth had turned into an upside-down U.

He put a hand to his chin. 'Like the beard?'

'Love it. Love it. You look gorgeous.' She shook her head dejectedly, feeling like she might cry. 'Are all the girls falling in love with you? I bet they are. They are, aren't they?'

'There aren't any girls here. I'm staying in a monastery.' He grinned. 'And this reaction is exactly why I have to be so far away. You wouldn't be reacting like this if you'd seen me yesterday.'

'But—'

'No buts. I'm missing you too.'

She blinked. 'You are?'

'I am. Even with you looking like the undead.'

'Oh God, I'm disgusting!' she wailed, pulling her hands down over her face, distorting her features like Munch's *Scream* and not doing herself any favours.

Matt laughed. 'You are not disgusting. You are just very badly hung-over. Fumes are coming through the screen this end.' He peered closer. 'Have you shrunk?'

'No!'

'Well, what are you wearing? You look like you've been dressed by giants.'

She pouted. 'They're your clothes.'

'*Why* are you wearing my clothes?'

She sniffed. 'Because they smell of you.'

Matt cast her one of his stern looks as she started smelling the collar of his shirt – it smelt mainly of beer and cashew nuts now. '*Still?* Ro, you cannot wear my clothes the whole time I'm gone. At some point – really quite soon – you are going to have to wash them and then you'll find you're actually just wearing clothes that are way too big.'

'Nooooo,' Ro wailed, tipping her mouth back down into an upside-down U again.

'Yes, Ro,' he chuckled, amused by her dramatics. She never coped with hangovers well. 'Wash them. Better yet, wear your own clothes. Mine swamp you.'

She gave a sigh, too broken to argue further.

'So how is it over there? Nice bunch?' Matt's eyes swivelled the screen, trying to take in her surroundings.

Ro leaned closer, her nose scrunched up like she was smelling something bad. 'We're worried about Bobbi and Greg,' she stage-whispered. 'They've got a biology thing going on.'

'Biology?' Matt arched a quizzical eyebrow.

'I mean chemistry. But Bobbi forgave me for blowing my nose on my face in yoga—' she continued.

'*What?*'

'She said she'd been more distracted by the woman next to her who always farts in the tranquillity pose. She holds her breath in readiness, she said.'

Matt blinked back at her, his mind racing, vague panic on his face. 'Did you mix your drinks? You know champagne and wine destroys you.'

'And Hump's lovely. Such a pudding.'

'A pudding? Well, I guess that's something,' Matt said with relief.

Ro just nodded, her eyes fixed on his even though there

KAREN SWAN

were nearly 9,000 miles between them. The screen flickered, then froze for a moment and she knew the signal was going. Already?

'How many days till you're back?' she whispered, her head tipped to the side.

'One hundred and fourteen.'

'One hundred and fourteen,' she echoed.

'You can do it.'

'I can do it,' she repeated, without conviction.

'I love you, Ro.'

Her eyes teared up instantly, knowing this was goodbye again. They only ever seemed to say goodbye these days. 'I love you.'

'We're leaving for Bayon tomorrow – more jungle trekking – but I'll call you as soon as I can, OK?'

She nodded bleakly. One hundred and fourteen days.

'Flash me your boobs as a parting gift.' He winked.

Ro chuckled, in spite of the tears, and pulled her (his) shirt over her head. She could hear him draw in his breath.

'God, I miss you. Behave yourself, baby.' His voice warped as the signal wavered again. 'And remember to wash!'

From beneath the cocktail-spattered linen shirt, she heard the connection between them break again and she fell back on the bed, closing her eyes and curling up into the foetal position. In under a minute, she had succumbed to oblivion and her brief call with Matt was as fleeting as a dream.

'Try this,' Florence said with knowing eyes, pushing a mug of green – green what? Algae? – towards Ro.

Ro smiled quizzically, trying to look baffled by

Florence's concern. She thought she was doing an admirable job of passing herself off as bright and perky. 'Really, it's just the tail end of jet lag.' She sipped the unidentified liquid while mastering her gag reflex and refusing to acknowledge that it had taken four attempts just to get her feet and the pedals working in unison on the twelve-minute bike ride over. (It should have taken three.) She had slept solidly for another four hours after Matt's call – stoutly refusing to respond to Hump's knocks on the door that she should go kayaking with him – and although she was far from well, she could at least keep her mouth closed for minutes at a time now, and her eyes were working together too. Bobbi had looked pleasingly broken as they'd passed on the landing, but Ro had no idea who the other brunette was emerging from Hump's bedroom, her shoes in one hand as she'd tiptoed down the stairs. As for how Greg had fared on his morning after the night before – and, more importantly, in which bedroom he had slept – well, Ro couldn't wait to get home for the lowdown.

'Your home is beautiful. Have you lived here long?'

She looked around at the kitchen she was sitting in. Glass-fronted pale blue cabinets were topped with a giant slab of rococo-cut white marble, the floor laid with white ceramic tiles. Blue gingham pelmeted curtains framed the many paned windows, with a large kitchen table running alongside them, and the window seats were upholstered with cushions in the same pretty check.

From the island unit, where she was sitting on a tall white stool, she could look through the row of arched floor-to-ceiling windows to the terrace and the vast, steam-rolled lawn beyond that boasted densely planted beds on either side and was fringed at the far end by the dancing grasses on the beach dunes. An ocean view in East Hampton? Even Ro knew she was probably housed, right now, in $10 million.

'It'll be thirty-one years in November. My late husband, Bill, and I moved here from Manhattan when our daughters were born. We used to come down for weekends and holidays anyway, and it seemed the perfect place to raise a family. New York's no place for children in my opinion. They need backyards and beaches to play and explore.'

'Oh, I completely agree,' Ro replied, aiming for all out jauntiness. 'Most of the pools I've seen out here are bigger than my entire garden in London. Matt and I could maybe have one child where we are now, but we'd have to move before the second was born, and I honestly don't know if we could afford to upsize in our area. Prices are just going through the roof again.' She rolled her eyes in a 'what can you do?' gesture. 'I imagine we'll be moving out sooner rather than later.'

'So you're planning on getting married?' Florence asked from her position by the sink. She was tending a row of kitchen herbs that released their aromas as the watering can nosed their leaves.

'We're getting engaged when he's back.' She closed her eyes for a second – one hundred and fourteen days. This time tomorrow, one hundred and thirteen . . .

Florence seemed surprised. 'How long did you say you'd been together?'

Ro interlaced her fingers round the mug. 'Since university.'

Florence seemed even more surprised. 'How lovely.'

'He is.'

A buzz on the intercom made them both turn, and

Florence put down the watering can. 'I wonder who that could be,' she murmured to herself. 'Excuse me, please.'

'Of course.'

She heard the sound of metallic voices in the hallway and, a moment later, saw a delivery van speeding up the drive. Ro looked down at the shallow trays on the worktop before her, with new batches of seed bombs rolled and ready to throw. She picked one up and rolled it in her palm absently. She had enjoyed her slice of 'guerrilla gardening' yesterday and she had a feeling a long, brisk walk into the wind after this meeting was what her body needed. It wasn't going to be enough to merely metabolize last night's alcohol – she had tried sleeping it off; now she was going to need to work it off and have it blown out of her too.

'It's good to see some people still have manners – he brought up my mail from the gate too,' Florence said, coming back through carrying a small box and a clutch of letters. 'I'm really so glad you could come over this morning,' she continued, opening the top letter with a steak knife she pulled from a drawer. 'The seed bombs generate so much attention and support whenever I take a stand at the local food fairs, but it's not enough. Long Island has a hundred miles of coastline, and almost all of it is at the mercy of the Atlantic. I can't get enough people mobilized from food fairs alone, and we have *got* to get these dunes replanted as quickly as possible. The thicker, more established the dune vegetation, the more resilient the dunes are to coastal erosion and the safer we all are. Those hurricanes, they just blow their way across the water, getting stronger and stronger, and *we're* the first thing they hit! The dunes down there were the only thing stopping this house from being five feet underwater.'

Ro glanced down the garden, horrified by the image dancing in her mind.

Florence, quickly reading the letter and putting it down on the worktop, looked at Ro and shook her head. 'Others weren't as lucky as us. Montauk was hit worst. They lost almost all their beachfront, and they had a dicky of a time trying to dredge the sand from the Sound before the April 30 cut-off. The channel had become almost completely blocked off.'

'On 30 April? Why then?' Ro asked, sipping the Green and watching as Florence opened the next letter with the steak knife.

'That's when the piped plovers come to nest in the dunes – yet another reason why the dunes are so important, you see. They're severely endangered and protected by federal law. All beach conservation work has to be finished before they migrate here for the summer,' Florence said, sipping on her own green smoothie.

'So you want me to help you with dispersing the seeds?' Ro asked, watching as Florence glanced at the letter before crumpling it in her hand and tossing it into a recycling bin.

'Heck, no. I need you for something far more important than that.' She looked up at Ro, resting her hands on the worktop in front of her. 'Beach retreat, dune erosion and hurricane risk all combine as the single biggest problem facing this entire area. Our local economy depends upon those beaches bringing in visitors from far and wide, but not everybody is civically minded. They don't care about what's right, or best for the long term. On the one hand, we've got residents inland who don't want their taxes being spent on what they see as merely protecting the ocean-front properties, and on the other, we've got those beachfront homeowners pushing hard for protection simply so that they can maximize their real-estate values and move on to something bigger and better – "flipping", they call it – and to hell with what they leave behind.' She shrugged. 'The dunes are nature's way of keeping both camps happy, and they cost a *lot* less than constantly dredging and rebuilding beaches, which seems to be the fashionable answer du jour. People seem to forget we're barely out of a recession.'

'But what can I possibly do to help you?'

'It's quite simple. When I talk, it sounds like a rant and people switch off. What I need is the power of *one* image to convey more than a thousand of my words.'

Ro straightened up, flattered, albeit disbelieving, that Florence thought she was up to the task. Florence was passionate, well informed, articulate, intelligent and persuasive. What made her believe Ro – barely more than a stranger on the beach – could encapsulate all those qualities visually?

'You mean you want a marketing campaign?'

Florence nodded back at her intently. 'Absolutely I do. It has to capture the beauty of the area but also the fragility. It has to make people understand how everything that defines this area is in jeopardy – and that apathy is the most corrosive element of all. We need to mobilize the town and really get this programme underway before the next storm season is upon us.' She beamed at Ro, a dazzling smile that stripped ten years off her in an instant. 'Think you can do it?'

Could she? She photographed families for a living, editing and filing their old forgotten media files into bite-size films. She'd never done anything that needed to convey a message before.

Ro bit her lip. 'I'd give it my best shot.'

'That'll do for me.' Florence smiled, her eyes twinkling as they had on the beach yesterday afternoon, as her hands found the small parcel that was left on the worktop. She slit the sellotape bindings with the knife. 'I have a feeling we're—' She stopped speaking abruptly as she saw, inside, a duck-egg-blue box. Tiffany. Florence raised a quizzical eyebrow as she lifted it out and removed the lid.

Ro, unable to hide her curiosity, leaned forward on her elbows, trying to seeing in. She'd never had anything from Tiffany before and the iconic blue box held a powerful mystique for her.

Slowly, Florence lifted a single-strand pearl necklace from the box, letting the pearls ripple over her fingers and warm against her skin. They were magnificent, each and every one notably larger than the pea-sized pearls Ro remembered her own mother wearing. Her eyes fell to the clasp – a gold oval studded with a ruby and encircled by tiny pearls, the scarlet as vivid as a pinprick of blood on snow.

'Wow,' Ro whispered, as Florence laid the necklace back in the box and picked up the small blue envelope instead. 'You've got a nice husb—' she started to say, before remembering Florence's earlier reference to him as 'my late husband'. She averted her eyes, embarrassed. 'Sorry, I . . . You said . . . Ugh, God.' She pinched the bridge of her nose between two fingers, the hangover too brutal to hide any longer. *Just shut up, Ro*, she told herself.

'It's fine,' Florence said, smiling kindly as she took in Ro's blush. 'He died seventeen years ago of a heart attack. I always told him he worked too hard and smoked too much.' She shook her head sadly. 'And he always told me not to nag him . . .'

Ro nodded silently, watching as Florence looked down to read the card. She herself was desperate to know who'd sent it – if not her husband, then who? Though of course their name would be no clue as to their identity to her anyway. She knew no one out here but Florence, Hump and Bobbi. Did Greg count? Probably not. She couldn't swear she'd recognize him if she passed him in the supermarket. Hell, the kitchen! She knew him about as well as she knew the hardware-store owner, and all she knew about him was that his name was Bob.

Florence looked up, meeting Ro's gaze with a strained smile as she replaced the card in its envelope and slipped it under the tissue paper in the box, beneath the necklace. 'Anyway, where were we?'

'Um . . .' Ro bit her lip, trying to think, trying to remember what they'd been discussing before this, but her mind had clouded like an English summer's day and she could think only of the $20,000 pearl necklace sitting in a box in front of her.

But it wasn't thwarted curiosity that was distracting her. It was the glimpse she'd caught of the look that had flitted over Florence's face like a phantom as she'd read the card – the tiny crease that had winkled in the furrow of her brow, the slight freeze that had set in the corners of her mouth. It wasn't the reaction most women would have to receiving such a beautiful gift.

'Oh, I remember! The dunes . . .' Florence cried, stabbing a finger in the air.

'Ah yes,' Ro nodded, catching sight of a diamond brace-let on Florence's wrist and immediately pushing the thought away. Florence was a wealthy, attractive, self-possessed woman who had doubtless received gifts of even greater beauty or worth than this necklace during her life. Ro, on the other hand, had been with the same man for eleven years and couldn't even get a ring on her finger. What the hell did she know?

'Hey!' Ro exclaimed in surprise as she looked down at the two prostrate bodies on the towels. 'Fancy seeing you here!'

Hump and Bobbi shielded their eyes to look up at her. Giant bottles of water were jammed into the sand next to each of them, a bright blue cold box locked shut by their heads.

'Hey, yourself! Where did you go to?' Hump asked, propping himself up on his elbows, the central groove deepening along his washboard stomach as he did so. 'I never heard you leave this morning. *For once.*' Ro's clumsiness was fast becoming the stuff of legend with her housemate, although she thought he could hardly talk! He wasn't one ever to shut a door if it could be slammed, and Bobbi was incapable of putting the cap back on the milk.

'Sorry – I had an appointment at eleven and had to dash. I woke up late.' Ro crouched down on her heels, hugging her knees with her arms. The sun was at its highest point in the sky now and the glare from the beach was blinding. She realized she'd forgotten her sunglasses.

'No, you did not wake up late,' Bobbi said in a low, contrary voice, turning her head fractionally to make eye contact with Ro. 'I heard you talking to someone in your room at six this morning.' A wicked gleam shone in her eyes. 'Did you hook up with someone last night?'

'No!' Ro exclaimed with such force she fell backwards onto her bottom, her feet accidentally kicking sand into Hump's face. 'I would *never* . . . You know I'm with Matt.'

Bobbi shot her a sceptical look – although whether she was sceptical that Ro hadn't hooked up with someone or sceptical that Ro really was with Matt, she couldn't be sure. She looked to Hump for support, but he was too busy coughing up sand to notice.

'I am!' Ro protested. 'It was Matt you heard me talking to. He Skyped this morning.'

'Huh. Shame,' Bobbi muttered after a pause, turning her face back to the sun and closing her eyes. She had recovered well from this morning's low point on the landing: her mascara was off her cheeks, for one thing, the green tinge in her complexion replaced by a becoming heat flush, and her hair had clearly made friends with a brush again – not that most people probably bothered to look much further than her yoga-honed figure in a knockout red halterneck bikini anyway.

'How was he?' Hump finally asked, loyally, sitting up fully and passing her a chilled Diet Coke from the cold box.

Ro shot him a look of gratitude. 'Great! He's loving it! Just loving it.' The can opened with a hiss and she drank with a rabid thirst. 'I mean, walking for days among man-eating monkeys and gripping the walls of ravines with his fingertips? Totally his idea of heaven!' She slapped a hand to her chest. 'My idea of hell, of course, but he's happy, so . . .' She shrugged, lost in the memories of him. 'Oh, and he looked *so* good. Y'know, he's got a tan now, bit of a beard. And he's lost a little weight – I suppose with all the humidity and the walking and only eating rice or whatever.' Her voice trailed away as she caught sight of Bobbi's expression.

'You got a photo of the boy?' Bobbi asked, a pained look on her face. 'If we're gonna hear about him all summer, we may as well know what he looks like.'

Ro fished in her pocket for her phone. 'Here.' She handed it over, showing her screensaver – a picture of Matt taken at Christmas as he ceremonially carried the overcooked, desiccated turkey to the table, a proud look on his face, the cleft in his chin pronounced as his mouth pouted in amusement at the chef's hat she'd plonked on his head seconds earlier.

'Oh my God!' Bobbi exclaimed, sitting up in one fluid movement and almost knocking the Coke can from Ro's hand. 'He is hot! You seriously let him fly halfway round the world for a year and you didn't go with him? Are you crazy?'

'Half a year. It's *half* a year. And in fact it's only one hundred and fourteen days now,' Ro corrected, feeling instantly panicky, her stomach twisting wretchedly as Bobbi's reaction confirmed her absolute worst fear – he was halfway round the world and women everywhere would be falling in love with him. They would be. It didn't matter that he was in a monastery – he wasn't going to be locked up in there for the whole time: they were leaving again tomorrow – or that he loved her. He was out in the world, away from her, and he was at risk from every woman he was going to meet on his travels.

'What's his sport?' Hump asked, having leaned over and looked at the photo with the merest hint of curiosity. 'He looks pretty buff.'

'Football.'

'As in soccer?' Hump clarified.

'Oh. Yes, right. Exactly. Soccer. He plays in a local team on Sundays. It's just a fun thing, but y'know, they take it really seriously.' She rolled her eyes, remembering all the times she'd spent sitting on the sidelines with the other girlfriends – well, they were all mainly wives now – not bothering to watch the game, buckets of sliced oranges at their feet as they chatted about work and kids and their new coats or boots. What she'd give now, though, to watch him running about, what she'd pay for that quiet luxury of being able to rest her eyes on him, letting the sight of him seep into her like a big view that touched her soul and became part of her somehow.

'He looks like a good guy,' Hump said, pulling his knees up and beginning to look around the beach, his eyes hidden behind blue-tinted mirrored aviators. 'Hey, you want to lie out properly? I got a spare here.' He pulled a rolled-up straw mat from the giant backpack to his right and threw it out so it unfurled beside him. 'I always carry one with me, just in case, y'know . . . I get company.'

Ro grinned and pocketed her phone again – allowing herself one last peek at Matt until she got home – then sat down next to him.

'Where's Greg, by the way?'

She asked the question to them both, but her eyes fell to Bobbi, who was lying on her back, her face turned away. She didn't move.

Hump spoke, after a beat, once it became clear Bobbi wasn't going to. 'Not sure. Woke up to a note from him on the kitchen table saying he'd pre-agreed to spend the day with his friends in Southampton. We'll see him again next weekend.'

'Oh, right,' Ro murmured, her eyes on Bobbi as she rolled up the cuffs of Matt's chinos to show off a little more calf. If only she could remember more of last night . . . She didn't recall actually seeing them kiss, but surely that was the way they'd been heading.

'You not brought your bathing suit?' Hump asked, watching as she rolled the arms of her T-shirt up to her shoulders too.

Thankfully not, Ro thought to herself, taking in the tiny string bikinis being paraded. 'I didn't dress for the beach. Like I said, I had that appointment to go to.'

'New rule for ya,' Bobbi drawled, still turned away. 'Always be beach-ready out here. Your bikini's basically your underwear. You never know when you might need to strip off.'

Ro bit her lip. How terrifying. She usually had to fast for two days and down a double vodka tonic before she stepped out in her swimsuit.

'So who were you seeing? A new client?' Hump asked, his voice fading out as a girl walked past particularly close to their towels, Hump clearly set in her sights.

He grinned, watching her pert derriere, before looking back to Ro like she was a partner in crime. Another bloke. 'And that's what I love about this place: ambition in a bikini, everywhere you look.'

Ro groaned. 'Am I going to have to hand this mat back already?'

'Nup, you're good . . . for now.'

A small timer beeped on Bobbi's phone and she turned it off, rolling onto her tummy in one swift movement. 'You were saying . . . the job,' she prompted.

'Oh yes. So, it's not a Marmalade commission, sadly. I

met a woman on the beach yesterday evening as I was on my way home. She's a local councillor—'

'Don't tell me – Florence Wiseman, right?' Hump interrupted, pointing his hand at her like it was a gun.

'Yes! How did you know?'

'Aaaagh, everyone knows Florence. She's one of East Hampton's matriarchs; what she doesn't know about this place isn't worth knowing. She knows everyone, is on the board of everything. She's not everyone's cup of tea, not once she gets on her soapbox, but I'll give her this: the woman's got balls.'

'Hump!' Ro shot him a disapproving look. She knew the point he was trying to make, but Florence had too much elegance to be described like that.

'What?' Hump shrugged, palms outstretched in sincerity. 'I mean it as a good thing. I can't even imagine the policies we'd end up with without her. She's old school. Cares about the town, not just the real-estate prices, unlike every other person on that board. I came up against some of 'em when I first floated the Humper concept.' He shook his head. 'They thought I was going to bring down the tone of the place; they didn't hear anything about me promoting local businesses.' He shook his head. 'She gets my vote, for sure. The gossip columns can go hang.'

'I don't know the woman. Heard of her, though,' Bobbi offered, her voice a protracted mumble.

'Well, I really like her. She's asked me to shoot her seed-bombing campaign.'

'Her *what*?' Bobbi drawled, lifting her head to break her near-comatose position.

'Seed-bombing. They're little balls packed with dune-plant seeds that you scatter randomly to help revegetate and strengthen the dunes. Florence says the dunes are one of the most effective defences against the storms that come in off the ocean.'

'Cool,' Hump nodded.

'No, not cool,' Bobbi contradicted, pushing herself up onto her elbows. 'Dunes can't do diddly-squat against a hurricane. People go on about this year after year. "What can we do? What can we do?" they cry. Jeez, they drive me crazy. They build jetties, they build revetments, they sink old subway cars to create reefs as offshore breaks, but the truth is, nothing's going to keep that ocean from creeping forward. And all those houses sitting on the shore? They're going to fall in the water sooner or later – ten, twenty, fifty years from now, they'll all be gone. I swear to God I could set up here specializing exclusively in strategic retreat. I've thought about it more than once.'

'Strategic retreat? What's that?' Ro puzzled, finishing off the Coke and unable not to stare at a girl walking past in a flesh-coloured bikini that was nothing short of alarming from a distance.

'Knocking down the existing properties and resiting them at the back of their own lots. Might buy you another hundred years before it's a problem again, but by then it ain't *your* problem, and in the meantime you've protected your real-estate value.'

'But surely that's incredibly expensive, knocking down and starting from scratch?'

'The lot's the thing, not the property.'

Hump gave a small snort. 'Besides, down the road in Southampton, they just raised a twenty-four-million-dollar levy against a hundred and twenty-five ocean-front house-holders to pump two and a half million tons of sand onto the beaches to replenish them. Twenty-four mill divided by hundred twenty-five? Now *that's* expensive.'

Bobbi tutted disgustedly. 'These people, they've got money to burn,' she shrugged, collapsing back fully on her towel again and turning her head away to tan the other cheek.

'Crikey,' Ro muttered under her breath. And to think she'd been working up the nerve to ask Matt to consider extending the kitchen with a side return. (Pre-pause, naturally.)

'You want some?' Hump was holding out some sunscreen lotion. 'You're going pink already.'

'Thanks. Celtic skin, what can you do?' she said, rolling her eyes and taking it from him. 'So what time are you heading back to New York, Bobbi?' she asked, squirting too much cream on her face. Way too much. It had warmed in the sun and now ran out of the tube like milk.

'I always get the seven thirty p.m. Jitney.'

'Uh-huh,' she said, vigorously smoothing it into her cheeks. 'And how long is the coach ride home?'

'Three hours that time of night? Depends on traffic. So long as I'm back at my apartment by eleven p.m. latest . . .'

Ro started dragging the cream down her neck, trying to find more surface area. 'Whereabouts are you in New York? Would I have heard of it?'

'Tribeca.'

'Oh. Uh . . .' No. She took some off her forehead and began rubbing it into her arms instead, distracted from the conversation by the laboriousness of such a seemingly simple task. Bloody hell, how much of that stuff had she put on?

Hump stood up suddenly, his eyes trained on something

further up the beach, like a gundog pointing. 'Hey, isn't that Greg? Yo, Greg!' Hump called, waving to a small group playing volleyball a few hundred yards away. They had a gazebo set up beside them and some smart teak portable loungers arranged in the shade. There'd be no sandy bottoms for them.

Greg, tanned and muscled in navy and red shorts, turned. Seeing Hump, he waved and said something to his friends, before jogging over like a model from a designer deodorant ad. 'Hi, guys,' he nodded, his hands on his hips as he stood above them all. 'I hope I didn't wake any of you when I left earlier. I tried to be as quiet as I could.'

'Well, that makes one of you at least,' Hump teased, and Ro dug him in the ribs with her elbow, knowing he was directing his words at her again.

She watched as Greg's eyes skittered over to Bobbi, who was still lying on her tummy and appeared to be pretending to sleep. He caught Ro watching him and smiled back, a quizzical expression on his face as he took in her alabaster-white complexion, and she hurriedly began rubbing her face again, this time using the heel of her hands to help drive the goddamned cream into her skin.

'So who you with, man?' Hump asked, jerking his chin towards the volleyball players.

'You know the Blaize brothers – Todd and David? And Shelley Anderton? She's a VP at Goldmans in derivatives; Grace Elliman, Kurt Styler's ex; and Erin Wesley.'

'*Your* ex?' Hump said with a small smile.

Greg nodded. 'Yes.' He looked back at his friends throwing themselves around athletically, long legs kicking up sand, arms outstretched, tummies taut.

'And that's all good?'

Greg looked at him, bemused. 'We've stayed good friends. She's with Todd Blaize now. Has been for a long time.'

'I remember,' Hump said neutrally, slapping him on the arm. 'You want a drink?' He pointed down to the cold box.

'I wish I could. It looks a lot more chilled over here.' He looked back at his friends again as though checking they weren't leaving without him. Ro saw one of the women, in an emerald-green bikini, jump high to punch down the ball, her limbs supple and elastic like a pro athlete. Ro tried to visualize herself in the woman's place – jumping around, tiny bikini – and gave a small shudder, rubbing the cream a little harder again. 'But I'd better get back. David and Todd can get way too competitive if someone's not there to diffuse them. You know what brothers can be like, right?'

'Totally,' Hump nodded. 'So when you heading back to the city? You coming back to Sea Spray later?'

Greg shook his head, but his stature deflated a little as though he was embarrassed. 'I'm booked on the seven thirty p.m. I figure I'll just shoot straight to the Southampton stop from the Blaizes' place. I've unpacked my stuff at yours now, so I can just leave it there. It doesn't make sense to double back when I'm already at Southampton anyway.'

Hump nodded excessively. 'Sure. Well, hang loose, bro. We'll get together again next weekend.'

'For sure,' Greg agreed, his expression intent. He looked down at Ro and Bobbi, frowning to see Bobbi hadn't moved – frowning more at the sight of Ro's shiny face.

They watched him jog away again, Hump remaining where he was and turning a slow circle on the spot, scoping the beach – no doubt for hot single girls. Bobbi, by contrast, sat up and reached inside the cool box for a fresh drink.

'Sounds like he's on the same Jitney as you, Bobs,' Hump said, finally collapsing back on his towel and fishing in the bag for his Kindle.

'No, I'm on the six thirty p.m.,' she clipped, setting another alarm on her phone.

'You said you were catching the seven thirty p.m. a few minutes ago,' Hump frowned.

'No, you're confused. I said the six thirty,' Bobbi sighed, rolling herself back down on the sand with impressive abdominal control. 'Six thirty p.m. Definitely.'

# *Chapter Ten*

Ro sat slumped on the steps outside the studio, a bowl of granola on her lap and the sun on her face as she watched the cars gliding past towards East Hampton Main Street in one direction and Montauk in the other, none of them stopping to browse in the pretty square. The designer homeware boutique seemed to make out like a bandit thanks to its highway frontage but if it wasn't for the faithful regulars darting into the spa and yoga studio, or the high school kids stopping by the ice cream parlour on their way home, she was certain no one would ever stop by it at all.

She spooned the food into her mouth with depressed monotony, and only the ceramic Chinese runner duck for company. She had been here nearly a week now and not one customer had even wandered in, coffee in hand and a curious look on their face. She paid her rent to Hump from the rent she collected from her own house in Barnes – after agents' fees, she just about broke even – but she still needed money for groceries and going out. All she had was the small advance she had been paid for Florence's commission, and she had started work on it already, cycling around the dune roads behind the beaches every evening after she'd left the studio, looking for angles and landscapes that sparked her creativity for the brief, although nothing was

KAREN SWAN

jumping out at her just yet. White sand – while pretty – looks bland when there's mile after mile of it, and besides, anyone could shoot that. Her brief was to find a way to get the viewer to engage emotionally with it; she had to make people understand the dunes weren't just somewhere people picnicked in films. They had a purpose, a real, eco- logical role; they were the town's first and last defence against the ocean's advance and that affected everybody who lived here, not just the ocean-front homeowners: no beaches meant no tourists, and therefore no jobs.

By her feet was a wicker basket filled with paper bags of the seed bombs, which Ro now collected every morning as she cycled past Florence's house on the way to the studio. It had become something of a habit, a new routine. Flor- ence left the bags out on trays for volunteers to take from a painted wooden barrow by the gates at the bottom of her drive. Ro had decided to keep a basket of them for her own customers to take too, but given that she didn't actually have any customers, she had taken to scattering them her- self on her sunset cycle back home as well, her camera swinging round her neck. She had worked out, just before she fell to sleep one night, that she was cycling on average eighteen miles a day. Matt wouldn't believe it when she told him.

'Hello there.'

Ro turned with a start to find a tall, rangy woman in orange leggings and a khaki jumper that slid off one shoul- der leaning against the porch post.

'I'm Melodie. I run Insala Yoga next door,' the woman said with a smile that reached her eyes. Her voice was deep and honeyed, and her skin had such a gleam to it, it looked like it had been polished. But her hair – her hair was thick and wiry, and didn't so much fall to her shoulders as spring just above them like bungee ropes, forcibly held back from her face by a thick, twisted navy scarf that knotted at the nape. Soulmate! Ro liked the look of her immediately, maybe because – she too – didn't fit the mould of a Hamptonite.

'Hi,' Ro said, clambering to her feet and slopping milk over her own flip-flopped feet. 'Ro Tipton, Marmalade Family Media.' Standing up, she saw how tall Melodie really was – six foot surely.

'Family Media,' Melodie repeated. 'I've been wanting to ask you about that since the sign went up. What exactly is Family Media?'

Ro smiled patiently. She spent her life explaining it to people – the downside of being first in on a new market. 'Basically? It's editing personal digital content and putting it into physical form that families can actually enjoy – so photobooks, portraits, calendars, short films, slide shows as laptop screensavers, that kind of thing . . . Otherwise all those images just sit unseen on a hard drive, and if the computer dies or is stolen, it's so traumatic . . . I've had clients come to me after all those memories have been lost and they've needed to start again from scratch. Their wedding photos or their pictures and films of their children as babies . . .'

'That sounds like a rewarding enterprise, Ro. You're really giving people something that enriches their lives.'

Ro was silent for a beat. Melodie's words were so . . . *warm* for a moment she wasn't sure whether she was being sarcastic.

'You teach yoga, you say,' Ro said, quickly changing the subject. 'Do you do the hot one?'

Melodie smiled as Ro's naivety on the subject was revealed in just those six words. 'No, I don't. Bikram is a bit too aggressive for me, and I find it attracts a certain type of client who is really only interested in the most superficial aspects of yoga – namely weight loss. I understand why some people might choose that, but I prefer to really focus on the connection between the body and the breath within the element of dynamic flow.'

Ro's head bobbed to the words as though she was having an Indian head massage rather than a conversation. She didn't know exactly what Melodie meant, but she felt so profoundly relaxed, did it really matter? 'Has anyone ever told you your voice is really amazing? It's so . . .' She searched for the word.

'Melodic?'

'Yes, exactly!' She laughed. The word was perfect.

'I know.'

'I mean, how clever were your parents to get your name so spot on?'

'Actually, they didn't. They named me Samantha, but everyone called me Melodie by the time I was three. Apparently my voice has an unusually high number of alpha waves, which make it sound so calming – useful in my job.'

'Yes, I'll bet.'

Ro saw a couple of women walk down the boardwalk towards them, rolled mats under their arms. 'Talking of which . . . I'd better let you go, Melodie. Your clients are arriving. It was lovely meeting you.'

Melodie turned as the women approached. 'Namaste,' she said softly, gesturing for them to go into the studio. She turned back to Ro. 'Would you like to join us? There would be no charge, of course, for business neighbours.'

Ro put her hands up immediately. 'No! No, thank you. I tried yoga for the first time last week. It's not for me.'

'May I ask where you went?'

'The SoulCycle Studio, I think it was called?'

Melodie winced. Actually winced. 'I wouldn't have thought bikram would suit you, no. From what I see Ro, you are *Kapha prakriti*.'

It sounded like a type of fruit. Ro wrinkled her nose.

Melodie smiled. '*Prakriti* means "body type". Vinyasa yoga is much more suited to your temperament and body type. I am certain you will feel better after the session than you do now.'

'Oh, but I feel fine.' What did she mean? Hadn't Ro come across as warm and chatty? Did eating granola on the steps somehow count as binge-eating out here? Were her emotions really so easy for everyone to see?

'I've seen you looking through the windows during the Guruji chants for the past few days. Join us. We can help you find what you're looking for.'

Ro cringed. They'd seen her?

'Just put a note on the door directing your clients to my studio – it's easy enough for them to come to get you, and the clothes you're wearing will be OK for now. They're loose enough.' Ro opened her mouth to protest again, but Melodie simply smiled, radiating a quiet certainty. 'We'll wait for you.'

Ro watched with a rising sense of panic as Melodie disappeared into the small white clapboarded hut. This is what came of eating in public; hadn't her mother always told her it was rude? People would get the wrong idea . . .

She stood on the steps for a moment, looking around the

deserted square. The sun was shining straight down on it like the landing lights of a spacecraft, but there was no one around to notice. Ha! Unicorns could have been surfing on rainbows and it would stay her secret.

Sod it. It was time to face it – no one was coming.

Jogging up the steps into her own studio, she scrawled a note with an arrow on it, pointing to Insala Yoga, five feet away, and Blu-tacked it to the door. A minute later, she was walking into the yoga studio with a look of trepidation on her face. Last week's encounter with the weekending Manhattanites had been frankly terrifying, what with their Barbie bodies and designer kit and hypoxic breathing techniques. But the first thing she noticed here was the light – or rather the lack thereof. In Bobbi's class, everything was bleached and blond and white – the walls, the floors, the customers, the candles, the mats, the potted orchids on the table in the corner – and two walls of the class were solid glass, drenching everyone in sunlight and vitamin D, and making their bodies look golden and honeyed, ready for the pools and tennis courts later. But here, the small windows were veiled with jewel-coloured sari silks that fluttered softly like tropical flowers below the air-conditioning vents and cast the room in soothing shade.

In Bobbi's class, perfumed candles the size of drums had competed with sticky Marc Jacobs scents, but in this room, Ro could see a lit oil diffuser and, beside it, a small bottle of lotus oil. The smell was heavenly – the one she'd been detecting all week – and when she closed her eyes in the cool, quiet, aromatic space, she didn't feel like she was in America at all, but across the ocean in Asia – with Matt.

The connection made her relax and smile. She opened

her eyes to find Melodie smiling back at her, a knowing look on her face. She nodded and gestured towards the empty mat near to her.

'Ladies,' Melodie said in her extraordinary voice, 'shall we begin?'

Ro sat cross-legged, resting her hands on her knees, and allowed herself a deep sigh. For the first time since arriving here, she felt at home.

Ro was just beginning to think levitation might actually be a physical possibility when she heard the knock. She had slipped slowly down into a black velvet hole and found happiness there – memories of her and Matt lighting her up from the inside, and she didn't want to leave. If she couldn't be with him there, she could be with him here. The scent of Asia, Melodie's voice, her incantations – indecipherable but suggestive – had led her into a deep meditation where their love didn't hurt or need to be numbed – as it had since he'd left – but felt good again, nourishing. For the first time since Matt had stepped out of her sphere, she didn't feel the profound shock of being alone.

But the knock . . .

She opened one eye and looked around the room. Without moving her head, she could see Melodie had risen from her mat. Moving her head, she could see she was walking towards the door.

She closed her eye again, relieved *she* didn't have to move; she wasn't sure she could, anyway; she actually couldn't feel her legs at all at this particular moment, as she cast her mind back to the breath in her body, which she had left hovering somewhere around her pancreas.

Why had she never noticed before how good breathing felt? She inhaled again, imagining the breath in her lungs as a rolling, gathering light, illuminating her from within.

'Ro?' Melodie's voice was by her ear, soft and rich like warmed caramel. 'Ro?'

Ro dragged open one eye. 'Uh,' she grunted, like a teenager being roused for school. 'Uh?'

'You've got a client. They're waiting outside for you.'

'Uh!' Ro was aware she sounded like a gibbon and really ought to try to articulate some words at least, but her body felt so deeply relaxed, her mind so thoroughly far from here that she was up and halfway across the room before she was even aware of it. 'Th-thanks,' she stammered, rolling towards the door like a drunk, trying to shake off the almost trance-like state.

She opened the door so that the outside world poured in and she blinked into the bright light and harsh day going on without her. It woke her up. She had a client?

She had a client! They weren't on the porch. She straightened up and marched noisily along the planks of the boardwalk connecting the run of small studios, running her hands through her hair and rearranging her shirt, which had become skewed round her body during the cat-cow poses.

She inhaled again – why had it felt so peculiarly good in Melodie's studio? – and opened the door with a flourish. 'Hi—' The smile died on her lips.

The Maniac, aka Long Story, held his hands up in a mollifying gesture. 'I come in peace.'

'I don't care if you come in twenty-two-carat gold. Get out.'

The analogy confused them both – Long Story frowned

in bafflement – but she stood her ground, out on the porch.

He took in her refusal to stand in the same room as him. She couldn't even look at him. 'Listen, I understand why you don't want to see me, but that's actually why I'm here – I've come to apologize. Last week on the beach, my behaviour . . . It was so completely out of character. I-I've never . . .' he stammered.

'I don't want to hear it. Just get out of my studio.' Her aura of deep calm had been shattered in an instant. The feeling of Matt was gone – because of *him*?

Long Story hesitated. 'I know what I did humiliated you.'

The memory of it brought bitter tears to Ro's eyes, but she'd be damned if she'd give him that as well. 'Not really. You were the one who showed yourself up,' she said quietly, her voice sounding calm, dignified even. 'Especially in front of your children.'

Her words hit their mark and she saw him wince. He blew out his breath slowly, staring down at the floor and clearly wondering what to say next.

'Please just go. I don't need your apologies. I would just like never to see you again.' She waved her arm before her, indicating for him to take a hike out on the boardwalk.

'I'm afraid it's not that easy—'

She froze. Oh God. He really was a maniac. He was stalking her.

'You see, I'd like to hire you – I mean *commission* you! I'd like to commission you. As a photographer. For my children.' He raked a hand through his hair nervously and her eyes automatically tracked the movement in bewilderment.

Ro stared at him for a long time, not sure whether to laugh, to cry, to call 911. 'So let me just get this straight:

when I met you, you assaulted me for taking pictures of your children.'

He looked taken aback. 'It wasn't assau—'

'It was assault!' Ro exclaimed angrily, shouting him down so that he fell silent. She took a deep breath. 'And now you're saying you want to pay me to take pictures of your children. Is that what you're saying?'

He stared at her for a long moment, his mouth flattening into a tense line. 'Yes.' He nodded. 'Will you do it?'

Ro laughed at the absurdity of the situation. 'Of course I bloody well won't! Do you think I'm completely bloody nuts? You are quite literally the last person I ever want to *see* again, much less work with!'

There it was – all her rage from the beach thrown back at him, her hands balled into furious fists, her breath coming fast and shallow. How did he have the nerve – the nerve! – to stand in her studio and commission her after his earlier stunt?

'I see.' He inhaled sharply, his eyes taking in the pictures all around them, other people's memories held up as totems of happiness and love and lives fulfilled, his hands stuffed into his pockets so that his shoulders were hunched. 'I'm sorry that I made you feel . . .' he said, his eyes on the floor. Ro thought he seemed exhausted by the confrontation, out of words, and as his eyes met hers, she could almost believe he really was. Almost. 'I'm truly very sorry.'

She watched him walk away, past the yoga studio towards the highway, his car keys bunched in one hand, his head bowed.

Melodie's head popped through the doorway. 'Is everything OK? I heard raised voices.'

Ro looked up at her. Where did she begin? 'It's fine.'

'You look really upset. I'm so sorry, Ro. He seemed so polite at the door.'

Ro tried to smile, to brush it off, but her face contorted with the mixture of shame and anger she felt in his presence. He had seemingly come in peace, but she felt as thrown by his apology as she had his aggression at their first encounter. She shook her head and put it down to still emerging from the meditation. She had succumbed to it too deeply – finding Matt there – and now felt like she did when she slept too long in the day and woke too suddenly – heart pounding, dizziness, vague bewilderment as to what the time was, where she was and why.

Always why. Because even when she was fully awake, the answer to that last question eluded her. Why was she over here when Matt was over there? Why hadn't he talked to her before booking his flights? Why . . . why hadn't she been enough?

# Chapter Eleven

Ro was in the shower when Bobbi turned up that Friday evening – she could actually feel the change in the house even under running water, as though the walls were vibrating with the extra charge – and she felt a flutter of excitement at the thought of seeing her sophisticated housemate again. It had been a long week – no other customers had looked in to the studio after Wednesday's unwelcome visit, no more contact from Matt – and she was eager to hear about someone else's news apart from hers and Hump's.

It wasn't to say Hump wasn't great. He was. With Greg and Bobbi back in Manhattan during the week, the downshift in energy in the house was welcome, and she and Hump had fallen into an easy rhythm together of quiet mornings where they didn't disturb each other (Hump was usually out first, kayaking on Georgica Pond) and hooking up at the studio at lunch after she'd finished Melodie's mid-morning class. Hump would bring her a coffee and a flagel, having handed over his shift to one of his team of drivers, and would spend some time at his computer, dealing with advertisers, printers and mechanics as she drifted around the studio, playing *Angry Birds* on her phone and watering the hydrangea. In the evenings, once Ro had come in from her nightly bike ride – provided Hump wasn't 'entertaining' a particularly pretty blonde/brunette/redhead he'd met on one of the Humper runs – they'd sit on the porch together, Ro rolling a bottle of Bud in her hands and taking ever bigger sips as she slowly began to acquire a taste for beer.

Ro loved how easy she felt in Hump's company. They had been living together for precisely eight days now and already they didn't feel the need to fill silences or talk incessantly, bringing each other up to date on their long and winding life journeys to this point.

Bobbi, on the other hand, had somehow managed to dominate the house even all the way from Manhattan, texting Hump the names of interior designers he hadn't asked for and filling the freezer with her special diet boxes of food, which were scheduled to be delivered to Sea Spray Cottage every other weekend. (No one had heard from Greg, of course. It seemed that when he was in Manhattan, he went underground, just working round the clock.)

Ro wrapped herself in a towel and stuck her head out through the bathroom door just as Bobbi ran up the stairs, two at a time. 'Bobbi? I didn't think you were coming out this weekend.'

'Yeah, that's what Hump just said,' Bobbi grinned, panting lightly as she winked back down at their housemate, who was standing below them with his hands in a 'what gives?' gesture. 'But the weather's so good and we . . .' She tried to get her breath back. 'Well, we had such a good time last weekend, didn't we?'

Ro remembered the disastrous yoga class, their coffees-on-the-go, the heavy Saturday night and lazy Sunday on the beach, and felt touched that feisty, indomitable Bobbi had enjoyed it as much as she had.

'Well, it had its high *and* lows,' Ro quipped, making Bobbi burst out laughing as Ro gave a giant sniff. 'You'll be relieved to hear I've moved over to vinyasa yoga.'

'Yeah?'

'Yes. It's got a lot more sleeping on the floor in a dark room. Much more my thing.'

'You just wait till I get you going to Tracy Anderson's classes. That'll wake you up. She's got a place over in Water Mill.'

'Who's Tracy Anderson?'

Bobbi burst out laughing, as though Ro had said something extremely funny. 'You kill me, Ro, you really do.' Then suddenly the smile was gone and it was back to business. There obviously wasn't time for laughing. Bobbi rarely had the time to laugh. 'So anyway, there's a season opener on at Wölffer Estate Vineyard tonight and that's why I had to come down. My boss is making me do it. We built their stables in Sagaponack and I gotta be there. Contacts, you know? But I was thinking, you could come with me and make your own contacts too? You can zoom in on the wives and talk about their kids and shit, while I talk phallic house extensions and offices with the husbands.'

*Kids and shit?* 'Well, to be honest,' Ro hesitated, 'Hump and I had planned to go over to Montauk tonight. They're showing old surf films at Navy Beach; it's a fundraiser for one of the Sandy charities.'

'But this is a fundraiser! This is totally a fundraiser,' Bobbi argued, her eyes wide and intense like someone was questioning her invoice. 'It's just a better-dressed one.'

'I'll bet.' Ro couldn't help but smile as she took in Bobbi's lean black Saint Laurent trouser suit and spike heels.

'What's Greg doing?' Ro asked Hump, who was still standing at the foot of the stairs. 'Is he down tonight?'

Hump shook his head. 'Working again.'

There was a momentary silence as both Ro and Hump's eyes slid over to Bobbi. Neither one of them had dared ask her what had actually happened between her and Greg last weekend, and Hump's memory was as fuzzy as Ro's.

'What do we need him for? We'll have a great time just the three of us,' Bobbi said, her eyes shining brightly.

Ro and Hump's eyes met. Not good.

'Hump, you up for a night of good wine and taking home a sexy chick in a little party dress?' Bobbi called down the stairs. 'You'll forgo me two nights' rent if I get you in there, won't you?' She put her hands together in a 'pretty please' pose that Hump was far too soft-hearted to refuse. 'It's for work, Hump. Otherwise I'd totally be in the city. Totally.'

Hump tried to look stern – technically speaking, this was breach of contract – but Ro could tell from the gleam in his eyes at the mention of women in little party dresses that he'd been reeled in. 'As long as it's not black tie.'

'It's not black tie. Just jacket and tie – with flip-flops, if you really must. But if anyone throws you out on account of 'em, you are not with me.'

'Deal.'

'Ro?' Bobbi turned triumphantly back to her.

'I don't have anything to wear for something like that. I've brought three pairs of trousers, three shirts, five T-shirts—'

'None of it yours either,' Bobbi nodded, frowning. 'We've *got* to take you shopping. I really don't think I can take looking at you in that Annie Hall get-up all summer. In the meantime, I've got a dress you can borrow.' She started marching towards her bedroom. 'We've got an hour to be out.'

Ro trotted after her in alarm, shaking her hands in frenzied little waves. 'We are not the same size, Bobbi.'

'No. But it's a DVF wrap – it's pretty much a one-size-fits-all,' Bobbi said dismissively, then as she saw Ro's expression, more encouragingly, 'Honestly, it'll be fine.'

It was not fine. The label inside the dress said, '4,' and whatever that meant, Ro knew it didn't equate to '14' in British sizing terms. There was a ten missing somewhere between the two women, and Ro had a feeling most of it could be found on her bust and hips.

She tugged the front edge of the skirt further round her thigh again and straightened up – slouching in her usual style only flashed her leg like Angelina Jolie's at the Oscars. She peered down her own décolletage sadly. Even she could see it was magnificent. If only Matt was with her now . . . he'd be so happy.

At least the dress wasn't red, that was one mercy – she was attracting enough attention at this party as it was. Rather, it was a chocolate-brown giraffe print with a wide Japanese-style obi belt, and if it had fit, she would have rather liked it. As it was, she felt conspicuous to have her figure so on display – Hump had actually choked on his Coke when she'd walked in earlier, and Bobbi's face had betrayed an envy that paid no heed to the fact she looked like a model in her ivory body-con sheath.

'Here you go,' Hump said, coming back with her drink.

'Thanks,' Ro murmured quietly, taking a sip.

'Not your thing?' he asked, noticing her discomfiture.

'Hump, I am in a dress ten sizes too small and wearing *flip-flops*.'

'And that's why you are the coolest woman here,' he grinned, checking out her lime-green Havaianas – the only option she had over her Converses and hi-tops. Like the rest of her clothes, Bobbi's shoes didn't fit.

At least he was wearing some too – a yellow pair, not so much in solidarity as in a branding exercise for the Humper.

Ro tried raking her fingers through her hair again, to calm it. She'd been so freaked out trying to cram her curves into the teeny-tiny dress, she'd not had time to blow-dry her hair.

'I wish we'd gone to Montauk,' Ro whispered. 'We could be wearing jeans and digging our fingers into cones of fries while watching surf dudes ripping it up.'

'Yeah, agreed,' Hump replied. 'We don't need to stay long if you don't want,' he said, just as his eyes pinned onto a glossy redhead sashaying past in a hot-pink mini kaftan and who held Hump's stare as she passed. Ro detected a slight change in his movements; she kept forgetting that not all women looked at him like a brother.

She stared into the crowd, feeling more alone than ever. Hump was with her – for the moment – but Bobbi, true to her word, had honed in on her contacts before she'd even had a glass put into her hand and was currently holding the floor with a group of men in blazers and chinos who were hanging on to her words with more than professional interest.

'Ro?'

Even before she'd turned round, Ro knew who was calling her. She'd know that voice anywhere.

'Melodie!' Ro exclaimed with delight. 'Look at you!' she cried, gesturing to Melodie's cobalt-blue silk jersey bandeau dress and sea-green turban. Her spectacular shoulders were on display – Ro had never met someone with dazzling shoulders before – a gold snake clasp wound round her upper arm and gold flat sandals wrapped round her calves. Almost just the sight of her – so exotic and serene amid the skintight dresses and plastic surgery – was enough to put Ro in a meditative state.

They had known each other only two days and yet it could have been two years, the women sharing an almost immediate and intense intimacy that Ro struggled to achieve with friends back home whom she'd known for over a decade. Yesterday and this morning, they had shared breakfast together, sitting on the steps outside their studios and chatting easily, Ro confiding in Melodie about Matt's abrupt absence in a way that she hadn't with a single other soul. Just putting a voice to her fears and anxieties – define 'pause'. What if he didn't come back? What if he met someone else? What if he didn't really want to marry her? – had seemed to lessen the burden of walking around with a bright smile, pretending that all this was *her choice*. And if their breakfast chats lightened the load in her head, Melodie's mid-morning class was like a recharging session to her heart, somewhere she could retreat and feel close to Matt, though he was nearly 9,000 miles away.

She linked an arm through Hump's proudly. 'Melodie, this is Hump, of Hamptons Humper fame, and also my housemate and landlord.'

'And friend!' he added.

'And friend. Of course.' Ro rubbed his arm.

'So you're the genius behind people getting Humped this summer,' Melodie smiled enigmatically.

'Yeah!' Hump grinned.

'The ads have struck a nerve,' Melodie added. 'I've been at quite a few lunches where it's come up. Outrage has generally been the common response by my friends.'

'That was the idea,' he beamed, eyes twinkling with delight.

'So you're actively courting controversy, then?'

He shrugged. 'You know what they say – the only thing worse than being talked about is not being talked about.'

'Oh, I know all about that,' Melodie sighed, looking down and noticing his unorthodox footwear. Bare toes weren't usually part of the 'jacket and tie' uniform. She smiled, seemingly liking him all the more for it. 'You know, I can hardly believe we haven't met before tonight. We've been neighbours for a few weeks now.'

'There's always chanting next door whenever I'm in the studio.'

'Oh? Feel free to join us sometime. Ro's become an immediate convert.'

'That's because it's a lying-down form of exercise,' Hump grinned, joshing her with his elbow and almost making her spill her drink. 'Personally, I prefer to go for the adrenalin rush.'

'Oh, but me too, every time.'

Hump looked a little baffled. 'Yeah, but . . . you can hardly say that sitting in a dark room chanting gives you that.'

'On the contrary, I've had some women report back that it was . . . transcendental.'

Transcendental? Her tone suggested . . . Ro's eyes slid over to Melodie, wondering whether she meant what Ro thought she meant.

Melodie looked back at her. 'You'd agree, wouldn't you, Ro? It's had a powerful effect on you, even just within a few sessions?'

'Well, yes, but not . . .' She cleared her throat, embarrassed. 'Not in *that* way.'

Hump looked thoroughly amused. 'Well, if I see any women wandering around the Square looking flushed . . .' he laughed.

'You'll make the most of it?' Ro offered, just as a man in a linen blazer came over to them, resting a shoulder gently against Melodie.

'Darling.'

'Oh.' Melodie smiled, turning slightly to open up the group. 'May I introduce my husband, Brook Whitmore?'

Ro looked at the man in surprise. Melodie hadn't mentioned him at all during their intense conversations, and she didn't wear a ring. 'Hi,' she said, holding out one hand and clasping the edge of her dress with the other. 'Ro Tipton.'

Brook Whitmore smiled warmly as they shook hands. He was suavely handsome in the mould of Pierce Brosnan or Alec Baldwin – all twinkly eyes and robust health, even though he must have been around twenty years older than her, judging by his bright grey hair. Melodie was forty-one – eleven years older than Ro – and he looked to be nearer his late fifties, early sixties, though he wore it well.

'Ro! It is such a pleasure to meet you finally. Melodie

has not stopped talking about this brilliant young British woman in the studio next door.'

'Oh,' Ro nodded, wishing she had extended the courtesy both ways.

'She was telling me all about your business. Family media, wasn't it you said, darling?'

Melodie nodded proudly, her eyes fixed on Ro.

'Very enterprising. I hope it's going well for you?'

'Mmm, well, hmm.' Ro pulled a face, her shoulders slumping. 'No, not so much, actually. But it's early days still – I know that. I'm going to put a sign up in Bob's hardware store. I need to be more proactive about getting people to know I'm there.'

'It's not always easy being ahead of the curve,' Brook said. 'Just you hang on in there. It'll happen. Sometimes folks just need a little while to get their heads round new ideas.'

Ro smiled, grateful for his kindness. She wouldn't necessarily have picked him out as Melodie's husband – he looked so conservative and old school in his brass-buttoned blazer – but he exuded a sense of generosity and calm that she could imagine had appealed to her new friend. 'What do you do?'

'Nothing that's anywhere near as exciting or glamorous as your world, I'm afraid. Insurance.'

'Ah,' Ro replied, with nothing whatsoever to say on that subject – unless her outrage at her car insurance premium going up counted as riveting conversation. 'Sorry, I'm being rude. Have you met my housemate Hump? Hump Slater. He runs the—'

'The Humpers, I'm guessing! I've seen them around. Certainly a distinctive fleet you've got there.'

'Thanks.' Hump puffed his chest out a little.

'Hump's turned his industry on its head too,' Ro said, proud of her friend. 'He makes his money from advertising, not fares. And so far all the businesses who advertise with him have reported thirty per cent surges in their takings the nights of their promotions in the Humper. How much did you say your base-level bids had jumped by?'

'Twenty-two per cent just in the first month, and we've not even hit Independence weekend yet. This is still very early in the season.'

'Those are impressive numbers, Mr Slater,' Brook said, regarding him closely.

'And there are four vehicles, with another two on order,' Ro added excitedly. 'Hump's going to try to get the Amagansett routes up and running before Fourth of July.'

'Clearly, I don't need a promotions team. Ro does it all for me,' Hump grinned, and Ro thought it was sweet to see him so bashful for once.

'Do you come up to the city much?'

'Occasionally,' Hump nodded.

'We should talk. I know a few people who'd be interested to hear more about this. I suppose you've considered franchise opportunities?'

'Absolutely. Miami, Palm Beach, Cape Cod . . . And that's just East Coast.'

'I assume you'd be looking for investors to really give you the capital injection you'd need for a large-scale roll-out? I might know a few people who'd be interested. Give me a call next time you're in the city and we'll have a drink. Here's my card.' And he reached into his jacket pocket and pulled out a calico-coloured business card.

'Great,' Hump beamed, pocketing it. Everyone paused

as a waitress stopped beside them with a tray of canapés, fingers reaching in delicately.

Ro saw Hump's eyes locate the redhead again. 'Does, uh . . . anyone need a fresh drink?' Everyone shook their heads. 'I'll just go get . . .'

'And if you ladies will excuse me, I'm going to the little boys' room,' Brook said.

Little boys' room? The words sounded so twee and undignified somehow coming from a man like him.

He kissed Melodie on the cheek. 'See you in a while, Songbird.'

Ro smiled politely as Brook wandered off, leaving the two women alone.

'Drives me mad too,' Melodie said quietly, her mouth fixed in a smile.

Ro looked at her in surprise – God! Could Melodie actually read her mind? She found it impossible to keep a secret in the woman's presence – but Melodie's eyes were on the crowd and the seething mass of women in too-high heels, their calf muscles bulging and the telltale rim of Spanx showing through on their thighs.

Ro turned in towards her, closing down their group to advances from strangers. She wanted Melodie all to herself. She felt understood by her, 'mentored' almost, and she didn't want to share it with anyone. 'You never mentioned you were married.'

'Didn't I?' Melodie paused. 'Well, I guess because it's not your average love story: we met pretty late, although we've been married for ten years now. My first, his second.' She bit her lip, her eyes on the crowd still. 'No children.'

'Oh. I'm sorry.'

Melodie smiled, but Ro saw the sadness shine in her

eyes. 'It's one of those things. Brook has children from his first marriage, so that's something.' Melodie's voice was quieter, less certain, less melodic than usual. 'I'm not sure it would have been a great idea in any case. God-awful genes running through my family – gamblers, alcoholics, adulterers . . . You name it, we've had it. My great-great-grandfather made a fortune in dredging on Long Island: he was a former fisherman who saw an opportunity . . . A real visionary.' She looked at Ro. 'He was an entrepreneur, just like you. Maybe that's why I'm so drawn to you.'

Ro flushed with pleasure to hear that Melodie valued their new friendship too.

'Unfortunately, it was pretty much all gone by the time my father died. Three generations of reprobate genes will do that. The repo men seized our family home in the middle of my eighteenth birthday party, two hundred guests watching on as they started walking past the pool with the TVs. Yeah, can you believe it? Talk about timing.' She said it with an amused tinkle in her voice, an indication she'd recalled it this lightly many times before, but that didn't lessen the humiliation in the words.

Ro regarded her statuesque friend through fresh eyes, Melodie's intense spiritual quest suddenly understood – she was looking for something deeper than material possessions, looking for a new path to the one her forebears had trodden.

'Melodie, I'm so sorry.'

'Oh, it was all a long time ago. And thankfully, I'm a lot more stable than my ancestors.'

Ro laughed, but the smile died suddenly on Melodie's lips and she leaned down towards Ro – Ro wished she was wearing something with more heel than a flip-flop:

Melodie was so tall – her eyes sternly fixed on something over Ro's shoulder. 'I don't wish to frighten you, but your unwanted guest is at two o'clock and staring.'

'Huh?' Ro said, trying to work out where two o'clock was and who the unwanted guest was at the same time. Both answers came at once.

Long Story was at the far end of the room, holding a wine glass by the stem in one hand, his other jammed in his trouser pocket. He was standing in a group of five other people. And Melodie was right – he was staring, his eyes darting from the person talking in his group to her, in rapid succession. When he saw her looking back, his surprise was apparent even from across the room and he looked away too quickly, too obviously, so that the woman next to him, a slight, grey-eyed blonde, put her hand on his shoulder and asked him something. He shook his head, and Ro could just see his jaw jut forward a little as he stood in profile to her.

Ro turned her back to him, safe in the certainty he wasn't going to try to approach her again – not here, not anywhere. She had bared her teeth and her message had been received, loud and clear. 'It's fine. He won't be bothering me again. I've dealt with that situation once and for all.'

Melodie looked impressed. 'I'm glad to hear it.'

'Oh, surprise, surprise,' Ro muttered, tutting lightly as she was diverted by the sight of Hump steering the red-head towards the bar. He had a cheeky grin plastered on his boyish face and looked even more handsome than usual, no doubt boosted by the confidence that Brook Whitmore's interest had engendered. 'I'll be eating breakfast with her tomorrow, then.'

'I take it Hump has lots of notches on the bedpost?'

Ro cast her a bored look. 'His bedposts look more like what beavers do to trees.'

Melodie laughed. 'Poor boy. He's obviously chasing comfort.'

'*Comfort?*' Ro spluttered. 'Yeah, right.' Melodie's world view of peace and love would change dramatically if she spent a week in Sea Spray. It wasn't comfort Hump wanted.

'Hey, what would you think about all of us getting together for dinner?' Melodie asked. 'I mean, just something casual. The boys seemed to get on well, and I'd like to get to know your other housemates too. They're going to be your family out here, really, aren't they?'

Ro swallowed. Bobbi as a sister? The thought was terrifying enough to make her leave home. Who could compete, or even cope, with all that energy and ambition and perfectionism on a daily basis? 'That sounds brilliant.'

'Good. So then I'll set it up.' A small sigh escaped her and Melodie looked back out into the crowd again, both of them watching from afar the scene they were enveloped in. 'That really will be something to look forward to.'

# Chapter Twelve

For the first time in a long time, Ro was woken nose first. She pushed herself up on her elbows, her hair falling over her face like a collapsed sail. The sound of a door slamming told her Bobbi was up, and she swung her legs out of bed, poking her head out of the door just as Bobbi was crossing the hall on her way back from the bathroom.

'Really, though?' she demanded, stopping in her tracks at the sight of Ro. 'Come on! You must have *heard* of hair serum?'

'Ugh,' Ro grunted. 'Don't start. It's too early.'

'Listen, you're a pretty girl, Ro, but you're not getting any younger. You have to make more effort as you get older.' Her pretty nose wrinkled as she took in Ro's unpedicured feet.

Ro shook her head, rubbing her face violently with her hands. 'Whatever. I'm going downstairs. If my nose is right – and it's rarely wrong – Hump is a man with a pan this morning.'

'I know! Right? I'm coming with you. I am so starved,' Bobbi beamed, forgetting all about Ro's feet and trotting behind her like a frisky pony. 'You coming to yoga with me later?'

'No. I told you – Melodie's is more my kind of thing.'

'What? You mean the napping-in-a-dark-room thing?'

'That's the one.'

'Tch. That'll never deal with your thighs.'

Ro frowned. What was wrong with her thighs?

'Hey, listen, I say that with love. So was she that woman I saw you with last night? The one in the blue dress?'

'That's her,' Ro replied proudly. 'Did you check out her shoulders?'

'Huh? What? No! Why would I check out . . . ?' Bobbi, confused by the sudden swerve of the conversation, drifted off. 'You two seemed pretty tight.'

'She's lovely.'

'She's loaded is what she is. Skin like that doesn't come cheap, and let's not even talk about the gold.'

'Please don't tell me that's what you notice when you meet people,' Ro grumbled.

'Hey, don't knock it. Where there's money, there's property.' She clicked her fingers intensely. Ro guessed that meant she was concentrating and stayed quiet. They padded down the stairs together. 'What's the husband like? I don't suppose you could introduce us?'

'I only met him for the first time last night myself.'

Bobbi hummed thoughtfully. 'Maybe I should come to the yoga class. Go through the wife.'

Ro slowed her pace. She liked Bobbi, very much, but she had the type of energy output that could charge a room, and Ro wasn't sure she'd ever find Matt in her memories with Bobbi beside her, plotting her next career move with an intensity that could short a power station.

'I'm not sure it's your thing. It's very mellow. Quite emotional.'

'Emotional yoga? What the hell is *that*?'

'Besides, Melodie doesn't do weekend classes.' Ro bit her lip. Melodie had explained she specifically kept her classes to weekdays so that her clients were locals and not the high-octane commuting Manhattan set, of which Bobbi was clearly a cheerleader. 'Besides, Melodie's going to set up dinner for us all. You can meet her husband then, schmooze him direct—'

The two girls stopped in their tracks at the kitchen door. The table had been laid with a tablecloth and cutlery, a jug of sweet peas, several glass carafes of sunrise-coloured juices, a heaped bowl of berries, Ro's marmalade and a rack of toast. And there was indeed a man with a pan, but it wasn't Hump.

'My two favourite housemates!' Greg said brightly, flipping a pancake into the air. He looked more like Gatsby than ever, dressed all in white, although Ro thought it was a shame to have missed seeing him in his pyjamas. He looked great in a suit, even better out of it, and she was wildly imagining him in pressed and piped Turnbull & Asser pyjamas, Savile Row's finest. 'Take a seat. Are you hungry?'

'*Famished*,' Ro said, noticing with delight a teapot warming on the trivet. He could almost be British! He'd thought of everything. She sat down and immediately helped herself to a glass of juice.

'How about you, Bobbi?' he asked, sliding the pancake from the pan onto a stack of them, his back turned to her.

'I never eat before yoga.'

Ro frowned. She was sure Bobbi had said . . .

She watched the way Bobbi seemed to have closed down; her sunny Saturday mood had dissipated in a flash. Greg, it seemed, couldn't meet her eye.

'Um . . . should I go wake Hump?' Ro asked, wondering if she should leave them alone.

'He's driving his date home,' Greg said quickly, clearly guessing her motives.

'Oh.'

'So what have you got planned today?' he asked, placing the plate of stacked pancakes on the table. 'Please, help yourselves.'

'Ha! Try and stop me!' Ro beamed, spearing a pancake with her fork and spooning out a tumble of berries and crème fraiche. 'What do you think, Bobbi? After you've done your yoga, shall we hit the beach? The forecast is for the high eighties today. You have no idea how exciting it is for me to actually be in a summer that's hot and sunny, as opposed to wet and windy.' She took the maple syrup and drizzled it over the pancake in ever-increasing circles. 'This looks amazing,' she said, taking an enormous bite and chewing on it with appreciation, before noticing that, alongside Bobbi's sudden abstinence, Greg wasn't eating either.

'Aren't you going to have some?' she asked quietly, her hand over her mouth, her eyes swivelling side to side between Bobbi and Greg.

'I'm saving myself for brunch,' he said apologetically.

'Brunch?'

'Yes, it's my summer weekend routine – brunch and tennis at the Blaizes' place – you know, my friends in Southampton? I think I pointed them out last week.'

'Bobbi? You're not going to have something?'

But Bobbi just shook her head, pretending to examine her hair for split ends.

Ro chewed more slowly, cross to be made to feel awkward – even if it was inadvertent – about having an appetite.

'You must enjoy getting time out from the office,' Ro said, her mouth still covered by her hand, her head bobbing as she tried to swallow. 'Hump says you work such crazy hours. Even worse than when he was a doctor doing, like, double shifts.'

'It can get a bit much,' Greg nodded. 'I appreciate my time out, that's for sure.'

'That must be tough for your girlfriend too.'

Oh no! Classic Freud! The words were out of her mouth before she could stop herself and she glanced quickly at Bobbi – as did Greg – who had moved on to examining her nails.

He hesitated. 'Well, I'm not really seeing anyone right now . . .' Bobbi's head jerked up. 'I mean, I kinda am, but . . .' he said quickly, before giving up with a rueful smile. 'It's complicated. Let's just say the only people who care about my hours are my bosses.' He smiled, before giving her a concerned look. 'Hump told me you're having a tough time, though, with your boyfriend being gone so long.'

'Oh well,' Ro faltered. 'You know, every day is a day closer.'

Greg refilled her fruit juice. 'That's the spirit. I'm a big believer in patience. We all get what we want in the end. It's just a waiting game, right?'

There was a rap at the screened front door.

'Come through,' Greg called, tipping back on his chair so as not to yell in Ro's ear. 'This'll be them now.'

'Who?' Ro asked, aware that Bobbi had stiffened beside her as a man and a woman walked in: she, a five-foot-ten brunette with a thoroughbred ponytail, slender as a pencil and wearing a green visor of the sort people used to wear in the 1970s. He was a similar height and stocky, with hairy forearms and a smile that warranted free sunglasses.

The woman stopped in the doorway like it was the end of a catwalk, draping a tennis racquet over one shoulder and laying her other arm over her companion like he was a resting post. 'Hey,' she smiled.

Ro choked on a blueberry and Bobbi obliged by smacking her hard between the shoulder blades. Slightly too hard.

Greg stood up to make the introductions. 'Ro, Bobbi, I'd like you to meet Erin and Todd. Guys, my housemates.'

Ro, who was still coughing, could only nod and smile wanly, raising a feeble hand in a wave. She felt strangely blessed, though, to be struggling to breathe, as it meant she didn't have to rise from the table wearing just Matt's T-shirt, which hung almost to her knees and – because she had worn it for a week and a half – came with its own atmosphere. Bobbi, on the other hand, dressed in her pretty lawn cotton camisole set, managed to convey a sense of equality with the two glamorous breakfast interlopers by merely nodding and popping a blueberry in her bored mouth.

'Hey, have we met?' the brunette asked Bobbi, a smile on her lips, confusion in her eyes.

'Us?' Bobbi's withering tone closed down any scope for discussion about it. She shook her head. 'No.'

'Oh,' the brunette said after a moment, her eyes widening with a sarcastic 'wow' as they met Greg's.

'So, you've got a nice day for it,' Ro said, after a tight pause.

Todd grinned. 'Yeah. You play?'

'Used to. Not as much as I'd like. Time.' She rolled her eyes.

'Talking of which,' Todd said, pointing his racquet at Greg, 'I just booked us in for a round at the Maidstone at two this afternoon.'

Greg looked pleased. 'On a Saturday? How d'you work that?'

Todd tapped the side of his nose with a finger and winked. 'So, you ready? The others are in the car.'

'You don't mind, do you?' Greg hesitated, seeing Ro's plate was only half finished.

'No, no,' she pooh-poohed, desperate for them to leave. 'You must go. You've set us up beautifully for breakfast. Thank you so much.'

'The pleasure was all mine,' Greg said, grabbing a large sports bag from beside the fridge.

Bobbi watched them go, merely shrugging her eyebrows as a goodbye gesture. She waited for the front door to fall on the latch, then leaned so far forward on the table that her hair dipped in the maple syrup. 'Oh my God, they are so fake. That guy is such a phoney,' she hissed.

'They seemed very nice to me,' Ro said, pushing away her pancake, which was now cold, and reaching for the toast instead. She wasn't entirely sure which guy Bobbi was referring to – Greg or Todd? But there was no doubt something was going on between the housemates. They'd barely looked at each other since that first night.

Ro's eyes flitted over to her as she buttered the toast. 'Listen, is anything the matter between you and Greg?'

'What? No. Why would you say that?'

Ro shrugged. 'You just seem a little . . . jumpy around

each other, that's all. It's a shame because you seemed to get on like a house on fire last Saturday night.' There was a silence and Ro looked up. 'What?'

'Did your hair just move?'

'What?' Ro laughed.

'I'm serious. I swear . . . I swear it just moved of its own accord. Have you checked it recently for hibernating animals?'

Ro couldn't help but grin. They were back to the serum conversation again. Diversion as distraction? Oh well, she knew intimacy couldn't be forced. 'Personally, I *like* the dormice. They create little hotspots on my head.'

'Ew, gross!' Bobbi cried, almost gagging, making Ro laugh harder as she handed her a plate and fork, and pushed over the pancakes.

Bobbi took one with a conspiratorial look and began eating with almost rabid hunger – safe in the knowledge that Greg wasn't there to see.

Ro was sitting on the bed, trying to get a flimsy green travel comb through her hair, when her mobile rang. She lunged for it, ever hopeful, her face falling as she saw the caller ID.

'Oh, hi, Florence,' she said, trying to mask her disappointment. 'How are you?'

She hoped Florence wasn't ringing for an update on the campaign. She had nothing to show her but 500 images of sand dunes taken in different lights and with different birds on them. No images, no ideas. If she didn't hit on something soon, she was going to have to pay back the advance and seriously consider buying a flight home with what money she had left.

'I'm sorry to disturb you so early on a Saturday, but I've just had a call, and, well, I wondered whether you might be able to help.'

Ro's hands dropped to her sides as she heard the fluster in the older woman's usually calm voice. 'Of course. Anything. What's up?'

'It's my great friend Nan Beckett. Her daughter's getting married today, but she's just had a call from a hospital in Boston. Their photographer was involved in an auto accident on his way down here early this morning. He's got a broken leg and is scheduled for surgery later today. I know it's a terrible imposition, but I didn't know who else to—'

'Of course I'll do it,' Ro interrupted, immediately walking over to her wardrobe and pulling out her trusty black work suit. She sniffed it and decided it could cope with one more outing, so long as she walked through a cloud of Febreze before she left. 'They can't possibly go ahead without a photographer. *Where* is it, and when?'

'Oh, you are a diamond! The service is at St Luke's Episcopal, just next to the windmill. The reception's at the Maidstone afterwards. Wait till I tell them – they'll be so thrilled.'

'Do they want some prep shots of the bride too? Shall I go to the house beforehand?' she asked, clamping the phone between her shoulder and ear as she stepped into her trousers.

Downstairs, she heard the front door slam – could no one ever shut a door quietly in this house? – and hoped it was Hump back from his chivalrous errand.

'Oh, would you? They're at West Meadows, Further Lane. The service is at twelve thirty, so they're beginning to get ready now, but they're in a terrible panic. Poor Lauren, it's the last thing she should be worrying about on her wedding day.'

'Well, tell her to wait for me. I'm on my way now.'

'Perfect. I'll see you there myself shortly.'

Ro hastily half buttoned up her white shirt and grabbed her jacket from the bed as she flung open the bedroom door and found Hump trudging wearily up the stairs. He was pale beneath his tan, and from the looks of things, hadn't slept last night.

'Hump! Thank God it's you. I need to ask a massive favour,' she said, wriggling into the jacket and just about popping the buttons off her shirt.

Hump recoiled, particularly at the stress she placed on 'massive'. 'I was just going back to bed.'

'No! Not yet. *Please* can you drop me at a house on Further Lane – via the studio?' She stuffed her foot into one of her Converse trainers and began tying the laces. 'I can't get over there with all my kit on the bike. Please. Pretty please.' She placed her hands in a prayer position and bent her knees for extra supplication. She figured she could tell him the rest when they got there.

A telltale ringing started up on the chest of drawers behind her.

What? No!

Hump eyed his bed from the stairs and sighed. He turned on the spot and started traipsing downstairs again. 'Fine. But let's go now. I'm so tired I'm seeing double.'

'OK,' Ro said slowly, her eyes and attention diverted to the laptop on the chest of drawers that had 'Matt calling' emblazoned in green letters across the screen. No! 'I'll just—'

She rammed her foot into the other trainer and hobbled

across the room, tripping on the laces and falling heavily onto the wooden floor.

'Jeez! *Why* are you so noisy? What are you doing up there?' Hump shouted upstairs. 'Come on, Ro. Now!'

She heard the scrape of his keys being lifted off the hall table and looked up at the screen. A gurgle of distress came from her throat – she had an absent boyfriend, panicking bride and exhausted sexed-out housemate all needing her *now*.

Why now? Why couldn't he have called even three minutes earlier? She got up and lunged for the laptop. If she could just say 'hi' . . . She caught sight of herself in the mirror as she passed and stopped dead – the green comb was still stuck in her hair. 'Bloody hell!' she spluttered, trying to tug it out.

'Big Foot!' Hump shouted, as it came free, along with several hundred of her hairs. She rubbed her head, swearing under her breath. 'I mean it! I need to sleep!'

'Urgh, I'm coming! I'm coming!' she shouted, looking at the screen, out of reach and out of time. She ran back across the room and closed the door behind her. With a slam.

Eight hours later, she found Hump slumped on the balustrade outside the bar.

'I owe you big time,' she said, patting his shoulder gratefully.

'Yes, you do.'

'Here. Drink this.'

Hump stared back at her with the look of the half-dead as he massaged a foot. 'Thanks, but I never drink when I'm working. There's a direct correlation between a blurry head and blurry pictures,' he said piously, echoing the words she spoke when she first met him.

'Drink it. That's an order from your boss.'

He took the bottle of beer and downed it in one, earning himself a foamy moustache and smacking his lips in appreciation. 'Any more orders you'd like me to follow?' he asked, hopeful there were more where that had come from.

'Sadly not. There's still the dancing to get through,' she said, patting his arm. 'We've got an hour off, though.'

The wedding breakfast was in full swing and she was grateful for the break. She leaned against him as they looked out at the ocean. The beach was all but empty now, just a few remaining dog-walkers and joggers catching the last of the light. At the foot of the dunes, a group of university students were digging a trench in the sand and lighting a fire, its grey smoke finger poking into the perfect uniformity of the violet sky.

'What are they doing?' she asked, watching a group of the girls staggering back up the beach, carrying several buckets between them.

'Clam bake.'

Ro tutted at him, resting her head on his shoulder. She was exhausted too, although rather more used to being on her feet for twelve hours at a stretch than her poor, shattered housemate, who was too big-hearted to turn down requests for favours. 'That's one of those obscure American things that English people hear about but have no idea whatsoever what they actually are – like sophomores and freshmen and sororities. I mean, we did create the language. We should get jurisdiction on these things, you know.'

Hump chuckled, the vibrations ticklish against her

cheek. 'We can have one tomorrow night if you like – before Bobbi and Greg go back.'

'Hmm.' She wasn't sure that was a great idea. Bobbi seemed intent on spiting Greg at any opportunity – and that was assuming Greg could be surgically separated from the Southampton crew, anyway.

She shifted position, looking down at the video camera in Hump's hands. 'So how much footage did you get?' she asked, pressing some buttons. 'Oh, seven and a half hours. Pretty good. We should definitely be able to put something together from that.' She squeezed his arm. 'You have no idea how grateful I am to you for helping me out. I know you're exhausted.'

'Don't worry – this is gonna cost you. It's breakfast in bed for me for a week.'

'Deal.'

A curl of laughter behind them made her turn and she looked into the honeyed glow of the clubhouse bar, where the regular guests were every bit as groomed as the wedding party.

'It's nice here,' she murmured.

'*Nice?*' Hump looked down at her, thoroughly bemused.

'What? What's wrong with that?'

'The Maidstone is one of the most exclusive clubs on the East Coast of America. It's so exclusive you have to be a member just to access the website.'

'Oh.' She shrugged, nonplussed. 'And how *do* you become a member?'

Hump paused for a moment. 'You know that saying "If you have to ask the price, you can't afford it"? Well, it's like that for membership here: if you have to ask how to join, you're not in the club.'

'Right,' Ro said, slightly lost. 'So are you a member, then?'

'My family is. I don't really bother with it. Not my scene,' he said, kicking up a foot to show off his signature yellow flip-flops, which had only been permitted here today as a one-off after Florence had hurriedly explained the pre-wedding crisis to the general manager.

'Mmm, me neither,' she said, slumping against him again, worn out.

He held up her hand, noticing for the first time it was empty. 'Haven't *you* had a drink?'

'No. I never drink when I'm working,' she replied automatically.

'Screw that,' Hump said, pushing himself to standing. 'I don't think you realize how hyperactive you are with that camera to your face. You're like a boxer sparring, all that fancy footwork and dodging and ducking. Gin and tonic coming up.'

She sighed gratefully. Maybe a drink would pep her up. She was still dejected to have missed Matt's call earlier. Of all the crummy luck . . . 'That would be great.'

He walked slowly inside and she lifted her camera, scrolling through the images on the display – she'd taken over 800 shots today.

She was at the 250 mark when a creak on the boards made her look up. The camera dropped from her hands and swung round her neck on just the strap.

'Are you *kidding*? First the hardware store, then my studio – *twice* – last night and now here? You're following me!'

Long Story stopped walking – seemingly as surprised as she – and turned slightly to show her the golf bag on his shoulder. 'Actually, I was just coming in for a drink . . .' An expression flitted over his face, as though he was going to say something but then thought better of it. 'But I can leave if you'd prefer.'

Ro narrowed her eyes suspiciously – why was he deferring to her? He hadn't left the party last night, and he'd only left the studio after she threw him out. Why now? And then it came to her – it was this place, with its snooty rules. He was probably worried she was going to make a scene; you doubtless got thrown out of clubs like this for things like that. She looked into the clubhouse. Hump was standing by the bar, chatting to a group of people dressed for cocktails and seemingly oblivious to how incongruous he looked among them in his jeans and surf T-shirt. At least he was in earshot.

'It's fine,' she mumbled. 'I don't care whether you're in there or not.'

She looked back down at the camera, trying to appear busy, but his feet – in her peripheral vision – didn't move.

After a few moments, she looked up again. 'What?' she demanded, disconcerted to find his eyes steady upon her.

'I just thought that seeing as we appear to keep bumping into each other, perhaps we should try to clear the air properly, once and for all.'

'No.' She looked down again.

'*No?*'

'That's what I said.'

'So you want to keep up this hostility every time we meet?'

'Trust me, we're never going to meet again,' she quipped, borrowing one of Bobbi's sarcastic smiles.

He shifted position, heaving the bag back on his shoulder. 'There must be something I can do to make amends.'

'A long walk off a short jetty would be a start—' She stopped. She realized there was something. But . . . no, no. She wouldn't give him the satisfaction of being able to make it up to her. After the humiliation on the beach, she was rather enjoying watching him wriggle on her hook now.

'What?' he asked, reading her expression.

'Nothing.'

'No, I saw – your face. You thought of something. Tell me.'

She stared back at him, but it was hard to keep her eyes on his, to keep the aggression in her gaze. Standing here, so polite and acquiescent, it was hard to believe he was the same man who'd manhandled her so brusquely. And the idea that had flitted through her mind – it was a good one. 'Fine. There is something you could do.'

'OK.' He planted his feet squarely like he expected her to start wrestling him.

'The images you made me delete on the beach.'

It was his turn to look wary. 'Yes.'

'I want your permission to use them.'

'What? But how? You deleted them. I watched you.'

'Yes, I did delete them, but from the camera, not the memory. I retrieved them when I returned to my studio.'

'You . . .' He stared at her for a long moment and a tremor of anger and confusion pulsed through his voice. 'Listen, I want you to know that I am sincere when I say I want to make things up to you, but I cannot let you use those images.' His voice had changed, taking on that thin, strained quality she remembered from the beach.

'They'd be for a good cause, a local cause,' she said quickly. 'And besides, no one can or would be able to tell that they're your children in the photo, if that's what you're worried about.'

Ten days' immersion in the extraordinary wealth that was seemingly everywhere out here had shown her that with wealth came paranoia; Bobbi had told her some of the kids at the summer camps had security guards. 'You saw the pictures yourself. They could be cardboard cut-outs for all anyone knows.'

He shook his head. 'I can't. I wish I could help you on this, but—'

'You owe me. What you did overstepped the mark and we both know it.' She crossed her arms and a defiant look came into her eyes. 'How do you think the management here would view the incident if I told them one of their members had behaved in that way?'

His reaction wasn't what she expected. He looked like he was almost going to laugh. 'So you're going to blackmail me?'

'No. I'm simply asking you to consider my request. I'm asking you to come down to my studio and look at the picture properly for yourself. Then, if you still don't want me to use it, I'll . . . I'll respect your wishes.'

He was silent. 'It doesn't look like I've got much choice,' he said finally.

'Ten o'clock tomorrow suit you?' she asked briskly, determined not to feel badly. She'd never blackmailed someone before.

'Eight thirty. I have plans.'

'Fine. Eight thirty.' Damn, that was an early start for a Sunday – especially after a long day like this had been.

He turned on his heel, walking away from her, away from the clubhouse.

'Hey,' she called after him. 'Aren't you going to have that drink?'

When he looked back at her, his eyes were cold. 'No.'

# Chapter Thirteen

She overslept, waking as she should have been arriving at the studio, and careering around the bedroom in such a loud panic that Bobbi banged hard on the wall. By the time she arrived at the studio, twelve minutes later – a new personal best; it had taken twenty when she'd first arrived – wearing a pair of Matt's chinos and a white shirt over her red swimming costume, her cheeks were as rosy as if she'd jogged on the beach, her hair vertical.

She pulled up on her bike, breathless, swinging one leg over the crossbar and freewheeling across the Square path. She could see him sitting on the steps outside her studio, his arms resting on his knees, his hands clasped and head bowed. Her approach was silent, so that she saw him before he saw her, and she was struck by the figure he cut. If they hadn't met under such unpleasant circumstances, she would have found it hard to believe that he was even capable of such aggression.

But they hadn't. And he was. She had to keep reminding herself of that.

He heard the sound of her bike chain as she was just metres away and he looked up, springing to his feet as he watched her hop off the lower pedal and grab her padlock from her backpack.

'Morning.' It was a polite greeting, rather than a friendly one.

Ro nodded and locked up her bike.

'Sorry I'm late,' she mumbled, refusing to look directly at him as she jogged up the steps and put her key in the lock.

'It's fine.'

She looked back at him as she put her shoulder to the door and opened it. He had an air of fatigue about him, down to having small kids, no doubt. She noticed his jeans and faded blue sweatshirt. They were supposed to look lived in but actually only looked expensive.

Dumping her bag down on the counter, she crossed the floor, pulling up the white linen blinds at the windows. Sunlight streamed in, spotting the floor with bright white rectangles. She noticed the hydrangea looked a little wilted on the centre table and she automatically refreshed it with water from the small copper can she kept beside the flowerpot.

She was silent the whole while. Usually, she'd be chatting away to a customer, offering coffee and a seat and whatever else might possibly relax them, but this wasn't a regular scenario. And anyway, it wasn't like he was trying to fill the silence either.

Ro walked back to the counter and he put away his phone. He'd been texting someone.

She booted up the computer, drumming her fingers impatiently on the wooden top as it ran through its usual early morning scans. Their eyes met, once or twice, as they waited in silence, no smiles or niceties coming from either of them.

Eventually, the desktop revealed itself, and Ro brought

the image she liked best up on the screen. The bow in the little girl's hair was caught at a good angle, enhancing the silhouette, and the children's hands could clearly be seen to be clasped. But Ro liked most of all the way the children's chins were tucked down, almost burrowing into their necks like roosting ducks; it had a pleasing symmetry to it.

'That's it,' she said, turning the screen so that he could see it from where he was standing on the other side of the counter. She didn't want him peering over her shoulder, like he had that day on the beach.

She watched him closely as he registered the picture – noticing the slight wince and the way his eyes narrowed as he looked at his own children through someone else's eyes – or rather, lens. He looked down for a second, as though thinking, before he looked back at it again.

'Do you think anyone would know that's your children?'

'Well, no, but . . .'

'There really is no breach of privacy here.'

'It's not about that.'

'That was what you said on the beach,' Ro countered, her tone bullish.

He sighed, looking back at the picture. 'I'm not disagreeing that it's a beautiful picture. It is. And you're obviously very talented.' He gestured vaguely with his arms towards the framed portraits on the walls.

'I really don't see what the problem is. The children are anonymous.'

'I don't see why you can't just set up a shoot to recreate this picture.'

'Because you could never capture it exactly – not the feeling. Yes, I could get some models and put them in similar poses, but good photography isn't about what you see;

it's about what it makes you *feel*. So many different elements came into play on that day – the offshore breeze, the light quality, the cloud cover, even the dress your daughter wore and how it caught the wind like that, the bow in her hair . . . It's a kind of alchemy.' She gave a nervous smile as she caught herself waxing lyrical about her passion. 'And for the record, it's for a good cause. A local cause.'

'So you said.' His eyes flicked over her and she sensed he was bemused by her fervour. 'What is it?'

'A campaign spearheading the regeneration of the dunes along the East Hampton beaches. The idea is to revegetate them with root grasses, which help strengthen them and protect against erosion, offering greater protection during the bigger storms.'

He raised an eyebrow, looking sceptical. 'Most people around here are of the view that the dunes – or lack thereof – are only a problem for the ocean-front homeowners.'

'And that's precisely the attitude this campaign is trying to redress. Protecting the dunes is in everyone's interest. Yes, maybe it is only the ocean-front homeowners who need the dunes during the storms, but the dunes help preserve the beaches too. And I'm not from here, but it's pretty obvious even to me that the Hamptons *are* the beaches. They're the local economy, the beating heart of the area. I've been here less than two weeks, but every day I see people out walking their dogs, jogging, playing frisbee or volleyball, having bonfires and . . . clam thingies. It's not just about lying sunbathing on the beach at the weekend. It's so much more than that. And people just assume the beaches are still going to be here ten, twenty, fifty years from now, but they won't be – not unless we take steps now to protect what we've got while we've got it.'

'We?'

'You.'

They stared at each other, neither one blinking. 'You should consider a career in politics, not photography.'

'This is Florence Wiseman's baby, not mine.'

'Florence?'

Ro nodded. 'You know her?'

'Of course.'

'You like her?'

He gave a wry smile. 'Of course.'

'So then help her.'

He exhaled wearily, his eyes tracking around the room, taking in the portraits again. 'I'm prepared to make a deal with you,' he said finally.

Ro bit her lip, intimidated by how Wall Street he suddenly sounded. 'Go on.'

'I'll give you permission to use the image – only that *one* – if you agree to take the commission I tried to hire you for last Wednesday.'

Ro frowned. 'And what is the commission, exactly?'

He began walking around the room slowly and she felt the balance of power shift to him. 'A photo shoot of the kids,' he said, pointing at the walls. 'Although not for another few weeks – Finn has had a bad haircut that needs to grow out a little.' He stopped by the centre table, flicking quickly through the photobooks. 'And some of these. One for each year of each child's life.' He looked up at her. 'Ella's just turned four; Finn's three.'

That was seven books.

'Plus I want two copies of a combined book of both children for each year, to give to their grandparents.'

Another four, times two.

He stopped and stared at the films that were running on loop in silence, headphones still hanging on hooks beside the screens. He walked up and placed one headphone to his ear, just able to make out the film's audio. Four children were running at a sports-day race, one chesting the winner's ribbon, the camera beginning to move up and down as the cameraman (or -woman) began jumping up and down, obviously celebrating.

'And a movie.' He watched, transfixed, as the images segued to the same child sleeping in bed that night, a gold medal with a blue silk ribbon hung round the top bedpost. 'They're made of home videos, right?' He replaced the headphones on the hook, walking back towards her at the counter.

Ro nodded. 'Highly edited.'

'So one of those.'

'That is a huge job. There's well over a hundred hours of labour just in the photobooks alone. And as for the film . . . How many video files have you got?'

He shrugged. 'But I wouldn't need them till September. My mother-in-law's birthday. Is that enough time?'

Ro looked away. The money she'd make from this would take away all her financial pressures. In fact, it would pretty much pay for the summer. But she didn't want *his* money – anyone's but his. It had felt so empowering rejecting his commission the other day.

'Time isn't the issue,' she said curtly. 'Let's just take a step back for a moment, shall we? The point of us meeting here today is that you did something wrong and you're supposed to be putting it right. All I need is your permission to use the image and then I will squarely let you off the hook for your disgusting behaviour the other week. We're not here to negotiate on what I can do for you.'

His expression remained steady. 'Everything in life is about negotiation, Miss Marmalade. It's all a question of balance and whether what you want is worth trading for what I want.'

Ro gaped at him, distracted. What had he called her? She wanted to laugh, but she was too busy trying to keep her poker face on. 'Well, it's not,' she shrugged finally.

He blinked at her, his expression impassive, but she could still sense his disappointment. 'So then we both lose. And you still get to think I'm an asshole.' He turned and walked towards the door.

Panic mounted in her immediately. Now that she'd hit on her idea for the campaign, she knew it was the right one. It was what she'd been waiting for and she'd been right when she'd told him it couldn't be restaged. Moments had to be captured, not recreated.

'Wait!' she said, looking down at the counter.

He turned, walked back slowly. No smile, and yet a smile just the same.

She met his eyes, resentment simmering in them. 'Fine. It's a deal.'

He held out a hand, but she just stared at it.

He lowered his head till his eyes caught hers. 'Shake or no deal. I know from bitter experience just how sly you can be.'

'Sly?' Ro gasped with annoyance, before seeing the smirk on his face. He was actually teasing her.

Reluctantly, she shook his hand and he gripped hers hard, like she was a man – his size, his strength. 'My name's Ted, by the way. Edward Connor, but everyone calls me Ted.'

'Rowena Tipton,' she muttered, furious to be forced into niceties with this man, of all men.

He didn't say anything about having called her Miss Marmalade and she wondered whether he had already known it wasn't her actual name. She bit her lip as it occurred to her: if he was Long Story to her, was she Miss Marmalade to him?

'So what next?' he asked, pushing his hands into his jeans pockets.

She cleared her throat. 'You need to send your photos and films over to me on an external hard drive,' she mumbled resentfully.

'Anything else?'

Ro looked down, beginning to jot notes in her notebook. 'No, that's it until we do the photo shoot. Unless you have any specific instructions for material you want to be included or an angle you want me to take.'

He was silent for a minute. 'No, nothing. I just want proof with my own eyes that it was all actually real.'

Huh? She looked up to ask him what he meant, but he had already turned and was halfway out the door.

# Chapter Fourteen

The water felt silken over her skin, air bubbles rushing past her ears as her fingers touched the wall and she turned without breaking cover. One more length. Every fibre of her body was straining for fresh oxygen now, one more breath on which to power, but she kept on kicking, fighting the urge that felt so natural and right, and going with the defiance that kept streaking through her like a wilful child: why should she breathe? Why should she stop? She could decide what she did and when.

The wall was there suddenly, her hand flat against it, and she burst through the water like a torpedo, gulping down air, her heart on a sprint her lungs couldn't keep up with. She collapsed her arms onto the side of the pool, resting her cheek on her arms, eyes closed as she let her body recover from the sudden, fierce punishment she had meted out against it. It was fair to say yesterday's meeting still rankled.

'I thought I was going to have to go in there and fish you out.' Florence smiled from her position at the table. A deep tray of what looked like soil was in front of her as she balled the seed mix into small 'bombs' and put them in brown-paper bags.

Ro raked her hair back from her face and waded over to

the steps. 'I don't know what came over me. I just . . .' She shook her head, her breath still coming hard. 'I don't know, I just wanted to really go for it. God, I haven't done that for years.' She blew out through her cheeks. 'Wow. Exhausting.'

'Come and have your smoothie.'

Ro climbed out of the water with wobbly legs and wrapped a striped towel round her. She picked up the glass with ghoulishly green contents, managing not to grimace this time, and took a sip. 'Mmm, that's surprisingly good.'

'It sets you up for the day like nothing else I know.'

Ro collapsed down on a curvy wicker chair opposite Florence. 'I'll help you with some of those as soon as my hands are dry,' she said, holding up her wet palms. One touch of the brown powder and it would turn into a gloopy mess. 'So, this is how you spend every morning, is it?' Ro asked, looking past the bottom of the garden to the dunes and the ocean beyond. It glittered like a sequin belt, thrown out over the horizon, and she could make out the red and blue sails of some windsurfers, jibing into the wind.

'Pretty much. There's something about the wind off the ocean . . .' Florence closed her eyes for a moment, enjoying the gentle breeze that pushed her silver hair away from her face.

'I feel like I'm in a film.' Ro looked slowly around the mature garden, which had clearly been developed over decades, with meadows in the furthest stretch of lawn leading down nicely to the dunes on the outer boundary, and wildflower arrangements in the artfully dishevelled beds.

Ro watched a man walking along the shoreline, a dog no doubt bounding somewhere ahead of him. His hands were raised against the sun as he looked up at the big houses with the bigger views, and she could imagine a lot of people stared up here, at Grey Mists, wondering what it was like to sit where she was sitting.

She turned back to Florence. 'So, I think I cracked it. The campaign, I mean.'

'I can't wait to see it. You're just a marvel to have done it so quickly.' Florence leaned over and patted Ro's hand. 'And thank heavens I got you when I did. You're going to be inundated when Lauren and Paul's pictures come out – they've been telling everyone, you know. And they're so excited about the idea of the movie and how you're going to add to it every year. Nan was saying the other photographer never even offered them anything like that. Did you get to talk to everyone you needed?'

'Yes, Nan was on the case. We set up in the library and interviewed people individually in there. There were some good stories and insights. I'm pretty excited with what we've got.' Hump had been a trouper with the footage he'd shot.

Florence leaned over and patted Ro's hand with her dusty one. 'What you did was very kind, stepping in like that when you no doubt had other plans yourself. It won't be forgotten, you know.'

Ro blushed, pleased to have done Florence proud.

'So, this big idea – let me see it.' Florence put on her half-moon reading glasses, which hung from a silk cord round her neck, and rubbed her hands together in keen anticipation as Ro reached down for the board-backed envelope she'd stolen from Hump's desk. Biting her lip anxiously, she pulled out the sheet of paper she'd spent all of yesterday working on after Ted had left.

'Now, this is just a suggestion, an example. I don't expect

you to go for it completely as is. I'm not an ad guru. I just wanted to clarify the angle I'm coming from.'

She took a deep breath and let Florence examine the poster; she had tweaked the colourings of the photo, printing it in sepia so that the sunset was amplified and the golden and bronze tones of the sand and ocean were deepened against the black silhouettes of the children, the dune grasses in the background picked out against the clear sky. 'Legacy,' was rendered across the top of the image in fine gold lettering and below it, 'Protect the dunes.'

'I thought that by bringing the children to the forefront of the image, it reinforces the idea that what we do now affects future generations. That we're doing this for them, not ourselves, not some philanthropic ideal – our kids. So that they can enjoy what we do.' She shrugged. 'It's the emotional link you need, in my view.'

Ro waited apprehensively as she watched Florence's eyes roll over the poster, the silence pregnant with expectation. Eventually, Florence looked at Ro over her glasses. 'You know, I had a feeling about you the day we met. I really did.' Florence smacked her hand to her chest, squinting as she looked at it more closely. 'And, oh my goodness! Aren't they just the most adorable children?' she asked, pointing to Ella and Finn, delight dancing in her voice.

'It was pure chance. They just happened to be playing there when I was out with my camera. Sometimes you get lucky like that.'

Florence sat back in her chair, nodding intently at the poster, unable to take her eyes off it. 'I just love it. I can't wait to present it to the committee. We have a meeting tonight. I'll take it with me then.' She smiled at Ro. 'It's just perfect. I'm not going to change a thing.'

'Really? Oh phew! I'm so glad you like it,' Ro laughed, mock-wiping sweat from her forehead and looking back down the garden again. She saw a man walking on the boardwalk that led over the dunes to Florence's garden from the beach. Ro watched him. It appeared to be the same man she'd seen just moments ago walking along the shore. He didn't seem to be looking for his dog, and from the surety of his stride, he didn't appear to be lost either. He was holding something in his hand, something he raised to his face. A camera? Ro squinted. No. Binoculars.

She glanced at Florence, who was still examining the poster, one hand on the arm of her glasses as though adjusting them like a microscope. Ro watched the man. He was definitely staring up at the house, gradually turning his view across the garden to the pool house and pool terrace where she and Florence were sitting.

She saw the man freeze and knew the two of them were in his sights. She stood up – as suddenly angry as she was uneasy. The man didn't hesitate; he turned round and marched quickly back down the boardwalk to the beach again.

'What's wrong, dear?' Florence asked, looking up at her.

Ro stalled. The man was almost out of sight already, not even a footprint in the sand to indicate he'd been there. 'Uh . . . cramp. I always get it if I don't stretch out.' She made a play of massaging her thigh, her eyes flicking back to the end of the garden repeatedly. But there was no sign of him. He had gone.

Ro sat back down, unsure whether to say anything. She didn't want to alarm the older woman. She lived here alone, after all. But then again – she lived here alone. 'Florence, that boardwalk. Is it private, or can just anyone use it? Is there a path that leads off from the beach to the lane down there?'

'Oh no. It only comes into our backyard. It used to happen occasionally. As you can see, our drive runs parallel to the dunes, along the bottom of next door's yard, before it comes up the side of the lawns and sweeps round to the front of the house. Well, a few times we'd get people who thought they could access the beach by walking along our drive and cutting across the boardwalk. That's why we put the electric gate in, and there's now a chain and a trespass notice at the bottom of the boardwalk steps, which has done the trick. Why? Was somebody trying their luck?' She frowned and turned in her chair, looking down towards the empty boardwalk.

Ro knew she had to say something. 'Well, someone did just come up, but they turned round again as soon as they saw us sitting here.' She bit her lip. 'I think they had binoculars.'

Florence shook her head sternly, her lips pursed. 'Some people are so damned *nosy*. It can be like living in a fishbowl sometimes. Everyone assumes the people in these houses must be billionaires or celebrities. We had one summer where that singer Jennifer . . .' She waggled her finger distractedly, trying to recall the name.

'Jennifer Lopez?' Ro suggested.

'That's her! Well, she took a house further up the lane and some enterprising Tom, Dick or Harry with a beach permit arranged drive-bys in his beach buggy. Every morning we had people with cameras looking in on us eating our breakfast.'

Ro bit her lip, hoping to goodness it hadn't been Hump.

It certainly had his stamp of entrepreneurialism all over it. No doubt he would have tried to seduce J Lo too.

'They never think we might just be ordinary people who happened to live here long before this crazy real-estate bubble started—' Florence stopped, as though catching herself. 'Tch, listen to me ranting on like a crazy woman and not stopping to count my blessings.'

'I think you're entitled to be angry if people are invading your privacy,' Ro said, the words catching slightly as she remembered Ted Connor's same accusation against her. But what she had done hadn't been the same, had it?

'Well, sometimes I do wonder whether I wouldn't be better moving to somewhere smaller anyway. It is a little ridiculous for me to be rattling around such a big house.' Her eyes gazed up at the building. 'But there are just so many precious memories locked up with this place. I worry that I might lose them if I left. Bill and I shared so many happy years here. I can look out into the backyard and almost see my girls playing leapfrog on the lawns.' Her eyes misted up as she retreated into the past, before quickly pulling herself back to the present with a bright smile that didn't quite touch the sadness in her eyes. 'And of course, now I get to see my grandchildren playing the same games as their mothers. It's like a second chance to live it all again.' She placed a flat hand against the poster. 'This house is *my* legacy.'

**05/23/2010**                     **04h38**
'Stop it. You can't video me *now*.' Laughter. The blonde woman leaning with her hands on the back of the sofa turns her head away. A look of pain crosses her face. Her long hair falls over

her face. She is flushed. The room behind is panelled in dark wood. The sofa is coral-coloured.

'Why not? You look incredibly sexy.'

She looks up. 'I look like a hippo!' Panting.

'Well, an incredibly sexy hippo. The sexiest hippo I ever saw.'

Laughter. A light pink cushion is thrown and hits the camera screen.

'You could be more useful, you know. We're never going to want to see this again, anyway. I know I certainly won't.'

'I will always want to look at you.'

'Oh no! Don't go Prince Charming on me. It's because of that that I'm standing here with my ass hanging out at all. Quit it. Put that thing down. Come and give me a pelvic-drainage massage.'

'Really? Because I was thinking I might hit the gym. You know, while we've still got time.'

The blonde woman's eyes narrow. 'Ted Connor, if you want to live long enough to actually meet your firstborn child, I suggest you put that thing down now and come and drain my pelvis. No, don't make that face.'

'Isn't there a massage that makes your breasts bigger? I'd rather do that.'

'You think they could get any bigger? Besides, nothing that is about to happen in the next twenty-four hours is going to be about what *you* want. In fact, scratch that – nothing that happens for the next twenty-four years is going to be about what you want. They call it parenthood, you know.'

A deep chuckle next to the camera. The room tilts.

'All right. Let's dredge your pelvis.'

'Drain it, you pig! Drain it.' Laughter. Panting.

Blackness.

**05/23/2010**                                              **10h48**

Whispers. 'World, welcome to the little girl who's going to change you forever: Ella Margaret Connor, so named after her grandmother and the singer to whom her parents danced their first dance at their wedding.' Pans in on sleeping baby swaddled in ivory blanket, a pink beanie pulled down, wisps of dark hair visible, tiny fists tightly bunched with long fingers, sharp nails.

'And her beautiful mother, Marina Louise Connor.' Camera sweeps in on the sleeping blonde, pink-cheeked, a pale blue nightdress, a tube coming from the back of her hand, a plastic tip attached to the end of her finger. 'Too clever for her own good, too pretty for mine.'

Pans back to Ella. 'My girls. Both of them. Always.'

An unseen door opens. Someone enters.

Blackness.


**05/24/2010**                                              **11h04**

'I don't understand how there can be so much of it. It's only been twenty minutes since the last.' Marina. Camera tilts. 'Is this on?'

Hospital bed. Bowls of water and cotton-wool balls. Two pots of cream. Wipes. Two tiny nappies. Ted squints at the camera. Hair upright. Pale. Unshaven. Grey T-shirt and jeans. Barefoot. Nods.

Camera steadies. 'So this is it: Daddy's first diaper change. This should be in-ter-es-ting.'

Ted pulls face at the camera. Leans back over the baby.

'You're not going to cry for Daddy, are you? You know Daddy's going to do this so well. Not like Mommy, who got your leg stuck, no.' Ella scrunched up small, knees in on her tummy, arms flailing to the sides sporadically. She goes red, looks set to cry. Ted rests hand lightly on her chest. Her breathing changes.

Camera zooms in on baby's face. Eyes dark, almost black, irises seem undefined. Like seal eyes. Small pointed chin. Mild rash on cheeks.

'Are all babies this beautiful?' Marina.

A foot comes into shot. Ted frowning. 'How did it get all the way up there? It's by her neck . . . Is it supposed to be green?'

Camera shakes slightly. Camera pans out. Nappy is off, Ella held on her side as Ted wipes her back.

'Tula-lula-lula-lula-bye-bye, in Daddy's heart you're dreaming . . .' he half sings, half whispers. Takes both Ella's ankles in one hand and lifts her bottom off the mat, quickly placing nappy beneath her. He glances at camera, triumphant look.

'Pleased with yourself, aren't you?' Marina.

'Well, I got you to marry me, didn't I?' he grins, fastening tabs at the sides of the nappy. Winks at camera. Handsome.

Rolls Ella onto her side again. Quickly places sleepsuit beneath her.

'Oh, I got this. Yeah, Daddy's got this, baby.' Gently places Ella's feet and arms into sleepsuit. Fastens poppers.

Slides one hand behind Ella's head, scoops her under the bottom with the other. Carries her tenderly towards the camera. His cheek beside hers. 'And that, ladies and gentlemen and Marinas, is how it's done.' Blinks, looks straight into the camera. Handsome. Turns and kisses Ella lightly on the nose. 'Who's Daddy's little princess? We said you wouldn't cry for Daddy, didn't we?'

'There's just one thing.' Marina.

Ted raises eyebrow. Invincible.

'The diaper's on back to front.'

Ted looks at Ella, back to Marina. 'No.'

'Oh yes.'

Ella strains. Goes red. Redder. Purplish . . . Begins to cry. Ted frowns, looks at his arm. Eyes widen. Holds Ella out towards the camera. 'Mommy's turn.'

Blackness.

**05/24/2010**                                                    **13h09**

'I'm not sure she's on properly.' Marina, head bowed, Ella in her arms, feeding. 'Ow.' She winces, hooks her little finger into Ella's mouth. Shifts position. Ella cries. Perfect breast exposed. 'Shh, shh. Let's try again.'

Ella starts feeding again.

'Is that better?' Ted.

Marina bites her lip. Looks up to camera with anxious eyes. Blue eyes. 'I'm not sure. It kind of hurts. But then, maybe it's supposed to? I mean, I've never had anyone chomp on my nipple before – except for you.' Smile.

'Hey!' Ted.

Silence. Ella feeding.

'Didn't they say she's not supposed to be actually on the nipple but the areola?' Ted.

'In theory, but what good is theory when I can't actually see? Can you look?'

Blackness.

**05/24/2010**                                                    **16h13**

'Look at the camera, Mom.' Ted.

Ash-blonde woman, early sixties, beige jacket, orange paisley shawl, pearl earrings, holding Ella, sleeping, arms angled to show her face to the camera.

'My first grandchild. And so beautiful.' Smiles. Looks back at baby. 'I'd forgotten how small they are.' Wriggles her pinkie into Ella's closed fist. Ella grips it hard. 'Just look at those divine little fingers.'

'Marina can't stop counting them. She's OCD about it. Every time I come back in the room, she's counting her fingers and toes.' Ted.

Marina. Sitting up in bed. Sticks her tongue out at the camera. Looks tired.

'I was the same with you, Edward. I couldn't stop inspecting you. I could scarcely believe you were as perfect as you appeared.'

'But I am.'

Both women look at each other, shake their heads.

Camera pans in on Ella. White sleepsuit and beanie embroidered with bumblebees.

Long silence.

Camera moves over towards man sitting in a chair, previously out of shot. 'How about you, Dad? You want to hold her?'

Man gets up. Sports jacket and patterned tie. Grey hair, tanned. 'I don't want to wake her up. Marina needs to rest.'

'I'm fine.' Marina smiles. 'Besides, sleep's impossible anyway. I can't stop looking at her.'

Man stands by his wife. Looks down at Ella. Cups the top of her head with his hand. 'It's like rolling back thirty years. She looks just like Ted when he was born, do you remember?'

His wife nods, carefully hands over Ella. He awkwardly holds her, his elbows sticking out at odd angles.

'Smile for the camera, Dad.' Ted.

He smiles.

'Mom, stand closer next to Dad.'

The man and woman angle their heads together, matching smiles, Ella between them.

'Perfect.'
Blackness.

**05/26/2010**                                              **17h41**
Silence. Slow zoom on Marina, eyes closed, cabbage leaf on her
left breast.

'Does that feel better?'

She nods. Sinks back into the pillow. 'Like you wouldn't
believe. I will never be able to look at a goulash without gratitude ever again.' She smiles, opens her eyes. Frowns. Gasps.
Pulls up her nightdress. 'Turn that thing off right n—'

'Yo, Big Foot!'

Ro turned with a start as Hump jumped through the
doors and threw his bag on his desk.

She hurriedly pressed 'pause' and took off her headphones, letting them hang round her neck. 'What are you
doing here?' She checked the time on her phone: 10.14 p.m.

'Just popped back to check on emails. I'm waiting to
hear from a dealer about a Landy import. Thinks he might
have something for me.' He sat down on top of his own
desk, squashing a day-old sandwich, the remains of yesterday's lunch, and scattering papers onto the floor. He took a
slurp of his iced coffee. 'And so much for breakfast in bed,
by the way! You sidled out of the house without fulfilling
your obligations.'

'You had company *again*! I'm not walking in on you
doing God-knows-what with God-knows-who.' She rolled
her eyes in mock exasperation, but it was beginning to bug
her that Hump was getting all this action while she was
suffering an enforced celibacy. 'Besides, I had a breakfast
meeting with Florence for the campaign.'

'Oooooh,' Hump said, giving it a 'fancy' spin. 'Success-ful?'

'Yeah. Yeah, it was. She liked my proposal, thank God.'

'You see?' He winked. 'You're getting there. The wedding and now this . . . it's beginning to happen for you. I knew it would. You're too good to stay a secret in this town.'

Ro kept quiet. She didn't want to tell Hump about her newest client. There'd be too much teasing and she didn't feel like it today. The combination of missing Matt's call on Saturday and a non-stop weekend had left her feeling tired and emotional.

Hump nodded towards the screen behind her. 'So is that the wedding you're watching? Please tell me I didn't leave the lens cap on. I woke at three a.m. in a cold sweat convinced I'd recorded eight hours of black and you were going to murder me in my sleep.'

'Don't even joke about it!'

Hump squinted at the screen. 'What *is* that you're watching? It's no wedding . . . It looks more like porno from here!' he grinned, getting up off his desk and leaning across her counter. 'Wow! She's a hottie!'

Ro turned back to the screen and saw she had freeze-framed Marina Connor, breasts overflowing, her nightdress half off. 'Hump, she is a breastfeeding woman with masti-tis.'

He pulled a face. 'Still a hottie. Who is she?'

Ro hesitated. There was no way she was going to be able to keep it a secret from him. No way. She may as well get it over and done with. 'Ted Connor's wife.'

Hump's jaw dropped open, exaggeratedly wide, his eyes bright with delight. '*Long Story?*'

'Please stop calling him that. It makes light of what he did and there was really nothing funny about it.'

'So why are you working for him if he upsets you so much?' Hump asked, hoisting himself up onto her counter to get a closer look at the screen.

Ro sighed and pressed the 'minimize' button to preserve Marina Connor's modesty. 'It's a long story.' The words were out before she could catch herself.

Hump threw his head back and laughed at her slip. 'You two have got some weird shit going on.'

'I'm not in any position to be choosy about who I do and don't accept as clients. I either take the money or . . . or have to fly back to London at the end of the month.' She knew she was being overdramatic, but if it shut him up . . .

'Is it that bad?' Hump asked, looking genuinely shocked and making her feel instantly guilty. It was like kicking a puppy.

'Tch, it's fine – if this tape is anything to go by, they've practically filmed the child's life in real time and I'm never going to catch up. I'll be busy watching them for the rest of my life, permanently four years behind.'

Just then, Melodie stuck her head round the door. 'Ladies.'

Ro giggled at Hump's expression. He was usually the one making the jokes.

'Madam, I am no lady,' he protested in a faux-Shakespearean voice, vaulting one-handed off the counter and landing just a metre away from Melodie, before flexing a bicep.

She was nonplussed. 'If you're not man enough to handle a yoga class . . .' She pinched his bicep with a look of withering disdain, leaning casually against the door frame in tight aubergine, navy and khaki layers, her silhouette thrown across the white floorboards like a painting.

'Yoga is for pussies – pardon my French.'

'Oh, really?'

Without a word, Melodie stepped into a handstand, her body as strong and still as Nelson's Column. After half a minute or so – though she could clearly go longer – she stepped down again. 'Your turn.'

Hump pretended to roll up his shirtsleeves – he was wearing a muscle vest – and stepped into one too, except his ankles were three feet apart, his knees bent down towards his head, and he had to start walking on his hands to stay upright. Just to show off, though, as he started to tip over, he flexed his arms and pushed off into a handspring, landing on his feet like a cat.

He looked very pleased with himself.

Ro watched, bemused, at her two new friends squaring up to one another, relaxed and informal together already, even though they'd only met for a few moments once before. She wished she could join in, but thirty years of British reserve wasn't going to disappear overnight, and besides, she just wasn't built that way: she didn't rush into relationships – being orphaned at twelve had been a cosmic warning about the dangers of handing over your heart – and she certainly didn't trust instinct. It was the opposite of security, as far as she could see.

'OK. Follow me,' Melodie said, this time getting down on the floor and resting on her elbows and toes, her body as straight as a plank.

Hump followed suit. 'Time us, Ro.'

Ro looked at her watch and then back at the two of them, immobile and silent on the floor.

Several minutes later, they were still going.

'Honestly, guys, if any clients walk in right now, they'll think you're coffee tables.'

'Ro, no clients ever walk in,' Hump quipped, his voice sounding strained and his arms beginning to tremble.

'Thanks!'

A minute and a half later, it was all over – Hump sprawled on the ground, groaning and out of breath.

Calmly, Melodie stepped out of the pose and stood over him, arms crossed, serenely victorious.

'Fine!' Hump conceded. 'Maybe it's not for *complete* pussies.'

'I'm so glad you think that.' Melodie smiled, satisfied, over at Ro. 'Your usual?'

'Yes, please,' Ro nodded, rooting in her purse to give Melodie her coffee money.

'I'll be back in five.'

Her shadow left the floor and Hump stared across the room at Ro. 'That's why she came in? For a coffee run?'

'Well, obviously for the great pleasure of making you eat your words too.' Ro shrugged, turning back to the video screen and clicking out of the Connors' baby videos. She really wasn't in the mood for it today, and besides, she had another deadline to fulfil first. She retrieved Saturday's wedding footage and booted it up. With her chin resting on cupped hands, she moved on from watching the first day of Ella's life to the first day of the rest of Paul and Lauren's lives. The irony wasn't lost on her that her own life was firmly stuck on pause.

# Chapter Fifteen

'Matt, you have to come home. This isn't working.' She hiccupped loudly, the phone clamped to her ear, and slid a little further down the pillow.

'And what's the point of that? *You're* not at home.'

'Be here, then – you know what I mean.'

'What, and crash the party?'

'It's not a party here. It's just boring old life.'

'That's not what Facebook's telling me. Your housemate keeps tagging you in photos – a cocktail party at a winery *and* a wedding last weekend. It doesn't sound very boring to me.'

'Ugh!' she cried in exasperation. 'It's not like that. Everyone's lovely. I'm perfectly content. I'm not crying myself to sleep at night. It's just—'

'You're crying right now.'

She gave a dejected sniff. 'That's because I'm talking to you.'

'Thanks!'

'No! You know what I mean. Stop twisting things. I'm crying with you because I hear your voice and I miss you so much. Don't you miss me? Don't you want to be with me?'

'Of course I do.' Pause. 'Look, we said from the beginning this wasn't going to be easy.'

'Matt, I am literally counting down the days till my life goes back to being *my* life again. I'm like a prisoner marking time on the wall. And besides, I never said anything of the sort. You were the one with all your theories about how amazing this was going to make us. I don't feel very amazing, do you? I haven't had sex in over two months, for God's sake. And I'm living with the biggest shagger on the East Coast. Hump by name, Hump by nature,' she mumbled.

'He hasn't tried anything on with you, has he?'

Ro felt gratified to hear the worry in his voice. 'Of course not. I'm the little sister he never had.'

'Good. I wouldn't want to have to fly out there and beat him to a pulp.'

'Yeah, right.' She stopped. 'Why? Would you?' There was an idea.

'Only if I genuinely believed you were in danger of being seduced,' he laughed, reading her mind even from nearly 9,000 miles away. 'You're not still wearing my clothes, are you?'

'. . . No, of course not.'

'Ro! You are an abysmal liar. They must look bloody awful on you.'

'You've clearly been talking to Bobbi,' she said sulkily. 'It wouldn't surprise me in the least if she somehow found a way to make contact with you in a Cambodian temple *just* to discuss my dress sense and hair.'

'How is the hair?'

'Disobedient.' She raised a hand to it to rake it back and her fingers got stuck. 'Tch.'

'Do you know what? It's the bane of your life. Just cut it off.'

'What? Just like that? Ha! I don't think so. Setting off round the world with two days' notice is one thing. Cutting a woman's hair is a whole other ball park.'

'I've shaved mine off.'

There was a long, crackly pause. 'When you say shaved, you mean . . .'

'Bald, yeah.'

'You're bald!' she screeched. 'Matt, are you bloody nuts?'

'It's so much cooler – the humidity's a killer out here. I think it looks OK, actually. I never knew I had a good-shaped head. And it feels nice. I like running my hands over it.'

'Stop it, stop it! I'm imagining your head as some sort of chicken's egg. Oh my God, it looks bloody awful, I bet. *That's* why you haven't Skyped. You don't want me to see you.'

'No. The reception is too patchy – there's not enough bandwidth, that's all . . . Seriously, Ro, you should try it. Put yourself out there.'

'Me? Bald? Frying pan to fire, no?'

'Not bald. Just have a radical cut. What's the worst that can happen? If you don't like it, let it grow out again. By the time I see you in September, it'll be almost back to how you've got it now. I'll grow mine back out for you.'

'I'm supposed to feel better talking to you. Instead I feel worse.'

'I'm sorry, baby.'

Baby. She fell quiet. '. . . Are we going to have a baby one day?'

'*Wha*— Of course we will,' Matt replied, sounding taken aback. He laughed – nervously. 'Where did that come from?'

'Nowhere.' Where had it come from? 'I was just . . . wondering if it's in the Plan. I guess I feel like everybody gets to just *do* their lives, whereas ours has to be mapped and plotted and planned beforehand.'

'There's nothing wrong with taking active control of our own lives, Ro. Look around you – most people are just drifting. They wouldn't know a life plan if it hit them in the face. There's nothing wrong with articulating your goals and ambitions, and organizing your life to make them happen.'

She counted to five. 'No. I s'pose not.'

'You could sound a little more enthused.'

'I'm just sleepy. It's only six thirty here.'

'Sorry I woke you. I really wanted to hear your voice.'

'Yeah?'

'Of course. Look, I know it sucks at the moment, but I guess this is the low we have to go through to get the high when we're back together. I'm missing you like mad.'

She smiled, delighted and appeased, cheered up that he was miserable too. 'How many days left?'

'Ninety.'

Ro gasped. 'Oh my God, I'm so excited.'

There was a pause. 'How excited?'

Ro grinned, hearing the shift in his voice. 'Well . . .'

'You're *where*?' Bobbi demanded.

'Downstairs. In the lobby.' Ro smiled, leaning against the wall. She had been in a good mood for the three days since Matt's call, reinvigorated to the extent that she'd finished editing the wedding film a day before she'd anticipated and had decided to give herself a day off. She had started by going early morning kayaking with Hump before he'd dropped her at the Jitney stop.

Bobbi didn't bother to reply. The line disconnected, and several minutes later, she was stalking towards her in four-inch heels and a magenta Roland Mouret dress, a look of utter disbelief across her face. 'What's happened? Just tell me.' She looked genuinely worried.

Ro laughed, amused by her housemate's melodramatics. Her life really was lived at a higher level. 'I just wondered if you fancied lunch.'

'Lunch?'

'Yeah.'

'You came all the way in from East Hampton for lunch?'

'Yeah.'

'Aren't you meant to be in the studio? What if you get a customer?'

'Hump's there all day today. He's going to look after anybody who stops by, but on the strength of how things have been, I'm not too worried.'

'Ha!' Bobbi rolled her eyes. 'Just wait till next week. You'll look back on this as a honeymoon period. The schools will be out, everyone will be there full-time, and you'll be mobbed.'

Ro shrugged again. The scale of Ted Connor's commission alone was going to keep her busy for weeks. 'So . . . are you free for lunch?'

Bobbi took a step back, scrutinizing Ro's outfit: a pair of boyfriend jeans, her green suede hi-tops and Matt's favourite khaki T-shirt, which she'd pulled from the top of his bag before he'd left for Heathrow. Her eyes narrowed and that scary look of deep, dark intensity clouded her face. 'Not for lunch, no.'

'Oh.' Ro shifted her weight, surprised by how disappointed she felt. She should have known better than to try being spontaneous. Like skinny leather trousers or straightened hair, it just didn't suit her. 'Well, that's OK. I thought you probably would have something booked in. I just thought I'd pop by on the off chance—'

'No, no. I'm quite free. But if you're in Manhattan for the day, there's no way we're wasting time eating. Wait here. I'll get my bag.'

'What are we doing if not going for lunch?'

'What you should have done the second you landed in JFK,' Bobbi called behind her, marching back to the lifts.

Got on the next plane home? Ro wondered.

'We're going shopping. You can consider yourself officially kidnapped. You're not going free till I say you're done,' Bobbi called in a raised voice, making everyone turn and stare, her finger pointed accusingly at Ro.

Ro nodded, mute with apprehension. A full-on kidnapping? She watched the lift doors close and wondered whether to make a break for it while she still could. But there was no point – she wouldn't put it past Bobbi to give her a makeover in her sleep. Instead, she sank into one of the high-shine black bucket seats reserved for guests and quietly awaited her fate. The Bobbi in her head was always so much gentler than the reality.

'It's looking good. I like it, I like it. You like it?' Bobbi asked, popping more sushi into her mouth as the manicurist efficiently buffed her nails into short squares.

Ro wanted to nod but didn't dare. The hairstylist was

wielding long, extremely sharp scissors next to her jaw, an alarming prospect not because of prospective injury but the fact that Ro's jawline was a full six inches above the point where her hair normally fell to. She gave a double blink in the affirmative instead.

She was grateful to be sitting down at last. By her feet were several laminated shopping bags containing two pairs of skinny jeans (with a *lot* of Lycra in them), one yoga ensemble (pale olive leggings with matching vest and neon-orange trim), several T-shirts, a striped sailor top (she had never dared try stripes over her curves before, worried she'd look like jelly wrapped in a barcode), a pair of suede wedges (the only thing Bobbi had compromised on, agreeing with Ro's assessment that she walked in heels like she had rickets) and a ruby-coloured sequin dress with a plunging V-neck and back split. Ro was privately convinced the only place she could wear a dress like that was on stage in Bangkok, but she had obediently handed over her credit card to the sales assistant anyway.

The manicurist working on Ro's left hand began painting her nails a soft coral colour that Bobbi had chosen.

'So, I'll be honest with you, I thought you were gonna be a whole lot harder work than that,' Bobbi said, drinking her coconut water. 'But you were surprisingly obedient.'

Ro resisted the urge to shrug – fearful of jogging the scissors any higher than they already were. 'I guess I'm just feeling more positive about things now that Matt and I are just past the halfway mark. We're on the countdown and I finally feel ready to have some fun. It's like the end is almost in sight.'

'The end? But summer's only just beginning. We haven't even had Fourth of July yet.' She winked and patted Ro's hand. 'Just you wait till you see how that goes down. You won't ever wanna go home.'

Bobbi threw herself back in her chair – to the alarm of her manicurist, who found herself painting a plastic tray in lieu of her hand – and watched as the hairdresser lopped another six inches off Ro's hair. 'I didn't think you'd buy into this bit at all.'

'This is nothing.' Ro arched an eyebrow and swivelled her eyes to the side to see Bobbi. 'Matt's shaved his head – did I tell you that?'

Bobbi pulled a face.

'Yeah, exactly,' Ro laughed. 'That's what I said. I keep trying to imagine what he looks like but – oh, surprise, surprise – suddenly, he can't Skype me, he has to call me.' She thought back to the phone call and how well it had ended. A small smile lit up her eyes. 'Anyway, he says I have to put myself out there. So that's what I'm doing. Having a trim.'

'This ain't no trim,' Bobbi guffawed, smacking Ro's thigh.

Ro bit her lip. 'No. Maybe not.' She watched as another loose curl fell to the floor, then studied her new reflection, noticing for the first time she'd actually got a bit of a tan. Were those freckles on her nose? 'Anyway, how come you've been able to just skip out of work to do this with me? We've been out for three hours now. Don't you have to get back?'

The hairstylist took Ro's head in his hands and angled her to look at the far wall – but not before Ro saw Bobbi's face fall. 'Things always quieten down this time of year. It's fine. Half the office is on the four p.m. Jitney anyway.

There's nothing going on that needs me back there urgently.'

'Oh, cool,' Ro murmured, but she wasn't convinced. She just about knew Bobbi well enough now to read nuance in her housemate's full-throttle approach and she heard the distinct undertones of pride bristling.

The sound of the hairdryer drowned out any further conversation and they sat in silence, Bobbi distractedly watching her nails being painted as the stylist began tousling Ro's hair with his fingers. Ro tried to read her horoscopes but didn't understand what 'Mercury Retrograde' actually meant. After a while, the hairstylist pushed the hairdryer between his knees and started snipping at stray hairs around the nape of her neck.

'So then if things are quiet at work, why don't you come out this weekend?' Ro asked, picking up their conversation where they'd left it.

Bobbi looked up at her from below her lashes. 'I don't think Hump would be too pleased. I've already gatecrashed one of my "off" weekends.'

'I don't see why not. You gave him tickets to that party as a trade-off, and he did strike it lucky that night, I seem to recall. I doubt he's going to insist on keeping to the letter of the law on your contract. He's far too chilled. And what's the point of your room just sitting there empty?' She leaned towards Bobbi slightly. 'The house isn't the same without you.'

'Yeah?' Bobbi straightened up, her eagerness almost puppy-like. 'What's it like there in the week?'

'Quiet. Mellow. Hump and I just flop on the sofa with a film, or drink a beer on the porch – except for when he gets lucky, of course. And on the weekends when Greg's around—'

'Let me guess: he's never around?'

Ro laughed. 'Yeah. Exactly. Most of the time it's just me and Hump – we go kayaking, hang out at the Surf Lodge if there's a band playing . . . He's even helped me do seed-bombing some evenings.'

'Oh, don't get me started—'

'I'm not going to!' Ro replied quickly, holding up her hands.

'It sounds like you got a good thing going with your yoga classes every morning too.'

'Yes, although I've missed a few recently. Now that I'm working again, it's harder to take the time off. It's a shame because I enjoy them . . . well, *need* them, actually.'

'What? You mean for your glutes?'

Ro smiled; she was becoming inured to Bobbi's bluntness. 'The classes are the only thing that make me still feel connected to Matt. Sometimes I think the meditation is almost medication: it keeps me going, you know? It's so hard to be this far apart for this long, with hardly any contact.'

'Right, yeah. I can't even imagine. So you're definitely gonna marry him, then? Matt.'

'I'm afraid so.'

'Why afraid?'

'Well, I know you must think I'm really dull and unexciting to have my future so clearly mapped out.'

'I admit it's kind of weird for someone like me who can't even see past lunch, but I figure there must be upsides to it . . .' She swished her mouth to the side. 'I suppose you got your dress picked out and everything?'

'No, none of that. I've never been much into that side of it. It's not the wedding bit; God knows I've covered enough of those to lose *that* romance. I just . . .' She sighed. 'I just can't wait to be Mrs Matthew Martin. I know it sounds soppy,' she said, shaking her head and making the stylist huff. 'I do. I hear myself and *I* want to gag . . .' She looked across at Bobbi, knowing she must sound insufferable. 'I honestly can't believe someone like you is single, though.'

'Believe it.' Bobbi shrugged, inspecting the colour of her nails.

'But there must be someone you're keen on?'

Greg's name hung in the air and they both knew it. Bobbi's eyes fleetingly met hers. 'I really can't afford to be distracted by a relationship right now. This is my year to make partner. I've got to put all my energies into that conversion.'

She straightened up suddenly as the hairstylist grabbed a handheld mirror and angled it behind Ro's head to give her a 360-degree view. 'Oh, baby, take a look at you.'

Ro chewed on her knuckles as the stylist slowly rotated the mirror, showing her the choppy bob he had not so much cut as carved into her hair. From root to tip it could only be nine inches long, but the gentle curls that turned to frizz at ten inches onwards looked silky and textured, her neck slim and elegant. She realized she had never once, in her life, noticed her neck before, just as Matt had said he'd never noticed the shape of his own head. Even her eyes seemed defined by having the hair cut around her face rather than hanging beside it like a bagged pheasant.

'Look at me,' Bobbi ordered, and Ro turned, striking a jokily saucy pose – one eye winking, her mouth open – as she correctly anticipated Bobbi's phone camera pointed at her. A flattering photo for once!

'Watch out, East Hampton!' Bobbi giggled, letting out a small whoop and pinging it straight to Facebook. 'Summer just got hotter.'

# Chapter Sixteen

**09/01/2010**                                    **18h24**

'Listen to this.' Ted. Whispering. Dark hallway, door jamb. Door is pushed open gently.

Nursery. Dimly lit by a white rabbit light. Narrow wardrobe with pink gingham fabric doors, a crib with a lace-frilled hood.

The camera moves towards the crib. Rocking. Cooing sound, like a pigeon.

Ella, lying on her back, chewing on her own foot. Hair fuzzy and dark. A fluffy pink pig beside her. Eyes look large in her head. Blue now.

She sees the camera – or the person behind it – and coos.

'My little love dove.'

She coos again. And smiles. One tooth.

Blackness.


**09/17/2010**                                    **10h38**

'And here we see the Marina in her natural habitat – an air-conditioned boutique with dense growth of overpriced clothes. Watch how she moves, fleet of foot, eyes alert to every colour offer and sale sign, the wheels of the stroller in perpetual motion, never stopping lest the dominant male should try to oust her from the store.' Ted. Low-voiced.

Marina looks over. Holds up a pale lemon fake-fur coat with matching bonnet. 'What do you think?'

'Too small for you.'

Rolls her eyes. 'For Ella.'

'Too big for her.'

Marina picks up similar coat in ivory. Holds them up side by side.

'The blue.'

Marina narrows her eyes, turns back to the rack. Camera zooms out.

'The male is in danger now. The first of the warning signs has been emitted and he must proceed with caution or risk incurring the wrath of the female, who is never more deadly, more ferocious than in this arena.' Camera swings to a couple of women chatting by the tills. 'Witness how the females guard the area, patrolling in packs and keeping the males away.'

'You are a child.' Marina.

Camera swings back. Marina is looking down at him. Navy overcoat. Blonde hair swept onto one shoulder. Shades worn like Alice band. Smile.

'I'm going for the yellow.' Holds up coat and bonnet.

'My clear favourite.'

'It's such a great colour on her. Very few babies really look good in it. Ella is one of the lucky few.'

'I agree.'

Marina narrows her eyes again. 'You will say literally anything to get out of here, won't you?'

'Literally anything.'

Laughter. Yellow fuzz on screen.

Blackness.

**09/19/2010**  **12h57**

'Look at him, Ella. Does Daddy look funny?' Marina.

Camera zooms in on Ted, running, orange kite bumping on ground behind him. Park. Speed-walkers. Runners. Small dogs. Ted waves back to camera.

Camera jogs. Waving back?

Dog is chasing after Ted, snapping at the kite.

'Hey!' Ted. Pulling on string, trying to lift kite into air. No wind.

Camera jogs. Giggling. Marina.

Ted running faster. Dog owner joins chase. Dog gaining on kite.

'Oh my gosh . . . no . . . ' Marina.

Dog leaps. Catches kites. Owner reaches him. Dog won't release kite.

Camera pans to path. Navy buckled flats. Laughing. Hard. Marina. 'Oh no, don't look at Daddy, Ella. Don't look.'

Camera swings back up. Ted remonstrating with owner. Hands on hips. Dog holding on to kite. Owner lifts dog. Dog still holding kite. Ted pulls on kite. Rips. Throws hands in air. Dismissive. Owner walks off, stroking dog's head. Dog holding kite. Ted, alone. No kite.

'Oh, baby, may you never remember seeing your daddy lose against a pug.' Marina laughing.

Camera pans round hood of buggy. Ella sleeping. Lemon-yellow bonnet and coat. Thumb in mouth. Pink pig, less fluffy. Rosy cheeks.

'Aaah. Lucky Daddy.'

Blackness.


'What do you think? Too much?'

Bobbi was standing on Ro's bed, trying to see her shoes

228

in the mirror on top of the chest of drawers. She was wearing a peacock-coloured short silk kaftan with turquoise feathered sandals that laced up her slim calves, Pocahontas-style, and large gold hoop earrings with tiny beads on them, flashing in her hair.

'No, I . . . Amazing.' Ro shrugged, wondering whether she was underdressed – 'casual' to her meant jeans that fit and a clean T-shirt, so she was wearing her new red skinny jeans, new striped Breton top and new wedges. It was this or the sequin dress.

Bobbi jumped off the bed, beaming. 'Great. Great.' She rubbed her hands together distractedly. 'Or maybe . . . Do you think the peach shorts suit?'

Ro shook her head. 'No. That's perfect.' She felt strangely protective to see Bobbi so nervous. 'Come on. The boys are waiting,' she said, picking up one of Matt's jumpers from the bed and tucking it under her arm.

'Why the hell is Greg coming, anyway?'

'Because he's our housemate and Melodie invited the whole house,' Ro sighed.

'But he doesn't belong with us and we all know it. He's using Hump's house as a hotel.'

'And technically speaking, he can. I agree it's a shame we don't see more of him, but he's paid for his room and there's no contractual obligation for him to hang out with us.'

'He's only going so he can add Brook Whitmore to his contacts. You know who Brook is, right? You Googled him yet?'

Ro gave her an 'as if' look that didn't appear to translate – or compute.

'It'll just be something for him to brag about in the office on Monday.'

Ro tutted and gave her a stern look. What was tonight about if not for Bobbi to add Brook to *her* own list of contacts? Hadn't she already said she wanted to tap up Brook through Melodie's yoga classes?

Ro put her hand on Bobbi's arm as they paused at the door. 'Look, you don't need to be best mates with him, just be tolerant. I don't want anything to be awkward for Melodie tonight.'

Bobbi sighed dramatically. Relations between Bobbi and Greg had plummeted from cool to downright chilly, and whatever had drawn them together so fiercely that first night was now just as fiercely repelling them. Something had happened either at the club or back home afterwards, even Hump agreed that, and the atmosphere between them was becoming – as he had feared – openly hostile. Ro was half convinced that it was Bobbi's attitude that meant he was spending more and more time with the Southampton crowd every weekend.

'Fine, fine. I'll be civil. But for one night only.' She grabbed Matt's jumper from Ro's grip. 'And gimme that,' she said, throwing it across the room, out of sight and out of reach.

They wandered downstairs, where Hump and Greg were leaning against the porch veranda – Greg in his usual preppy chinos and white Oxford, Hump in long check shorts, a linen shirt and yellow flip-flops. Greg stood to attention as the girls joined them; Hump wolf-whistled.

'Go, Ro!' Hump crooned, *not* calling her Big Foot for once, as he walked round her like she was a vintage car, his hands bouncing her bob lightly. Her extreme haircut had rendered him speechless for a full seven seconds when she'd hopped off the Jitney yesterday, but she had persisted in wearing Matt's clothes at the studio today, and this was the first time he, or anyone, was seeing her as Bobbi had truly envisioned. 'Hey, so you are a girl. I just couldn't be sure before. You sure you're going to be OK walking in those shoes?'

She should have known! There was always a tease with him. 'Bog off, Hump,' she grinned.

Ro saw Greg's eyes slide over to Bobbi. There was a natural opportunity for him to compliment Bobbi too – especially for someone with manners like his – but whether or not he intended to say anything, he didn't get the chance.

'House photo!' Bobbi ordered, getting her phone out of her bag. 'You can take it, Greg.'

'Sure.'

Ro shot her a look – Bobbi's point was clear – but Bobbi just smiled back with innocent eyes, sending the photo out into the ethernet as soon as the phone was back in her hands again. Just as Ro needed a camera lens to validate her life, so Bobbi, it seemed, needed social media.

'And I'm sitting in the front,' Bobbi said bossily, climbing into the front seat of the yellow Defender before Greg could.

Ro deliberately pulled her hair as she got in, in the back. 'Ow!'

'Sorry.' Ro smiled, but messaged, 'Behave!' with her eyes.

Hump rolled the car down the drive and they swept through the wide lanes in the early evening sun, shades on and the radio blasting. They passed a large, gold-tinted pond with a family of swans gliding across it, waving back at the cyclists in bikinis and board shorts who cheered at the sight of the Hamptons' already-beloved Humper. Ro closed her eyes happily. It was the all-American dream she'd been sold in films all her life, and here she was doing it, living it. The only thing stopping it from being perfect was Matt not being here to share it with her.

Greg, on her right, kept checking his phone.

'What are your friends up to tonight?' Ro asked, leaning in to him slightly.

He looked up bashfully and pocketed his phone. 'They're at a gala charity dinner. It's a couples thing.'

'Oh . . . Well, it's great you could come to this. Melodie's become a really good friend.' She felt like she was bragging, but she couldn't hide how proud she was to have someone like Melodie in her life. 'Do you know her?'

'By family reputation only. Barrington Dredging is a big local company. I'm looking forward to meeting her husband too. He's an influential man and has really put a voice to all those people worst affected by Sandy. You know there's a grass-roots campaign to get him to run for senator next year?' Greg added.

Bobbi whipped round in her seat, an accusing but silent 'See?' in her eyes, just as Hump pulled up a short pitch to a pair of reddish solid-wood gates at least two metres high. Nowhere was far from anywhere in the Hamptons. He leaned over and spoke into the intercom. The gates swung back and they rolled in.

Everyone was silent as they parked in front of an angular building so low slung its roof couldn't be seen from the road. The house was constructed from the same reddish wood as the gates and had huge plates of green-tinted glass. It looked, to Ro, like toddlers' stacking cubes on a giant scale, the upper levels set at seemingly random angles and overhanging the ground floor to create shaded loggias below.

'Fuck . . . me,' Bobbi muttered not so under her breath, fiddling with her seat belt. 'That's only a Moji Fukayama design. You know who he is, right?' She looked across at Hump, who shrugged. 'He won the International Architecture Award – it's the most prestigious mantle out there. He takes on, like, one project a year. One! We're all scrabbling around trying to do bigger, bolder, more, and he takes one per year and even then not always.'

'Uh-huh,' Hump nodded, clearly totally disinterested and spotting Melodie waiting for them by the door. She was looking radiant in a lipstick-pink origami-folded silk dress, her lustrous hair left down. Next to her was a handsome young waiter who looked like he did day shifts in the Ralph Lauren store and bench-pressed ponies, holding a tray of pink champagne. 'Now let's party.'

'I thought we said "casual",' Ro said under her breath as she and Melodie kissed their hellos. 'Casual to me means marmalade on toast, not –' she gestured to the handsome waiter who was waiting for Bobbi to choose a drink '– *him*.'

Melodie patted her arm. 'This is casual. Rather than me stressing about it, I delegate. You see? Casual.'

Casual, Hamptons-style maybe. What would every person here think if they saw what passed for casual back home? Lap trays, pyjamas and fleecy socks, and a box set of *Borgen*.

Ro made the introductions to Bobbi and Greg, and they all followed Melodie through into an open-plan all-white sitting room that was, Ro imagined, just like walking into heaven. On the angled, vaulted ceiling, a ghostly pink haze rippled along it like a light show. There was no music playing, but there was sound and she saw, to her left, a wall with pink-lit water skinning down the length and width of it. Her eye followed the water's fall and she saw how it fed into a deep, narrow groove that was cut through the polished concrete floor like a Mondrian line, dissecting it with arrow-straight precision to the glass wall opposite, where it dashed underneath to the pool outdoors.

Ro had never seen anything like it, and she looked over at Bobbi to check she was still remembering to breathe in and out. It was debatable – Bobbi was rotating on the spot, open-mouthed. The house somehow appeared to have two fasciae: inside the house, the irregular angles of the walls were in contrast to the cuboid parallelograms of the exterior, and Ro could almost see Bobbi's mind whirling at the engineering and advanced maths involved in building a house like this.

'Would you like me to pinch you?' Melodie asked her, bringing her over the drink that she had been too distracted to collect on her way in.

'I just can't believe it. I can't believe I'm standing here. I can't believe this is your *home*. It's part of architectural legend.' Bobbi smacked a hand over her heart. 'It is because of buildings like this that I do what I do.'

'It's official. She really does love her job more than I do mine,' Greg murmured, watching from the sidelines.

'It's certainly a very interesting house to live in.' Melodie smiled modestly.

'Did you and your husband commission it, or did it come onto the market? I know that the architect is incredibly controlling about who he will build for. I mean, he actually interviews his clients first, right?'

'Well, it never came onto the open market, but we bought it quite soon after it had been built. The previous owners divorced and couldn't afford to keep it.'

'Luckily for us,' Brook said, picking up the conversation as he walked into the room. 'So long as *we* don't divorce,' he grinned, squeezing the back of Melodie's neck affectionately.

'That's not likely, darling,' Melodie said, a wicked gleam in her eye. 'Obviously, I only married you for your money.'

Brook laughed expansively. 'The other way round more like.' He turned to face the small group, all looking on politely. 'Now, you must be Bobbi,' he said, beaming with bonhomie and holding out a hand.

'Yes, Bobbi Winkleman. A pleasure,' Bobbi said, stepping smartly forward from the group and staking her claim.

'And Ro, of course,' Brook said, turning to her. 'Well, I say of course, but . . . your hair.'

'I had a dramatic cut this week, yes. I guess I must look quite different from when we met at the Wölffer party.' Ro's hands patted it soothingly.

'Indeed, but all for the better if I may say.'

She smiled and relaxed.

Hump held out his hand. 'Hump, we met last weekend too at the—'

'I remember. The entrepreneur. We're going to have lunch, aren't we?'

'Yes, we are.' Hump grinned, clearly delighted that a suggestion of drinks had been accidentally upgraded to lunch. 'I'll set it up.'

Greg held his hand out, in turn. 'Greg Livingston.'

Brook looked at him through interested eyes, immediately discerning Greg's more reserved manners and professional demeanour. He never seemed fully 'off', as though he could chair a board meeting at any moment. 'Now, we haven't met.'

'No, sir.'

'And what is it you do, Greg?'

'I'm senior attorney at Overy & Chambers.'

'Overy & Chambers. I've heard of them. Environmental practice, right?' Brook said thoughtfully.

'I'm flattered you know that. Most people have never heard of us. We're below radar compared to the corporate behemoths.'

'Ah, but you guys are smarter than them. You're at the coalface of federal policy. Leave those sharks to chasing paltry dollars in discrimination lawsuits. The future is environmental – global warming, carbon emissions, polar navigation rights, natural-disaster relief . . . They're the big issues that affect the planet's billions of normal people, not just multinationals. You guys are the G8 of law.'

'Well, I've not heard it described like that before. I'll have it put on my cards,' Greg laughed. 'Which field are you in, Mr Whitmore?'

'Call me Brook. I'm an insurance man, I'm afraid: the grey man in the grey suit.'

'You're so not grey,' Ro said, looking at his deep tan. He was certainly well into his late fifties, if not early sixties, but looked fitter and better than most forty-year-olds.

'That's because of the twice-monthly trips to Bermuda to play golf,' Melodie said, patting her husband's arm.

'My wife doesn't believe me when I tell her ninety-eight per cent of my business is conducted on the golf course.'

Melodie rolled her eyes. 'Meanwhile, most other people are out there working for a living . . .'

'As I recall, you don't seem to mind the trips yourself, Songbird. And besides, you do play a little golf too.' He stepped back to his wife and rested his arm over her shoulder. 'Her yoga flexibility gives her a wonderful swing.'

Melodie's smile seemed to fix in place. 'Well . . . why don't we go outside and enjoy the fresh air rather than standing in here?' she suggested, motioning towards the terrace.

Hump joined her, his large foot straddling the groove in the floor; Bobbi followed, but – still distracted by the avant-garde building – she stepped without looking and her thin heel caught in the gap as she walked. She shrieked as her forward momentum was thrown and her ankle twisted, her knee buckling.

'I've got you!' Greg said, lunging forward and catching her one-handed – for he was holding his drink too – by the elbow. He held her still for a moment while she recovered her balance. 'Are you OK?'

'Yeah,' Bobbi murmured, embarrassed, as Brook rushed over and took her by the other elbow. Bobbi stood between the two men, both her elbows supported, until Greg, realizing the ridiculousness of the situation, took a step back, demurring to their host.

'Is your ankle hurt?' Brook asked solicitously at the sight of her foot completely free of her shoe and attached only by the calf straps.

'I'm good, thank you. It was entirely my own fault,' Bobbi replied, clearly on her best behaviour, bending to slip her foot back into the shoe.

'No, it wasn't at all. You're not the first person that's happened to. Melodie's always telling me to infill it. The "crack", she calls it. She says it's a safety hazard, even though neither she nor I – you'll be relieved to hear – wear high-heel shoes. I suppose she does have a point.' He scuffed the groove lightly with his shoe, an almost loving gesture. 'Clearly I'd hate for anybody to come to any harm, but . . . it's a Fukayama house. That doesn't really mean anything to my wife, but—'

'Oh, but it does to me!' Bobbi gasped. 'He's my absolute hero. I studied him obsessively at college.'

Brook looked surprised. 'Really? No one ever usually knows what I'm talking about when I mention his name. It's like I'm speaking in tongues.'

'Oh, I do. I'm an architect, a VP with BES Associates.'

'I know them well! Dick Eastman is one of my oldest friends. We were at Varsity together.'

'He's a great man, a true visionary. I've learned so much from him,' Bobbi gushed, eyes sparkling at the news that her host was an old friend of her top boss. Ro could almost see the cogs in her mind working, wondering how to take best advantage of the situation.

'You know, I always find myself jealous of architects. I share your love for the discipline but lack the requisite creative vision myself. Of course, I can appreciate it when I see it –' he gestured to the award-winning house surrounding them '– but it's not quite the same.' He cleared his throat. 'I don't suppose you'd like a tour?'

Ro thought Bobbi was going to swoon on the spot, and as Brook led her out of the room, Ro almost had to wonder whether Bobbi hadn't sabotaged herself on purpose.

'Well, I guess we should go out too,' Ro smiled, looking over at Hump and Melodie, who were already standing by the pool.

Greg looked back at her. 'Sorry, what?'

Ro hesitated. He was clearly straining to hear the conversation between Brook and Bobbi in the next room, as Bobbi's laughter kept drifting through in coquettish fragments.

'Shall we join the others?' She jerked her thumb behind her and he nodded, following behind reluctantly.

She carefully picked her way over the groove in the floor, and they walked towards the terrace, Ro trying to take in the immaculate garden. It was like a modern-day Versailles, with box balls and trees planted in rigid symmetry, and parterres criss-crossing the lawn in a saltire. It was certainly impressive and clearly very high maintenance, although not to her taste – she preferred Florence's house, where beach balls lay strewn on the grass and pool towels were stretched messily across the old-school plastic loungers.

They joined Melodie and Hump's conversation – seemingly on ZZ Top, of all things – Ro trying to adjust to this new context in which she had to view her friend. They had met and bonded in a small, dark yoga studio where Melodie had brought Ro along for the ride on her hunt for spiritual riches; but seeing her here – in what had to be one of the most spectacular properties in the Hamptons – it was hard to reconcile that humility with such lavishness. What could the woman who lived in *this* possibly be searching for?

A peal of laughter rippled over to them and they all looked up to see Brook and Bobbi in an upstairs bedroom, Bobbi folded over with amusement at something Brook had said, her hand resting on his arm. Ro glanced back at Melodie, who had looked over too, an inscrutable expression on her smiling face. And she thought, then, that perhaps she knew.

'I can't tell you how much I'm looking forward to seeing your posters up,' Melodie said as the waiter set down her lobster salad. Only a sliver of flame-red daylight was left in the inky night sky. They were seated now at a slim glass table beside the illuminated pool, which was flickering like candlelight, the dark garden dotted with discreet uplighters.

'It's funny, I've never done anything like that before. I wasn't even sure if I could do it. It was really interesting having to find a single image that can communicate a specific message.'

'Sorry, what's this? Greg asked, putting his hand over his wine glass as the waiter came round with a bottle of Pouilly fumé.

'Ro's in cahoots with Florence Wiseman for her kooky seed-bombing campaign,' Hump explained, a devilish look on his face.

'Hey! It is not kooky! There is sound reasoning behind her objectives,' Ro said defensively. 'And I hardly think we're in cahoots. She was doing me a favour because I hadn't got any work on and she had to commission someone anyway. It helped us both out.'

'Is this the project to replant the dunes?' Brook asked her, the first time he'd spoken to her since the introductions at the beginning of the evening. Ro was sitting to his left, Bobbi to his right, but Bobbi had monopolized his attention all night, barely pausing for breath, much less food.

'It is.'

'A noble idea,' he replied, sipping his wine thoughtfully. A pause bloomed after the comment. *Noble?*

'But?' Greg prompted, picking up on the same scepticism as Ro.

'Well, I admire the sentiment, I really do, but it's going to take more than grass to protect this town when the next northeaster comes.'

'What's a northeaster?' Ro whispered to Greg on her left.

'The storms that hit us throughout the winter come from the northeast, the prevailing wind and tide direction,' Melodie offered, overhearing.

'So what do you think should be done?' Greg asked, clearly interested as he leaned in on his elbows.

'Well, *something*, for a start. For too long now, the town's been paralysed into inactivity by the damned LWRP,' Brook said.

Ro looked to Melodie for help again. 'The what?' she mouthed.

But before Melodie could help, Brook butted in. 'It stands for the Local Waterfront Revitalization Program. A town citizens' committee drafted it in the late 1990s and the town adopted its recommendations when the Department of State authorized it in 2007. Basically, they advocate an "elevate or retreat policy": either lift or relocate vulnerable structures—'

'Oh! Strategic retreat, right? I've heard of that!' Ro said excitedly, remembering Bobbi's comments their first afternoon together on the beach.

'Exactly,' Melodie nodded. 'The problem is—'

'The problem is, they wouldn't know consistency if it hit them on the ass,' Brook interrupted. 'Policy states they're outlawing rebuilding in certain areas and yet after every storm, there they are handing out emergency permits for owners to repair their properties. It's too expensive. At some point, we're going to be hit by a super-storm that'll leave us with a clean-up cost that even Lloyds of London can't cover.'

'But what are you saying – that these people aren't entitled to protect their homes? That the State doesn't have an obligation to help them? They're taxpayers; these are their homes, their businesses,' Greg argued, eyes shining. 'Are they just to be left to the elements without either support or recompense? When the LWRP was drafted, there were only half as many hurricanes as there have been since 1995, and the problem's only going to get worse.'

'How do *you* know that?' Bobbi demanded, a sneer in her voice.

Greg looked at her coolly, the first time he had looked at her all dinner, Ro thought, though she may have missed a glance as she fiddled with the claws. 'I'm an environmental attorney, Bobbi. It's my job to know.'

'I agree with you, Greg,' Brook nodded, pulling Greg's gaze back to him. 'I advise on the National Flood Insurance Program and we're all in accord that new thinking is needed; new policy is needed. It's already coming from the top. As you're probably aware, a bill has just passed from the House of Representatives to the Senate with $50.7 billion in Hurricane Sandy aid and long-term hazard reduction. I know Senator McClusky is absolutely focused on making damn sure some of that money comes our way, but we're on the frontline here, and Montauk more than anyone.'

'They were worst affected by Sandy,' Melodie said kindly, for Ro's benefit again. 'Their beaches and dunes were all but destroyed, only to be hit by another north-easter a week later.'

'Oh no,' Ro mumbled.

'It's an emergency over there, that's for sure,' Hump said, pulling apart a bread roll and scattering crumbs all over the table. 'The surf's great, but . . .' he shrugged.

'So you're saying shelling out for repairs is too expensive – but what's the alternative?' Greg persisted. He lived for the cut and thrust of debate, it seemed.

'Well, that's where there may be progress. I'm on the Coastal Erosion Committee.' This time Brook looked directly at Ro. 'It's an advisory council that was set up by East Hampton Town Board in December, after Sandy. I'm on it, some town officials, local business owners, environmental advocates, engineers, you name it . . . We report our recommendations directly to the board.'

'By which you mean to Florence Wiseman,' Melodie said quietly.

Brook looked across at his wife. 'As the town councillor, darling, yes.'

'Well, you're already on a hiding to nothing, then. She's a lovely lady but hardly the steadiest boat in the harbour.'

Ro frowned. What did that mean? But Greg wasn't interested in personalities or reputations. He wanted theories, ideas. 'So what's your consensus, Brook?'

Brook turned back to him, holding one hand up, index finger outstretched, to indicate for more wine to be poured. 'Well, our interim proposal is that measures currently considered "hard structures" – such as sandbags – are redefined as "seasonal structures". That would mean they could be put in before the winter storms hit and removed in the spring.' He reached for his refilled glass.

'And your long-term objective?'

'We're pushing for a programme of soft measures.' Brook cleared his throat and took a sip of wine. 'Beach nourishment, in other words.'

'Rebuilding the beaches? But that's just throwing money away,' Bobbi scoffed, launching herself into the debate. 'You're dredging or importing sand – whatever – at these colossal costs only for it to be dragged out to sea during the next storm.'

'No, no. Not at all,' Brook countered. 'Beach nourishment isn't just a matter of relocating sand to beaches. When storm season hits, a nourished beach can absorb a storm's energy.'

'But how?' Bobbi frowned. 'I don't get it. The sand just gets pulled out to sea again.'

Brook put down his glass, a pleased smile on his face as he patted her hand. Ro saw Greg's eyes watch the gesture. 'You see, Bobbi, a nourished beach is all about the angle and the volume of the sand.' He tried to show it for her with his hands. 'As a storm hits land, yes, the waves will carry the sediment offshore, but where it shoals further out, the waves break, weakening their force *before* they hit the shoreline, protecting dunes and the properties behind them from wave attack and limiting how far ashore the storm surge will travel. Do you see?'

His tone of voice was worryingly close to patronizing and Ro shot a nervous look at her volatile housemate, looking for danger signs. But Bobbi, to Ro's astonishment, was nodding back at him, her mouth parted a little in studied interest. For Brook's benefit, though, or Greg's? She was putting on a fine show and seemed oblivious to the fact that both Melodie and Greg were staring daggers at her.

'Are you really in insurance? You sound like a geography professor to me,' Hump grinned, looking more like he wanted to start a food fight with the bread rolls than debate environmental policy.

Brook threw his head back and laughed. 'I only know all about it because of the savings it generates for my industry. Did you know that after Hurricane Isabel in 2003, an estimated one hundred and five million dollars in damage was prevented because it struck a nourished beach? The project was designed to stop a nine-foot storm surge – and it did! Over a hundred million dollars *saved*. Isn't that incredible?' He looked around the table in genuine amazement. 'Don't get me wrong. It's not a permanent solution – nothing ever will be – but I do passionately believe it is a long-term vision that can protect our backshore assets and coastal communities for decades to come, and really help restore confidence in the real-estate values and property sectors there.'

'And insurance industry,' Greg added drily, well able to see that Brook's interests weren't purely philanthropic.

'Exactly!' Brook agreed. 'Everyone agrees coastal ecology and economy are closely intertwined.'

'Well, *I'm* not holding my breath,' Melodie said, grasping her wine glass lightly. 'It'll all get tied up in the usual red tape. Look at the fiasco over the Montauk lighthouse. The rock face has been severely eroding right in front of everyone's noses for years, and even though they've had the plans and money in place to build an abutment that will shore up the cliffs, some archaic law has prevented the State from transferring the funding to the lighthouse's owner. The tip of that coast has come in from three hundred feet, when the lighthouse was built, to only fifty feet today. And all because it never occurred to anyone to actually transfer ownership to the town. I mean, it's laughable,' Melodie exclaimed with a high, brittle laugh, shaking her head.

'I think what my wife's trying to say is that a life in politics is not for her,' Brook joked.

'I just don't have the patience for all that wrangling and procrastination. Either do it or don't, but don't spend ten years talking about it.'

'Local politics are never that straightforward, darling.'

'But that's precisely why Florence's campaign is so exciting,' Ro offered, keen to be able to contribute to the conversation. 'She's not just content to let things get caught up in bureaucratic tangles. She's out there doing something about it right now.'

'I agree her campaign is part of the solution – just not all of it,' Brook said, managing to agree and yet disagree with her at the same time, something she noticed he'd managed with Greg and Bobbi too. He was indeed a skilled politician: slippery and hard to hook. 'Sandy eroded some dunes that were thirty feet high to just two feet. The dunes can only do so much. Beach nourishment is the answer.'

Oh. Ro fell quiet again, feeling out of her depth, and she concentrated on her food, deciding to wait for the conversation to change topics. No one discussed local politics with anything like the same passion back home – although why would they when the most pressing thing on their agenda was introducing kerbside recycling and e-bills for utilities?

She wondered what Matt would think to see her sitting with these people who had all been unknown to her not so long ago, discussing important issues in such lavish surroundings. She tried to imagine him sitting here too – contributing with *Blackadder* quotes and factoids he picked up from reading the miscellanea book in the loo. She tried to imagine him drinking with Hump, debating with Greg, agreeing with Bobbi, but it was like trying to picture him with a shaved head. She just couldn't see it.

# *Chapter Seventeen*

**10/01/2010**                                                    **07h27**

Closed door.

'Anything?' Ted calls.

'Gimme a minute!' Marina. Behind the door. Cross.

Audible sigh. Camera shifts slightly. Glimpse of grey silk walls. Pans across room, past vast double bed, to crib. Zooms in. Ella sleeping. Thumb in. Pink pig in her other hand.

Door opens. Camera switches back. Marina wearing a thin blue dressing gown. Holding a small white stick.

'Well?' Ted. Anxious. Impatient.

Marina pale, hair unbrushed. Slowly places a hand to her belly.

Audible gasp. 'Does that . . . ? Are you saying . . . ?' Ted. Voice thick.

'It's so soon, Ted . . . You are never coming near me again. Do you hear?' Marina.

Smiles.

Camera angle changes. Ted. Stands up.

'No, no, no!' Squeals as camera gets closer. 'You've done quite enough damage! Ted!'

Whoop. Ted.

Blackness.

**11/06/2010**                                                              **17h19**

'OK, let's give it another go.' Marina. Scene out of focus, deep blue. Camera pulls back. Focus sharpens. Pair of legs. Jeans. Tanned feet. Pedicure. Wooden floor. Coral sofa.

Angle swings up to show Ella sitting on the floor, cross-legged and wobbly. Surrounded on all sides by pink cushions.

'And there we have it!' Triumphant. 'Ella is officially sitting— Oh! Oh!'

Scene out of focus. Coral. Muffled voices. Crying.

Blackness.


**12/25/2010**                                                              **02h17**

'You are crazy.' Marina.

Camera on Ted, cross-legged on floor, screwdriver in mouth. Fronds of Christmas tree in background. Presents in red foil paper with snowmen. Leaning against coral sofa. Wearing boxers. Bare chest. Beer beside him on the floor.

'It'll just be so much better if she gets it pre-assembled.'

'But you've been doing it for five hours now. She'll be up soon.'

'I've nearly got it.'

Camera zooms in on elaborate wooden doll's house.

'I don't think you have, Ted. Is that a window or a door? It looks like a window to me.'

Frowns at the window in the doorway. 'Nearly there.'

'It's not like she'll remember if it's not pre-assembled anyway.'

Ted looks up to camera. 'You go to bed, then. There's nothing stopping you. You don't have to stay up.'

'What? And miss you taking a chomp out of Rudolph's carrot? You have to be kidding.'

'I told you. I don't like carrots when they're cooked. I'm certainly not eating one raw.'

'But it's for Ella. What will she think to come down and find Rudolph hasn't eaten the carrot she left out?'

Ted. Straight to camera. Eyebrows up. 'Like you say, I doubt she'll remember. Besides, *you* need the folic acid.'

Sigh. 'Fine. Pass it over.'

Ted picks up carrot from plate on table out of shot. Holds out carrot.

Marina's hand comes into shot. Reaching.

Ted pulls back carrot.

'Hey!' Marina reaches closer.

Ted grabs her wrist. Pulls her towards him. Leans up. Face inches from screen. Closes his eyes. Kisses her.

Blackness.

Ro opened her eyes, startled to find they'd even shut, her heart pounding as her fingers found the soft pucker on her own mouth, reflected back to her on the screen.

She sat in silence, calming herself down. W-why . . . why had she . . . ? She shook her head and pushed herself off the stool angrily. She was overtired, that was it. It was gone eleven and she'd worked far too late, that was what it was. It was only Monday and she'd already worked fourteen hours this week.

Hump had said he was out tonight, which was all the more reason for her to stake her claim on the sofa. She switched off the screens with fierce stabs, grabbed her bag and went home. She needed a beer.

It was 11.35 a.m. and Ro was sitting in the child pose, breathing like a professional, like she'd been doing it all her life, when the door opened and someone entered. The lesson was more than halfway through – what was the point of coming now? she wondered irritably – but she kept her eyes closed, desperately and determinedly trying to find Matt in her subconscious. She had to find him today. She'd slept badly, agitated and upset by her body's own betrayal last night, trying to understand why she had imagined kissing Ted back as he moved in to the camera while she sat alone in the studio in the dark. Were kisses like yawns – contagious, maybe? For God's sake, *him*, of all people!

If she could just connect with Matt, it would overwrite the moment . . .

But she couldn't sink down thanks to the sudden hard slap of expensive shoes hitting the wooden floor. She couldn't float away as she heard the gentle pad of mani-cured bare feet lightly running over. She couldn't drift into her subconscious over the jingle of pretty hippy bracelets as hair was quickly tied in a topknot, and by the time Ro felt the soft breeze as a mat was thrown out and unfurled beside her, she knew the intruder by name.

'Hey,' Bobbi whispered.

'What are you doing here?' Ro whispered back, still keeping her eyes closed and privately giving herself a brownie point for putting on her new sleek olive yoga kit. 'It's Tuesday morning.'

'I know *that*. I've got a meeting in an hour. Thought I'd try to chill beforehand.'

A meeting out here? Ro listened to the sound of Bobbi inhaling deeply and knew from her movements that she was running through some warm-up stretches.

Melodie began moving the class through some

salutations and Ro got onto her knees, looking across finally at Bobbi, who was wearing a white crop top and navy hot-pant-style shorts, her body doubled over, her nose taking a well-earned rest on her knees.

'It's so dark in here. What's with all the gloom?' Bobbi whispered again, turning her cheek onto her knees so that she could look at Ro.

Ro, who was upside down in downward dog, tutted lightly. 'It allows the mind to rest from external stimulation and helps with the meditation. We all like it.'

The 'we' sounded cliquey and she flashed a brief smile to take any sting out of the words, but Bobbi wasn't looking. She couldn't take her eyes off Melodie. Ro closed her eyes again, trying to engage with the light inside her.

'She looks good for her age, don't you think?' Bobbi whispered, sitting up from her stretch and joining in with the rest of the class.

'She's only forty-one. Hardly a pensioner,' Ro whispered as they slid from downward dog into a plank.

'Check out her toe ring. That stone's citrine. Pomellato, if I'm not mistaken. Probably, what, eight thousand? Just on her *toe*.'

'You are obsessed. Melodie isn't remotely acquisitive. She's a very spiritual woman.'

'With a very rich husband.'

Ro fell quiet, still disquieted from the dinner party at the weekend. Bobbi and Brook's continued high spirits and private conversations had persisted throughout the meal, long after the open-table topics had ended and the plates had been cleared. Bobbi had insisted she had only been 'being polite' as Hump teased her all the way home. Greg hadn't said a word, and Ro had a bad feeling about what might happen if Brook's showman ego and Bobbi's ambition were given further opportunity to merge.

The class repeated the sequence, pushing back into a downward dog again. Ro felt the sense of calm trickle down her as she focused on her breath, trying to loop it in one continuous, fluid motion, and by the time they started on the salutation seals, ten minutes later, she wasn't even aware of Bobbi's competitive meditation beside her. It was beginning to happen again, the peace that settled upon her during the class transporting her across continents and time zones . . .

'How much longer?' Bobbi whispered.

Ro sighed, losing her concentration again. 'We're nearly done. Honestly, I don't know why you bothered coming.'

'Well, it never hurts to consolidate contacts.'

Ro stiffened. What did that mean?

'Who's the client?' she asked casually, willing her not to say Brook.

'Can't say yet – don't want to jinx it.'

'Where did you meet, then?'

'I gave him my card at the Wölffer party.'

The Wölffer? The night Ro had met Brook for the first time – and Bobbi had been there too. Could they have met there, *before* the dinner? Was that why Bobbi had been so curious about him? Why she'd been so nervous about what to wear?

Bobbi looked across at Ro. 'If I can pull it off, it's just the kind of new business I need to bring in to make the partners sit up and take notice.'

'Bobbi, how could anyone not notice you?'

'I know, right?' Bobbi deadpanned, as they rolled onto their backs to the bridge position, hips in the air, arms by their sides. 'Hey! Is this giving me a double chin?' Bobbi demanded.

'Can't. See,' Ro muttered, more concerned with not being smothered by her breasts, which had slid up her chest and were making breathing difficult. What was it with yoga that made apparently reflexive behaviour strained?

They relaxed into the final pose – the Shavasana – lying flat on the floor, palms up, and Ro closed her eyes for the last time, trying to forget about Bobbi's ambitions and push herself back down into a lucid mental state. She *had* to find Matt today; she had to have some feeling of connection with him to hold on to. What had happened in the studio last night was nothing to do with Ted Connor, she knew that. It was just a reflection of her loneliness. The affection she saw between Ted and Marina was a mirror to her and Matt, and she missed his touch. She missed being touched so badly she wanted to cry – back slaps from Hump on the way to the fridge didn't count. Matt had been so certain that their reunion sex would more than make up for his absence, but she had never counted on feeling so physically isolated that a yoga class would be her only escape from the loneliness.

She inhaled as deeply as she could; her ribcage spread gratifyingly wide with each inhalation, the lotus oil and gamelan background music pulling her to a land that was as dark and ancient as this one was bright and shiny and new. Matt was in there somewhere; she could sense him, like smoke in the mist. But even as the familiar feeling of safety settled over her, something was wrong – she couldn't see his face.

The class had ended now. People could get up when they felt ready to. Most took advantage of the peace to lie there for a few minutes longer, but beside her, she heard Bobbi jump up and dash across the room, determined to be first at the water cooler. Ro opened her eyes, jolted back to reality once again, and stared bleakly at the ceiling. No matter what she did, it was going to be yet another day without him.

'The very person!'

Ro turned, her newly purchased yoga mat on her shoulder narrowly missing knocking over a white mannequin in a $1,000 dress. Florence was walking towards her down Newton Lane, a cardboard roll under her arm.

'Guess what I just picked up!'

'The posters?'

'The very same! Are you free for a bit or rushing off?'

Ro beamed, grateful for yet another diversion to keep her from going back to the studio – the scene of last night's crime. She didn't want to see Ted Connor's face when she hadn't been able to find Matt's, and she'd hopped on her bike straight after Melodie's class, adamant that she couldn't go another minute without owning her own yoga mat. She'd do anything to delay pressing 'play' again.

'I'm free. I was just putting up my ads, at last.' She pointed to her advert, now hanging in the window of the hardware store, and showed off one of the high-quality cards Hump had sweet-talked his printer into doing as a small run, for her to leave in the smarter galleries.

Florence nodded approvingly. 'Well, we'd better hurry, then – before your phone starts ringing off its hook.' She tapped the large tube under her arm. 'This warrants a coffee and a muffin – my treat. We need to admire the fruits of our labour.'

They wandered into the Golden Pear, Ro grabbing them a table at the back where there was more space and the tables were larger, while Florence poured them each a coffee from the orange-rimmed percolators – signifying the French roast – and carefully chose the two best-looking gluten-free banana muffins.

Ro, who had picked up a free copy of the *East Hampton Star* on the way in, began absently scanning the news as she waited.

### Suspicious School Visitor Is Arrested

East Hampton Village's police chief this week explained the sequence of events that led to the arrest of a father who visited the John Marshall Elementary School on June 29 and allegedly identified himself in the parking lot as a New York City police officer . . .

Her eyes flicked to the next panel.

### Sandy Left Vacationers Wondering, How Are the Beaches?

It's the first question being put to employees working the phones at Montauk's beachfront motels this summer. The good news is that reservations are strong. The scary news is that such a strong tourist season has such a shaky foundation . . .

She wondered whether Brook Whitmore had read this.

**Vigorous Debate Over Town Manager**

The question of whether a manager or administrator is
appropriate and advisable for the town of East Hampton
was the subject of a lively debate at the village's Emergency Services building on Saturday. The ninety-minute
forum provided residents with a range of opinions from
elected officials and others . . .

Ro was about to move on to the next story when her eyes
caught sight of a name in the text. She leaned in closer.

Support for a change in the organizational structure has
argued that since its inception, the local town government
has grown in complexity to the point where it is believed
management of the administrative details of government
should be in the hands of professionals. The Town Board
spends 'an inordinate amount of time on administrative
details, many of which people are truly not qualified to
do, but it's part of the job', said one reformer, who asked
not to be named. Supporters cited the $24-million deficit
that pushed the town to the brink of bankruptcy, accrued
three years ago under the leadership of Florence Wiseman,
saying it would not have occurred under the steer of a
qualified administrator and that questions were still un-
answered over the handling of the issue, particularly the
$3-million black hole that remains unaccounted for . . .

'Here we go,' Florence said, setting down a tray with the
coffees and muffins.

Ro looked up, quickly folding the paper away, but not
before Florence caught sight of the headline.

'Oh.' She drew her lips into a thin line as she sat down

slowly, her back to the room. 'Well, that ruined my breakfast this morning.' She shook her head slowly.

Ro blushed, embarrassed that Florence had caught her hunched over it, reading it avidly as though it was a gossip column. Florence had been one of the first people to show her kindness and friendship since arriving here and this was how she repaid her? But a $3-million black hole . . . ? She couldn't not ask about it.

'May I ask what happened?' Ro took her coffee cup and wrapped her hand round it.

Florence busied herself with stirring her coffee and was quiet for a long while. 'We made some bad calls,' she said finally. 'Invested too heavily in a highway-maintenance scheme that was later badly damaged by Sandy anyway, so that was money down the drain. We privatized the recycling programme hoping to make some savings, but it was a complete fiasco during the changeover: some people had no collections for over a month, and with the costs of trying to put it right, we ended up spending more than we ever could have saved . . .' Her brow furrowed. 'It was just a bad year. We couldn't do right for doing wrong. We overspent, borrowed too much . . . There were too many people writing cheques. It was shambolic – I readily put my hand up to it . . .' She inhaled sharply, meeting Ro's gaze with watery eyes. 'And I was having problems in my personal life. I was there in name only. I was grieving and . . . not myself.' Her voice faltered, but she stared back at Ro with wet, determined eyes. 'It was the first and only time I've ever given less than my all to the town, but I take full responsibility. It happened under my watch. When we discovered the money was missing, I offered to resign, but the board gave me a vote of confidence.' She shrugged. 'Well, nearly all of them, anyway. Some members saw it as the perfect opportunity to try to get rid of me; they see me as getting in their way. I'm a stickler for making sure our rules are fair to everyone – not just the rich weekenders – and that they're rigorously enforced. It doesn't always make me popular, especially when there's money involved.'

'But what about the missing money?'

'It's still missing. We've brought in a team of forensic accountants to try to trace it.' She shrugged. 'It appears to have been taken in small deposits, rather than one lump sum – that's why it's taking so long to trace. There's just so many accounts to work through . . . Hundreds, in fact, some moving just a few dollars. There's been a full investigation and inquiry. I was exonerated of any wrongdoing, but . . . mud sticks, doesn't it? And until they find the money, the whiff of suspicion hovers over me.'

Ro put her hand on Florence's arm lightly. 'But that's terrible. Surely no one who knows you could think you're capable of something like that . . .'

'My true friends don't, of course, but to those for whom I'm just a public official . . .' Florence chewed her inner cheek. 'I think it's the size of the loss that makes people wonder whether maybe there's some truth in it.'

'What do you mean?'

'Well, doesn't it strike you as odd that the number's so . . . *small*? I mean, if you were going to defraud the town accounts, why take such a measly sum?'

Ro thought that only in the Hamptons could $3 million be considered measly.

'If you're going to go to the trouble and risk of stealing it, why not take thirty million dollars? That would still be insignificant enough to stay below radar for a long time, certainly long enough for the thief to cover their tracks and disappear. But three million?' She pursed her lips together tightly. 'It's almost a domestic sum.'

Ro frowned again; she couldn't fathom this world where $3 million was almost considered pocket change. 'So what are you saying?'

'I'm saying that I don't think whoever took the money actually wanted the money. I think they took it either hoping to frame me for it or, at the very least, make me look incompetent slash suspicious – delete as appropriate.' She shrugged. 'Either way, my reputation's shattered.'

'But surely the police were able to discount you as a suspect early on?'

'Transparently, yes. The authorities were able to establish pretty quickly that I don't have it in any of my accounts, unless of course I'm secretly some technological mastermind capable of siphoning money through hundreds of offshore accounts.' She smiled. 'And given my callouts to my IT support company for help with my email account, I don't think that's an avenue they're actively exploring.'

'So then you're saying that someone took the money to discredit you?'

'Exactly.'

There was a long pause as Ro digested the hypothesis. Frankly, it seemed almost egoistic on Florence's part to believe that someone would go to such lengths to smear her, that they would steal $3 million and not even *want* it.

'I know it sounds far-fetched, but it's—'

The sudden scraping of a chair being pushed back made Florence stop, sitting straighter in her chair as she looked across at the people sitting nearby. A middle-aged couple were standing up, a newspaper rolled under his arm, sunglasses on the top of her head.

'You were saying,' Ro prompted, looking back at Florence again.

But Florence just shook her head. 'No, I'm being a blabbermouth, forgetting myself. I'm too indiscreet sometimes,' she said, shutting the conversation down as though remembering where they were. 'This is neither the time nor the place for this conversation, but . . .' She patted Ro's hand. 'I do appreciate your loyalty, Ro.'

Ro felt disappointed that she had to let the matter drop. Florence's theories were almost more dramatic than the actual crimes. 'Well, I think you and I got the measure of each other very quickly, Florence.' Ro shrugged lightly.

Florence looked touched as she reached down for the cardboard tube. 'Anyway, on to some fun business,' she said brightly, pulling out the poster and pinning it flat at the corners with the saucers and plates.

'Ace!' Ro gasped, taking in the lustrous quality of the finished product, which her printout hadn't been able to achieve. Ro looked at Ella's image – her blacked-out silhouette telling nothing more than that she was going to be tall, and her hand around her brother's revealing that she was kind. It was strange seeing her again, now that Ro had been privy to such seminal, intimate moments in her life. Ro smiled at the recollection of Ted engaged in the tug-of-war with the pug over the kite, her grandparents' pride as they took turns holding her, her beloved pink pig, Binky. Did she still have it?

'Hey! Lady!'

The sudden shout made Ro look up, just as she saw a man advancing towards her, his face twisted in a vicious sneer. He was wearing jeans and a blue hoodie – the hood pulled up, his arms up in the air like he'd thrown out a sheet across a bed. Ro saw something coming towards her. She couldn't work out what it was: there was no time. She was just up and out of her seat, blocking Florence from the impact of whatever was coming.

She screamed as, in the next second, her skin stung like it had been ripped from her face and arms at once. Florence screamed too, rising from her chair, trying to support Ro as she toppled back against the table, coffees and muffins crashing to the floor, making more noise, more mess, more heat.

Ro felt like her skin was on fire, taut and raw. Someone grabbed a tablecloth from the neighbouring table and ran at her again. She blanched, unable to react in time, paralyzed now. She heard a man shout, 'Get this off quickly!' and felt hands rip her T-shirt away like it was made of paper, the tablecloth pressed against her scalded skin.

'Soak another one in cold water! Get it out here now!' the man demanded, sending the waitress running out to the kitchen.

Ro began to shake as the shock set in. What had happened? Her skin felt scorched and tight, several sizes too small.

'Oh my God, how could this happen? Who would do this?' Florence was crying, the manager's arms around her as everyone clamoured for a better look, some people taking photos on their phones.

'We've called 911,' a waitress said.

'Did anyone see his face? Do you have CCTV?' the man demanded. He still had his arms around Ro, holding the tablecloth to her.

'I'm sorry, sir.' The waitress shook her head.

'For Chrissakes,' the man muttered furiously. 'It's OK, Ro, we'll find out who did this.'

He knew her name? Ro looked up and saw that she was in Ted Connor's arms. Again.

Ro stepped out of the cool bath, shivering, wrapping herself carefully in the pima cotton dressing gown that someone had just happened to have bought from the Monogram Shop over the road and generously given her as a cover-up. The cotton felt good against her vulnerable skin, and she could tell just from the feel of it that it would have been expensive. The kindness of strangers. They weren't all bad, then?

She felt the tears flow again and sat on the edge of the bath, letting them fall. Her hand, forearms and neck had been worst affected, her face mainly protected – bar a few drops – by her instinct to raise her arms. Thankfully, Florence hadn't been hurt at all. The situation would have been even worse if it had been her thinner, more fragile skin that had been scalded.

The paramedics had said she'd been lucky – she had mainly first-degree burns, apart from on her arms, which had second-degree severity and would probably blister within the next few days. She didn't feel lucky. A stranger with a coffee pot? Wrong time, wrong place. Bloody unlucky.

Ted Connor had driven her and Florence back to Hump's house, Florence increasingly agitated by what had passed and Ro's injuries. They were downstairs now, Hump trying to soothe the older woman with cups of camomile tea and Rescue Remedy as he'd ordered Ro into the deep, cold bath he'd drawn for her. The shock on *his* face as he'd opened the door to them had almost been one of the worst things.

She wiped her eyes and opened the bathroom door, pausing to listen for noises downstairs. Hump's voice drifted to her ear and she could tell from his tone he was calming Florence down, fully back in the doctor mode he'd walked away from, apparently without a backward glance.

She walked lightly over the landing to her bedroom, dodging the creaky boards – she knew where they all were now – not wanting to alert them that she'd got out of the bath. It was Matt she wanted to speak to, Matt she wanted to comfort her. Much as she loved Hump, only Matt could make her feel better.

She walked straight over to the laptop set up on the pine chest of drawers and pressed the Skype button, waiting for the distinctive bubbly underwater-sound dial tone to fill the room. She held her breath, staring at his Skype ID picture on the screen, as it rang. She needed him desperately now. More than she'd ever needed him. He had to be there. He had to be. Pick up.

Pick up.

Pick up.

Pick up!

PICK UP!

'Dammit, Matt, where are you?' she screamed, kicking at the chest of drawers furiously as the line disconnected, all her pent-up rage and frustration and fear tumbling over each other in a tangled ball that left her breathless and exhausted. 'I need you! Where the *fuck* are you? You can't not be here. You can't!' she cried, her hands balled into fists, tears streaming down her face as she leaned on her forearms – forgetting – before crying out from the pressure against the burns. 'Ow! OW! *Bastard!*' she railed, sinking to the floor in dejection, sobbing.

'Rowena.' The voice was quiet, so quiet she hardly registered it over her sobs and the sound of blood rushing in torrents through her head. She felt so unbelievably angry, as though the heat in her skin was boiling her blood, and she realized she was pounding the floor with her fists.

It was only the soft touch of skin on hers that made her stop. She looked at the hand closed gently round her wrist and knew she had seen it before. On the film . . . She opened her eyes. Ted Connor was kneeling beside her, his head dipped beneath hers, trying to get her to look at him. His face as close to hers now as it had been on the screen last night as he'd leaned in for the kiss.

The shock of the visual echo stunned her into stillness. 'Hey,' he said, a ghost of a smile on his lips, his voice so quiet she was forced into silence to hear him. She watched his eyes travelling over her face and knew she must look hideous – as red and blotchy from crying as the rest of her was from the scald.

He blinked. 'Let's get you into bed. You need to rest.'

He helped her stand, his arms supporting her as she walked to the bed. For some reason, her legs couldn't stop shaking and she felt as boneless as jelly. She got to the side of it and hesitated. She was nude beneath the robe.

'I'll turn round while you . . .' he said quietly, turning his back to her.

Quickly, she slipped off the robe and slid between the sheets. They felt cool against her skin, which felt like it was trapping fire beneath the dermis.

'OK,' she croaked, holding the sheet close to her neck, still shivering slightly, paradoxically.

He turned back, handing her a white caplet and the glass of water from the table. 'Painkiller. Hump says to take these regularly, every four hours, OK?'

She leaned up on her elbow, swallowing the pill like an obedient child as her body began to realize it was spent – Matt's absence the proverbial last straw on today. Ted took the glass from her, and she lay back on the pillow, silent tears streaming from the outer corners of her eyes, forcing them shut.

Occasional hiccups punctuated the silence, but she was too far removed from herself to care about little indignities today.

'I'll let you sleep,' Ted murmured after a moment, intruding into her oblivion, and she realized she'd already forgotten he was there. Sleep was claiming her fast, as adrenalin gave way to a smothering exhaustion.

'Don't go. Not yet,' she mumbled, and she turned her hand so that her fingers caught his. 'Please stay, just a little longer.' She felt sleep rolling up from her feet, making her body heavy, drowsy, even her mind just filling with a tempting empty blackness. She felt him hesitate, then relax, felt the weight of his body dropping onto the side of the mattress.

'I'm so tired of being alone,' she murmured, almost incoherent now, barely aware of his hand lightly stroking the back of hers.

She couldn't be sure. She couldn't trust her own ears when her body was so fugged with pain and fright and shock. But she thought she heard him say two words as she dropped into the chasm she so desperately craved. 'Me too.'

# Chapter Eighteen

'You made the wrong call, Hump.'

Hump, who was applying a bandage to her left forearm – the blisters had burst, as predicted, and were prone to infection – raised a querying eyebrow.

'I'm serious. You must have been a brilliant doctor.'

He shook his head. 'No. Too many rules and regs.'

She watched him closely as he expertly wrapped her arm, keeping it clean and protected from invisible but omnipresent bacteria, which he treated with a sombre respect, knowing he would change it again tomorrow and the day after that. Tension infused his face, his happy-go-lucky grin but a distant memory these past two days. Since the attack, he had hovered over her with a concern she'd have expected for 90 per cent burns, not 15 per cent. He had delegated his shifts among his other drivers for the rest of the week and wouldn't let her off the sofa, much less out of the house.

'*Rules and regs?* Hump, no one walks away from God-knows-how-many years of post-graduate study and the thousands of pounds – I mean, dollars – it would have cost because of *rules and regs*.'

His eyes flickered to hers quickly and back down again. 'I'm just not suited to it. It's a personality thing.'

'But what about the people? You're so good with people. I mean, the way you're looking after me—'

'You're my friend. You get special treatment. Anyone else?' He pulled a face. 'I'd just let the arm rot.'

Ro laughed, not fooled. 'Everyone loves you. Think how much nicer it would be for people to be given bad news by you rather than someone like . . . I dunno—'

'Ted Connor?'

Ro stopped in surprise. 'Don't say that,' she said in a quiet voice. 'He was really kind.'

'Yeah, he was. Quite the revelation,' Hump said quietly, his eyes meeting hers briefly as though she was supposed to say something back. 'So I take it you're friends now, then?'

'Well, I wouldn't go that far. I hardly know the man.'

'Well now, we both know that's not true,' Hump replied, alluding to her almost constant watching of the Connors' home videos as she lay on the sofa, a notebook beside her covered in scrawls of timings, dates and scenes. 'Sometimes I think I'm living with a spy.'

'It's my job, Hump,' Ro spluttered, laughing in spite of herself. 'He's paying me to watch them! Besides, what else have I got to do when you're forcing me to rest all week? I need to keep on top of things. It's ridiculous – I've gone from famine to feast in just over a week and I can hardly keep up with all the enquiries coming in.'

Whether it was the ad in the hardware store, her cards in the galleries or, most probably, her overnight, highly dubious fame after being splashed on the front pages of the local newspapers, which had featured some of her work, to show what a talented, hard-working victim she was, suddenly people were stopping by the studio every day and

Hump was run ragged trying to deal with her business (as he enforced her absence), as well as his.

She put her head to the side and smiled sweetly. 'Surely I can just pop by the studio with you while you make your calls later?'

'Out of the question,' Hump said shortly, straightening up and putting away the first-aid kit.

She exhaled loudly in protest. 'Strictly speaking, you're not my doctor, Hump.'

He looked at her sternly. 'Yes, I am. You're not going out. Not yet.'

'Well, when, then?' she demanded, as he rose from the sofa.

'Not before Saturday at the earliest. Trust me, the very last thing you need is for these to become infected. Just rest, drink water, sleep lots. And don't argue!' he bossed, pointing a finger at her as she was stopped, open-mouthed, from doing exactly that.

Hump wandered back into the kitchen with the depleted first-aid kit, and Ro slumped sulkily back to her reclining position.

'There's no food in the fridge,' he called through.

'I'll go out and get some,' she said quickly.

'Ha, ha! Nice try, Big Foot. Shall we get a pizza delivery tonight?'

'S'pose.'

'We can watch a movie. Of your choosing.'

'Great. More films,' she muttered, as she pressed 'play' on the remote – she had rigged the home media direct into the TV – freeing Ella from her holding position of bear-walking across the living room, smiling as her attention was immediately diverted back to her. She was one of those babies who didn't crawl on their knees but with their bum in the air, and she was surprisingly fast at it. Hump had made her rewind the tape several times a few days earlier, when he'd walked in on an earlier video of Ella bottom-shuffling – her knees out, her feet pressed together like a yogi – and traversing the room at great, comical speed without any apparent friction burns. The two of them had got the giggles really badly, watching it become funnier on every replay, tears streaming down their cheeks until eventually Hump had had to run to the bathroom.

Marina had taken this video, her voice cooing and aahing softly next to the microphone, as Ella circuited the room, heading towards bright plastic toys that were scattered all over the floor and broke up the interior designer's carefully conceived scheme.

Ro watched impassively as the camera angle swung up, surprise in Marina's voice, and Ted came into shot. He was wearing a suit and was pulling off his tie, his eyes fixed on his wife, just to the left of the screen, it seemed. He winked at her, sharing the private smile that Ro recognized as 'theirs' now, his eyes travelling down to her belly – Ro quickly calculated Marina was seven months pregnant by now and recorded it in her notebook on the cushion beside her.

Ro watched as he looked down at his daughter bombing towards him across the floor, bottom in the air, before clinging on to his trouser leg. He laughed, bending down to pick her up. Ro gasped – worried – as he threw her high in the air above his head, their eyes locked on each other, Ella gurgling with delight.

The laptop, also sitting on the sofa beside her, began ringing and Ro started in surprise, looking down at the

Skype screen she'd needed to see so desperately the day of the attack. It was Matt. Obviously. He was around now. Finally. He was there; she was here. The stars had aligned again – it was their fortnightly chance to be together again. Only . . .

A peal of giggles made her glance back at the screen. Ted was holding Ella above his head and blowing raspberries on her tummy.

A shot of anger tunnelled through her again as Matt's photo stayed belligerently on screen, demanding she pick up because he was ready now and everything they did went according to his rules, right? Her own stubborn streak kicked in. Well, where had he been when she'd needed him? The attack had happened two days ago – the culprit still unidentified – and Matt knew nothing about any of it. She crossed her arms and looked back determinedly at the TV screen. It was his turn to wait.

The next day, she was still in the same position – cross-legged on the sofa, the notebook now on her lap, the remote in her hand, the house phone ringing laconically on the side table to her right. She picked it up with an eagerness that betrayed her mounting desperation to talk to someone, see someone, *do* something other than obsessively watch the Connor family videos.

'Hello?'

'Yo, Ro.'

'Hey, Bo.' Ro smiled down the phone – pleased with her riposte but more pleased to hear her housemate's voice. Bobbi had been on the Jitney back to Manhattan straight after her meeting on Tuesday and hadn't learned of the attack until later that evening, when Hump had rung her while Ro slept upstairs. Several times Ro had overheard Hump in the kitchen on the phone, updating her on Ro's progress, and she was touched by Bobbi's long-distance concern. 'How are you?' She sat forward, rearranging the cushions behind her and getting ready to settle in for a chat.

'Do you have whites?' Bobbi demanded, skipping all the usual niceties most people bothered with. She was busy, busy, busy.

Ro, who'd been anticipating 'Oh my God, how *are* you?' was so wrong-footed it took a moment for her to respond. 'White . . . ?'

'Whites. Tennis whites. Wimbledon whites.'

'Uh, no. No, didn't pack those funnily enough. Why?' She dragged the last word out slowly, suspiciously, trailing it over three octaves.

'I've entered us into the Fourth of July tournament this weekend. Biggest tennis event of the season.'

'You. Have. Not.' Ro closed her eyes.

'What's up? You said you play tennis. You told Greg that morning—'

'I told him I *used* to play tennis. Past tense. Long time ago. When the dinosaurs still walked the earth.'

'And I already got Hump's approval on it. He says you'll be fine to play so long as you take your pain meds beforehand and make sure not to get whacked on the arm by a ball.'

Ro winced at the thought. 'Ha! A likely story. As if Hump's going to let me play in some ritzy tennis tournament when I'm not even allowed out of the house. I don't think so.'

'That's different. He just doesn't want you going into town until they find the psycho who did it. He says you're better off at home where the only thing that can hurt you is his cooking.'

The joke fell flat, outgunned by the shiver already trammelling down Ro's spine. Bobbi, true to blunt form, had put voice to the fear that neither Ro nor Hump had been able to articulate all week – that she had been targeted, that someone had deliberately set out to hurt her. Hump had insisted over and over it had been a random attack – he'd repeated it every time she woke with a short scream as her mind snagged on the twisted sneer, the faceless figure, skin on fire – but he'd clearly said differently to Bobbi.

Ro blinked slowly, blindsided by the thought. The level of hatred that fuelled an act of that sort brought tears to her eyes – what had she done to deserve it? – and she covered the phone receiver to sniff discreetly, not wanting Bobbi to know that she was so on edge.

'Well then, if that's his thinking, why let me play in the tournament? If it's the biggest tennis event of the summer, there'll be loads of people there, any one of whom could be the . . . nutter,' she mumbled.

'Nuh. All the eyewitnesses said the guy looked like a tramp – you know, stood out from the crowd. There's no way he could afford to get in. The security will be insane on account of the cars and tennis bracelets alone. You'll be totally safe there.'

Ro looked up to the ceiling. Only in Bobbi's world could a potential crime not happen because the assailant couldn't afford the entry ticket. 'So then, how are *we* supposed to afford it? You know I'm stony broke.'

'It's fine – we're going on a corporate account. One of our clients sponsors it and it's a prime networking opportunity.' Bobbi's voice became muffled suddenly and Ro could make her out talking to someone in the background. Then she was back. 'So listen, I actually just rang to say I'll get you some kit up here and bring it down with me tonight. Unless I can trust you to go into Lulu Lemon on Main and do it yourself?'

'What?' This was Bobbi's definition of kindness?

'No, thought not. How you feeling, by the way? Bandages off?'

'Uh, wel—'

'Good. Great. Glad to hear it. Gotta go. Meeting in three. Ciao.'

The line clicked dead. Ro felt like someone had just boxed her round the head.

She sat in silence for a moment, before putting her headphones back on and returning to the business of envying the Connors their perfect family life. They had what she wanted – well, once she'd forgiven Matt for not being here, anyway. She was angry with him now, yes, but once Matt came home and life was back to normal again – this whole crazy experiment just an odd, slightly eccentric memory that they'd laugh about one day – her life would be like this too. He'd made a promise. There would be no coffee-throwing strangers or guerrilla gardening or this ever-present urgent need to meditate or medicate herself into a calm state of mind. Her life would be full of the little moments she witnessed on this screen – low-key family lunches and walks in the park, birthdays and Christmas Days with bright eyes and little hands scrabbling at wrapped presents. She settled into a comfortable position, stretching her legs long and resting her head on her hand, determined to watch and learn.

'Hump, I'm just popping out!' Ro yelled from the drive, her foot already propped on the pedal.

'What? *Where?*' she heard Hump's voice call back from deep inside the house. 'Ro! Where are you?'

But Ro just wheeled down the steep slope of the drive onto the lane, relishing her freedom again; she couldn't wait even another hour for Dr Hump to grant her outside access. She thought she'd go mad if she spent another hour robbed of smelling the salty wind, seeing the pound of the waves, hearing the sunlight skipping over the grass.

Besides, she was feeling bolder now, after a furtive outdoor dash into town earlier – in strict contravention of Hump's rules – when he had popped over to the office for an hour's paperwork.

It had been a muted success and not quite the jubilant escape she'd been anticipating. She'd been astonished by the sheer volume of pedestrians on the pavements for one thing. Bobbi had been right about the town filling up once the schools were out, and she could scarcely believe the difference in just one week; it was as though she'd come back from a trip to the moon – every day she'd spent on the sofa equating to a week out here, and it felt like high summer now, with beautiful kids hanging around outside Ralph Lauren and Starbucks, the doors to BookHampton (the bookstore) and Citarella (the smart deli) opening and closing with a ring of bells, every parking spot taken at Waldbaum's (the supermarket), every single one of the outside tables taken at Café Collette, traffic snaking down Main Street, past the windmill and all along the highway towards Amagansett and beyond.

But it wasn't just the volume of people, the face of the town had changed too, with new shops – 'pop-ups', Bobbi had called them – seemingly having opened overnight. She clocked the distinctive orange of a Hermès boutique and a Michael Kors. The contrast made her realize how sleepy East Hampton had been to this point. Up until now, it had been like a bear emerging from hibernation, groggy and slow-moving. But now it was like a hive with everyone buzzy and busy, intent and focused. This town was ready to party, and so was she – at least in theory.

Bobbi's words, Hump's theory, hadn't let her rest, no matter how hard she'd tried to shake them from her head, and they had ignited a rebellious anger in her. She was no victim. Why *should* she stay holed up in the house, hiding out while she waited for the police to arrest someone on the strength of eyewitness reports and a willing confession? On that basis, she could spend the rest of the summer locked away.

No. That might have suited her a few weeks ago, but to her surprise, she'd found she wanted to get going again, to resume the new life she'd been building up brick by brick. Lightning didn't strike twice, right?

That was what she'd told herself, anyway, as she shuffled through the crowds, her head down and body hunched, her heartbeat louder than the traffic as she scanned for feet getting too close, moving too fast . . . More than once she had pressed herself to the wall as men and boys in hoodies and caps marched past without even noticing her, leaving her watching after them – just in case – with big eyes and flaming cheeks; it had been the first indication that her burns would possibly heal faster than her mind.

This, though, this was different. She felt safe in her solitude on the bike, and she pulled out carefully into the new, heavy traffic as music carried in the air like the buzz of mosquitoes, making cars vibrate and the occupants move their heads in time to the beat, like nodding dogs. Ro cycled slowly along the wide lanes, taking the long way round, enjoying counting the numbers of Stars and Stripes flags flapping on flagpoles, and the matching bunting strung along the street intersections. She was enthralled. The closest thing Britain had to an equivalent day of national celebration was a royal jubilee, and those only came every quarter century or so . . .

She felt her spirits rising with every revolution of the wheels, the past week beginning to slip from her shoulders as she basked in the liquid sunlight, her skin soothed by the cool, rippling breeze, and she realized she was beaming as she flew along, hair out behind her. Hump would be furious with her when she got back, but she knew she was right to do this – and there was someone who'd be pleased to see her out and about again.

She screeched to a stop in front of Florence's tall gates five minutes later. 'Hi!' She smiled brightly, waving into the intercom, knowing her image was being beamed into the lofty blue and white kitchen.

'Ro!' Florence sounded shocked. 'C-come in.'

There was a pause before the hydraulics purred behind the cedar timbers and the gates opened. Ro cycled quickly up the drive – out of the saddle – which ran along the length of the back lawns before sweeping round graciously to the front of the house.

Florence was waiting for her by the front door as Ro freewheeled round happily. She jumped off the bike, dropping it on its side by a flowerbed and jogging over, feeling strong and wanting to show Florence how well she was again. 'Florence!' Her smile faded as she approached. 'Have you lost weight?' Even in the course of three days, her friend was noticeably thinner.

'No,' the older woman said, waving Ro's concern away and turning back into the house – but not before Ro saw her lower lip was trembling.

Ro followed her silently into the house, taken aback and wondering whether turning up unannounced like this had been a bad idea after all. It had been one thing defying Hump with her spontaneous outing, quite another turning up here completely unexpectedly.

Florence walked over to the kettle and filled it up at the sink, her back to Ro, who was settling herself on her usual stool by the island. 'You must think me very thoughtless not to have been to see you yet,' Florence said, her voice sounding strained. 'You were the one injured and I've been . . . I've been so selfish not coming to see you.'

'Oh, please don't worry about that,' Ro said dismissively, keeping her voice bouncy and bright, though she was frowning at the sight of the wilted sweet williams sitting in pots on the windowsill. 'You would never have been able to get past Hump, anyway. He's been like a jailer, not a doctor.' She waited for a chuckle from Florence, but none came. Her concern deepened.

Florence turned, but stayed by the worktop, as though reluctant to get too close. 'Are you in pain?'

'Not so much. I'm down to painkillers every eight hours instead of every four, so getting through it.' She tried to make Florence meet her eyes. 'How about you? You had a shock too. Are you OK?'

'Me? Oh, I'm . . .' There was a long silence. 'I'm . . . I'm fi—' The words wouldn't come, Florence's shoulders inching up to her ears.

'Oh, Florence, I'm so sorry.' Of course she wasn't fine: a retired widow, living in this enormous house on her own, after witnessing a trauma like that? Ro wanted to kick herself for not having come over before now. She jumped off the stool and rushed over, but Florence drew sharply back.

'No, you have nothing to apologize for. It is I who should be apologizing. It's all my fault – I know it is.'

'What? Florence, don't be crazy!' Ro argued. 'It could have happened to anyone. How could you possibly know that some lunatic was going to walk in and chuck coffee over a pair of complete strangers?' She shivered and quickly tried to turn it into a careless shrug, even though every step she'd taken in town earlier had been with her ears pricked and her feet ready to run. 'It was bad luck, that's all, and it certainly wasn't *your* fault. I'm just glad it hit me and not you.'

She watched as Florence took a teabag from the caddy and held it in her hand, seemingly unsure of where to put it. After a moment, she replaced it in the tin and closed the cupboard, her hands shaking.

Ro watched her confusion before taking Florence by the shoulders and steering her over to the table. 'Come on, you sit there and I'll bring the tea over.'

Florence did as she was told, sitting wringing her hands as she looked down the garden.

Ro brewed the tea quickly, glancing continuously at Florence before carrying it over and sitting down opposite.

They sat in silence for a moment, Ro watching her new friend, who was usually so indomitable, so *sure*. It was painfully clear Florence was still traumatized from the attack. Trembling, not eating, not sleeping . . . She clearly wasn't coping.

'Florence, I'm worried about you. Have you had anyone looking after you?'

Florence looked down at her tea. 'Ted's been round every day.'

'Oh.' Ro swallowed, taken aback by the news. It hadn't occurred to her that he might have checked up on Florence after the attack – that he had thought to do what she hadn't.

And then irrationally, unexpectedly, she felt a sharp jab to her pride that he hadn't felt the impetus to check up on her too. She hadn't seen him since Tuesday, when he'd put her to bed, and she felt embarrassed now to think she'd been such a baby – having a tantrum on the floor, asking him to stay.

'Well, g-good. He was exceptionally kind in the immediate aftermath. Thank heavens he was there. The paramedics said my burns would have been a lot worse if he hadn't acted so quickly.' The memory of him ripping her T-shirt away from her, so easily, came back to her. She tried to keep a smile on her face. 'Is there anyone who can come and stay with you for a bit?'

Florence shook her head silently.

'But what about your family?'

Florence fell still, her body rigid suddenly, every muscle in her face straining to hold back the tears. 'It's all too much . . .' Florence whispered in a voice so frail it sounded like it had been snapped in two, her hands rubbing over one another in a frantic, agitated fashion.

'What is? What's too much?' Ro asked gently, but growing more alarmed by the moment. Had Ted Connor seen this behaviour, or had she hidden it from him?

But in the next instant, Florence shook her head again, inhaling sharply, growing taller, returning somehow to herself. 'Nothing. It's just a bad day. That's all.'

Ro watched her look back out to the garden again, watching the wildly see-sawing emotions raging in her friend as she strove for dignity. 'Florence, look – these feelings are completely normal. There's nothing to feel ashamed about. I had them too. Hump said I was in shock for the first two days. I just couldn't sleep properly, kept bursting into tears for no reason. But you know what helped? Having someone around looking out for me. You're here on your own, Florence. This is a big house . . .'

'Yes,' Florence said sharply. 'And that's precisely how they want me to feel, like it's too much for me.'

Now Ro was confused. What was too much for her? And who was 'they'?

'Do you mean the guy in the cafe?'

Florence pinned Ro with a look that made shivers run down her spine. 'No. I mean the people *behind* him. The people who set him up to it.'

Ro sat back as they looked at one another, Florence's gaze unwavering.

Paranoia? Ro tried to list in her head all the classic symptoms of PTSD. She was no doctor, but Hump would know, he could tell her. She had to get him over here. 'Florence, I think you should see someone, a doctor I mean, even if it's just to talk.' She spoke slowly, aware that a patronizing tone was colouring her voice. 'I think you're under enormous strain.'

'You don't believe me. You think I'm delusional,' Florence replied, a thin vein of anger in her words. 'I'm not some dotty old woman, Ro.'

'Of course you're not. I've never for one moment thought so.'

'But I can see you don't believe me.'

Ro was quiet for a moment. 'I believe that you believe it, but I think your feelings are stress-related from the attack. I really do think you should see someone; they could help you make sense of all these emotions. It's only natural to feel overwhelmed or anxious after something like this.'

'No.' Florence's voice was firm. 'They'll just call me depressed or confused or demented, when I'm not any of those things.' She tapped the table with her finger. 'I know what's really going on here; I just can't prove it.'

'Prove it?'

'I've tried, believe me. But they're untraceable.'

Ro tried to keep the frown from clouding her face. '*Who* is?'

Florence didn't reply; she just stared back down to the bottom of the garden, watching the dune grasses flattening in the wind, the muscles in her face quivering like plucked strings. Ro watched the conspiracy theories crossing over her face and wondered whether Florence was aware of her own words. She certainly seemed lucid enough, but . . . she's '*hardly the steadiest boat in the harbour*'. The words, forgotten till now, floated through her mind.

Ro swallowed discreetly as something else came to her too – that day in the cafe, seconds before the attack, Florence had been talking about the missing money. '*I was*

*. . . not myself.'* Those fantastical theories about the missing money and how it was secretly all about her.

Did Florence have a history of mental disturbances?

Ro decided to take another tack. 'At the very least you should stay with someone for a while. Why don't you come to ours? You'd be more than welcome. Hump would love nothing more than confining us both to the house.' But even as she said the words, she knew Florence wouldn't want to stay in a house full of thirty-somethings, with Bobbi's organic face creams pretty much the only edible things in the fridge.

Florence shook her head with a firm look.

'Or call a friend, then.'

'I don't want to endanger anyone.'

Good God. Ro forced herself not to react. 'Your friends and family would want to help you through this, Florence.'

'I will never leave here.'

'And you don't have to. I'm just talking about you getting a change of scene, some fresh company for a few days, that's all. A little space can bring perspective.' Ro covered Florence's hands with hers and she saw the suspicion, the doubt in the older woman's eyes. 'Do you have any plans for Fourth of July this weekend?'

Florence didn't answer for a long time. 'I'm supposed to be spending it with the family,' she said finally.

'Here?'

'No. We take it in turns to host. I did it last year.'

'So where will you be, then?' Ro was anxious to know of Florence's movements. She couldn't shift her uneasiness about the frailty of Florence's mental state. She had definitely lost weight, and judging from the depths of the shadows around her eyes, she wasn't sleeping either. She couldn't be left alone.

'At my daughter Casey's. She lives on Dunemere Lane.'

'OK. Good. Well, that's something.' Being a quarter of a mile away wasn't quite the break Ro had intended, but at least she'd be with her family. 'Do you want me to take you over there? I could ask Hump to drive us.'

Florence looked back at her for a moment, her expression different again. Some strength had come back to her gaze but something else too that Ro couldn't quite read. After another moment, she shook her head. 'Casey said she'd come by for me after Little League at six. I'll wait for her.'

'Why don't I—'

'I'll be fine. *Really*,' she insisted, noting Ro's sceptical expression. 'I'm tougher than I look. I don't scare easily.'

Ro let herself out, fifteen minutes later, having persuaded Florence to drink her tea and eat half of a ham sandwich, but doubt still chased after her like a following wind. How could it not? Florence was paranoid, unsteady on her feet and suffering erratic mood swings – strong one minute, crumbling the next – and she resolved to look in on Florence on her way to the studio on Monday. Hump would be able to advise her on the best approach. She cycled home, knowing he and Bobbi would be waiting for her so they could kick-start the weekend's festivities, but as the setting sun shone gold on her face, she couldn't help but feel cold on the hot summer's evening.

# Chapter Nineteen

'I cannot believe you went ahead and signed me up for this just because you want to network and make new contacts. I mean, who does that? Your ambition has an almost psychotic element to it,' Ro muttered, tugging at her form-fitting tennis dress again as she stared into the mirror disconsolately. The skirt barely grazed her bottom; the V-neck plunged like a waterfall, although it had been something of a revelation to detect actual muscle tone beneath the performance fabrics. All the cycle rides, yoga and sporadic kayaks with Hump were clearly having more than just a therapeutic effect on her. 'And why is it that I wouldn't wear a dress like this in a million years, not under any other circumstances, and yet because it's white and I'm accessorizing it with a tennis racquet, it's deemed OK?' She bit her lip anxiously. 'Be honest. Do I look like a porn star?'

There was no reply.

She turned back to Bobbi, who was sitting cross-legged on the bed, her long thighs flopped out easily as she frowned at some plans on the bed. 'Mmm.'

'You aren't listening to me.'

'Mmmmmm.'

'I need your honest advice, Bobbi.'

'Mmm.'

Ro humphed, planting her hands on her hips. 'You know you look fat in those shorts?'

'Mmm . . . *What?*'

Ro grabbed one of her sweatbands – which she had honestly thought Bobbi had bought as a joke – and pinged it at Bobbi's head. 'Yeah! Now you're listening!'

'Sorry, I was—'

'Working. I know! But you're the one who got me into this mess. The very least you can do is listen to me whine about it.'

'You're right.' Bobbi sighed, carefully folding the plans away, her eyes still scanning the drawings. 'I just want so badly to land this deal, but I can't think how to make the house work on the lot. The client wants to get five beds in, but . . .' She blew out through her cheeks, squeezing her eyes shut and pushing her fingers to her temples. 'New local law, which came into effect in April, means there has to be a 125-foot buffer between the building and the crest of the dune, right? But that pretty much squeezes the house into the top corner of the lot, which – would you believe it? – is triangular! And naturally the height of the roof can't exceed thirty-two feet onto the road, and that's not taking into account the two-foot flood zone *underneath* that we need to incorporate within that. I simply can't get that many rooms in the cubic area when I'm squeezed front, back, above and below!'

Ro pulled a face, hopelessly lost. 'It sounds complicated,' she offered weakly.

'It is,' Bobbi sighed, pushing away the plans and looking up at Ro properly for the first time. Her eyes popped. 'Holy crap!'

'I know! That's what I was trying to tell you!' Ro wailed, all her worst fears instantly confirmed.

'No, no, no! You look great. You just . . . Wow, there really are no straight lines on you, are there?' she chuckled.

'That's it. I'm not going.' Ro stomped her foot as Hump hollered up to them both through the floorboards.

'You are too . . . Here, I've got a cardigan you can put on as a cover-up.'

'So then you agree I need to be covered up?' Ro panicked, as a silky ecru cardigan sailed through the air and landed on her head.

'Don't worry about it. Everyone's in the same boat,' Bobbi said, opening her bedroom door and pulling Ro by the wrist. 'You'll relax as soon as you're there. It's like having to put on a bikini for the first time after winter. Fine after the first five minutes.'

'Yeah, right,' Ro muttered miserably.

'Oh, but—' Bobbi stopped abruptly and turned back to her, one finger in the air, like she'd remembered something. 'Whatever you do, avoid Wes Turner at all costs – especially looking like that.'

'Why?'

'Slimy.' Bobbi shook her head. 'Just slimy.' She turned and walked quickly across the landing, bouncing down the stairs two at a time.

'But who is Wes Turner?' Ro asked, jogging after her, panic-stricken as she held the bottom of her skirt down to stop it from flashing her knickers.

'Finally! I thought you were never going to get dressed!' Hump said, standing in the hall, his racquet in his hand, and swiping an impressive backhand through the air. He fell still at the sight of Ro, in her teeny-tiny dress. 'And I see you still haven't.' He sighed, tutting, his eyes flitting briefly over her newly exposed arms. After he'd finished telling her off for her 'Houdini act' yesterday afternoon, Hump had agreed she could go without bandages today. The blisters had sealed now, but the skin was a bright, rosy foetus-pink and suspiciously shiny. He swallowed at the sight of them before turning away. 'Shall we get on?'

Ro held on to the roll bar of the car as Hump changed gear and they bunny-hopped through the decorative wrought-iron gates that owed more to Pacific Palisades than Bridgehampton. Her grip tightened along with her stomach as she saw the McMansion ahead – pink, turreted, *moated*, a parking area that was as flashy as the Maidstone's was discreet.

They drew quizzical stares as they rumbled along the drive – the Humper as loud as a tractor and alerting unwitting pedestrians to its presence behind them, making them hop daintily out of the way. The guests here, from the look of things, were most definitely not Hump's clientele, and as Hump looked for somewhere to park, Ro looked for somewhere to run.

But they were trapped – as locked inside the estate as any would-be attackers without five grand in their pockets were locked out. They all jumped down, the old yellow Defender looking comical beside the buffed, pimped-up sports convertibles and Italian marques. Something rustled suddenly in the hedge behind them and Ro jumped back, almost knocking Bobbi off her feet. A cat holding a bird in its mouth stalked past with an unimpressed glare.

'Stop looking so shifty! Jeez, you look like you're here to

case the joint,' Bobbi groaned, before affectionately nudging Ro in the side. 'Come on.'

Ro followed Hump and Bobbi, who strode ahead, arms
swinging, trotting up the steps at the entrance of the house
like they owned the place. She walked in, only able to
absorb the scene in flashes: giant shiny ceramic black pan-
thers just inside the hall; a split curving staircase that
looked like a drug dealer's attempt at class; a crudely
painted oil of a nude woman that forced you to look away
first; swagged silk on poles above the giant windows but
no curtains.

'Hideous, ain't it?' Bobbi murmured through one side of
her mouth.

'An abomination,' Ro murmured back, her eyes struggling to adapt to such a radical departure from anything
sludgy green or wainscoted. She realized now how spoilt
she'd been these past few weeks.

They marched straight through the central spine of the
house and out onto the terrace at the back. From where
they'd parked the car, Ro realized it would have been
quicker to follow the path round the side of the house, but
that clearly would be to miss the point. Today wasn't about
tennis or even charity – it was about showing off.

Her stomach lurched as they took in the scene below
them – Bobbi was looking for contacts, Hump checking out
the women. Ro couldn't see anything but the heaving,
interwoven crowd, just hundreds of strangers all in one
place, eyes beginning to notice their little group at the top
of the steps, notice her. Ro looked around, scanning for an
exit, just in case, her hands automatically covering the still-
tender skin on her arms. She saw a huge open-sided
marquee had been erected on the far side of the pool, and

on the other side of the marquee was the tennis court. But why was it glinting?

There must have been a hundred people there, wearing white and drinking pink, and throwing out dazzlingly bright smiles that indicated of all the many friends they had, the hundred here were truly their favourites. The ambient noise level was incredible, shrieks of laughter peppering a loud, urgent hum in which everyone vied to be heard. Ro wanted to be sick.

'You OK?' Hump asked, looking down at her with concern, and she wondered whether he too had been searching for the same thing in the crowd: a too-intent stare; tight-stretched lips; fisted hands . . .

Ro nodded, trying to smile. Bobbi had been right about the security. Beefy guards were positioned at regular intervals, and she'd clocked a 'dog-patrolled security' sign on the gate as they'd come in. What was the worst that could happen? They couldn't burn her with champagne. Would being pelted with ice cubes count?

'Follow me, then.' Hump winked reassuringly, resting his racquet on his shoulder and bounding down the steps. Ro followed after in mild bewilderment – she still couldn't get used to seeing him in socks and shoes. She had half supposed he would play tennis in flip-flops too.

The three of them made their way down one side of the curved steps, Hump and Bobbi greeting acquaintances and contacts as they passed. Ro kept her head down – she had no friends to greet here, but she could feel stares landing upon her anyway, and she was sure that anyone who was looking recognized her from the coverage of the attack in the papers. Her grip tightened on her skirt again; her palms felt sweaty. She didn't want to be here, among all these bodies, all these strangers . . . Suddenly, her safe place on the sofa seemed like the perfect place to be.

'Right.' Hump stopped by a large easel upon which an order of play had been posted. His finger slid along the sheet as he searched for their names. 'Ah, there we are. I'm first up against . . . Oh look! Greg's playing too.' He turned and looked into the dense crowd before giving up with a shrug. Unless Greg had been standing immediately before them, it would have been impossible to see him, as you couldn't see even five metres back. 'Well, he's in there somewhere. I expect we'll run into him at some point.' As ever, Greg hadn't come back to Sea Spray Cottage last night for their Fourth of July house dinner, infuriating Bobbi even further.

Bobbi was peering closely at the order of play. 'Hmm, Carolynn Young's in your draw, Ro. Bad luck.'

'Who's she?' Ro asked, taking her suspicious eyes off the crowd for a moment to lean in (as much as she dared with her skirt) and squint at the sheet.

'Defending champion.'

'Oh.' Ro went straight back to eyeing the high-level mingling going on around them, shooting unfriendly looks at anyone who came too close. She didn't like having her back to the crowd.

She wished she could have brought her camera with her, but Bobbi had told her the *Hamptons Magazine* had the exclusive on the event and no other photographs were permitted. It was a shame, as it would have calmed her down. She always felt safe behind the lens. 'So, you've got Emma Clarkson in the first round – fine, but erratic serve,' Hump said, generously serving up some insider information. 'Um, then either Nica Washington or Lauren Oliver in the second

. . .' He nodded interestedly. 'Let's hope it's Nica. She practically lies down on the court and cries if you put any spin on the ball. I don't know Lauren.'

But Ro had stopped listening. Was that Melodie over there?

A sudden piercing whine made them all wince, some especially delicate ladies covering their ears with their hands. They turned as one to see a short man with sandy-blonde hair the consistency of candy floss standing on the terrace with a microphone in his hand.

'Ladies and gentlemen,' he said in a deep, expansive voice that belied his small, round, tight body, 'thank you all for coming to our tennis benefit today in honour of Long Island Cancer Care. I know each and every one of you is besieged with requests for patronage and funds to many other, equally needy good causes, and it gladdens my heart to see that you feel – as I do – that LICC warrants your support.'

He held his arms out wide in an inclusive, clubby gesture and the crowd applauded, some whooping.

'I know from personal experience, when my beloved Cynthia was struck down with the disease, just how valuable the services they provide really are. The moment that cancer diagnosis is confirmed, your life changes and suddenly you're on the outside looking in. No one else can possibly understand the isolation you feel in a crowded room, or the terror you feel in the dead of night, not knowing if every cough or cold is just that, or the beginning of the next stage. But LICC did. With them, we weren't alone, Cynthia and I, and I thank every one of those personnel who banished the darkness and made us smile. Even on the day Cynthia passed, I was able to smile. Yes, really,' he nodded, drawing more applause. More whooping.

'So today is all about giving back and helping them to continue to help the other poor souls who find themselves on the wrong side of the glass. Thanks to your generous . . .'

Ro tuned out, doing another security sweep and looking around the crowd. Now that everyone was standing still and listening to the speaker, it was easier to make out faces. She could see now – it was Melodie on the far left. She wasn't dressed for tennis, but was wearing a long, burnt-orange silk kaftan and giant, deep red beads at her neck.

Ro gave a small wave, trying to get her attention, but she was looking straight ahead.

'Thank you, ma'am.'

Suddenly, the entire crowd shifted, their curious eyes coming to rest on Ro, some clapping politely, others slowly withdrawing their hands from the air.

Ro froze. What?

'What the fuck did you do that for?' Bobbi hissed in her ear.

'What did I do? What did I do?' Ro asked desperately, trying not to move her lips as one hundred pairs of eyes settled upon her.

'Jeez! I told you back at the house,' Bobbi hissed. Everyone was clapping and appeared to be waiting for her to do something. 'Quickly! You'd better go up, then,' Bobbi said, pushing her into a walk.

'What for? What did I do?'

Oh no. Oh no. The crowd parted for her as Ro hesitantly stumbled through, gripping her skirt, her cheeks a neon pink, willing a sinkhole to open up, right here, right now.

The applause strengthened as she climbed the steps and more people took in her scanty dress and fulsome curves.

The man was standing on the terrace waiting for her, his arms outstretched like a preacher's, and she knew she had no choice but to walk towards them.

'What's your name, honey?' he asked creamily in her ear as he took her hand in his.

'Rowena Tipton.'

He turned back to the crowd. 'This year, I am delighted to announce Rowena Tipton has kindly agreed to co-host today's tournament with me.'

More applause. Ro looked out over the sea of faces in mortification. She had agreed to do *what*? She saw Melodie looking back at her with disappointment, Hump with astonishment, Bobbi with a frown as she mimed to Ro in silent fury, 'Wes fucking Turner?'

Ro's mouth formed a little 'O' as she looked across at her co-host in surprise. This was him? She knew nothing about him – other than that he was screaming rich and his wife had died – but as his thumb gently began caressing her palm, she could make a decent guess as to why Bobbi had advised her to steer clear.

The touch revolted her and she pulled her hand abruptly from his, having to mask the gesture with a flurry of head tosses and pretending to bat away a wasp.

A ripple of amusement gusted over the crowd looking up and watching her, and she fell suddenly still, eyeing them back with naked distrust, her scrutiny nervous and skippy as she scanned their expressions for the aggression she was braced for, ready this time at least. She was sure they could see her heart hammering against her sternum, such was the number of eyes fixed on her chest.

A few lines back, she found Greg, the only other friendly face that she knew in this crowd. She could see him easily from her privileged vantage point, but he hadn't seen her. He wasn't even looking: he was oblivious to everything that was going on around them, so deep was he in conversation with the glossy brunette she'd met over Greg's pancakes that time. Erin, was it?

Ro continued to watch as the little man beside her talked on. She couldn't take her eyes off her elusive housemate. Something about Greg and his friend drew her eye as they chatted to each other, first him bending to her ear as he talked, then her to his, their bodies close, their eyes linked. And . . . somebody in front of them shifted and Ro saw their hands clasped – not that she'd needed the confirmation. It was all there, clear to see.

She frowned, able to see Erin's toothy boyfriend making his way over to them, only a few metres back in the crowd and carrying three fresh glasses. Greg and Erin, detecting the parting crowd, smoothly – as though they were well practised in the deceit – unlocked their hands, no sudden movements or guilty stares to give them away, the secret still theirs for another day.

Ro felt her stomach tighten as she watched Greg chat easily, laughing at something Todd said, a viper in the grass. She looked away. The betrayal felt like a personal strike. It was none of her business who Greg did or didn't sleep with, but it was a shock to realize that Bobbi's estimations of him had been closer to the bone than hers. She'd been so taken in by his manners and intelligence and smooth confidence that she had never once thought there might be some justification in Bobbi's violent antipathy towards him, as though the lack of vision about him was Bobbi's limitation and not hers.

She looked around her, wanting to get off this stage. She didn't want Greg to see her up here and realize she'd discovered his secret. But before she could make her excuses, everyone erupted into applause again and she felt a hot, sticky hand close around hers once more. She looked across to find her co-host watching her inquisitively. Everyone was beginning to disperse, shuffling through the marquee and out the other side towards the tennis court lying behind it.

'Come,' Wes smiled, shaking her hand playfully so that her arm waggled limply. 'As the emperors were wont to say, let the games begin.'

Ro shifted position again, trying to keep her eye on the ball as it was volleyed across court like a bullet, but she was too aware of Wes Turner's left thigh inching into her peripheral vision again.

'Another drink?' he asked solicitously, leaning over with the Pimm's and, she knew, trying to glimpse down her cleavage.

Ro shook her head and crossed her legs, angling them away from him. 'No, thanks. I'm on court next.'

Her line of sight was angled 110 degrees away from him, but she could still feel his eyes on her.

'Do you play regularly?'

'Yeah . . . every ten years or so,' she replied, keeping her eyes dead ahead.

He gave a low laugh. 'What's your shot? Your killer blow.'

'A knee to the nuts usually,' she said with a too-sweet

warning smile, her eyes on the players. At least, she told herself, she was safe from the crowd here. From their thrones – actual gold-sprayed thrones set apart from the rest of the grandstand seating on the opposite side of the court – she could easily see everyone.

'And in tennis?' She heard the amused smile in his voice and it made her skin creep as she realized he thought she was playing hard to get.

'My backhand, I s'pose.' She looked at him properly. He was dressed in beige shorts and a red polo shirt. No whites. 'Why aren't you playing?'

'It's not my game.' He leaned forward, so close that she could feel his breath on her neck, and whispered a secret. 'Between you and me, I can't stand the sport.'

'Why do you host this, then?' she asked scathingly.

'Just doing my bit for the charity,' he replied, trying to lock his eyes on hers.

Ro looked away, revolted by him and disgusted that her seat beside him seemed like some sort of proclamation of intent. More than once she'd caught some of the younger girls staring over at her with openly hostile faces.

She stared ahead again – it was safer – shielding her eyes from the glare coming from the court lines.

'Why are the lines in gold?' she asked finally, determined to force his eyes off her chest.

'The gold leaf?' he asserted. 'The guests appreciate a little decadence. It's just a bit of fun, although quite literally at my expense – every touch from the ball costs me four hundred dollars.' He pulled an 'ouch' face and gave a laugh that was more like a whimper.

She looked at him in bafflement. 'So you thought you'd have a tennis *tournament*?'

He shrugged, enjoying the largesse he believed her shock imbued him. 'People enjoy the extravagance.' His eyes roamed her face, looking for signs that she was turned on by this reckless display of wealth.

'You're mad.'

'And you are sexy.'

She shot him a tight, unamused smile. 'Well, my boyfriend thinks so.'

There was a half-beat as she looked back into the crowd and she sensed the tempo between them had shifted gear now that he'd played his card. 'Is he here?'

'No.'

'Well then . . .'

Ro arched an unimpressed eyebrow, instantly shooting down his implied suggestion.

She felt the weight of his stare again.

'Do you love him?'

'Very much.'

'Does *he* have a gilded tennis court?'

'No. He has taste.'

Wes laughed at that, a loud, obnoxious sound that drew the attention of everyone nearby, prompting them to look at her and wonder what she had said that was so very amusing.

'You have a cruel wit, Rowena. Usually when girls raise their hands to co-host with me, they're a little more friendly.'

'I was waving to my friend, not you.' She looked back at him, sensing an escape. 'Perhaps I should just leave and you can find someone who's better at this than me.' She put her hand on the armrest, rising to leave, just as the crowd erupted into applause at the conclusion of the match on court.

'I wouldn't hear of it,' he said quickly, his hand slapping down firmly upon her forearms and blanching her fresh, still too-pink skin, so that she winced with pain. 'I'm enjoying your company. It's fun to have a sparring partner.' His eyes gleamed. 'Besides, everyone saw you walk up to the terrace of your own volition and accept your role today. We wouldn't want them to talk, now would we? From what I gather, you've had more than enough headlines recently.'

Rowena stared at him, feeling the cold chill that had accompanied his casual words. Everyone was talking, pointing . . .

Her name was called on the speaker system, but neither one of them moved.

'Looks like you're up,' he smiled, pleased with his verbal counter drop-shot. 'I'll be rooting for you all the way.'

Ro picked up her racquet and slowly walked towards the court, only vaguely aware of the wolf-whistles in the crowd as she and her opponent shook hands at the net. She watched dispassionately as the coin was tossed and she won – choosing to serve first – her mind filled with the frozen image of the assailant's twisted face, Florence's frightened tears in the kitchen, the horror of the event reduced to mere gossip by this toad of a man.

Everyone had fallen quiet. She stood at the baseline, bouncing the ball slowly, nine, ten, eleven times, trying to slow down her breathing and quell her anger. She caught the ball in her hand and put it to her racquet. She looked across the court at her opponent and then fractionally right, tossing the ball high in the air, her arm thrown back and ready for the drop.

When it did, she smashed it hard and fast over the net, where it landed, to her immense satisfaction, smack bang in the middle of the service line.

'Right, now you have to focus,' Bobbi ordered, her face only inches from Ro's. 'Don't get tight.'

'I feel perfectly floppy,' Ro countered, pulling back and trying to reclaim some personal space even though they were sitting in a bathroom so large a tennis court and all the guests could have been fitted in there too. Certainly, there was enough gold-leaf trimming already.

'Yeah, but she slices like a bitch. Have you seen the angles she's getting?'

'Is that supposed to make me feel better?'

'I just want you to know what you're up against. She obviously plays, like, *all* the time. And you said you've barely played since school.'

'Yes, but I *was* in the team. And besides, I'm in the final, aren't I? It doesn't matter what I have or haven't done for the past ten years; today, I'm playing well.' She shrugged, bending down to retie her laces.

'You've just got to beat her. And not just beat her, *thrash* her.'

Ro looked up at Bobbi, bemused. 'Competitive much?'

'Just win. That's all I'm sayin'.'

Ro nodded. 'I shall do my best. Now can I go to the loo, please? In private?'

'Oh yeah. Right. Sure.' Bobbi pushed herself away from the marble basin and checked her appearance in the mirror again. She walked to the door. 'But just make sure you win. I don't care what it takes.'

'Yes, Tiger Mum,' Ro nodded, shaking her head the second the door was closed.

She locked it and ran cold water over her pulse points, trying to cool down. The truth was, her heart was clattering like a tin pot, and she felt anything but floppy. Anger had fuelled her to this point – Wes Turner's lackadaisical bile precisely the trigger she had needed to find her game after a decade's dormancy. By her estimates, she alone had cost him well over $10,000 in repairs. Hitting the lines was her target, not outgunning her opponents, and it had taken her mind off the spectators, who were supposedly gossiping about her or waiting for her to fall out of her dress. Almost without meaning to, she had blitzed her two qualifying matches and both quarter- and semi-final matches. But now here she was, hiding out in the loos, and all out of anger. She had rotated Wes Turner, her attacker and Matt – she was appalled to admit – on the ball, smacking her racquet hard against them for their wrongs against her. (Matt wouldn't see his abandonment of her like that, of course.) But after over two hours on court (each match was best of seven games), she had run out of fire and the thought of all those people watching was beginning to get to her again. Everybody *knew*.

She washed her face, trying to bring down her high colour. At least her almost continuous play had meant she'd been able to dodge Wes Turner's attentions ever since their 'spar' and she hadn't been forced to return to sitting ostentatiously with him in the throne.

She checked her reflection in the mirror, turning her head interestedly as she noticed her hair – still sharply styled by the good cut – was steadily lightening into a golden blonde, like an autumn leaf. Her legs were brown now too, for the first time in her life, and it helped her feel a little more covered up than she really was. She stared at her arms for a moment, the one part of her that didn't conform to the Hamptons aesthetic. There wouldn't be any scars left, thankfully, but that also meant there'd be nothing for Matt to see, when he got back, of what she'd been through, and that thought alone angered her.

The clock on the opposite wall told her there were five minutes till play. It was time to go back out and see whether her luck could hold for one last game – she'd never won anything before.

Unlocking the door, Ro started down the glossy corridor, heading back towards the atrium that fed front to back and would lead her out onto the terrace. The polished limestone floor shone like a mirror, glossy, heavy walnut doors set back in deep recesses that showed off the fortress-like thickness of the walls. The house may be tacky, but it wasn't flimsy, at least.

Ahead, waiting staff buzzed back and forth with large round trays, stacked with newly popped bottles and sparkling glasses. One waiter stopped in his tracks ahead of her.

'Have you seen where my date's gone?' a man asked him in a demanding tone. He was standing just round the corner from where Ro was approaching and she froze. There was no doubt in her mind it was Wes Turner. *Date?*

The waiter glanced down the hall, taking in her shocked expression.

'No, sir. I'm afraid not. I believe I last saw her by the order of play board five minutes ago.'

'Goddammit! She's a slippery one.' He was silent for a second. 'Where are you taking that Krug?'

'To the service area in the marquee, sir.'

'Take it to the Gardenia Suite. And more ice.'

'Yes, sir.' The waiter took a step back – as though moving out of the way – and glanced down at Ro again. She realized he was warning her and every instinct told her not to be either alone or in a confined space with that man.

Without hesitating, she ran to the nearest door on her left and tried the handle. It was unlocked and she darted in, silently pushing the door to, just as she heard Wes's soft-soled shoes squeaking past a few moments later.

She pressed her ear to the door, listening out for the sound of the bathroom door closing further down the hall. But that wasn't what she heard.

Voices.

'. . . you going to say "yes"?'

'What do you think? I've spent the past ten years getting down on my knees to make this happen.'

Pause. 'But you don't love him. Sometimes I think you don't even like him.'

Ro turned. She was standing just inside a huge room with zebra-hide sofas and Perspex tables, a row of open French windows opposite looking out onto the terrace and the party below. Two women in tennis whites were standing together by one of the windows, their backs to her as they surveyed the scene like chatelaines.

'You are such a fantasist, Shelley.' The woman's voice was scornful. 'I get all that on the side. But a Gin Lane address? That's hard to come by.'

They lapsed into silence as the shrill sound of an announcement on the PA system rose up the steps.

Shelley shrugged. 'Well, c'mon. You'd better get back down there. Seeing as you're so hung up on fortunes, here's a chance to get some more silverware.'

303

'Tch, let's face it – I scarcely need to turn up. Have you seen the girl? Dressing like a hooker, practically lap-dancing Turner courtside.'

'And I mean, hello? Has she even heard of foundation?'

They both laughed, wandering off into the sunshine and leaving Ro shaking in the shadows on the opposite side of the room.

Five minutes later, she stared at Erin across the net as she aced her first serve, the fire back in her belly. Her father had once told her revenge was a dish best served cold, but sometimes, there was nothing better than serving it up still smoking hot.

# Chapter Twenty

'Can you reach?' Hump asked, behind her.

Ro leaned over further, as far as she dared, her hands grasping at the seaweed covering the rocks. 'Got. It,' she managed, pulling it towards her like rope and throwing it quickly into the bucket on her knees. She shuddered at the feel of it, still childishly squeamish about touching it. 'Surely that's enough?' she asked, taking hold of her paddle again as Hump pushed them away from the rocks with his.

'Almost.'

'But we've got five bucketfuls already.'

'I told you. The joy of clam-baking is that you have to work for your meal. You appreciate it all the more afterwards.'

'Hmph,' Ro pouted, looking back towards the shore and seeing Bobbi lying on the beach, occasionally prodding the fire with a long stick. 'It looks like some people got the better end of this deal.'

'Actually, Bobbi had already dug the pit by the time I got there, which was another fifteen minutes before you got there,' Hump said, poking her on the shoulder. 'Just because you're a famous tennis champion now, don't start thinking you can play the diva.'

Ro chuckled, still delighted by yesterday's win. She'd tried calling Matt to share the news with him, to no avail, and she'd celebrated instead with Hump and Bobbi at the Surf Lodge, where they'd drunk margaritas and danced in the sand as a DJ out from LA played the decks.

'Did I tell you I served up eleven aces throughout the tournament?'

'Many, *many* times,' Hump drawled, steering them towards another cluster of rocks as Ro held on to the bucket.

'Ha!' she giggled. 'I got so lucky. If you played me tomorrow, I'd have to do drop serves.'

'Yeah? So what brought on your A game, then?'

'Oh . . .' Ro blew out through her cheeks, wondering whether to mention her concerns to Hump. She looked back to shore, debating. Almost every fifty yards, she could make out smoke twisting in the air from other fires, tanned bodies hunched over, digging the pits and hunting for rocks to cook on.

'Ro?'

'I always play well when I'm angry.'

'Yeah? Go figure. What the hell do you have to be angry about?'

'You mean apart from my boyfriend doing a disappearing act on me for six months?' she deadpanned, pleased that at least she could take the mickey out of her situation a little now.

She felt his hand squeeze her shoulder. 'Yeah, apart from that.'

'And you mean apart from Erin and her friend bitching about me?'

'Really? What did they say?'

'They called me a lap dancer and a slut.'

'No shittin' way!' Hump howled in outrage, as they drifted alongside the rocks. 'I should be so lucky!'

Ro laughed out loud at the joke, loving his loyalty – he was like the lion in *The Wonderful Wizard of Oz*, all bluster and puff and wobbly legs – as she began pulling off the rockweed and putting it in the bucket.

'So apart from that . . .' Hump prompted.

She sat up and sighed, wondering where to start, wondering whether she even should. The day's revelations had completely coloured her view of her housemate and she wasn't sure she could hide her disapproval. 'It was something they said about Greg.'

'*Greg?*'

'I don't know for sure. I walked in on the end of their conversation. They didn't know I was there.'

'Were you creeping around in the shadows again, 008?' She could hear his grin over her shoulder as he deliberately rocked the kayak so that Ro gasped and had to hold on. 'I knew you were a spy!'

'I was hiding from that odious little man, you nutter!' she laughed as the water splashed around them, wetting their legs.

Hump guffawed behind her. He and Bobbi had not stopped teasing her about putting her hand up to 'co-host' with Wes, which was a well-known euphemism to the local crowd for sleeping with the man and auditioning to become the next Mrs Turner.

'So go on, then, what made you so mad about Greg?' he asked finally, after they'd stopped messing around.

'Well . . . they were talking about whether Erin should say "yes".'

There was a short pause as Hump tried to understand. 'You mean "yes" yes? As in, marry-me "yes"?'

'I think so.'

'So then she's gonna marry Todd Blaize at long last. The only thing that's surprising about *that* is that it's taken him this long to ask. But I don't get what that's got to do with Greg.'

She took a deep breath. 'When I was standing on the terrace with Wes, I could see absolutely everyone, right? And I saw Erin and Greg holding hands. Her boyfriend had gone off to get drinks and . . . well, the way they were looking at each other, Hump, they're so having an affair.'

Hump didn't reply.

'Hump?' she asked, twisting round in her seat to get a better look at him. 'Why aren't you saying anything?'

He wasn't smiling. 'Are you sure? I mean, you couldn't have . . . misread the situation?'

'Hump, I nearly grabbed the mic and told them to get a room.'

'Oh Jeez,' Hump groaned, pulling his hands slowly down his face. 'Not again.'

'*Again?*'

Hump slid down his seat a little, his legs bent into mini mountains as he looked up at the clouds. 'Greg's nuts about the girl. Always has been. I mean, properly lost the plot, can't think straight about her.' He narrowed his eyes. 'I *knew* it was trouble, him seeing them this summer. Jeez, poor guy.'

'Poor guy? *Poor guy?* Hump, she's his mate's girlfriend!' Ro cried in outrage. 'What he's doing – it's just wrong!'

Hump sighed wearily. 'Yes and no. There aren't many

ethics in this tale. It's complicated – Todd stole Erin off Greg in the first place.'

'*What?*'

'They were a couple at Penn. It was serious. Greg was going to propose to her the night she broke up with him. Had the ring in his pocket and everything.'

'Oh my God, poor Greg!' Ro's hands flew to her mouth.

'He went completely off the rails – boozing, sleeping around, failed his senior exams and had to retake the entire year again. Trust me, you wouldn't recognize him as the man he is today! He managed to turn it round, but at the time, everyone was surprised he didn't drop out altogether. He just couldn't accept that he'd lost her.'

'I can't believe it. How can Greg even bear to be in the same room as Todd? *Or* her?'

Hump shook his head. 'Maybe he decided to play a long game. Todd's the heir to some agricultural-plant company in Minnesota; Greg's just a regular guy who's good at everything he turns his hand to. My brother always said it was so obvious Todd was jealous of Greg – he was the guy everyone loved, top of the class. He's got the golden touch, but he didn't have enough of the golden stuff – not back then, anyway.'

'Is that why Greg works so hard? To try to win back Erin?' Ro asked, seeing how his parallels with Fitzgerald's Gatsby went further, much further, than just sharp suits and smooth manners. She remembered his distracted behaviour that night too, when Erin and Todd were at a gala – 'a couples thing', he'd said – and he couldn't stop checking his phone.

'I reckon so. He's up for MD this year, and if he gets it, he'll be made.' He was quiet for a second. 'It's probably no coincidence that it's only *now* that Todd's proposed to her, just when she's within Greg's reach again. He's a sick bastard like that. It's just the kind of power-trip bullshit he'd pull.' He peered over her shoulder. 'You good?'

'Yup, it's pretty full now,' she said, steadying the bucket as he pushed them away from the rocks again and steered the kayak towards shore.

'So what should we do?' she asked as small splashes of water off his oar speckled her shoulders.

'There's nothing to do. It's their mess.'

'But don't you think we should tell him what I heard? I mean, if she's getting engaged to Todd and stringing Greg along . . .'

Hump sighed. 'Does he know you know about him and Erin?'

'I don't think so. And Erin doesn't know I overheard her conversation with her friend either.'

'Jeez, what a fricking mess . . . Hold on to the bucket – I'm jumping out,' he told her, and she felt the kayak rock as he plunged into the water like it was a bath. Slowly, he walked them into shore, steadying the boat against the breaking surf, Ro holding on to the bucket of rockweed.

He took the bucket with one hand and held out another to pull her out of the kayak, his eyes falling to her forearms exposed in the T-shirt. 'The seawater will have done the skin good, but you need to get a long-sleeved top on now,' he said, no trace of jollity in his voice. He took his care of her way beyond duty.

'Hump, it's boiling!' she protested, indicating to the clear blue sky above them. But Hump just shot her one of his stern doctor looks and she conceded. 'Oh, fine, fine.' She didn't want to be relegated to the sofa again.

They stood together in the shallows, both of them ponderous as Bobbi shielded her eyes and watched them suspiciously from the beach. Whatever happened, *she* couldn't know about it most of all.

'So, Greg . . .' Ro prompted.

Hump shook his head slowly, a worried expression on his usually happy-go-lucky face. 'It wouldn't do any good. He'd just think we were meddling. Everyone's tried to warn him off her in the past; he's better off without her, but he doesn't see it. And at the end of the day, he's a big boy. When he got involved with her again, he would have known it would get ugly, and someone would end up hurt. It's obviously a risk he's prepared to take. We're better off out of it.'

'But—'

'No buts, Ro. My brother tried telling him once and it all but destroyed their friendship, so we're not going there. Greg's his own man. We're just his housemates.'

Ro frowned, just as Bobbi stomped over. 'Are you guys coming over or not? I'm just about fried from stoking that fire,' she said with a look of annoyance.

'You should try sitting in a damp kayak for an hour. That'd cool you down,' Hump grinned, abruptly changing the subject and beginning to walk up the beach with the heavy bucket. 'Has the wood charcoaled yet?'

'Only about twenty minutes ago,' Bobbi stormed. 'I've been sitting on my own watching you two messing about on the water while everyone else on the beach is partying.'

Hump threw his arm consolingly around Bobbi's shoulders, indulging her tantrum as he winked at Ro. Both of them knew her well enough now to understand that what she was trying to say was that she was lonely.

They stopped at the dug-out pit inside which the drift-wood had disintegrated into smouldering cinders, revealing the super-heated rocks beneath. Hump and Bobbi started laying the seaweed over them, before carefully arranging the lobsters, clams, mussels and corn cobs on top, and covering that too with seaweed.

Ro watched on, transfixed. Hump ran down to the shore and soaked a tablecloth in the ocean before running back again and draping it over the steaming seaweedy hump in the middle of the pit and gently kicking sand over the edges to keep it in place.

He planted his hands on his hips and looked up at her, a satisfied smile on his face. 'And that's how we clam-bake.'

'And to think that the Brits consider any food that doesn't come out of a Marks & Spencer packet competitive picnicking,' Ro said with a smile. 'So what now?'

'We wait . . . and we drink.' He handed her a beer and sank down onto the driftwood log Bobbi had cleverly appropriated earlier as a bench.

'How long will it take to cook?' she asked, taking a swig and sitting down in the sand, hugging her knees.

'About two hours.' He shrugged with a Gallic 'comme ci, comme ça' air, his eyes on some windsurfers further out on the water.

Bobbi pulled her beach dress over her head and settled down on her Hermès towel in her bikini, determined to catch the last heat of the day.

'Aaah, now this is how we do it,' she sighed. 'I love Independence Day.'

Ro rooted in her bag for a long-sleeved cover-up. 'I thought it was going to be like Thanksgiving. I thought everyone spent it with their families,' she said, slipping a kaftan over her swimming costume before lying down beside her, relaxing as she felt the sun on her skin and the wind in her hair.

'That's right,' Bobbi murmured sleepily.

A few seconds passed.

And Ro smiled.

'Now your turn,' Bobbi said, slurring slightly.

'OK, well . . .' Ro took a deep breath. 'When I was eleven, I stole a car.'

'Shut the front door!' Hump exclaimed, falling off the log bench. '*You* did?'

'Yeah!' Ro giggled.

'I never saw that one comin',' Bobbi muttered, shaking her head. 'Nope.'

'What was it?' Hump's eyes were alight with fascination across the campfire. He had used the remains of their woodpile to get the flames going again after their shellfish feast, providing them with light, as well as heat, on the beach.

Ro grew a little taller, revelling in the infamy. 'A red Mini Cooper with white stripes.'

'Shut up!' Hump yelled. 'You never can tell!' he said to Bobbi, who was still shaking her head.

'It was a one-to-fourteen-scale Tonka model from my local toy shop,' Ro admitted, laughing madly at their expressions as they realized they'd been had. 'Gotcha!' she shrieked.

'You . . . ! You . . . !' Hump laughed, out of words and almost out of beer. He passed the girls the last two bottles. They were all out – the entire box of beers depleted and the empty bottles clunking around on their sides in the sand.

'I'll go get some more from the bar,' he said, rising.

'No! *I'll* go,' Ro insisted, handing him her untouched beer. 'You've done everything today, Hump.' She saw Bobbi's mouth open in indignation and hurriedly corrected herself. 'Both of you have. It's the least I can do.'

'You sure?'

'Well, you're sure they'll let me in the clubhouse?'

'Yeah, I signed us all in for the day. But don't go up to the clubhouse itself. Use the beach bar.'

'You think of everything!' Ro sighed, slurring a little, clapping her hands on her thighs.

'I am the clam-bake pro!' he replied, thumping his chest, Tarzan-style.

'Toodle-pip, peeps,' she said merrily, walking in erratic zigzags on the sand as Hump and Bobbi collapsed in fits of laughter behind her.

'Toodle-pip!' they echoed, sounding like Monty Python characters.

Moving felt good, the soft crush of sand cool beneath her bare feet as she made her way past the neighbouring parties that were strung along the miles-long beach like Chinese lanterns, fiery speckles of ash whirling into the night sky. Everyone's food had long since been demolished, and music drifted on the breeze, conversation drowning out the thump of the surf, people beginning to wander between encampments now, the night but young.

Ro smiled as she passed by, wondering to herself how it had come to pass that her life had been hijacked by this version – a glossier update with glamorous settings and new friends. The last time she'd asked these questions on this beach, she'd doubted the wisdom of her actions in coming here, but now, tonight, even in spite of the past week's horrors, she didn't want to be anywhere in the world but here.

Was Matt having as much fun? Was he as happy as he had hoped? Or more so? What if it was even better than he'd dreamed? A spike of anxiety pricked her happy bubble as she wondered suddenly, What did it mean for them if they were both so happy apart?

A peal of laughter made her turn and she saw a guy running towards the water, a girl in a miniskirt over his shoulder. Ro turned and looked back along the twilit beach scene: people were dancing, playing with fluoro frisbees . . . She had never felt more removed from her leafy suburb, working out of the spare room and catching the bus to the local studio, feeding the fish at five on the dot and nipping into the corner caff once a week for a flapjack treat. How could the life she shared with Matt stay alive or real if neither one of them was living it?

She turned in from the beach, her head hanging low as the questions knocked against her and her beer-induced merriness slunk into familiar melancholy – even feeling happy made her feel sad.

She walked on the boardwalk between the dunes towards the low-lying hulk of the private club. It looked more discreet from the beach side, with none of the witch's-hat peaks of the grand front facade.

The members were having their own Fourth of July party on the terrace around the pool, with the underwater lights flickering ambiently, a live band set up beside the steps as men in dinner suits and women in jewel-coloured cocktail dresses whirled past in a blur of thrown-out arms and kicked-up legs.

Ro hesitated at the sudden sight of the crowd and made

herself take a few deep breaths. She watched the heaving mass, trying to break it down, process it in bite-sized chunks. It was clear no one would be interested in *her* here. It was Gatsby again – this smart, WASP world she kept bumping into and was never once dressed for. She looked down at her bare feet, denim cut-offs and coral-coloured swimsuit (Hump had let her take off the kaftan when the sun set) versus all the Louboutins and Michael Kors dresses. She should have let Hump do the beer run after all. He would have just ambled past, squeaking in his yellow flip-flops, smiling easily, bare-chested, his baggies hanging so low on his hips all the women's eyes would have followed him.

Why hadn't she anticipated this? Of course there would be a crowd here tonight.

She closed her eyes and tried to think like Bobbi: this was the Maidstone. You couldn't even *pay* your way in here. It was the club of all clubs. The coffee-thrower had no chance of getting her here.

She stepped warily into the mass, her eyes darting rapidly, processing every movement in her peripheral vision, turning slightly too sharply as strangers approached – and passed on by.

She saw the white-painted beach bar and picked her way over to it quickly, making sure no one came too close. It was surprisingly quiet in there and she was served promptly.

While the barman filled a cardboard crate with beers for her, she watched the party through the folded-back glass doors. On the outer flanks of the pool were smart blue and yellow painted cabanas, and almost all of them were open tonight – members hosting parties within the party. The mood seemed to be different over there, she thought – more louche and cliquey (if that was even possible) as the VVIPs lounged elegantly on the expensive wooden benches, a few important metres away from the pool's hoi polloi. Society out here was as tiered as a Vera Wang wedding dress.

The barman handed over the crate and she paid cash, eager to get back to the cool, dark beach and her happy-go-lucky friends.

'It's heavy. You going to be OK with that?' the barman asked her. Ro suspected he modelled too.

'I'll be fine,' she smiled, her arms straining as she took the weight. 'Thanks.'

She walked quickly, keeping her eyes on the ground and off the crowd as she made her way towards the beach again. If anyone lunged for her, she'd simply drop this on their toes.

'Rowena?'

She looked up in surprise.

Ted Connor was jogging towards her from one of the cabanas. He was wearing cream trousers and a crumpled white linen shirt, and looking like the drink in his hand wasn't his first. Five-o'clock shadow darkened his cheeks. 'I thought it was you.'

'Oh. Hi.' She stopped where she was, the beer crate banging painfully against her knee. She hadn't seen him since the attack, since she'd embarrassed herself so badly, and as always in his presence, she felt an overwhelming urge to get away. It would just be easier if she could avoid him altogether. Their relationship was so stiff and creaky, constantly shifting in ways that left them both awkward – hostile, angry and aggressive one moment, kind and even heroic the next. It would have been so much easier if he could have just left her hating him, but he had made that impossible and now . . . well, now she didn't know what to feel about him or how to act. He was clearly a gentler, funnier man than she had wanted to admit – the home videos had shown her that over and over again – and she couldn't deny she'd felt a stab of hurt pride that he had been to visit Florence and not her. But still, if they could have just stuck to hating each other . . . A simple life was all she asked for.

'So how are you?' he asked, stopping just short of her, one hand in his pocket. She saw him taking in her beach-ready outfit – clearly not at one of the club's parties – and she badly wished she'd kept on her kaftan.

'Fine. Yes, fine, thanks. You?'

'How are your burns?' he asked, ignoring her question about his own well-being, as though the answer interested neither one of them.

'Oh, all healed now. Hump was a good doctor.' She smiled nervously. 'Strict.'

He nodded, watching her. 'He's very protective of you. A good housemate to have – you chose well.'

'Yes.'

'You haven't had any flashbacks or . . . ?'

'No, no, nothing like that,' she said quickly, the lie falling off her tongue easily. 'Um, but Florence . . . I looked in on her yesterday.'

'Yes. I'm worried about her.'

Ro relaxed a little. So it wasn't just her, then? 'Me too. I was wondering whether she might be suffering from PTSD? I mean, not that I really know about these things, but . . .'

'No, I agree. I'm trying to talk her into seeing someone.'

'Oh, you are? That's good.' She nodded, looking around vaguely at the cabana scene. Everyone seemed very tall. 'She said you'd been looking in.'

There was a short silence. 'I'm sorry I didn't look in on you too. I wanted to, but I wasn't sure whether you would—'

'Oh no, no problem. I mean, I wasn't expecting it or anything.' She gave another nervous smile, itching to go, but knowing she hadn't acknowledged what he'd done for her yet, not even a thank you. 'Uh, but I did want to say thank you, you know, for what you did that day with the . . . first aid . . .' She couldn't bring herself to mention the T-shirt ripping. 'And then . . . after . . .' She tried not to think about how much she had humiliated herself in front of him in her bedroom either. Pounding the floor? Seriously?

'It would have been more helpful if I'd gotten to him first.' He frowned. 'I should have realized when he walked in; he looked so jumpy and out of place in all those clothes. I mean, it was a hot day. I should have realized.' He shook his head, clearly frustrated.

'God, no, no! You were . . . What you did . . . The paramedics said my injuries would have been a lot more severe if you hadn't acted so quickly. I'm very grateful.'

They stared at each other, the party jumping around them, music booming from the speakers.

'So anyway, thank you.' She shrugged, trying to fill the silence that surrounded only them in the middle of the thumping party. 'Um . . . but I'd better get back. The others are waiting for these.' She indicated to the beers, just as someone dashed towards her and she gasped, her body frozen all over again.

'Hey, it's OK,' Ted said, instantly stepping between her

and the drunken dancer who'd overestimated his abilities and was now picking himself up from the floor, six feet away from her. 'I've got you. Here, let me take that for you. It looks heavy.'

She looked back at him, her body rigid with tension, only vaguely aware of the weight leaving her arms as he easily took the beers. 'Come on, I'll walk you back. Are you on the beach?'

'Yes, but—' Over his shoulder, she saw a glamorous blonde in black silk walking towards them. Ro couldn't see her clearly in the dim lights, but she knew who it was, of course.

She straightened up and braced herself to meet Marina at last. She must have spent over forty hours going through the videos already and she felt strange that she was going to be introduced as a stranger when she already knew her so intimately.

'Hi, darling,' the blonde smiled. 'I was wondering where you'd got to.'

'Oh.' Ted was startled by her silent approach, distracted momentarily by her hand snaking around his hips. 'This is Rowena Tipton, the photographer I was telling you about.'

Ro couldn't speak.

'And Rowena –' he looked back at her, a new expression in his eyes '– I'd like you to meet Julianne Starling.'

# Chapter Twenty-One

**02/05/2011**                                      **21h19**

Bedside light on. Double bed. Pale grey silk walls.

Ella sleeping. Thumb half in open mouth. Pink pig tightly gripped in her fist.

Ted sleeping beside her. In his suit. Jacket and shoes off. Storybook on his chest.

'My sleepyheads.' Whisper. Marina.

Blackness.

**03/09/2011**                                      **13h19**

Ella sitting in high chair. Red velvet dress. Red velvet bow in her hair, growing out lighter.

Beside her, grey-haired man in sports jacket and tie holding up her pink pig. 'Did you drop Binky, Ella-moo?'

Ella claps, kicks her legs. Chubby now.

'Dad, see if you can get her to say "El-la".' Ted.

'Can you say "El-la"? El-la?'

Ella stares at pink pig. Out of reach. Bottom lip pushes out.

'The other babies in the group are talking already.'

'Talking?' The grey-haired man keeps his eyes on Ella, waving her pink pig. 'El-la.'

'Well, they're not having conversations.' Chuckle. 'But single words. Like Mama, Dada. She's ahead of the curve on everything else. Marina's worried, thinks maybe we should take her to see a specialist.'

'A specialist? She's nine months old, for Pete's sake.'

'Yes, but Marina says a lot of the other babies in her group are making sounds already. They start at any time from six months, you know.'

'Listen, if she's not talking yet, it's because she's developing in another area instead – like memory or motor control. There's nothing wrong with her grip, that's for sure. You worry too much, son.'

'I guess.'

'El-la.'

'Tada!' Marina. Out of shot. Camera swings over a dressed dining table. Marina walking through doorway carrying a heavy plate with a roast chicken. Silver-haired woman behind carrying tureen.

'Lunch is served, everybody—'

'Ta-da.'

Collective gasp. Marina looks over at Ella. Camera swings back.

'Say that again, baby!' Ted. Excited. 'Ta-da. Ta-da.'

Ella reaches for pink pig, legs kicking. 'Ta-da.'

Collective cheer. Clapping. Ella claps. Giggles excitedly.

'Ta-da.' All the adults, cooing. 'Ta-da.'

'Oh, Ted, her first word. I can't believe it.' Sound of plate being set down. Walks back into shot.

'Ta-da, my sweetie. Ta-da. Ma-ma says "ta-da".'

Ella goes quiet. Red. Redder.

'Uh . . .' Dad.

'Oh . . .' Mum.

Ella cries. Marina wrinkles her nose.

Camera shakes. 'Tada!' Ted. Laughing.
Blackness.


**03/28/2011**                                              **11h18**

Beach. Bright day. Heavy sea. Dunes. Egypt Beach?

Shaky zoom onto Ted running to the water. Rolled-up red trousers, a jumper and a down sleeveless jacket. Ella on his shoulders wearing a toddler snowsuit. Shrieks.

Runs into the shallows. Runs back out. Runs back in. Runs back out.

Ted looks up at camera. Waves.

Points camera (or Marina?) out to Ella. Ella points at camera. Soft laugh. Marina.

Runs back into water. Runs back out. Runs back in . . .
Blackness.


**03/28/2011**                                              **14h33**

Same day. Ted hunched over with bucket and spade, digging deep moat round intricate sandcastle. Three towers. Cocktail umbrellas as flags. Shells for windows. Wearing red trousers – rolled up over bare feet – and a grey Ralph Lauren down gilet.

'Are you sure the tide's going to come this high?' Marina. Bare feet just in shot. Raspberry-pink pedicure.

'I checked this morning. Should hit here by three thirty-six p.m.'

'Thereabouts.'

Ted looks up. Winks. 'Thereabouts.'

Ella sitting on blue check blanket. Wearing pale pink snowsuit and bobble hat, with light brown tendrils peeking through. Sandy hands. Hitting empty bucket with small green spade.

Ted sits back on haunches, inspecting castle. 'It's missing something.'

'National Guard? White knight?'

'Ha, ha.'

'Working drawbridge?'

'Working drawbridge!' He clicks fingers, points at Marina.

'Ted, I was kidding!'

'But you're right. It's just what it needs.'

'It's made of *sand*, Ted.'

'Don't be so defeatist. Where there's a will, there's a—'

Ella staggers into shot like drunkard. Small, lurching steps. Unbalanced.

'Ted, the trench!' Marina. Gasps.

Ella straddles moat. Sheer luck. Loses balance on castle wall. Falls down hard on bottom.

Castle crushed. Ted crestfallen. 'Oh.'

Ella cries.

Blackness.

**04/01/2011**                                                  **14h21**

Ella. On a swing. Park. Pink striped dress and cardigan. Marina pushing her. Heavily pregnant.

'Why don't you let me take over with that?' Older woman's voice behind the camera.

'It's OK — I've got it.'

'You are worn out.'

Marina looks to camera. 'Mom, I am fine.'

Ella kicks excitedly, little fists gripping the chain links. Pink pig on her lap.

'When are you stopping work?'

'Next Friday.'

'The baby's due a week Tuesday.'

'I'm aware of that.' Tight smile.

'I'm just worried about you, mine heart.'

'Mom! I have had a baby before. I do know how this goes.'

Silence. Ella swings back and forth.

Blackness.

Ro took off the headphones, niggled by something, and stared out into the square distractedly. There were no shadows on the grass today. A front had come in off the Atlantic, the sky colour-washed in an eau-de-nil tint and the air wet, gently misting her on her frequent coffee runs over the road.

She just couldn't settle. The weekend's revelation had left her reeling, although she didn't understand why – people got divorced all the time, especially around here where more money and younger bodies were the commodities traded as a matter of course. But still, she just couldn't reconcile what had been plain enough on Saturday night with what she was seeing on film here.

Granted, the last films she'd seen had been shot three years ago now. But could everything have fallen apart *so* spectacularly between Ted and Marina in that time? There was no hint of it on screen – the cheeky winks, private looks, fond teasing . . . It spoke absolutely of a couple in love and in love with their family. She thought of Marina's mother's comment that Marina was exhausted just looking after Ella. Was this what having kids did to people – sapping them of energy, vitality, freedom, time and destroying their relationship in the process?

She sighed, stretching her arms above her head and wondering where Melodie was. If she had been gently slipping out of her yoga routine before the attack, now it had

come to an abrupt halt altogether: her recuperative confinement at home had coincided with Melodie reducing the
class roster to every other day as the summer social season
really kicked in and she was cornered into chairing endless
swanky lunches for Brook's business clients and charity
commitments instead.

She heard the slop-slap of flip-flops coming along the
boardwalk and looked up in readiness of Hump's easy-
going presence appearing at the doorway, coffees in his
hands. Instead, a woman trailing two kids walked through
the door, eyes widening with delight – even behind her
Chanel shades – as she took in the portrait of the two
young brothers on the wall immediately opposite. Ro rose
from her seat and gave a big smile. Another client, sold.

'Why don't you come into Manhattan for the day? We
could have lunch again.'

Ro flopped onto the chair and extended her legs, putting
her feet on top of the chest of drawers. 'Because I'm
snowed. And as I recall, we didn't have lunch last time:
you trapped me in a dressing-room cubicle for three hours,
walked me at gunpoint to the till, made me spend all my
money and then cut off my hair.'

Bobbi snorted with laughter. 'Exactly. It was great fun!'

Ro chuckled, reaching up to her toes with the nail-polish
brush and trying not to paint her skin. 'It was, but I'm still
snowed. I just had another commission yesterday from one
of the guests at Lauren and Paul's wedding. Besides, I
thought you were flat out working on that house that
didn't fit the plot.'

'I solved it.' A ring of triumph sounded in her voice.

'You did? How?'

'Steps.'

'Stairs?'

'No, steps. I've stepped the house with the lowest dimension looking onto the road boundary, and the top one at the back looking onto the beach.'

'Ooh, clever. Not just a hot bod.'

'Thank you,' Bobbi preened.

'Did the client like it?'

'He hasn't seen it yet. I'm submitting it tonight.'

Something in Bobbi's tone vibrated like a tuning fork. 'Tonight?'

'We're doing it over dinner.'

'Oh. Right . . .' Ro felt her voice thin out. Bobbi had been deliberately oblique about her new mystery client, refusing to name him. And now she was pitching to him over *dinner*? 'Is that standard practice?'

'Well, strictly speaking, no. But we're all crazy busy and we gotta eat, right? This way, two birds, one stone.'

'Uh-huh,' Ro muttered, not buying that excuse for one moment. 'And is he attractive?'

Bobbi giggled. 'Maybe! He's got that older-guy groove going on.'

Oh no. No. No. 'What, you mean nose hair and prostate problems?' She tried to keep her tone light. It couldn't be Brook. It couldn't be. What if it was?

'I mean a Carrera S and handmade suits.'

'Wow, he sounds perfect,' Ro said with sarcasm.

'No, not perfect. He's a bit pigeon-toed, if you really want to know.'

'Oh. So you like him because . . .?'

'Listen, technically he's a realtor but actually he's way

more diverse than that. He's a really top-flight business-man, a non-exec – I checked out his LinkedIn page – and I've always wanted to date a non-exec.'

'Bobbi! That's dreadful! Why would you even care about that?'

'Because it means he's already made for one thing.'

'That is so the wrong reason to date someone!' Ro splut-tered. God, did everyone out here think like this? Was that why Ted and Marina had split – both of them trading up? She thought about Greg and wondered what was happen-ing with him and Erin (who clearly did think like that). He hadn't come over to the house at all during Independence Day weekend, although Hump had heard through friends that Greg had been in Southampton for the celebrations. (Neither of them had dared to tell Bobbi that.) His clandes-tine relationship with Erin was obviously still going on, but there had been no announcement made of the engagement between Erin and Todd, and Hump was beginning to think she'd entirely misunderstood the conversation.

'Listen, there's nothing wrong with being practical while you still can be. Make these decisions before you fall be-cause once you've fallen, it's over, done – you'll put up with anything. I mean, look at you! Would you have gotten together with Matt if you'd known he was going to string you along for eleven years and then take a hike?'

'Bobbi!' Ro shrieked, half cross, half shocked that Bobbi could be *that* insensitive. She had built up some immunity to Bobbi's bluntness but not a rhino hide.

'Hey, listen, I say that with love. You are wasting your summer, not to mention your life, waiting around for him. It's about time you start seeing the situation for what it is.'

'I see perfectly well what it is! It's a pause!' Ro snapped.

'A pause,' Bobbi echoed. 'You ever hear of anyone else ever having a pause?'

'Y-y- . . .' Ro stammered, wanting to say 'yes' but unable to think of an example.

'No!' Bobbi answered for her. 'And that's because there is no such thing.'

'You do not know Matt. You can't say that. I have no problem with him taking a bit of time to himself before we settle down. You're the one who's got a problem with it,' Ro cried furiously.

There was a long silence – really long – Bobbi's attempt at tact coming rather too late. 'Well, it just makes me sad watching you, that's all. You deserve better.'

Downstairs, Ro heard the front door slam, Hump shouting out for her. She could hear him bounding up the stairs. 'Yeah, right. Look, enjoy dinner tonight. Whatever.' Her tone was surly. 'I'll see you on Friday.'

'Hey, Ro—' Bobbi started to say.

But Ro had already hit 'disconnect' and was pressing her hands to her eyes, trying to stop the frustration from coming out as tears. She would not cry. She would not.

Hump burst in, almost falling through the door in a clatter of ungainly limbs.

'Hey! Knock, why don't you!' she spluttered, watching the surprise unfurl on his face as he took in her red eyes and tense posture.

'S-sorry.' He had stopped in the doorway and was hunched over, leaning his hands on his thighs for support. He was panting.

Ro sniffed, watching him and feeling the hairs on her arms bristle. Something was wrong. Hump was fit. He could run for miles without tiring. 'Why are you out of breath?'

He looked up at her and the apology she saw in his eyes was chilling. 'You have to come with me . . . It's Florence.'

Ro felt clutched by cold hands. 'What about her?' she asked, her voice small and hollow. It was Tuesday already. She had last seen Florence on Friday and she suddenly realized she'd forgotten to look in on Monday morning, too hung-over from the weekend's celebrations, too shocked by Ted's surprise girlfriend, to make the short detour.

'She's in the hospital.' He swallowed hard as though the words were rocks in his throat. 'In a coma.'

# Chapter Twenty-Two

Doris, the nurse behind the station, shook her head again. 'I'm sorry, but if you're not family, you can't go into ICU.'

'But . . .' Ro continued protesting. She was sure she could wear her down. Surely the fact that they'd endured the attack together counted for something? It had clearly meant something to *them*, to Florence. If they had been naturally warm with each other before, now they were bonded in a way that went beyond words or age difference or the few weeks they'd been acquainted.

Hump put his arm around her, pulling her away. 'Come on. It's no good, Ro.'

'But we can't just leave her alone!' she cried, rubbing her forearms distractedly. The skin tingled beneath her touch, still sensitive, still shocked by its sudden premature exposure to the world.

Doris arched one eyebrow as she recognized the signs of severe burns, and softened slightly. 'She isn't alone. Her family is with her.'

'Oh. They are?'

Doris nodded reluctantly.

'So there you go, then,' Hump soothed her. 'We can see her tomorrow. She's probably just in ICU overnight for observation and they'll move her to a general ward in the morning. Wouldn't you say, Doris?'

'I wouldn't say any such thing,' Doris replied, clearly not taking kindly to Hump speaking on her behalf.

'Thank you, Doris,' Hump smiled, refusing not to smile, refusing to be defeated by her stern demeanour. The smile would win out. It always did.

'He's a doctor, you know,' Ro said crossly. 'He knows what he's talking about,' she said, as Hump dragged her away from Doris's unbending gaze and led her slowly across the waiting area, Ro looking around her at the milling scene – some people sitting on the plastic leather chairs reading the paper, drinking coffee. One man was hunched forward, his head in his hands, his fingers tugging at the hair by his temples. Nurses were criss-crossing the waiting area with speedy efficiency, some carrying clipboards and files, their soft shoes squeaking on the floor.

She stopped, looking up at Hump with her doe eyes. 'How could this have happened, Hump? How could Florence be in here? I only saw her on Friday.'

Hump squeezed her shoulder. 'That's the thing about accidents – you're never ready for them to happen.'

'But we don't even know *what* happened yet.'

'I promise you we'll find someone who can tell us more.'

'Not if Doris has any say in—'

'The Humpster?'

They both turned. A young doctor was walking towards them, his chin tipped down but his eyes firmly on Hump and a devilish grin on his face.

'Peter!'

They shook hands, the doctor laughing quietly, aware that his white coat brought attention like a red flag. His hands gripped the stethoscope hanging round his neck. 'Are those your cars I've been seeing around? The name's too much of a coincidence. Plus the yellow.' He nodded towards Hump's signature yellow flip-flops.

'Kerching.' Hump grinned.

'Going well, then?' Peter asked.

'Going really well.' Hump nodded. 'Looking into rolling it out along the East Coast next summer.'

'Bet it's good being your own boss, huh?'

'Yeah.'

'Still, you must miss this?'

'Nope.' No hesitation. No delay.

'Well, we miss you, man.'

Hump shrugged lightly. 'You? Last I heard you were in Boston,' Hump said.

'Ortho rotation. Here till October.'

'Swerving summer in the city, huh?'

They both laughed, and Ro tried to imagine Hump in the white coat – with yellow flip-flops. He seemed so at home in this environment.

He remembered that she was standing there, with them, and rested a hand on her shoulder. 'By the way, this is my housemate Ro. Be careful – she's British.'

'Oh? Is it catching?' Peter grinned, shaking her hand briefly, his eyes too expertly, rapidly, assessing her arms.

She felt Hump's fingers squeeze her shoulder a little harder, as though he could tell that she felt more exposed and scrutinized here than in any other place since the attack. The police report may as well have been tattooed on her skin.

'It's nice to meet you, Ro. I hope for your sake Hump's table manners have improved since med school?'

She tried to think of a witty riposte, but her tongue felt leathery and leaden in her mouth, her mind solely on Florence, just metres from where she was standing. In a *coma*.

Peter looked from Ro back to Hump, recognizing shock in all its guises. 'Why are you in here? Not bad news, I hope?'

'A friend of ours has been brought in to ICU. Florence Wiseman.'

Peter grimaced. 'Oh yeah. The lady who was electrocuted, right?'

Ro felt herself sway as the word splashed over her, and Hump's hand clamped to her arm tightly, as though keeping her upright.

Hump leaned in to Peter, lowering his voice. 'Can you tell me anything? The nurses are sticking to protocol – we're not family, but she's a good friend and we're concerned. Ro's mind is going into overdrive.'

Peter looked around their group before lowering his own voice. 'Well, I'm not on that case, so I really shouldn't obviously, but . . . just don't take any of this as gospel. From what I heard, it happened in her pool house when she turned on the shower.'

'The shower . . .' Hump's voice sounded different, weak, and Ro watched his expression change, like a child looking to its parent for reassurance. 'But it shorted, right?'

'Well, yeah, but . . .' Peter's eyes flicked to Ro quickly and she sensed there were things neither of the doctors was saying out loud.

'What are her chances?' Hump's voice had almost flat-lined, as though he didn't want anyone, not even Ro – especially not Ro – to hear.

Peter angled his head, scratching his ear awkwardly. 'Just can't say yet. She's been unconscious since getting here. Her heart rhythms and blood pressure are all over the place, and we're monitoring a small haemorrhage in the brain. We'll know more in—'

'Twenty-four hours, yes, right . . . Jesus,' Hump muttered, glancing back at Ro. 'Anyone know how long she was under there for?'

'Long enough obviously. The electrics fused and the other person in the house went to investigate.'

'Who was that?' Ro frowned. 'She lives alone. She's widowed.'

Peter shrugged. 'I'm afraid I don't know the finer details. Like I said, she's not my patient.'

Hump nodded. 'Listen, can you text me if her condition worsens? Even if we still have to sit out here.'

Peter hesitated. 'Sure. OK. Same number?'

'Yep.'

'I'll write, "Bad weather forecast," OK? I need to be careful with patient confidentiality.'

'Of course.' Hump slapped his arm gratefully. 'Thanks, man. I owe you.'

'No worries. Let's grab a beer sometime.'

'On it.'

'You looked worried when he was talking,' Ro said nervously, as Hump caught her by the elbow and gently led her out of the waiting area.

He glanced down at her, taking in her pale complexion. 'She's lucky to have made it in here, Ro. She's not going to be out of ICU tomorrow.'

They walked in silence through an automatic door and

out into the car park, easily finding the canary-yellow, angular Humper amid the hundreds of round-shouldered silver coupés.

Hump opened the door and Ro climbed silently into the passenger seat. She had just clipped her seat belt and was turning off the radio – she couldn't bear to listen to anything – when she did a double take.

'What's he doing here?'

'Who?'

She pointed wordlessly to Ted Connor, who was walking towards the hospital entrance, a huge spray of flowers in his arms.

'He's obviously visiting someone.' Hump shrugged, starting up the engine.

Ro watched as the huge plate-glass doors closed behind Ted and he disappeared from sight. But not from mind.

It was three days before Florence was moved out of ICU, and Ro and Hump were standing in front of Doris again on the dot of two o'clock, the start of visiting hours.

They were led through to Florence's room with solemnity, Doris having warned them that they couldn't stay for more than five minutes.

'Don't agitate her, stress her or excite her in any way. Her heart rate is still erratic,' Doris said bossily.

'Of course not,' Ro replied. 'I just want to hold her hand.'

'No, don't hold her hand either.'

'Why not?'

Doris glanced at her like she was a defiant toddler. *Why not? Why not? Why not?* 'She's in here.'

They had stopped at a closed door, 'Florence Wiseman' written into the temporary door plate.

'You ready?' Hump asked, stalling her with a hand on her arm.

'Of course.' She frowned.

But she wasn't. She wasn't ready for the blackened skin on Florence's hands and forearms, for her yellow complexion or the number of tubes coming out of her. More than anything, though, she wasn't ready for Florence to be looking back at her through entirely red eyes that weren't so much bloodshot as blood-soaked.

Ro gasped, tears instantly falling from her eyes – she could never have envisaged this – and Hump squeezed her arm as they stood in the doorway.

'Be strong. For her sake. She won't have seen her reflection,' he whispered in her ear.

Ro nodded fractionally, feeling her resolve stiffen. Her reaction mustn't be allowed to frighten Florence further. She must be terrified enough.

'Hi.' She smiled, walking over and looking down at Florence's arm for somewhere to touch or squeeze in greeting, but there wasn't anywhere safe and she looked back up quickly. 'How are you feeling?' What a ridiculous question, she thought to herself, as the words came out. How would anyone feel after God knows how many volts had surfed through them?

It was hard to meet Florence's eyes; they were too graphic an indicator of the internal bleeding and bruising and haemorrhaging that had occurred as her body had been gripped in the electricity's warp.

Florence opened her mouth to reply. Slowly. Painfully. God, she was so weak. Suddenly, Doris's overbearing attitude was given perspective. Florence would never manage five minutes of conversation today.

Hump leaned forward fractionally. 'Don't try to speak too much, Florence. Keep resting. Is there anything we can get you?' His voice was as warm and comforting as a tumble-dried towel.

Florence shook her head lightly, her eyes meeting Hump's for politeness's sake only, constantly returning to Ro's.

'Is there anyone we can contact for you?' he asked.

She shook her head again. 'My family knows.' Her voice was tissue thin, almost transparent, and without any power behind it. 'What . . . happened?'

'Don't worry about that now.' Hump smiled. 'You just need to concentrate on getting better.'

Florence pinned her all-red eyes on Ro. 'No one will tell me. Worse *not* knowing.'

Ro looked up at Hump, distressed by the thought of Florence imagining the causes of her injuries – although *was* there anything worse than being electrocuted in your own shower?

Hump saw Ro waver and talked quickly. 'You had an accident in the shower, but it's all OK, Florence. They've established the cause – an earth wire had become detached, but everything's been fixed now. You can go home as soon as you're better.'

Florence looked back at Hump, expressionless, before she slid her red eyes over to Ro. What passed between them was wordless, but Ro understood. She had seen that expression before.

'Anyway, we'll leave you to rest and you'll be home before you know it. Close your eyes now and we'll come back tomorrow,' Hump said, taking charge yet again in his medical capacity.

But Florence's eyes didn't close; they never left Ro's as Hump gently steered her out of the room. Ro slumped against the wall, shaken by her friend's condition.

'She's still frightened, Hump. I'm not sure she wants to go back home, not yet anyway. I think we should tell the nurses to inform her family. They need to look into making alternative arrangements.'

Hump shook his head. 'No need. From the looks of her vitals on the screen, she's going to be in here for several weeks at least. And even if she was discharged, she wouldn't be allowed back to the house.'

Ro went very still, Hump's tone setting her on alert. 'Why not?'

He sighed, running his hands through his hair. 'I didn't want to tell you this, and we certainly can't let Florence know, but the house is a crime scene.'

'*What?* But you said in there it was an accident. You just said it.'

'Because I was hoping you wouldn't have to know. You've been through enough yourself recently.'

'Hump, tell me what you know,' she demanded crossly. 'You can't keep wrapping me up in cotton wool. I'm not a child.'

Hump looked back at her as though he didn't believe that, but he knew too well that he was going to have to tell her the truth.

'One of my drivers saw the yellow tape going up outside the house this morning. He spoke to the officer on duty.'

'About what? What's happened?'

'They traced the faulty earth wire to one on the pole, on the street outside the property. And it hadn't simply come loose, Ro. It had been cut.'

# Chapter Twenty-Three

'I'm coming home.'

'No.' Ro shook her head. 'Don't.'

'No?' Matt's blue eyes widened. 'You've been telling me for the past four months you wanted me to come back and now when I offer to get the first flight back, you say "no"? You can't stay there, Ro.'

'I can, Matt. I have to. I can't leave Florence – not while all this is still going on.'

'And what about what happened to you? Listen, I feel bad for what's happened to Florence, I do, but this isn't your problem. You've had enough going on without making her your responsibility too. She's got her own family to look after her. You've only known her a few weeks.'

Ro stared back at him down the screen, rankled by his certainty that her relationships here were temporary, flighty and meaningless: 'just passing through'.

'You don't understand. I care about what happens to her, Matt. What happened in the coffee shop – it's a sort of tie between us. I can't just scarper and leave her to it. I'm involved in this now whether I like it or not.'

'Ro, listen to yourself. You're not being rational. This is not the time for some noble sense of loyalty. The fact of the matter is, someone tried to hurt her. No! More than that. If they tampered with the electrics – well, don't you see? They're obviously prepared to *kill*, Ro.' She heard the tremor in his voice and watched as he began chewing on his cheeks, which he always did when stressed. 'No, I'm sorry. You can't stay there. I won't let you. Christ, it's bad enough you kept what happened to *you* a secret from me for two whole weeks, much less this.'

'I didn't keep it a secret,' she fibbed, remembering how she'd ignored his call on the sofa. 'I just couldn't get hold of you. It's not as simple as simply calling your number. Nine times out of ten when I ring, you never pick up. You're never there. And besides, the two things aren't related. What happened to me was just . . . just a freak thing. I got unlucky.'

Ro looked away from the screen. Outside the window, two pigeons were perched on the telephone line strung to the roof, their feathers lightly ruffling in the breeze. The sky behind them was streaked peach, the sun setting on yet another beautiful day. She had cycled to work after an early morning walk seed-bombing the dunes on Wiborg Beach on Florence's behalf – for some reason, she felt even more compelled to continue Florence's work while she was recovering – snaffled a yoga class with Melodie, had lunch with Hump and spent the afternoon in the grounds of a glorious estate on Further Lane photographing twin boys climbing up a giant fir tree as a surprise for their father's fortieth birthday. It had been glorious, idyllic, wonderful, even with the unexplained horrors lurking in the background. She was surprised to realize she actually didn't want to leave this and go home. Not yet, anyway.

'Hey, don't pretend I'm not here.' His tone cajoled her into looking back at him.

'But you're not, are you? I am. I'm the one here, living this, part of this. And the only reason for that is *because* you are all the way over there. You just shrugged off our life together like it was an old coat that made you too hot, so you don't get to boss me around or order me back. You've forfeited that right for the time being. Who says I have to live by your rules, anyway?' She looked at him, as though seeing him properly for the first time in the conversation. Until now she hadn't laid eyes on him in almost a month, and his appearance hadn't done anything to comfort her. He was indeed – and still – bald, and had grown a goatee too, something he'd omitted to mention on their last phone call.

It wasn't that it didn't suit him. It did. He had a beautifully shaped head, it was true, but his blue-shock eyes didn't seems so intense without his dark hair framing them, and the goatee hid the cleft that she loved so much. He looked lean, rangy and tanned, exuding a raw sexiness, but he didn't look like hers. Not *her* Matt – the Matt she had unwittingly styled for over a decade, picking out his pants and socks, buying his shirt-and-tie combos for work, approving his jeans . . . He had gone native. Free-range Matt. She could picture him now in beads and batiks, tie-dye and rags, recycled flip-flops and a hookah in his backpack.

'For God's sake, you've got to let this go, Ro,' he sighed impatiently, a dark spark of anger in his eyes. 'I haven't abandoned you or dumped you or left you. We've been over this, like, a million times. I explained my reasons to you. I am coming back, so just stop playing the victim card.'

'*Victim?*' Ro felt her anger flare. 'That's rich coming from the man who's camped along the Irrawaddy tracking sodding river dolphins! What would you know about any of what I've been through? I've been the victim of bigger and badder things than just you leaving.'

'Exactly! Which is why as soon as we hang up, I'm rebooking my flight, and I want you to do the same.'

Ro stared at him, able to feel every single one of the almost 9,000 miles that separated them. 'I said no!'

'Why? Why not?' he demanded, cross now.

'Because I'm not ready to leave yet. I like it here. I've got friends. Work is taking off finally.'

'You've got better friends at home, and work has already taken off back there. You've got customers who are waiting for you to come ba—'

'And!' she interrupted, losing her temper now. 'If you really want to know, I will not be responsible for you cutting short your dream trip, OK? Because what would it mean further down the line? When we're married with two kids, will you suddenly up and off again because you didn't get the chance to really get it all out of your system? I'm not taking that chance, Matt. We do this now. We get this bloody "pause" out of the way, and then we go back to our lives, the way they were.'

'What? You really think I'd do that? I'd just walk away from my own family?'

'You've done it once, Matt,' she said tightly. 'So let's just get this done once and for all.'

He watched her for a moment, as though finally hearing what she was saying, his eyes finding the new distrust in hers. 'You'd really rather stay there, even with all that shit going on?'

'That's right. Even with all that.'

They stared at each other's pixelated images on the flickering screen. 'Then I'll call you when I can,' he said finally.

'Fine.' Her heart was pounding triple time, her breathing shallow.

'Fine.' He had dropped his gaze from her and the top of his newly bald head was the last thing she saw of him before he disappeared from view again. The screen went black and Ro found herself alone in her room in her new life that didn't include him.

She jumped up and began pacing madly, her hands balling into anxious fists, her feet coming down so hard on the floorboards that she knew the small wooden ceiling light downstairs would be swaying slightly, disturbing Hump from his position on the sofa as he groaned that Big Foot was on the prowl.

Regret was already snapping at her heels like a nervy dog. Oh God, why had she said those things? It had been the opportunity she'd been waiting for since he'd left and she'd just thrown it back in his face, rejected it. Rejected *him*.

She dropped her head in her hands, confused by her own actions. She said she wanted one thing and yet inexplicably did another. She felt caught between two worlds, trying to keep one leg planted in each life, like a giant straddling continents. It should have been easier than this, just a light-hearted summer of weekends at the beach and driving on the right; but she hadn't counted on the sapling friendships that were springing up around her and steadily turning into oaks. Florence, Bobbi, Hump, Melodie . . . Each of them brought a new dimension to her life – spiritual wisdom, motherly advice, sibling rivalry and peace – and she knew it wasn't Matt's fault he didn't know that.

He heard only the headlines, not the behind-the-scenes stories. Yes, she'd been attacked, but if he only knew how tenderly Hump had put her back together again. And he wouldn't implore her to leave Florence if he knew how isolated she was already – he knew that she understood better than anyone what it was to be alone.

No. Ro straightened up, inhaling decisively. She was right to see this through. In less than two months, summer would be over and the contract fulfilled. Everyone would be gone from here, and she and Matt would be back together in their cottage in Barnes. That was the plan they had agreed upon and were working towards. They needed to stick to it, even if . . . even if it was *that life* that felt like the foreign concept now.

Ro sat on the bench, looking out to sea, her hair trying to blow in her face, but it wasn't quite long enough these days. Rubbing against her left shoulder was a small brass memorial plaque, given by the grateful family of one of the nursing home's former residents, and she shifted position slightly, feeling its corners catching against the thin cotton of her T-shirt. She noticed there were quite a few benches like this one in the gardens – everyone, it seemed, wanting a rest or a view. Or to be remembered.

She watched as, overhead, the precious piping plovers that seemed to be so famous in these parts wheeled on the thermal currents, gliding and swooping with a freedom she found dizzying. They made it look fun, even to her, and freedom had never been something to celebrate in her book. It was the dark undertow she was constantly fighting. Sometimes she felt like her entire life was a battle to

345

belong to someone. Was it really too much to ask for the quiet happiness of someone to love and to love her back?

Her thoughts drifted to Matt, as ever. They hadn't spoken since the fight, six days ago, but she, for once, wasn't hovering by the phone. She hadn't changed her mind about leaving here. In fact, she was more convinced than ever that it was the right thing to do. It had been a revelation to realize that as much as she missed him, she didn't need him – at least, not in the way that she used to. Just over four months ago, he'd been her oxygen, the engine that powered her heart, and she couldn't function without him. But he'd left her alone, left her to fend for herself while he went off chasing dreams, and to her surprise as much as his, she wasn't sinking.

She looked at the birds again. It did look fun up there, flying.

A sudden shriek – a joyous, playful sound – made her turn and she saw Florence just inside the building, sitting in a wheelchair, watching two little boys fist-pumping the air like they'd won the Superbowl. They ran out into the garden together, away from where she was sitting, holding what looked like a piece of paper between their hands. A young woman – their mother presumably – was crouched down beside the chair, her hands resting gently on Florence's, eyes locked on her face. She was talking intently to her and Ro took in the similarities of their profiles: small, deep-set eyes, rosy complexions and high foreheads, with hair that naturally swept back, as though a lifetime of Alice band-wearing had conditioned it to grow in that direction. Ro thought she'd seen her before. But where?

Florence appeared to say something, and it made the woman – her daughter surely? – laugh, the sound as sudden and arresting as the childlike noise that her sons had made moments earlier, piercing the thick skin of convalescing silence that blanketed the nursing home like an anaesthetic. But then something changed and the young woman had her hands cupped over her face; her shoulders were shaking in small hiccups. She wasn't laughing after all – she was crying. Ro watched Florence's hand lift slowly – the effort clear even at this distance of fifty metres – and she began slowly stroking her daughter's fine, blonde hair, the woman shaking her head all the while, seemingly embarrassed by the strength of her emotions but unable to stop them.

Ro looked away, feeling intrusive, and watched the boys instead. She was pretty sure they were twins – same height, same build – but one of them had a shock of orange hair, the other blond. Ro guessed they were around six or seven. They were standing close together, heads almost touching, one hand linked. She peered closer – were they thumb-wrestling? Both seemed oblivious to their mother's tears, their grandmother's infirmity.

By the time she turned back, the woman was standing, wiping her hands lightly on her khaki shorts, her face flushed but nothing more telling than that about the storm that had just raged through her.

Then, suddenly, they were looking over at Ro, and Ro felt herself blush, embarrassed to have been caught intruding on their private moment. Should she turn away? Stand up and walk over?

The decision wasn't hers to make. In the next instant, Florence was being wheeled through the doors and along the smooth path to where Ro was sitting, pretending to enjoy the view.

'Ro.'

The weak voice could barely be heard above the breeze and Ro didn't pretend, for pride's sake, that she hadn't heard.

She jumped up from the bench. 'I'm so sorry. I didn't mean to interrupt. I can always come back another time if—'

The woman stepped forward. 'Not at all. It's a pleasure to meet you at last. I'm Casey.'

Her voice was softer than Ro had anticipated. She looked just like one of the yoga bunnies from Bobbi's class, with tight skin and stealth-wealth style, but she had Florence's warm, expressive grey eyes and a welcoming smile.

'Ro. Hi,' she replied, lightly shaking her hand.

'Mom told me what happened to you too. I'm so sorry. Are you OK now?'

'Absolutely. It was nothing really,' Ro said, not wanting any sympathy distracted from Florence's plight, before realizing she was rubbing her arms and forcing herself to stop.

'It was not nothing,' Florence said, and the fragility of her voice made Ro look down in alarm, all manners forgotten. She took in the sight of her, up close now, cushions plumped all around her like airbags, a blanket covering her legs.

'Are you out of the wind, Mom?' Casey asked, positioning Florence's chair to a different angle.

Florence nodded, not wasting her strength unnecessarily.

'Well, then I'll leave you both to talk.' Casey looked at Ro. 'She's been very anxious to see you. I'm sorry we've hogged all the visiting slots up to now.'

'You're her daughter,' Ro smiled. 'Frankly, I'd have been alarmed if you hadn't.'

Casey called the boys over, introducing them quickly as Freddie and Jude, before restraining them from throwing their arms around their grandmother's neck. 'Remember, you need to be gentle with Grandma now.'

Ro waited for them to walk away before she sat down. She felt suddenly nervous.

'Well, it's official. I'm now old,' Florence half-whispered, pointedly smoothing the blankets on her legs. Her voice may be weak, but her spirit clearly wasn't. Ro leaned forward, lightly touching Florence's shoulder, too scared still to touch her hands, forearms or face. Her eyes were clear grey again – thank God – and her complexion all but free of the liverish pallor. 'Not old. Temporarily below par.'

Florence smiled at the vast understatement.

'Are they looking after you properly?' It seemed to Ro that Florence had lost more weight.

'Well, the cook clearly thinks everything tastes better when it's covered in vinegar.'

'Oh dear.'

Florence glanced back at her. 'No, I'm not complaining. I know I'm lucky to be here.'

Ro kept quiet. Florence had no idea *how* lucky. She had to assume her family were protecting her from the truth of what had happened. 'The posters are up, by the way. I saw one by the cinema earlier. They look really good.'

'Thanks to you.'

'*You*, you mean. Your idea.'

'Your concept.' Florence smiled weakly.

'Team effort, then.'

'Team effort.'

They fell silent again, Ro's brain overloaded from feeling like she was going to trip over the ugly truth that had to stay hidden. She looked over and smiled as the silence lengthened, and was surprised to find Florence already watching her.

'How much longer must I stay here?' Florence asked.

Ro swallowed. Her inability to lie was almost spectacular to watch. 'Until the doctors are satisfied your s-skin is healing properly and there's no risk of infection. Septicaemia could be a risk if that happened,' she said quickly.

Florence blinked patiently. 'The real reason, Ro.'

Ro hesitated, staring down at her own hands, trying to hide the lies in her eyes. 'Florence, it's really not for me to—'

'I may look frail, but I know what's happening. You know I know. I tried to tell you, that day in the kitchen.' She paused until Ro looked back up at her. 'I always knew *you* were never the intended target. And this was no accident either.'

Ro frowned, shifting in her seat slightly. 'You mean . . . you're saying you think the two events are linked?'

Florence nodded slowly.

'But why, Florence? What proof is there that what happened in the Pear wasn't a random attack? Why should the two things be related?'

Florence sighed, a deep, heavy sound that echoed through her shrunken body. 'Because there had been other things before. Warnings, I suppose.'

Ro felt her temperature drop. 'What?'

Florence was quiet for such a long time, Ro wondered whether she was even going to answer. 'They started off as sweeteners, inducements – offers for first-class flights anywhere I wanted to go, jewellery, donations to my charities in my name, that kind of thing . . .' Her eyes narrowed in concentration. 'I think you were there when the necklace arrived, were you not?'

Ro nodded. 'Yes, the pearl necklace from Tiffany. I saw your expression change when you read the note.'

Florence gave a tiny snort of contempt. 'Yes, well . . . I stuck to my guns and sent it back. I refused to budge, and that's when things grew uglier: I received dog excrement in the mail—'

Ro gasped in disgust. 'But you never said!'

Florence blinked slowly. 'And why would I have done? Would it have made it any less terrible burdening you with it?'

Ro looked away; she knew the real reason why Florence hadn't told her – Ro hadn't believed her when she had tried to bring it up. She realized now what she had seen in Florence's eyes that day in the kitchen – disappointment. 'What other things were there?' she asked quietly, ashamed that she had effectively turned her back.

Florence watched her for a moment, as though reading her like a book. 'They were clever – making sure they left no trace, changing it up. A few silent phone calls, and I'm pretty sure that for a few weeks someone was watching the house – I could see on the CCTV by the gates, the same car, always parked just forward enough that I couldn't see the plates or the driver. By the time I'd opened the gates they'd be gone. Then there were other things that were more nuisance than anything – my appointments would be changed without my knowledge, making me look disorganized and incompetent in front of my colleagues; not to mention the missing money from accounts that only I can authorize. I'd come in from being out and find the alarm off, even though I knew I'd set it. I'm not senile, Ro. I'm sixty-two, not ninety-two.'

'I know, I know.'

'But they were trying to confuse me. Making me think I couldn't live on my own anymore, that I wasn't responsible, wasn't safe. Trying to force me out.'

'Who's "they"?'

'The people who want the house.'

Ro blinked at her, not understanding, desperate to keep up. 'Your house?'

'Yes. The house next door is empty, has been for a few years. It was up for sale for a long time and the realtor did quite a lot of work to it, trying to upgrade it to match the rest of the street. Then, finally, quite suddenly, it was sold just before Christmas – and that was when everything became unpleasant.'

'So you think the people in that house want you out of yours – what, for the land?'

Florence shook her head. 'For the drive. My driveway runs along the bottom of their backyard, meaning they don't have beach access. Historically, their lot was part of my property, but it was sold off years ago – probably a previous owner needed the money. I offered to cut down the hedges to improve their ocean view, but . . .'

'The house is worth more with direct beach frontage.'

'About five million dollars more.'

Ro's mouth dropped open into a silent 'O'. 'But, Florence . . .' she puffed, trying to make sense of everything she was hearing. 'You nearly *died*! You were very nearly killed! Surely they wouldn't go to those lengths just for five million.'

'An *extra* five million. The house itself is already worth twenty-five million dollars.'

'Even so. I know it's a lot of money, but surely—'

'People have killed for a lot less.'

There was a pause.

'Well, have you met the people next door? Had any face-to-face contact? I mean, who the hell are they?'

'The house is still empty. It's been bought by a company, not a family.'

Ro frowned so hard she thought she could feel her eyebrows touch. 'So then you have to tell the police.'

'I tried. They think I'm a paranoid, confused old woman. When I told them I had been the intended target at the cafe, one of them even suggested I was just looking for attention.'

'Because the coffee hit me and not you?'

'Yes.'

Ro felt her annoyance grow. 'But what about the bribes? Surely they had to take account of those?'

'As they told me – very patiently and like I was deaf – there's no law against sending someone a necklace. And stupidly I didn't think to keep the gift from the dog.' The corners of her mouth turned up fractionally. 'Besides, I didn't keep the necklace – I sent it back. There's no proof now I even received it, much less that it was a bribe.'

'Then *I'll* tell them. I was a witness. I was with you when it came.'

'I appreciate it, Ro, but I can assure you it'll be falling on deaf ears. They're not interested. As far as they're concerned, what happened to you had nothing to do with what happened to me.'

Her hands gripped each other tightly and Ro watched the blue veins bulge slowly.

'What else do you know about the company that's bought next door?'

Florence sighed, looking exhausted, and Ro worried that this was too much for her, that she was pushing too hard. 'Only that it's called SB Holdings Ltd. They're registered offshore in Bermuda and therefore untraceable. There's no way of finding out the people involved behind that name.'

Ro slumped, prickles of fear running up her back. If this nameless, faceless organization wanted Florence out, they had already proved they had the resources, contacts and appetite to keep going until they achieved their aim. The man on the boardwalk suddenly came back into her mind as it occurred to her: had he been the one to cut the wire to the pool house? And how many others were there out there like him? 'So then what are you going to do? You can't go back to the house if these people are invisible and remain at large. They're dangerous, Florence.'

'I know. Ted wants me to sell.'

'Ted?' Ro's voice rose an octave. 'Ted Connor?'

'You remember, he—'

'Yes, yes, I know Ted. But why would *he* be advising you to sell your home?' she asked in alarm, wondering why he was becoming so closely involved not only with Florence's well-being but also, now, her financial interests. If Ted was positioning himself in Florence's life to the degree that he could dictate the disposal of her (very considerable assets), what else was he persuading her to do?

Florence seemed to read the suspicions clouding her face. 'He has my best interests at heart, Ro. If it wasn't for him finding me in the shower and calling for help, I wouldn't even be sitting here now.'

The alarm bell began clanging even more loudly, as she remembered seeing him walking into the hospital the day of Florence's accident. He seemed to be around her almost all the time. 'So Ted was with you when the . . . the accident happened?' She did her best to keep her voice and face neutral, but she felt a growing unease in the pit of her stomach.

'He was in the main house. He saved my life, Ro.'

Ro nodded but didn't reply. Ted had been – at a safe distance – in the house when Florence had been electrocuted, just as he'd been – at a safe distance – in the cafe when Ro had been scalded. Was that just coincidence? Or something more?

She looked back at Florence with a vague smile. 'Listen, don't rush into any decisions just yet. You're safe here and the police will be running their own lines of enquiry. Remember, they've got access to resources you don't. You never know, they could have it all wrapped up by the time you come out.'

'I know you don't think that.'

Ro smiled, busted. 'No. But at the very least the people doing this may be frightened off now that the police are involved. Then you wouldn't have to sell.'

A silent tear crept down Florence's face. 'I don't want to do it, but people are at risk. Not just me.' She looked back at her. 'You've been hurt already. And Ted said . . . he said, what if next time it was my grandchildren?'

Ro sat back, frightened by the thought of young children becoming entangled in this nightmare, but even more shocked that Ted Connor was prepared to use Florence's own grandchildren to manipulate her emotionally like that.

'Do you see? I can't take the risk. I can't,' Florence quaked, shaking her head, her discoloured hands gripping the armrests of the chair.

Ro nodded. 'I understand. I do,' she said quietly, one hand resting gently on Florence's arm, almost hovering above it. And she did. She knew Florence doted on her grandchildren; she wouldn't take any risks where they were concerned. She remembered that morning by the pool when she'd spoken about her happy family life in the house and the legacy she'd wanted it to leave for her grandchildren in turn.

But someone was trying to stop her, someone Florence thought was hiding behind a paper trail. It didn't seem to occur to her that there was one person who was linked to everything that had happened so far, who seemed far too good to be true. But he had a face and he had a name, and Florence wasn't the only one who knew it.

# Chapter Twenty-Four

'Do you think I should say anything? To the police, I mean?' Ro asked, shadowing Melodie round the studio as she lit the oil burners.

Melodie looked back at Ro, who was wringing her still-pink hands. 'It's a tough call, Ro. I mean, do you *really* think this guy would be capable of something like that? You're talking attempted murder. That's as serious as it gets. He didn't look like a murderer to me.'

'No? What does a murderer look like?'

Melodie smiled, amused. 'Touché.'

'Oh God.' Ro grimaced, as though she was actually in pain. 'I know it sounds so ridiculous when I say it out loud. Most of the time he's tender and caring and really funny—' She clocked Melodie's arched eyebrow. 'I'm referring to his behaviour on the home videos!'

'Oh.' Melodie continued round to the next window. 'Well, for what it's worth, he didn't strike me as the aggressive type, that day he turned up here. You were the one I heard shouting, not him.'

'Yes, but you see, you wouldn't say that if you'd seen him on the beach on my first day. He was livid, properly out-of-control furious then. When I think of him like that, I think maybe he *could* be capable of violence. And no matter what I may think about him, when you get down to the nuts and bolts of who, what and where, he is always there, always involved, right at the heart of it.' She thought about Florence's condition when she'd visited her in ICU in the hospital – discoloured, fried, shrivelled. If someone was responsible for it, they had to be held to account. 'I mean, that's just too much of a coincidence, isn't it?'

'I suppose it is a little weird. But still ... *attempted murder*?' Melodie shook her head, leading them both back to the mats. 'All I can say is that if you're going to go to the police with your suspicions, you need to be certain. If he gets wind of what you're accusing him of, you could find yourself on the wrong side of a slander case. You have to be absolutely sure before you go down that path.'

Moments from the home films flashed through Ro's mind: Ted sleeping beside Ella after reading her bedtime story, the look on his face (visible only from the reflection in the mirror) as he'd shown Marina into the white roses-bedecked dining room at their apartment the night of their seventh wedding anniversary, the attempt he'd made at being 'artistic' filming Marina and Ella's shadows in profile on the ground as they walked through Central Park – Marina's pregnant silhouette caught by the wind, Ella's arm upstretched, their hands clasped . . .

She sat down in a cross-legged pose and sighed heavily, confused and anxious. She just couldn't get a handle on him. What she saw in the videos – a devoted husband and father – wasn't what she saw in real life: single man with a trophy girlfriend and a dangerous temper.

'I just don't know what to do,' Ro moaned, holding her feet together and jigging her thighs up and down, more in agitation than relaxation.

'Then I'd suggest you hold fire. Keep a close eye on him by all means, but you've got to remember there are plenty of other people who have a grudge against Florence . . . Namaste,' Melodie smiled, nodding to some regulars who were padding barefoot through the door now.

'What? Like who? Why?' Ro whispered.

Melodie looked surprised by Ro's question. 'Well, I don't think I'm revealing any secrets in saying that Florence has made many enemies over the years. She heads up the Town Board; she's sat on numerous citizens' committees . . . She's directly helped to shape and enforce a lot of our local laws, and many people resent her for it.'

'Such as?' Ro pressed, wanting names, identities, flesh-and-blood people that could be held to account.

Melodie shrugged. 'Such as . . .' She thought for a second. 'Well, Brook said there was a heated argument at the Zoning Appeals Board just the other week. A couple over in Gardiner's Bay applied to build a bulkhead to protect their property – as I understand it, they actually *have* water on the land now, but their plans were rejected because town policy is strategic retreat. So their home will effectively be washed away in the next northeaster.'

'That's dreadful.'

'Yes and no. They knew town policy when they bought the property a few years ago. Apparently, there's another abandoned house, on stilts, actually ten feet out from the shore now, so none of this can be a surprise to them.'

'But what would that have to do with Florence?'

'Because she chaired the LWRP that brought in strategic retreat and now she's the head honcho on the Town Board, enforcing her own recommendations in the report. She's the town figurehead; it's her name on the rejection documents. To a lot of people, she's public enemy number one.'

'Making her an easy target,' Ro murmured, remembering how she and Florence had been examining the Legacy poster – her latest campaign initiative – when the first attack had happened. Ro fell silent. It seemed hard to reconcile this impression of a divisive public figure with her passionate, articulate friend who applied herself selflessly to her town and family. 'And does everyone know all this about her?'

'Well, it's not a secret, although I suppose I'm privy to more than most because of Brook being on the Coastal Erosion Committee in Montauk. He's always butting heads with her over something. He loses a lot of sleep thanks to her.'

There was a bitter edge to her words and Ro remembered the fractious note in Melodie's voice the night of the dinner party when Florence's name had come up.

'Look, I know she's your friend and . . .' Melodie reached for the right words. 'Just because she and Brook don't see eye to eye, it doesn't mean I don't see the goodwill behind her intentions. But she's a seasoned politician, Ro. She knows how to win votes and influence people.'

Ro frowned. 'What are you saying?'

'I'm saying that you shouldn't rush to get too close to her, that's all. Things may not be what they appear with her. Florence's track record has been . . . erratic lately. She's never far from a scandal, it seems.'

'So you're saying you think what happened to her is her fault? That she somehow asked for all this?' The anger made Ro's voice quiver and Melodie shrank back a little, her eyes flitting to the other class members stretching on their mats or meditating.

'No. I . . . I'm obviously not explaining myself very well. I just mean you're in a vulnerable place right now, Ro. You're trying to set down roots and find your way. I can see how Florence could be an attractive . . . mother figure to you, perhaps. It's understandable. But she's not a dear, sweet thing, and you'd be foolish to place all your trust in her without knowing her better.'

Ro and Melodie exchanged loaded looks. This was their first disagreement and Ro felt distinctly patronized.

A man in 1970s green running shorts that curved up to his hip bones and were going to be alarming during the child pose sat down on the mat next to her.

Melodie quickly changed the subject as the last stragglers padded into the room and mats were unfurled around them.

'Is Bobbi going to come to any more classes?' Melodie asked, new levity in her voice as she pressed each ear towards her neck in a stretch. 'She's very limber.'

'I doubt it,' Ro muttered. 'She just had some time to kill before an important meeting.' Ro knew she sounded truculent, but she couldn't help it. How had they moved from debating whether to report Ted Connor to the police to a character assassination on Florence?

'I hope it went well?'

'Yeah, she got the commission.'

'And the guy?'

Ro met her eyes in surprise.

Melodie smiled, trying to tease her out of her sulk. 'What? I overheard you both talking. You weren't very quiet.'

'Oh. Sorry.'

'On the contrary, tell me more.' Melodie pinned her with beseeching eyes, trying to make up.

She shrugged, a little less moody. 'I really don't know much. I haven't met him yet – she's been very cagey about him. All I know so far is that he's older and drives a Porsche.'

'Sounds perfect,' Melodie quipped light-heartedly.

Ro budged. 'That's what *I* said – although he's a bit pigeon-toed apparently. But Bobbi's prepared to forgive him that because he's also a non-exec. Her *first*.'

Melodie frowned and Ro rolled her eyes. 'I know – her ambition is boundless, but it's impossible to hate her for it. She's actually very sweet when you get to know her, a pussycat really,' Ro protested, before mumbling, 'just with very sharp claws.'

'Uh-huh.' Melodie nodded, but her eagerness to bond had slipped a little now, and Ro knew she profoundly disapproved. As if her opinion of Bobbi hadn't been low enough after sitting through an evening of watching her flirting with her husband . . .

'Hey, it's really not her fault. She's never been in love. Until that happens, she chooses her boyfriends according to spec.'

Melodie had to grin. 'Ro, you are loyal to a fault. You see the best in everyone, even when they don't deserve it. She's lucky to have you as a friend.' Melodie stretched her legs in front of her. 'We all are.'

She winked at Ro – peace seemingly restored – and a small, flattered smile sat on Ro's lips like a kiss as Melodie began leading the class in the warm-up incantations. Ro chanted in unison, determined to relax and find a little peace. This was her safe place, a refuge from the pressures pushing in on her in the outside world. But when she closed her eyes, it wasn't Matt she found drifting through her subconscious.

Ro trailed in Bobbi's wake, racks of clothes fluttering like flowers in the wind as her hand trailed over them, her keen eye trained for the print, colour, fabric or shape that would transform her from 'date' to 'hot date'.

Ro didn't touch anything. Ironically, in spite of the fact that she was working almost round the clock and nearly at the point of having to turn work away, she was still broke after her splurge in New York. Obviously, with Florence in such a weakened state, the last thing she was going to do was hand in her invoice for the Legacy job, and she had had to wait till the newlyweds had returned from honeymoon only two weeks ago before she could even present them with their images for the first edit, much less a bill. She had a small payment due imminently for the surprise fortieth shoot, but that was it so far. The Connor job was huge, of course, and dominating her working days, but she was still only a third of the way through it, having completed the film run-throughs and annotations, and was now editing and splicing them. Next up were the photobooks, which would involve going through all their stills (she dreaded to think how many tens of thousands there might be), and then finally, she had to set up the shoot of the children – once Finn's hair was suitably photogenic. She wouldn't see any money before September, at the earliest. If, indeed, she ever would. Her suspicions about Ted's actions around Florence persisted, no matter how she tried to arrange the facts – there was just too much coincidence involved – and she found it almost perverse to be editing a film that showed him as the perfect family man. Irony in motion.

Something waggled in front of her line of vision, drawing her out of her head. Bobbi was holding up a dress for her opinion – black, skater-style, sort of knitted, with little peekaboo holes in rows along the bust, waist, hips and down the skirt.

Ro frowned.

'It's lined, you prude!' Bobbi chuckled, showing her the inside of the dress.

'Oh. Well, in that case, be my guest.'

'Aren't you going to try anything on?' Bobbi asked, as she marched towards the dressing room.

Ro absently picked up the price tag of a folded T-shirt: $330! 'Nope. Don't have that kind of money. Don't have that kind of life.' She wandered over to where Bobbi was changing, sat down on a leather chair and waited.

'So, is this for anywhere in particular?'

Silence emanated from behind the curtain.

'Bobbi?'

Bobbi poked her head through, her hands clutching the fabric below her chin. 'It's for Kevin.'

'Kevin?' A name! She had a name – and it wasn't Brook's! She tried not to appear elated. 'He's the older man, is he?'

'Uh-huh. But don't tell a *soul*.'

'Of course not,' Ro agreed solemnly. 'So then, the pitch at dinner went . . . well?'

'It did go . . . well.' Bobbi grinned, winking and disappearing into the changing room again.

'I thought you seemed perky!' Ro was quiet for a moment, slightly depressed that even Bobbi – who by her own confession was concentrating on her 'conversion' to partner – was getting some action while her enforced chastity soldiered on. 'And nobody at work suspects anything?'

'Why should they? We know how to be professional about it. Kevin doesn't want it getting out any more than I do.'

'Right.' Ro hoped that wasn't code for 'married with kids'. She inspected her fingernails. Grubby, broken, unmanicured. Over two months in the Hamptons and what had she learned? 'So are we going to get to meet him? Are you going to bring him to the house for Hump and me to inspect?'

'What are you, my parents?' she laughed. 'You've got to be kidding me! He'd run a mile if he met you guys.'

'Hey!' Ro protested, just as the curtain whisked back and Bobbi stepped out like a Lipizzaner – all high steps and dainty ankles. 'Oh wow!' Ro laughed, her hands flying to her mouth in amazement. 'That looks incredible on you.'

'You like?' Bobbi asked, turning to admire her reflection in the mirror behind her.

'Like? I love! You've got to get it. Got to!'

Bobbi pouted thoughtfully, jamming her hands onto her tiny waist. 'It's kind of expensive.'

'Whatever it is, it's worth it. Get it,' Ro said, waving her hands dismissively.

Bobbi hitched up an eyebrow. 'Like eighteen hundred dollars expensive.'

'Shut the front door!' Ro burst out, using Hump's favourite phrase, something that had started to become a habit of late. Wasn't that the same as a wedding dress?

Bobbi preened, swishing the skirts left to right, showing off her tight thighs, her arms lean and sculpted. She looked stunning, but then, with her figure, she'd look knockout in an $18 dress too.

'Yeah. He's worth it,' she decided, nodding her head firmly and sashaying back into the changing room.

'Blimey. You must really like him.'

'I do.'

'I mean, really, really, really like him.'

'I told you he's a non-exec, right?'

'Bobbi!'

Bobbi's head stuck through the curtain again. 'What? Listen, don't get all preachy on me, Miss Childhood Sweetheart. No guy gets to pull a number on me. *My* terms. Sentiment gets you nowhere. Jack shit.'

Ro shook her head, wondering how it was they managed to share a conversation, much less a house.

They walked up to the till together, Bobbi holding out the dress like it was an offering to the gods. Ro tried to read the label, but couldn't pronounce it.

'How d'you even say that?' she asked.

'Azz-ed-ine A-lai-a.'

But Ro still couldn't get it. 'I'll stick to Gap. It's more A-B-C.'

'Anything so long as you're not in Matt's clothes.' Bobbi rolled her eyes. 'You have *no* idea how much it stressed me out looking at you swaddled and swamped in your boyfriend's stuff. It was like some sad, desperate, "abandoned ex" look. I mean, I say that with love, right? You know, you look pretty hot now. You got a tan, dropped some weight—'

'Cut out the animals nesting in my hair.'

Bobbi chuckled, then winced as she handed over her credit card. 'Oh Jeez, I must be mad – it'll be noodles for me for the next month.'

'Like you said, he's worth it. But I've got to meet him. You're spending nearly two grand on looking nice for him! I mean, come on!'

'OK, maybe. But just you. Hump'll go into his thumb-wrestling, shoulder-bumping, surf-dude mode and Kevin's not like that. He's fifty-one, for Chrissakes. He wears cuff-links!'

'Enough said. It can be our secret.'

'Well, it's only fair we have one. I reckon Hump's keeping one from us,' Bobbi said confidingly, taking her receipt and the tissue-wrapped dress.

'Why do you say that?' Ro frowned as they sauntered out of the boutique together, back into the sunshine. They stopped on the pavement, their mission accomplished and wondering where to go next.

'Coffee at Colette's?' Bobbi asked rhetorically, looping her arm through Ro's and leading her towards the turquoise-umbrella-ed cafe on the opposite side of the road. 'Because I was in the kitchen when he came in this morning and I asked him where he'd been.'

'And?'

'He said he'd been kayaking.'

'Well, yeah, I go with him sometimes. He goes most days.'

'Maybe he *used* to.'

Ro turned to look at Bobbi, who was wearing a mysterious smile on her face. 'What are you getting at? Just spit it out.'

'I saw his kayak propped against the shed in the back-yard, where he always keeps it.'

'*So?*' Ro cried, laughing at Bobbi's long-winded tease.

'So, I saw it when I filled the kettle when I first came

down – at least forty minutes before he came in.' She looked across at Ro meaningfully. 'He was out, but he wasn't kayaking. I think he's got himself a girlfriend and he doesn't want us to know.'

'Ha! That's it? Listen, Bobbi, Hump *always* has someone on the go. You've got no idea what he's like during the week. It's a new girl at breakfast three days of the week.'

Bobbi clamped Ro's arm closer in to her. 'Yeah, so why keep it a secret, then?'

'Same reason as you?'

'He's self-employed! He doesn't have any bosses to hide it from,' Bobbi shrieked excitedly as they crossed the wide road, trucks stopping to let them pass. 'Nope, he lied for a reason, Ro. And I, for one, am going to find out why.'

Greg was lying out in the garden when they got back, muscles gleaming like each one had been individually polished. Both Ro and Bobbi stopped talking and walking at the sight of him.

'Hey!' he said, shading his eyes from the glare of the sun. 'Where have you been? Hump wanted to try to put a four together for tennis. Now that we have a champion in the house –' he grinned, displaying his perfect teeth '– we thought we could show off at the Maidstone.'

'They have courts there?' Ro asked, walking out onto the veranda. Bobbi followed at a distance.

'Grass. Perfect for *your* game.'

Greg's eyes tracked Bobbi in the shadows. 'Get anything nice?' he asked, clocking the expensive boutique bags.

'Not really.'

'Not really?' Ro laughed in disbelief. 'She just spent nearly two grand on *one* dress!'

Greg's eyes stayed on Bobbi, but his expression was cooler. 'It must be an important event.'

'It is.'

'Care to share?'

'Nope.'

Greg looked back at Ro and gave a small half-shrug. Whatever. 'Thirsty, Ro?' Greg asked, leaning down and pulling a Coke from the blue cold box beside his lounger.

Ro turned, just in time to see Bobbi storming through the back door, bags bustling about her knees like balloons.

What could she do? She'd already taken on Melodie on her behalf, but she couldn't fight all Bobbi's battles for her, and no one could say she hadn't provoked Greg into this eventual retaliation.

He handed her the drink as she clambered onto the squeaky sunbed beside him and she picked up the well-thumbed copy of *Dan's Papers*, the local newspaper. It had a colour-magazine cover, and Hump's adverts were always prominently displayed on the inside front page. She began rifling through it noisily.

'So, what are you up to tonight?' she asked, scrutinizing the pretty girl in this ad. Ro was pretty sure they'd break-fasted together at some point. Laura? Lauren? Lowri?

'It's a big one, actually. I shouldn't really be here. I ought to be helping out, but . . .' He tipped his head back, angling his face to the sun for a moment. 'Man, it feels so good just to stop for a moment, you know? Things are going to get crazy later and I really need to take a bit of time out and just get my head straight . . .'

'Uh-huh.' She flicked towards the back to the 'House & Home' section, where she'd paid for her Marmalade Media advert to be positioned between a custom closet company and . . . a rentable mechanical rodeo bull? She was sure they'd said it was an ad for an annual radio ball. She shrugged. There *might* be an overlap in their customer base . . .

'. . . I hope you'll join us. I'm sorry it's such short notice now. I don't know what happened to your invitations. I wrote them myself, but Erin's just had so much to oversee, as you can imagine. They must have been put down somewhere and—'

Ro squinted, paying more attention to what Greg was saying again. 'Sorry? What invitations?'

'For the charity cocktail party we're throwing in Southampton tonight. Didn't Hump tell you about it?'

'I haven't seen him yet today.' He'd been too busy sneaking into the house, keeping secrets if Bobbi's hunch was right.

'Oh. Well, can you make it? It's for a good cause, and I'd like you to really meet my friends properly.'

'It sounds . . .' She wanted to say 'lovely', but after the fiasco at the Gilded Heights – Hump's affectionate nickname for Wes Turner's place – tennis competition the other week, she wasn't sure anything 'big money' was her bag.

'It's not going to be like the Wes Turner gala, if that's what you're worried about,' he said. Thanks to Hump convincing his printer mate to run up a banner printed with 'Ro *hearts* Wes' and tying it to the stair banister, she hadn't been allowed to forget that particular weekend. 'In fact, it couldn't be further from that. Tonight will be much more . . . subtle. And Hump's coming.'

'Are you going to ask Bobbi?'

He seemed to freeze a little before he looked away, back to his paper. 'She's already out, right? The dress?'

'Well, yes, but . . . it might be nice to invite her anyway.'

Greg raised a sceptical eyebrow. 'We both know she'd rather eat wasps than say yes.'

Ro's mouth flapped as she tried to find a silver lining. 'She'll come round eventually.'

He shook his head. 'It's the end of July and we only have another six weekends here all together. I'm not going to hold my breath. I think it's fair to say that friendship has sailed.'

'That is terrible!' she groaned, as he chuckled beside her. 'Wow, have we really only got six weekends left, though?' When she'd arrived, time seemed to have dragged, every day feeling like a week, the days long and empty, but now she was rushed off her feet and falling into bed at night like she'd been clubbed. Sometimes she didn't even try to Skype Matt. How could time be so elastic, snapping away from her just as she was finding her rhythm?

'I know,' Greg nodded. 'And I feel like I'm only just getting to know *you*. How are you doing, by the way? You know, since the—' His eyes flickered down to her arms.

There was nothing to see now. Her skin had returned to its usual unexfoliated pink and, guiltily, she was sleeping better since Florence's revelations that the attack had been intended for her. It had abated her fear of crowds, at least, although of course now her mind was still worked up with conspiracy theories of one sort and another.

'Fine, thanks. The sensitivity's really settled down. Although I think Hump's missing bossing me about.'

'Yeah,' Greg chuckled.

She looked across at him, squinting into the sunlight so that she had to raise her hand to her eyes. 'You know, I still

KAREN SWAN

can't understand why he jacked in being a doctor. I mean, he's good at the whole entrepreneur thing, I can see that – he's got that buzzy energy and so many off-the-wall ideas. And any job that allows him to wear flip-flops day in, day out, *of course* he's going to go for it. But I don't know . . .' she sighed. 'It just seems to me that he was born to do medicine.'

Greg let his paper drop. 'But you never can tell how people are going to react to a curve ball like that.'

'Curve ball.'

'Hmm?' He took in her puzzled expression. 'It's a base-ball term.'

'We play rounders.'

'Right.' He'd clearly never heard of it. 'Yeah, when—'

There was a sudden slam from inside the house. 'You ready?'

They both looked up. Bobbi was standing on the back steps, looking fierce in tennis whites.

'But you don't play!' Ro spluttered, sitting to attention.

'Not *formally*. Not, like, when people are looking. You said you wanted to play.'

'Uh . . .' Actually, she hadn't. Greg had said Hump wanted to, but she saw the way Bobbi's leg was jigging quickly as she stood there, her gaze flighty, a mottled stain growing on her cheeks.

'You'd better go,' Greg said under his breath.

'Oh, right.' Ro jumped up from the lounger and jogged across the lawn. 'Where are we playing?'

'The Maidstone. Hump's at the court now, waiting for us.'

'All of us?' Ro turned back to Greg inclusively.

'Actually, I'm on my way out,' Greg said.

372

'Hump's got one of his driver friends to make up the four,' Bobbi said at the exact same moment.

There was a tense silence, Greg and Bobbi trying to shoot each other down with cold stares. Suddenly, those six weekends were feeling l-o-n-g again.

'OK,' Ro muttered, grabbing Bobbi by the elbow and steering her back towards the house. 'Well, while I get changed, why don't you . . . I dunno, refill the ice-cube trays?'

'The fridge makes ice,' Bobbi frowned.

'So humour me!' Ro shouted, bounding up the stairs.

Five minutes later, she was doing her best Diana Dors impression in her tennis dress again, both of them hopping onto their bikes, racquets slung over their shoulders. They freewheeled towards the sun with smiles on their faces – Bobbi felt she had 'won' that encounter – the question that had been on the tip of Ro's tongue before all but forgotten.

# Chapter Twenty-Five

'Oh well. It's all clear now, isn't it?' Hump said laconically, as they chugged up a carriage drive that had been designed for sweeping up only.

'Absolutely. Thank God you were able to help him out,' Ro murmured back, staring up at the old colonial-style ivy-covered mansion, two floors of arched windows centred with a portico, hatted with a slate roof that was the same depth as the walls, with dormers and four tall chimneys that acted like sirens – intended to be seen from a distance or from the air – heralding the incredibly grand fireplaces within.

Hump stopped in the queue for the valets and looked across at her. 'Todd so didn't want Greg sleeping under the same roof as his girlfriend.'

'Nope.' She sighed heavily.

They reached the front of the valet queue, just beyond the front steps, and Hump handed over the keys as one of the other valets moved to open Ro's door. 'It's OK – I'll help her down,' Hump said quickly, running round to Ro's side. The combination of a tight dress and a high car wasn't a good one, and short of hiking her dress up round her waist, she couldn't get in or out without assistance. He put his hands round her waist and lifted her down, a grin on his face. 'Trust me, you're going to need some protection tonight in *that* dress.'

He laughed as he saw her expression change, Ro more worried by the compliment than flattered – there was nothing subtle about her figure, and if her teenage years had taught her one thing, it was that men lost their senses in her skintight and upholstered presence. She nervously smoothed the cherry-red sequins of her dress. It was all she had to wear that remotely fit the brief, but judging by the turn-of-the-century house, she had a feeling the women here would be wafting around in old-rose chiffons and nude silks and wearing white kid gloves.

Hump held out his arm for her and she slipped her hand through, hugging him gratefully as they walked along the grassy garden path. 'We should have just gone to the Surf Lodge,' she mumbled, as they passed white-jacketed waiters holding gleaming silver trays. She loved their Saturday nights, dancing barefoot in the sand.

'Agreed,' Hump mumbled back, no more comfortable at these grand occasions than she. 'We still could. We could duck out of here before anyone sees us.'

'We can't. We have to support Greg. We told him we'd come.'

'Yeah, but there'll be hundreds of people here tonight. He'll never know if we—' They came round to the terrace. 'Oh crap.'

It was perfect. Majestic oaks ran down the length of an enormous five-acre lawn, each blade so immaculate it would have made Wimbledon's groundsmen weep. Deep, Andrew Jackson Downing-designed beds led back to mossy brick walls that opened up suddenly to archways cut through ancient domed yews, grassy paths behind curving round to private nooks that framed bronze sculptures. But it was the ocean that was the centrepiece, the perfect stretch of deep blue accessed first by a strip of pure white sand that – unlike Florence's wild, grassy horizon – looked like it had been combed.

Ro didn't approve – far from it – but at least it was now obvious why Erin had chosen Todd over Greg. Hump had told her during one of their evening seed-bombing walks that Todd was the elder twin to David by three minutes. That three minutes meant all this was going to be his one day. That three minutes meant he got the house *and* the girl. If he'd been the younger twin, things would have been different – for his brother and probably for Greg.

'Come on, let's get a drink.'

They walked slowly down the steps, Ro holding on to Hump's arm and keeping her eyes down as usual. Normally she felt underdressed; today she felt overdressed – would she ever get it right? The tenor of this dress was wrong and she was going to stand out like a geranium in a bowl of white roses tonight.

At least the grass was firm beneath her feet – a small mercy, as she found it difficult enough walking in heels, even wedges; she and Hump had had to make a pact before leaving that he wouldn't wear flip-flops if she wouldn't wear trainers.

Hump retrieved two glasses of pink champagne, both of them looking around discreetly for Greg. Ro saw Erin first. She was standing with a small group of couples, wearing a mocha-coloured chiffon number that cascaded down her tiny frame in stepped tiers, bronze pearls at her ears and on one wrist. She was listening intently to another woman talking, her head nodding ever so slightly, her eyes sliding over the woman's shoulder every few seconds, checking the new arrivals on the terrace. Ro watched as she graciously placed a hand lightly on the woman's arm, stopping her mid-flow and excusing herself to greet a couple coming down the steps; Ro realized she and Hump had been 'allowed' past without a special greeting.

'So what's this in aid of, anyway?' Ro asked, tearing her eyes away – reminding herself of her own, actual victory over Erin – and looking out to sea.

'Who knows? There's one a week in this lane alone. It's hard to keep up.'

'Why's it called Gin Lane? Because the bored, spoilt women in these houses pour it on their cornflakes?'

Hump laughed. 'Probably. This is the pinnacle, baby. Old-school WASP. Anything goes here. They've seen it and done it all.'

'Hmm.'

Ro let her eyes roam the crowd. There was enough space here for her not to feel overwhelmed by the proximity of strangers, although it wasn't a stranger who made the hairs on the back of her neck stand on end, and he was looking straight back at her.

'Well, well, I see Long Story's here,' Hump drawled, noticing as she turned away with a start and following the line of her sight. 'I thought you two were friends now.'

'We . . . we're not. I mean, we were never friends. He's a client.' The truth was, she didn't know what he was anymore – he had been at various times her enemy, her client, her hero, her suspect. He was still that, even if he did look good in a dinner suit.

Her eyes fell to his hand, intertwined with Julianne's: a casually protective, reassuring, loving gesture, one that belonged to the man on the videos. How could that same hand belong to a man capable of manipulating – possibly defrauding – her friend? Then again, she thought, as a waiter approached their group with fresh drinks, didn't the titanic fortunes required to fund estates like this almost invariably require crossing lines of one sort or another? Was he one among many tonight?

'His wife's pretty.'

'She's not his wife. Well, not his first one, anyway,' Ro snapped, her eyes flitting over to Julianne, who was looking elegant and discreet in an ivory satin dress that stopped mid-thigh, the hint of breeze making it cling to her revealingly and showing off a lean physique Ro hadn't even had as an eight-year-old.

Ted nodded by way of greeting to them both across the lawn and Ro nodded back. The last time she'd spoken to him had been at the Fourth of July party. Things had been cordial back then; she had still been in the dark about his actions around Florence at that point, and she couldn't afford to alert him to her new suspicions. Not yet. But why had he been invited? Who did he know here? Was it Todd? Was it Erin?

She bet it was Erin. They looked like they should know each other; they probably went way back. She could just imagine the two of them growing up together, playing state-level tennis at the Maidstone's perfect courts before sipping chilled cocktails overlooking the ocean. Maybe they had dated each other. Probably long ago lost their virginities to each other and been the prom king and queen thingies.

'And I guess that's another long story, is it?'

Ro turned back to him, remembering suddenly Bobbi's

words this morning. A smile flickered on her lips. 'I'll tell you what's a long story, Hump. The one Bobbi told me this morning. She thinks you're seeing someone.' She jabbed his chest lightly with her finger.

'What? Me?'

'Yeah. Bobbi reckons you lied to her this morning, but I know you wouldn't lie to *me*.' She grinned, holding him with her eyes, determined to leave him nowhere to hide.

'I never could, nor never would lie to you,' he replied earnestly, slapping a hand over his heart by way of oath.

She cocked an eyebrow. 'That's not an answer.'

'What was the question again?'

She laughed – certain now that Bobbi was right – just as Greg made his way over, his eyes alive with delight. 'I'm so glad you came,' he beamed genuinely, kissing her on each cheek and gripping Hump's hand firmly, one hand on his shoulder. He looked so handsome in his dinner suit. Ro felt a rush of pride to be connected with him, even if it was just for a summer.

'Dude, why didn't you say something before? No wonder you've been running back to Sea Spray Cottage at every given moment!' Hump remarked drily. 'I mean, what a dump!'

Greg laughed, a strong, exuberant sound that made women turn. 'I know. Just keeping it real.'

'So, what's this little gathering in aid of, then?' Hump asked.

'Lungworm.' He held up his hands. 'Not the fashionable choice, I grant you, but there needs to be more awareness of it. Erin lost her schnauzer to it last year, so it's a cause very close to her heart.'

Ro and Hump's eyes met, both of them clearly wanting

to laugh, both of them clearly itching to ask, *And are you?*

'She's worked so hard on it. The treasure hunt was all her idea.'

'Treasure hunt?' Ro echoed.

'Mmm-hmm. It gives people a chance to explore the grounds and she thought it would be more exciting than the usual, y'know, silent auction or –' he shrugged '– Rihanna playing a set.'

'Oh, thank God you said that,' Ro deadpanned, amused by this clique's ennui. 'It's beyond tedious. I, personally, would drop down dead if I had to endure another private performance by her.'

Hump burst out laughing, hugging her into him fondly. 'You're a riot!'

Greg's eye was caught by someone over their shoulders – Erin probably – and he held up a hand to indicate he'd be right with them.

'So what do we have to do?' Hump asked, straightening up, remembering his manners.

'Well, I give you one of these,' Greg said, handing them each an envelope from the pile in his hand. 'The clues are in there. You're looking for a quarter-mill Harry Winston diamond bracelet. It's hidden somewhere in the gardens.'

'Behave yourself!' Ro burst out, making several people nearby turn round. A quarter of a million dollars' worth of diamonds? Hidden in the shrubs?

Hump was more circumspect, for once. This wasn't his first time at one of these events. 'And what's the buy-in?'

'It's twenty-five thousand dollars.'

'Twenty-five grand?' Ro echoed, shocked. She turned to whisper to Hump, 'What, is that just to play?'

'Each,' Greg added.

Her jaw dropped. Hump handed back the envelope, but Greg pushed it towards him again. 'No. Do it – it's fun. No one'll know . . . Just don't win!'

'Oh, I couldn't wear that much money, anyway,' Ro said earnestly.

Hump hugged her again. Greg rubbed her arm. She felt like a teddy bear.

'I need to circulate and hand these out to the people who've signed up, but I'll catch you later, OK?' Greg winked, wandering off.

'Sure thing,' Hump nodded, eagerly opening the envelope and pulling out a glossy postcard showing a headless winged figure. 'Oh great,' he groaned. 'Good start. Should've known it'd all be about showing off their expensive educations.'

'No, wait – I've seen that statue,' Ro said excitedly. 'In the flesh, or rather, in the marble. It's in the Louvre.'

'Really? But what is it?'

'You've got me there. I was there on a school trip – I spent most of my time snogging French boys by the vending machines.'

Hump chuckled, hurriedly taking out his smartphone and Googling it on images.

'Isn't that cheating?'

'Well, given that we're technically not part of this game, I don't think anyone will care, do you?'

'Guess not . . .' She peered over, resting her chin on his shoulder – one advantage of wearing heels. 'What's it say?'

'Something to do with the Goddess of Victory . . . It's supposed to commemorate some naval victory?'

'Hmph. Means nothing to me,' Ro mumbled. 'Let's walk. Maybe we'll see something that makes sense of it.'

They began walking towards the main path to the left that led off the lawn. It seemed the most natural place to start.

'Anything?' Hump asked, as they shuffled along, not sure what to look for.

'Gimme a chance. I am *dredging* my brain for archived useless knowledge.' She went quiet as she remembered the clip of film where Marina was in labour and their joke about dredging her pelvis. Four short years ago, and now she was out of sight and her husband had some dolly on his arm with God-only-knows-what plans up his sleeve. She shook her head like a spaniel, throwing Ted Connor straight back out of her thoughts.

It felt good in the shade; the evening sun still had impressive warmth in it and Ro felt overheated in her dress, tiny as it was. They followed the narrow paths that meandered among old fruit trees, passing other couples who were also walking slowly with cream envelopes and pink champagne in their hands. They kept their eyes on low-hanging branches and peering through longer flowers, looking for a hint of gold, a wink of a diamond. They found themselves walking towards a sculpture of a globe worked from bronze bars like a cage, with an arrow shot through the middle of it.

'Any idea?' Ro frowned, staring up at it. 'It doesn't look very naval.'

'No. But it's nice to see the Great and Mighty can be as messy and disorganized as the rest of us,' Hump grinned, pointing towards a stray white tennis shoe peeking out of the far flowerbed.

Ro stared at it. 'Hang on a sec . . .' She didn't think for one moment that that shoe was there accidentally. Ro had met enough Type-A brides to know Erin wouldn't have let anything as imperfect as a lost shoe mess with her manicured landscape. 'Isn't the Goddess of Victory in Greek . . . ? Isn't it Nike?'

'You know that?' Hump's eyebrows shot up. 'Goddam, Ro, I think you really might be my dream woman.'

'Well, I might be talking complete tosh. You'd better check. Is it a Nike trainer? I bet it isn't. It's probably Adidas or something.'

Hump retrieved it, looking back at her with an amazed and impressed smile. He held up the tennis shoe so she could see the black tick along the side. She jumped up and down on the spot excitedly, but Hump's eyes almost jumped out of his head at the sight of her and she quickly stopped again.

'You want to do the honours?' he asked, inviting her to reach inside.

Ro shrugged and put in her hand. As she'd suspected, it wasn't sweaty or smelly. No doubt Erin's feet were rose-scented and soft as cashmere cushions. She pulled out the small, folded piece of blue writing paper that had been pushed into the toe.

'Tada!' she cried, her smile fading as she remembered how that had been Ella's first word. For heaven's sake, this was getting ridiculous! That family had taken lodgings in her head.

She opened up the paper, staring at the cryptic clue.

> *I am the key to let you in,*
> *What you need for this game to begin.*
> *So hurry, make haste –*
> *It's emergency.*
> *Come and find me so that I can go free.*

'Helpful, not,' Ro muttered, pushing the clue back in the shoe and turning round in a circle. 'Well, at the very least I would assume we continue down this path rather than doubling back on ourselves.' She pointed towards the shaded path that she suspected was leading them towards the ocean as Hump replaced the shoe in the flowerbed.

'Come along, then,' Hump said, taking her by the hand again and pulling her along. 'Sounds like we need to look out for a key.'

They sauntered along slowly, enjoying the breeze that had picked up in strength a little. Ro closed her eyes and shook her head lightly, enjoyed the feeling of it against her bare neck now that her hair was jaw-length and no longer clung like a scarf round her at all times.

'How can you look if you're walking along with your eyes closed?' She opened them to find Hump grinning at her. 'We've got a competition to win, remember. You're the brains in this outfit.'

'Not in this outfit I'm not,' she quipped, her eyes flicking down to her showgirl dress. 'I feel like I dropped thirty IQ points between here and the shower.'

They laughed, Hump jerking her hand lightly and making her arm wiggle.

'Besides, we promised not to win,' she reminded him.

'We're not going to win the bracelet. We're just going to take quiet satisfaction in knowing that we beat everyone else and found it first.'

'Competitive much?'

Beyond the beds, on the other side of the crumbly wall, they heard a silky voice over a PA system, asking for everyone's attention.

'Sounds like Erin's in da house. Think we should go

back and listen?' Hump asked, jerking his thumb towards the path they'd been walking down.

'What, and lose our lead? You've got to be joking! Besides, what's she really got to say that we need to listen to anyway? She's only going to be thanking all her rich mates for paying twenty-five grand each to play in the garden. I'd rather not if it's all the same.'

'Yeah.'

They carried on walking, feeling poor but clever at least.

'Oh look, pretty,' she said, pointing out an old, weathered dovecote set high against a crumbling brick wall that appeared to be mainly held up by pride and thick ivy. Two pure white faces peered out of two of the round holes. 'Why am I not surprised that they have doves when the rest of us have one-legged pigeons with fleas?' Her eyes fell to a small door on the bottom right that was padlocked shut. 'Hang on, what did the clue say again?' She repeated it in her head, her eyes closed. '"*So that I can go free.*" Think it could be referring to that?' she asked, pointing to the tiny locked door.

'Doubt it. We're looking for a key, and that's got a combination lock.'

'Hmmmmm.' They looked around the bushes and ground near to where they stood, searching for the glint of a key – although to unlock what still wasn't clear.

Ro repeated the clue out loud again:

*'I am the key to let you in,*
*What you need for this game to begin.*
*So hurry, make haste –*
*It's emergency.*
*Come and find me so that I can go free.'*

'What do you think it means by *"It's emergency"*? It seems a little bit contrived,' she mused.

'Unlike the rest of it. Because Erin always talks in iambic pentameter.'

Ro laughed, nudging him in the ribs. 'Oooh, get you!' she teased.

'What? We do study Shakespeare here, you know,' he said, trying not to laugh.

A thought came to her. 'What if . . . what if it's not an actual key we need? I mean, hotels have cards as their keys now.' She looked at the locked door. 'What if the combination code for that padlock is the key to opening it?'

'So then . . . emergency . . .' He walked suddenly towards the dovecote and turned the numbers on the lock to 911. The padlock unfastened.

'Brilliant!' Ro squealed, as they high-fived.

He opened the door.

'Carefu—' she cried, just as a dove flew out in a drumbeat of wings, trying to find loft in the air right in front of Hump's face. 'It did say something had to go free,' she laughed, watching Hump splutteringly bat feathers away from his face.

Tentatively, worried there may be more, he reached his arm inside the nook and pulled out a cream envelope.

> You're nearly there.
> It's the end of the day.
> To find this next clue
> Will be child's play.

'Oh, that's too easy,' Ro puffed disappointedly.

'Is it?'

'Yeah. Child's play? Where are we heading to?' She pointed towards the peek of blue between the trees. 'Bet you we find a bucket and spade or something on the beach.'

'*How* are you so good at this?' he asked, replacing the envelope in the door and closing the padlock. (Although Erin could think twice if she thought he was going to recapture the dove again.)

'A childhood spent reading *The Times* crossword – sets you up for anything.' She winked.

'The *New York Times* one is harder,' Hump replied, being controversial.

'So isn't,' Ro grinned, hooking her arm through his as they carried on down the path towards the beach.

Sure enough, a spade was sitting on an upturned bucket, just beyond the grassline of the garden. Ro let Hump do the honours, preferring to look back up at the house from this viewpoint. It seemed even bigger from a distance, the elegant, slow-moving guests like confetti petals on the lawn, Erin but a pretty dot on the concentric steps.

Hump came back, carrying a small paper US flag. 'Good luck with this one,' he said, reciting the clue aloud:

> '*The final one.*
> *Don't be undone*
> *By the boastful looks*
> *Of history books.*
> *See the roots for what they are.*
> *This story started from afar.*'

'That's it?' Ro grimaced.

'Other than telling us to take one of these flags.' He

pointed to a cluster of small paper US flags flapping at the top of a sandcastle.

'So then that's telling us we've got to find something in the garden that relates to stars and stripes?'

'I guess so. Or "old glory", or "star-spangled banner".'

She looked around – there was no way Erin would risk hiding a $250,000 bracelet in the sand. It had to be back in the garden somewhere, and the garden was symmetrical; another path ran up the opposite side of the lawn. 'Well, then I suppose we head up this way.'

Applause swept down the lawn like a rushing tide, just missing them as they disappeared into the glades again, the tiny paper flag pinched between Hump's fingers.

They walked in easy silence, their glasses empty in their hands, eyes peeled for a glimmer or a clue, and Ro realized she had forgotten to be self-conscious in her dress now – it actually fit better than when she'd bought it, having dropped a few pounds somewhere over the weeks – and although she was the only woman there both with cleavage and a cleavage that was natural, actually, that was OK. Hump had been right earlier when he'd said he would protect her. She did feel protected with him. She didn't need to be perfect or tiny or fragrant around him. He saw her at her worst – drunk, first thing in the morning, shocked, dunked in the sea – and still brought her coffee every morning and passed the pepperoni. In most social situations, he was the odd one out, like her: always just slightly too loud or clumsy, like her; his heart too trusting, like hers. They fit together.

She looked across at him, watching as he absently spun the flag in his fingers and wondered who it was he was seeing. He had been deliberately coy with her, clearly as reluctant to share her identity with Ro as he had been with Bobbi, and she felt a stab of jealousy that she wanted his confidence and didn't yet have it.

They came to a break in the wall, where the path fed back to the lawn through a pudding-bowl yew.

Hump looked across at her. 'Sorry, but I need to go to the washroom. Give me your glass and I'll get us some fresh drinks on my way back. This is thirsty work.'

'Why not? I think we've got a good enough lead on everyone to permit a quick diversion,' she said, turning to walk with him.

'No. You stay looking. We can't afford to lose our lead. I'll bring them over.'

Ro rolled her eyes at his competitiveness, but knew she was no better. 'Well, you'd better give me the flag, then. We can't have that lot out there picking up on our clues.'

'You're right,' he winked, handing it over and sauntering off.

She ambled at a snail's pace, not wanting to leave him behind, even though the path had one main artery, with the only tributaries short and leading to occasional nooks for the sculptures. She soon came to one, a circular spot with a magnificent red rose planted in the middle and a life-size military figure set into a niche in the wall at the back.

History books? That had to be it. She ran her hands over and around the statue, searching keenly for anything that stood out. It should have been relatively easy. Everything was so perfectly maintained and in order that anything rogue or stray would flash like a beacon. But there was nothing.

She planted her hands on her hips and exhaled in

concentration, the clue running over in her mind: *The final one. Don't be undone, By the boastful looks of history books.*

'"*Don't be undone*,"' she murmured, looking up at the bronze general. 'So then it's saying that it's *not* on him.' She looked down at the flag again, trying to do free-association as she turned slowly on the spot: 'Stars . . . stripes . . . spangles . . . glory . . . military glory . . . wars: civil, Independe—'

Ted Connor was standing by the entrance to the nook, watching her. Fear rippled through her like a sonic pulse to find herself alone with him in this remote spot.

'Hi,' he smiled, his voice benign, though she found his position aggressive – did he know he was blocking her exit? Was it deliberate?

'Hi.' She crossed her arms over herself, a defensive posture that, unfortunately, only deepened her cleavage. She saw his eyes just barely follow the movement and quickly dropped her arms.

'How are you?'

'Fine. I'm fine.'

'I've been meaning to drop by the studio and see how you're getting on with everything, but I've been rather overtaken by events recently.'

She bet he had. 'There's no need. Everything's fine. I'm almost done editing the films now and I'm starting on the stills next week.'

He smiled. 'Good luck with that. There are thousands. We were trigger-happy to say the least.'

His words sent a shiver down her. *Were.* Past tense. Gone. Dismissed. Forced to make way . . . Ro's eyes scanned for Julianne, knowing she must be near. But there was no sign of her.

He saw her look around for Julianne. 'She's making a call.'

'Oh.' She nodded, unsure what to say next. It was too much to stand here making small talk with him knowing they were both talking in riddles. She'd never been a good liar. Did he sense her suspicions about him? Had he seen it across the lawn earlier? He knew she was close to Florence too; he must have known they'd talked. 'Are you . . . um, doing the treasure hunt?' she asked, wishing Hump would hurry back.

'Yes. Although it looks like you've beaten us to it.'

'No, no, I'm not doing it,' she said, seeing her opportunity to get away. 'We couldn't afford to play. I'd better leave you to—'

'Wait.' He side-stepped in front of her, blocking her path directly. There was nothing accidental about his positioning now. 'Is it just my imagination or are you always trying to escape me?'

*Escape?* Odd choice of word.

'No.' She shook her head, knowing full well that she blushed when she lied and having to resist the urge to put her hand to her cheek to check. 'I just need to get back to Hump.'

She moved to step past him, but although he wasn't touching her, his hands by his sides, she couldn't get past without squeezing herself against him, and that was *not* going to happen.

'Rowena . . .'

She swallowed, refusing to look at him. He was too close. Far too close.

'I just wanted to . . .' She felt his hand hover above her

arm, not touching, but able to feel the charge of his body against hers, like magnetic north to south.

'How's Florence?' she blurted out. 'Have you seen her recently?'

The words fell like tiles on the ground between them as she watched his response.

'Uh, yes. Yes, I saw her earlier, actually.'

'Really?' Ro inclined her head a little, trying to come across as surprised.

'She asked me to be with her when the police came to report the conclusions of their investigation with her.'

'What? You mean they've finished already?'

He nodded.

'And?'

He put a hand in his trouser pocket and leaned against the wall, his eyes never leaving her.

Another house on the street had work done recently and they think it happened then. Her wiring system was over thirty years old and there were none of the safety cut-outs you'd need now. But Florence has still been advised to get a good lawyer. She'll be due millions in a civil lawsuit.'

Ro's heart was beating double time. 'But . . . she's convinced it was cut.'

'And it was. Just accidentally. There's no criminal case to answer.'

Ro looked away, feeling winded by the update. She had believed Florence that day on the bench. Everything she said had seemed plausible, and Florence had been coherent and calm.

'Don't worry, Ro – she'll get justice. This episode won't

go unpunished. Florence is going to be a very rich woman after this.'

Ro looked back at him, seeing the picture beginning to emerge now, like an image onto film. The lawsuit.

He looked at the ground briefly. 'If you don't mind me saying, you look very beautiful tonight.'

'What?' Was this the charm, the flattery that ran rings round Florence? She looked up in surprise, his eyes catching hers like a pinned butterfly, and what she saw – fear ran through her, fast and cold. All her worst thoughts reflected back at her, right there . . .

'Oh! Sorry!'

Ted stepped back smartly at the voice, revealing Hump standing behind them, no glasses in his hands.

'Hump!' Ro's relief rang out like a bell between them all, prompting Ted to glance back at her.

Hump picked up on it too, stepping more confidently into their circle now, protective as ever. 'Hope I'm not interrupting anything . . .' His eyes slid between Ted and Ro, resting on Ro.

'No, no. I was just coming to find you, actually,' Ro said quickly, almost wanting to cry with relief. She looked pointedly at Ted. 'The bracelet's in the rosebush.'

'What?' Ted asked, astonished, looking over at the full-flowering red rosebush in the middle of the nook.

'"See the roots for what they are. This story started from afar."' This is a rose, the symbol of England. The American War of Independence fought for separation from England . . . hence the flag,' she said in a manic rush, the words falling over each other as she tried to look calm in front of them both. 'Hump, where are our drinks?' she asked, posting an innocently curious expression on her face.

KAREN SWAN

'We've got a small problem.' Hump shook his head for-biddingly.

'What sort of problem?'

He looked across at Ted quickly, but it wasn't him Ted was watching. 'Just come with me.'

Ro turned back to Ted, more confident now that Hump was here. 'Well, bye, then,' she said.

'Bye,' Ted said quietly, his hands in his pockets, his eyes steady upon her, discerning the obvious upbeat change in her behaviour.

She took Hump's hand as he led her up the path, taking three strides to his one. She kept her chin high, refusing to look like she was running away, knowing – absolutely knowing – Ted was watching her the whole way. Because it wasn't charm that she'd felt between them in that last moment alone together. It had been far more dangerous than that.

# Chapter Twenty-Six

'Hump, are you going to tell me what's going on?' she hissed, as soon as they were out of sight, struggling to keep up with his fast pace in her wedges as they crossed the lawn and jogged up the steps towards the house.

Hump, who'd been keeping a polite 'nothing to see here' smile on his face, looked across at her. 'He's in here,' he said, striding through the French doors and into a gracious drawing room decorated in salmon-pink and pistachio tones.

'Who, Hump? Who?' she asked, dodging bullion-fringed ottomans and Victorian side tables.

He pushed open a door and Ro gasped to see Greg slumped on the floor, his arm resting on the loo, his head lolling on his chest.

'Oh my God, what's happened?' she whispered, running in and crouching down in front of her housemate. He was barely conscious. 'He was fine half an hour ago.'

'That was before he necked a bottle of vodka.' He pointed to the empty bottle beside Greg's legs.

'*What?* But why?' Ro mouth hung open in surprise. 'Greg, wake up. Can you hear me?'

'He's out of it. We need to get him to the hospital and have his stomach pumped. That level of spirits could give him alcohol poisoning.'

'Oh God, Greg, what have you done?' she whispered, cupping his handsome, catatonic face with her hand.

'Ro, we need to get him out of here ASAP – and discreetly. His career will be destroyed if this gets out. Half the people here are clients or industry benefactors. I need you to get the car brought round to the front doors. Can you divert the valets?'

'Yes, of course,' she replied without thinking. How? How was she going to do that?

'Good.' He handed her the valet ticket. 'Be quick. He's a dead weight like this. I can't hang around once I've got him on my shoulders. OK?'

Ro nodded nervously. 'I'll be as quick as I can. See you in two minutes.'

'Don't run. You don't want to attract anyone's attention.'

'Right.' Gripping the ticket firmly in her fist, Ro slipped out of the bathroom, checking the hallway was clear. It was. Everyone was outside, including the staff, who were rushed off their feet.

She crossed the gleaming parquet floor, her sequins rustling lightly from her hurried movements. She didn't have time to notice the blowsy floral arrangements of old roses and sweet peas, or the silver Tiffany photo frames that housed black-and-white snapshots of an idyllic life shared over several generations. All she was focusing on were the enormous front doors, which were at least ten feet high and double width, and which she hoped weren't locked.

They weren't and she opened them soundlessly, trotting down the steps and turning right towards the side garden path they'd entered by and to where the valets' booth was set up. There were five of them in there, leaning and playing on iPads, enjoying their lull before guests began leaving again in a couple of hours or so.

She gave a tight smile as she handed over the ticket and waited for one of them to bring the Defender round from the adjoining paddock, her eyes flicking back restlessly towards the house. How was she going to help Hump get Greg in the car without the valets seeing? He was one of the hosts and too conspicuous tonight to be seen in this state by anyone. This couldn't get back to Erin or Todd.

She heard the Humper long before she saw it and twitched restlessly, sure she was going to let down Hump and Greg. What could she do? What could she do?

'Cool car, ma'am,' the valet said, as he jumped out, leaving the engine running. He couldn't have been more than nineteen.

From the corner of her eye, Ro saw the front door beginning to open.

Out of time!

'No!' she shrieked loudly, and the front door's progress halted. The valets jumped. 'What's that?' she asked, adopting her poshest British accent and trying to sound like the queen. An imperial attitude might be an asset right now.

'What, ma'am?'

She pointed towards the paddock just beyond the trees. 'Is that *kids* messing about in there? Don't they know the value of the cars? You do have security in there, don't you?'

All five valets bucked up, straining to lean over the booth counter and make out what she was pointing at.

'Surely you can see them? They're *right there*.' She jabbed her finger with annoyance.

The valets clustered out of the booth, not wanting to contradict her, but clearly there was nothing to see.

'Oh, good God, don't say they're . . .' She frowned and looked at the nineteen-year-old. 'You have insurance, I take it?'

'Why, ma'am?' He looked terrified.

'Well, they're plainly keying the cars.'

'Mother fuckers!' one of the valets cried, forgetting he was in the presence of a customer. 'Come on!'

'They're behind the navy Maserati,' she cried after them, as they all raced across the drive, vaulting the white post-and-rail fencing into the paddock. 'Quick! Now!' she hissed to Hump, who had overheard her diversion and stood back from view from the open door.

She watched as Hump staggered down the steps, clearly straining to carry the full weight of his semi-conscious friend on his shoulders. A small step by the back door was just low enough that she could climb up in her dress and stand in the cab, taking the weight of Greg's head and upper body as Hump gracelessly flopped him forwards, like a badly tossed caber, onto one of the bench seats.

'You hold on to him. Make sure he stays on his side. If he starts throwing up, he'll choke.'

'Oh God,' she muttered, steadying Greg by the shoulder as Hump jumped into the driver's cab and pulled away in second gear, sending a spray of gravel onto the rose beds and mullioned windows. They hurtled down the drive as Ro saw the valets peering beneath and around the cars in the paddock, their arms outstretched in confusion.

'Is he all right?' Hump shouted over his shoulder. With the sound of the gravel and the engine, it was hard to be heard. Shouting was the only option.

'Yes! Did anyone see you in the house?'

'No! Don't think so!'

398

They pulled out of the gates at the bottom and Hump went through all the gears again, Ro keeping her hand on Greg's arm to steady him from the movement.

'Hump, why has he done this? He was fine when we saw him earlier.'

'Yeah, but that was before the evening's big announcement.'

'What? Thanking sponsors and supporters?'

'Erin and Todd announced their engagement.'

'No!'

'Yep. Straight back to the old days.'

Ro looked down sadly at Greg, his superb body limp, his handsome face slack, his objective clearly achieved as the pain, any feeling at all in fact, was numbed – for now at least.

'Can you get him under the other arm?' Hump panted, trying to take Greg's weight along with his own.

'Yes, sure.' Ro ran back down from unlocking the front door and tried propping Greg from the other side so that he was – marginally – more balanced.

Greg laughed, an indistinct, undefined sound that he had neither energy nor sense of mind to punctuate. They had been in the hospital for several hours as Greg's stomach was pumped and he was fed a saline drip to rehydrate him, but the damage had already been done and he was as drunk as a skunk in drag. 'You guys . . .' he slurred, his feet leaden and useless beneath him as they part carried, part dragged him up the porch steps and into the house.

'How are we going to get him up the stairs?' Ro cringed, panting from the effort after only fifty yards.

'We're not. He'll have to sleep it off on the sofa,' Hump groaned, for he was bearing most of Greg's weight. 'I'll stay down here with him.'

They turned to drag him into the sitting room, just as a pretty pair of toes appeared on the stairs. They looked up. Bobbi was tying a dressing gown around her, although it had slipped on the shoulder and her black bra strap was visible.

'Sexy . . .' Greg slurred.

'Fuck! What the hell happened to *him*?' she exclaimed in astonishment at the sight of Greg so incapacitated.

'A bottle of vodka in under two minutes. Give us a hand, would you?' Ro panted. She could only take pigeon steps in her tight dress.

Bobbi ran down the stairs, thighs flashing, and helped the others get him to the sofa. He fell onto it, almost face first, and Ro would have laughed if she hadn't wanted so badly to cry. She felt distressed to see her dignified house-mate in this state.

Bobbi sat beside him on the sofa, unable to stop staring at the sight of him, his dinner jacket lost somewhere – probably still back at the estate – his dress shirt untucked and only fastened with two buttons, his face pale and streaked from the tears that had caught up with him in the hospital as he'd revived just long enough for the pain to catch him up, burying his face in Ro's neck, her soft skin a universal comfort men remembered from their mothers.

A creak on the floorboards upstairs made them all look up. Ro hitched up an eyebrow.

'Kevin's here?'

Hump stood in front of Greg defensively. 'I don't want

anyone seeing Greg like this. You'd better keep Kevin upstairs.'

'Can you just tell me what happened to him?' Bobbi asked, looking up at him, unconsciously stroking Greg's hair from his face. Even she didn't like to see her sparring partner so wounded.

Hump lowered his voice, not wanting to distress Greg further. 'Erin announced her engagement to Todd Blaize at the fundraiser tonight – even though she's been secretly having an affair with Greg all summer.'

'You're fucking kidding me?' Bobbi gawped.

'Wish I was,' Hump sighed, looking down at his old friend.

Greg's eyes were open, although unfocused, rolling up occasionally before he snapped them back with a sudden jerk of his head. He looked at Bobbi as she took his hand in hers, rubbing his palm gently with her thumb.

'You're going to be OK, Greg. We'll get you through this,' she said firmly, brushing back one particularly floppy forelock that kept falling over his eye.

He grinned, a daft, wolfish grin that he couldn't quite control and which tipped him over into tears in the next instant. 'Have we met?' he asked her, his face telling two stories at once as silent tears slid down his appled, smiling cheeks.

'Unfortunately for you, yes. I'm Bobbi, your stroppy housemate.'

Greg stared at her as she wiped away the tears with her thumbs. His hand closed round her wrist. 'No, that was what *she* said to you.'

Who? Ro frowned as Bobbi pulled back. It was easy

enough to wrest her arm away from his grip; he had no strength to speak of right now.

'I'll go make sure Kevin doesn't come down.'

'Thanks,' Hump said, as she rose and walked across the room.

'I think you have!' Greg called after her, every word linked to the next one like joined-up writing.

But Bobbi didn't turn back. ''Night, everyone,' she said, as she started climbing the stairs. 'Sleep tight.'

Ro's sleep was anything but tight. It barely held her through the night, its bonds loose around her, her mind frantic and racing – only one degree below waking – her ears pricked for sound, her body ready to run. The night was too hot for one thing; there was no breeze. And she was worried about Greg. Worried that he'd poisoned his own blood, worried that his fragile glass heart, which had already been patched together once before, had now been smashed for good. She could glimpse a fragment of that emotional landscape he was now wandering in and she pitied him: the past four and a half months without Matt had offered her occasional moments of clarity as to what life would look like without him, and it was a desolate and bleak world in which she faded into her own shadow.

But what finally nudged her from her gauzy slumber wasn't Greg or Matt at all, but another man's face close to hers, too close to say to 'no', his lips on hers—

She sat up, her heart pounding like a bass drum, her lips still parted as she'd kissed him back. She threw the covers off and walked straight over to the window, furious with her brain for betraying her like that *again* even if it was simply a mash-up of last night's events. She poked her head out, like one of the doves at the dovecote – albeit less fresh and pure-looking – and looked out onto the fresh day budding up.

The sea mist hadn't yet rolled back, telling her it was still before six, although the flags were already in the pins on the greens at the Maidstone. People gladly sacrificed extra hours in bed for a round there.

A car parked outside the cottage suddenly started up and slowly pulled away. Ro looked down and watched it go. A Porsche. Wasn't that what Kevin drove? Maybe it had been the sound of him leaving the house that had awakened her after all, not . . . not . . . Dammit. She rubbed her face hard, pulling down on her cheeks with the heels of her hands, trying to wake herself up fully.

She watched as the car indicated left, then immediately right – meaning he was either going to the beach or the Maidstone. It was a shame to have missed him by only a few moments. She was curious to see what type of man had tamed – at least temporarily – her feisty friend. Feeling nosy, and because it was too early to go downstairs and risk disturbing the boys, she remained by the window. If he was playing golf, she'd see him in a few minutes. The first green was visible from this spot.

She grabbed the laptop and fell into her usual early morning position at the window – sitting on the deep sill, legs jammed up in the frames, her knees level with her nose, the laptop on Skype speed dial.

She and Matt still hadn't spoken since their fight ten days earlier. She'd been determined up till now not to be the one to call first. But last night had been a wake-up call and there was more at stake here than pride. She and Matt needed contact: they needed to talk to each other and see each other and make their old jokes, because she couldn't find him on her own anymore – not in her yoga meditations, not in her dreams. She was getting too used to being without him. She needed to need him more.

The connection timed out and she pressed 'call' again, her eyes tracking a beaten-up pickup truck that idled slowly past on the road below – no one ever seemed to be in a hurry out here, no tail-gating or frustrated overtaking, and she realized again she was going to miss this. She had only six weeks left – six weeks of waking up to blue skies and an ocean breeze, bike rides and yoga, and housemates who may slam doors but always chilled the beer.

She saw a buggy bounce over the grass towards the first green, two men inside. One was wearing claret-red trousers and a hat, the other an emerald-green jumper, and was bald as a . . . well, a Matt. She hoped for Bobbi's sake that Kevin – if he was either one of these guys – wasn't the short bald one. Matt could carry it off; this guy couldn't.

She watched as they climbed out, one of them inspecting the position of the pin by crouching down on his haunches, the other beginning to rifle in his bag for his clubs.

'Ro?'

She jumped, startled to hear Matt's voice rumbling against her tummy.

'Matt!'

'No need to look so surprised. You did call me.'

She stared down at him, not sure whether he was still prickly with her, but then he winked – 'Thank God,' he murmured – and she felt relief loosen the tension in her shoulders.

'You're growing your hair!' she grinned, taking in the dark fuzz that crested his head like duckling's down.

'I got the impression you didn't like it last time we spoke.'

'I didn't mention it.'

'Exactly.'

'I could level the same charge at you,' she said archly, tipping her head to the side slightly to indicate her bob.

'Looks amazing. It annoyed me how good you looked. It looks very . . . sleek.'

'*Sleek?*' Ro spluttered. 'Can hippos be called sleek?'

'Stop putting yourself down. From what I can see, you're looking altogether different. Kind of . . . glossy.'

'OK, stop it. You're confusing me with a magazine.'

He laughed, a sound that soothed her, and she preened slightly. 'I have, however, broken the habit of wearing your clothes.'

'What? Even my T-shirts in bed?'

She nodded triumphantly. 'Even your T-shirts in bed.'

'When?' He looked almost crestfallen.

'Oh, a while ago. Hump was about to evict me; Bobbi was on the edge of a breakdown.' Actually, it had been Erin and Todd's unexpected breakfast visit that had marked the beginning of the end for that phase.

'Well –' his eyes roamed her face '– guess I'll see for myself six short weeks from now.'

'Six weeks,' she echoed, remembering Greg's words yesterday, everyone keeping time. 'Flying by now, huh?'

'Yeah? That's how it feels for you now?'

'Why? Doesn't it for you?'

'Oh no, no . . . I'm loving it,' he demurred. 'But looking forward to getting home obviously.'

'Oh yeah. Obviously. It'll be so weird going back to the cottage again. Everything's so . . . big and airy here.

Victorian proportions are going to take some getting used to again.' She thought of their narrow dog-leg hallway, the tiny cellar, the double reception room with walk-through arch . . .

'I'll be struggling enough with just sleeping in a bed again. Almost five months in a sleeping bag . . .' He cricked his neck.

Ro pulled a face. 'You have washed it, I hope?'

'Of course.' He grinned, simultaneously shaking his head. 'I'm passing washing machines every third bamboo tree out here.'

She giggled. Both of them would have big readjustments to make, slotting back into their old life. It felt like they were both going to have to scale down to fit into it, somehow.

'Where are you now?'

'En route to Tonlé Sap. It's like an inland sea. There are literally hundreds of floating villages there. The residents conduct their whole lives on the water, can you imagine?'

She shook her head. She really couldn't. She wondered whether he would be able to imagine her dressed in sequins and hunting for diamonds in the bushes.

He pointed to his cheek. 'You've got some mascara . . .'

'Oh.' Ro wet her finger and made vague, blind sweeping motions. 'Gone?'

He pulled a so-so face. 'Pretty much. So what were you up to last night, then? You only ever wear mascara on high days and holidays. Unless maybe that's what's different about you. You wear make-up every day now?'

'No. God, no!' she protested. 'I'm like a rescue dog compared to the women here. I don't know where they get the energy, looking so clean and perky all the time. No, we were just out last night.'

'Let me guess: the Surf Lodge again?'

So he'd been reading her Facebook updates, then? 'Actually, no. It was a fundraiser thing over in Southampton. Big money, free booze. A rather fun treasure hunt in the garden.' She leaned in closer to the screen. 'You'd have liked my dress.' She winked cheekily.

'Yeah?'

'Yeah!'

'Well, then I hope no one else liked your dress.'

She remembered Hump's big-brotherly protectiveness, Ted's eyes tethered to her like guy ropes. 'Don't be silly.'

'Is that it?' He jerked his chin up, his eyes behind her, and she turned. The red sequinned dress was hanging outside the wardrobe.

'It is.'

'Hold it up. Let me see it properly.' An unhappy note sounded in his voice and she knew he knew all too well what the dress would have looked like on *her*.

She jumped off the windowsill and walked towards the wardrobe, holding out the laptop so that the camera could show it more accurately. Matt didn't say anything and she felt her nerves rise. 'Anyway, Greg got bladdered, so it was all a bit of a disaster to be honest and we ended up back home by nine o'clock,' she gabbled, wandering back over to the bed and flopping down on it. She could still feel her own body heat on the sheets.

'Right.' A tense moment passed.

'Don't be jealous.'

'I'm not jeal—' he began, before deciding to change the subject instead. 'How's Florence?'

'Much better. She's recuperating in a nursing home, but you were right – there's been nothing since. Whoever was behind it seems to have been frightened off.'

It was technically true, at least. There hadn't been any further threats – not since she'd appeared to fall in line with Ted's 'advice' to sell the house.

'Thank God for that! I was freaking out with worry. You don't know how hard it's been being so far away from you when you've had all that crazy shit going on.'

'I'm fine. Honestly. Things have quietened down completely. It's just beaches and beer on the porch.'

'Since when did you start drinking beer?'

'Since . . . since about three days after I got here. Hump's been on a mission to turn me into a proper American girl.'

'You have picked up a bit of an accent, actually. Just now, when you said . . .' A sound in the background made Matt turn his head. 'Bugger, I've got to go. Dinner's ready,' he said reluctantly.

'Oh. Well, I guess I should investigate the severity of Greg's hangover.'

'Don't envy you that. Sounds like it's going to be bad.'

'Mmm.' Bad wasn't going to be the half of it. 'I love you.'

'Love you too. Just six more weeks.'

'Forty-two days!' she clarified excitedly.

'We can do this thing.'

'Yes, we can.' She nodded firmly.

'Bye, baby.'

'Bye.'

He kissed the screen. She leaned in and kissed hers, slightly self-conscious as she remembered the last time she'd done this, inadvertently, in the studio not with him.

When she opened her eyes, the screen was black again.

She fell back on her pillows, staring up at the ceiling and picking over the conversation, relieved they hadn't fought this time. It had been a good conversation, one of their better ones. Not one of their best, admittedly. Something had felt a little . . . flat? But that was probably just the last traces of the argument dissipating in the air between them. It would be gone the next time they spoke. The slate was clean again.

She pushed herself up from the bed, determined to start the day brightly. It was going to be an awful one for Greg, that much was certain, and if nothing else, she could take over from Hump's nightshift. He could probably do with a couple of hours sleeping in his own bed. Poor guy – for someone who'd retired from medicine, he still spent a lot of time putting people back together again.

She padded downstairs, everything still quiet in Bobbi's room. She stopped in the hall at the entrance to the sitting room, looking in on the two overgrown men, sleeping with their legs hanging over the armrests on opposite sofas. Greg didn't appear to have moved from where he'd fallen last night, a towel and a washing-up bowl strategically positioned below him on the floor – mercifully, still unused, although the alcohol fumes hung in the air like pea soup.

She walked to the front door and opened it, closing her eyes as the breeze swept in like a welcome visitor, freshening the house. She stepped out on the porch just as a police car raced past, its siren off but blue lights flashing.

No doubt it was responding to a house alarm, she thought, stretching – just as another police car shot by. And then another.

She frowned. That was no house alarm. Dropping her arms, she walked briskly down the porch steps and out through the front gate, standing on the small green and looking towards the beach.

But it wasn't there that the district police were congregating.

She watched in mounting apprehension as one patrol car after another, and then an ambulance too, sped in silence towards the pristine greens of the Maidstone, where a bright yellow privacy screen was being erected – at the tee to the first hole.

# Chapter Twenty-Seven

Ro blinked back at the police detective sitting opposite her, wishing she could stop wringing her hands together, her jigging ankles knocking the washing-up bowl still by her feet and making the detective look down at it with sporadic flashes of irritation.

Mainly the police officer was watching her closely, now that he had ascertained she was the nearest thing he had to a witness. 'Let's go through it one more time. Tell me what happened from the moment you woke up.'

Ro took a deep breath again, feeling the pressure of getting it right. 'I had had a . . . bad dream –' lie: it had been exceptionally good, actually '– and I woke up suddenly. I got up, walked to my window and looked out. A car was parked outside the house and it gave me a shock as it was turned on suddenly—'

'So you didn't see anyone actually getting into the car?'

'No.'

'So they could have been there for some time.'

'I suppose so. Maybe.'

'All night, even.'

'Why would someone sit in a car all night?' Ro frowned, before giving a little gasp. 'You mean they could have been spying on us?'

'Why would anyone spy on you?' the detective countered.

'Well, that's just the thing – I don't know. We're so . . . boring.'

The detective looked down at the bowl by her feet again; Greg's dinner suit was still strewn across the coffee table.

'Have you noticed anyone acting suspiciously outside the house? Anyone taking an unusual interest in you?'

Ro swallowed hard as Ted Connor flashed into her mind. He had taken an unusual interest in her last night – there'd been no doubt about it. She was worried he'd picked up on her suspicions, that she'd given herself away somehow; Matt always said she wore her emotions on her face, that she was as easy to read as a book. But he couldn't possibly be involved in *this*. Even she didn't think that. Her mind couldn't go there. 'No.' She shook her head. 'No one.'

The detective stared at her for a long moment, as though wondering whether to believe her. 'So you don't know how long the occupant had been in the car for?'

'No.'

'And you said the car was a Porsche.'

'Yes, a navy one. Soft-top.' She sat a little straighter, pleased she had caught this detail.

'But you didn't get anything of the licence plate?'

'Well, no, I wasn't watching it for that.'

'But you were watching it?'

She shrugged. 'It just drove slowly down to the junction and turned into Old Beach Lane. I was quite surprised that the driver would bother to drive such a short distance from here when it's just a few minutes' walk.'

'And what happened after the car turned into the lane?'

'Well, I figured if he was play—'

'He? Why did you assume the inhabitant was a male?'

'I don't know.' She swallowed nervously. His questioning style was intimidating, making her question her own mind. 'My flatmate's boyfriend had stayed over. I automatically assumed it was him. He drives a Porsche and it would make sense for him to have parked outside.'

He blinked at her and she sensed he didn't appreciate her making assumptions. 'Continue.'

Ro tried to remember her train of thought. 'Uh . . . so . . . oh yes, I figured if he was playing golf, I'd see him on the first tee in a couple of minutes. So that's when I got my laptop and started trying to Skype my boyfriend while I waited.'

The police officer looked at her through interested eyes that made her nervous. 'And why were you so intent on seeing your housemate's boyfriend play golf?'

Ro's eyes flicked upstairs. Bobbi was still sleeping. Hump and Greg had been relegated to the kitchen by another police officer as soon as Ro's status as a 'witness' had been identified on their door-to-door enquiries. 'Because I . . . I was being nosy. She hadn't introduced him to us yet and I was curious about him. He was older than—'

'How much older?'

Ro wrinkled her nose. 'Fifty-one, I think she said?'

'And—'

'Well, to be honest, I thought maybe the reason she was reluctant for us to meet him was because he was married, had a family. I was worried about her getting hurt. She's not as tough as she makes out.'

The detective watched her, his eyes moving side to side over her face like he could fathom the truth from her freckles. 'So you assumed that any person you saw coming out on the first tee might be him. Do you know for a fact that your housemate's boyfriend stayed here last night? Did you see him?'

'Well, no, I didn't actually see him myself. If I had, I would have known what he looked like, wouldn't I?' The detective's eyes clouded at her flippancy. 'But I heard him upstairs,' she added quickly. 'Bobbi told us it was him.'

'How do you know he didn't leave later in the night?'

She exhaled, weary now. 'I don't. Greg, our housemate, had had too much to drink –' her ankle kicked the washing-up bowl lightly '– and we were all trying to help him onto the sofa here. We heard someone upstairs. Bobbi said it was Kevin and we told Bobbi we didn't want some stranger seeing him like that.'

'Greg's the one with the bloodshot eyes in the kitchen?'

Ro nodded. It wasn't vodka that had done that, although there'd been no time for broken hearts this morning – even one as destroyed as Greg's. 'I went to bed straight after we'd got Greg sorted. Hump stayed down here with him. I fell asleep immediately and didn't hear a thing until I woke up this morning.'

'Can you be sure it was a bad dream that woke you?'

'It was a very . . . shocking dream, yes. It took me a couple of moments to recover from it.'

'But could it have been a sound – such as the front door closing, car doors closing?'

'I think it was definitely the dream. It frightened me awake.'

The officer nodded, not remotely interested in pursuing a conversation in dream psychology.

'Let's go back to what happened when you called your boyfriend.'

Ro brightened. 'Oh well, he picked up, which was nothing short of miraculous. He's in Cambodia, you see. Really dodgy connections. Half the time I can't get him.'

The police officer nodded again, bored by her diversions. 'And?'

'And so I started talking to him.'

'Were you still watching for the man to appear on the golf course?'

Ro frowned, concentrating hard. 'Yeah . . . Oh! No, wait, I'm getting it wrong. I saw the two men come out onto the first tee *before* my boyfriend picked up.'

'You're sure?'

'Yes.'

The detective scratched out something in his notebook with a suppressed sigh. 'What did they look like? Could you give me a physical description?'

'Well, not in any detail. It's too far to see clearly from here. I could just see that the taller man was wearing red trousers and a panama.'

'A panama?'

'It's a hat.'

'I know what a panama is, ma'am.'

'Right, yes, of course you do.' Ro shifted position on the sofa.

'What about the other man?'

'He was shorter, bald – from what I could see, anyway – and wearing a bright green jumper.'

'That's it?'

His tone suggested she had failed in some way and her shoulders slumped. 'I'm afraid so.'

'What were they doing? Were they talking? Did they appear to know each other?'

Ro hesitated, trying to think back. It had all been so innocuous, fractions of moments she had barely registered, even *with* her curiosity piqued about the possibility of finally seeing Kevin. 'They just came over on a golf buggy and one of them started, you know, crouching down and looking at the slopes or whatever. You know, like they do in the Masters and stuff—'

'Which one?'

'The bald one.'

'And the other one?'

'He was getting out his clubs.'

The detective's eyes narrowed and Ro got the impression he was holding his breath. 'And then what?'

'Well, that's when my boyfriend picked up and we started chatting.'

'That exact moment?'

'That exact one, yes. He gave me a bit of a fright, you see. I hadn't realized he'd picked up.'

'You didn't see anything further on the green?'

Ro shrugged, feeling thoroughly useless. 'No. My boyfriend wanted to see the dress I'd worn last night, so I left the window to show it to him and then I flopped on the bed.'

'Flopped?'

'Mmm-hmm.' She nodded vigorously and bit her lip.

'And then?'

'And then we finished chatting and said goodbye, and I went downstairs to see how Greg was doing. It stank of booze down here, though, so I opened the door first to let in some fresh air, and that's when I saw the police cars going past. I ran back in and woke up the boys, and then you started knocking on all the doors. And now here we are.' She shifted position, on tenterhooks to know what all this was really about. She'd told him hers; now it was only fair he told her his. 'Can you tell me what this is about now? I know it must be bad. I mean, the tent – I've seen those on the telly. They only go up when . . . when there's . . .' She swallowed hard, unable to get the words out. She'd been so focused on trying to help she hadn't allowed herself to think about what had actually happened.

The officer closed his notebook. 'We're investigating a homicide at the Maidstone Club.'

Ro sucked in her breath, feeling her blood pool at her feet. Oh God. Oh God. 'You mean . . . he d-died?'

'Someone died?'

They both turned to find Bobbi standing in the hallway, tying her dressing gown around her, her face puffy with sleep, but her dark eyes already slitted suspiciously.

The police officer stood up. 'Detective Bryant, ma'am. We're just making some routine enquiries for a live investigation. Could you come in here, please, and take a seat? I need to ask you some questions.'

'What's happened? Who's died?'

'There's been a homicide at the Maidstone.'

'The *Maidstone*?' Bobbi spluttered, almost laughing from the shock of it, as though the idea of anything so messy happening there was inconceivable.

'Take a seat, please,' he repeated, standing until the smile died on her lips and she walked in slowly, silently, her dark eyes moving between Ro and the policeman. She sat down on the sofa beside Ro, their legs touching. Ro felt a strong urge to reach out and take Bobbi's hand, but she didn't. She didn't dare.

'What is your name?' the detective asked Bobbi, sitting down himself and opening his notebook again.

'Bobbi Winkleman.'

'I understand you had a guest last night,' the policeman began.

Bobbi's eyes narrowed dangerously. 'Has my *mother* sent you?'

'Please just answer the question.'

Ro put her hand on Bobbi's leg. 'It's important, Bobbi.'

Bobbi took in the expression on Ro's face and looked back at the police officer. 'My boyfriend was with me.'

'And what's his name?'

Bobbi hesitated. 'Kevin Bradley.'

'How old is Mr Bradley?'

'Fifty-one.'

The police officer opened his notepad again and looked down at his notes. 'And at what time did Mr Bradley leave here?'

'Just after six this morning. Why are you asking me about Kevin? What is this about?'

But the detective ignored her. Right now, it was his questions that needed to be answered. 'Do you know where he was going?'

Bobbi scowled. She didn't take well to being ignored (as Greg had discovered to his cost). 'He said he had a meeting.'

'At six o'clock on a Sunday morning?'

'He's not a nine-to-fiver,' Bobbi retorted. 'He's a successful businessman. He works round the clock, round the world and not necessarily out of an office.'

Ro bit her lip, knowing the detective could be heading in one of two directions with these questions, and she hoped now – hoped really, really badly – that Kevin was going to turn out to be married with kids after all – that he'd left here to go back to his family, not some dodgy meeting or a game of golf. Especially not that.

'Do you have any photographs of Mr Bradley?'

Bobbi crossed her arms. 'Not that I'm prepared to show you until you tell me what's going on. I don't understand why you're asking me all these questions about Kevin.'

The police officer stared back at Bobbi levelly. 'If you could show me a photograph of your boyfriend, ma'am, it would help us in our enquiries.'

There was a long pause and Ro could see the pennies slowly beginning to drop in Bobbi's mind. 'It's on my cell,' she murmured finally, pointing vaguely to the ceiling.

'Do you want me to get it for you?' Ro asked her.

Bobbi looked across at her, but Ro wasn't sure her house-mate was actually seeing her. Panic was beginning to set in with the understanding.

Ro looked at the police officer, who saw what Ro saw and nodded subtly. Ro ran quickly up the stairs, her heart pounding as she darted into Bobbi's room and found the iPhone on the bedside table. She descended the stairs two at a time and handed it over to Bobbi, panting.

Bobbi scrolled through her picture gallery in silence. 'There. I took that last night. We had a reservation at Nick & Toni's. Table nineteen. You can check. And he was with me till an hour ago.'

The police officer took the phone, his eyes flicking from the screen to Bobbi and back again.

'Ma'am, I'm going to have to ask you to come with me.'

Bobbi stood up, anger bursting through her in one last defiant stand. '*Why?* He hasn't done anything – I can tell you that for sure. I've given you an alibi for him. I know he sails pretty close to the wind at times, bu—'

'Ma'am, you've misunderstood. Your boyfriend isn't a suspect in this investigation.'

'But . . .' Bobbi visibly paled. Ro threw her arm around her, squeezing her tightly, too tightly, but Bobbi didn't notice. Every fibre of her being was focused on the police officer.

The detective – for the first time since entering – looked apprehensive, his closed, suspicious demeanour giving way to something closer to regret. 'I'm afraid I have to ask you to come with me to the morgue. We need you to formally identify the body.'

The house had never been so quiet. Not a door had been slammed all day; the stairs didn't creak with one housemate or another bounding up three at a time, picking something up from their room en route to the beach or the club.

Greg stood by the window, looking like hell, his forehead pressed to the cool pane and enjoying the momentary chill. Temperatures had risen quickly once the sea mist had rolled back and the day's grisly proceedings had been revealed.

Hump was perched on the bottom step of the stairs, his elbows on his knees and his head dropped low. Ro was pacing. She reckoned she must have walked three miles just in the sitting room, trying to burn off her agitation as they all waited for Bobbi to be dropped back in the patrol car.

She had chosen to go to the mortuary alone, her manner subdued but efficient as she'd gone upstairs to get dressed, her eyes down and, when they did meet anyone's, dim. She hadn't cried, hadn't even gasped; her pretty knees had just discreetly buckled at the detective's words and she'd sunk softly back down on the sofa like a marionette whose strings had been cut.

Greg straightened up suddenly. 'She's here.'

They all stood up, ramrod straight and nervous, clustering together in the hallway, not wanting to crowd her on the porch. There were huge numbers of people already gathered at the police cordons further up the street, at the Egypt Lane junction, all wanting to find out what had happened and to whom, and how and why.

Ro watched Bobbi stop at the sight of their small gaggle through the porch screen, the lot of them divided by more than mesh now, united by more than an address. Bobbi blinked, her bottom lip trembling, as Greg opened the door and she crossed the threshold into six arms, tears running down eight cheeks, two hearts broken – a motley crew that had started out as strangers but somewhere along the line, through all the bickering and noise and mess, had become a family of sorts.

# Chapter Twenty-Eight

'Are you telling me you actually witnessed the murder?' Florence asked, her voice restored to its former power now that she was almost fully recovered. 'You actually saw the victim clubbed to death?' Her questions were back to full-strength directness too.

Ro saw a couple of well-dressed visitors twitch in their chairs slightly as Florence's voice carried over the tartan carpets, and she moved her chair closer to Florence's. 'No,' she said in a quieter voice. 'But the police think I would have done if I hadn't started talking to Matt and moved away from the window.'

'So then, technically, you were the last person to see that poor man alive.'

Ro paused, before nodding with a shudder. It was a hard thing to accept – that she had been the last person to see a dead man walking. 'Apart from the . . .' she couldn't bring herself to say the word 'murderer', 'perpetrator, obviously.'

Kevin's death had cast a shadow over the entire house. Fear and violence wasn't just something that lurked behind shadows or in the dark anymore; it was right in front of them, in the blazing sunlight, outside their own windows and part of the innocuous inanities of going about life – drinking coffee, taking showers, playing golf . . .

The story had dominated the local news every day for weeks now – many of the headlines focusing on the shock that this could have happened at the elitist and secretive Maidstone Club, rather than the horror of a life brutally cut short – and the police were convinced that the murderer was known to Kevin, either through his business or personal life. The police had spent a couple more days interviewing Bobbi about the relationship, and her recollections tallied with their own checks – Kevin hadn't been seeing anyone else, it appeared, and he wasn't married either, although he'd been divorced three times – and the police had concluded the murderer was most likely a business associate.

It was a relief of sorts, but Bobbi's grief was complicated and hard to manage for them all, especially in the first week after the killing, when both she and Greg had stayed down in East Hampton (Greg's own heartbreak a hidden torment that he suppressed after the humiliation of his vodka binge): the relationship had only been going a short while, Bobbi's motives for the hook-up had been more rooted in ambition than attraction (or at least they had started out that way), and her moods were erratic – shock blending with anger mingling with fear. Mainly fear: fear that the killing had happened within metres of where she slept, fear that it had happened within minutes of her kissing him, fear that her own ambition had propelled her towards someone whose even greater ambition had crossed lines where murder was the only answer. She had suffered from nightmares for the first few days and they had all taken it in turns to sit by her bed as she slept, Bobbi even accepting Greg's solicitations without rancour.

Florence twisted carefully in her position on the wood-trimmed sofa and rested her hand firmly upon Ro's. 'Ro dear, I don't want to alarm you, but . . . I do have to ask you something: you are quite sure the murderer didn't see *you*, aren't you?'

Ro stared back, dumbstruck. That thought had never occurred to her. 'Well . . . y-yes. I mean, I never had any sense that either one of them looked my way or saw me . . . I don't think.' She frowned. Was she absolutely sure about that? Could she swear to it? She hadn't tried to hide herself at the window after all. What if her movements had been picked up as she'd left the window to show Matt the dress?

Florence lowered her voice cautiously as a nurse passed by. 'I only ask because if the murderer is still at large . . . Well, you know what I'm saying.'

Ro stared at her, feeling her heart beginning to gallop. 'But . . .' Ro swallowed. 'What happened to you and what happened to Kevin are entirely unrelated. There's no suggestion, is there, that—'

'No, no. I'm not suggesting that. It's just that violence, once unleashed, seems to always drag innocents into its path. Just look at what happened to you in the cafe, when that coffee was intended for me. There's been too much suffering already, Ro. I couldn't bear it if you were to get hurt again. Just be alert.'

'I was just sitting quietly at the window,' she murmured, thinking how she had yet again been at the wrong place at the wrong time. If only she had stayed sleeping, if only Ted Connor hadn't invaded her dreams and made her waken with such a fright . . .

'I'm not trying to frighten you. Be safe, that's all I'm saying. Both you and I have found to our cost that some people will stop at nothing to get what they want. Keep out of their way.'

Ro looked at Florence quizzically, a furrow deepening in her brow. That sounded like surrender if ever she heard it. Did Florence still think that selling the house was the only way to secure her safety? 'You have reconsidered on selling the house, haven't you?'

'On the contrary, being stuck in here has really given me time to think and I've completely come round to Ted's view on this. He's a prudent man and I'm just being foolish if I think that sentimentality over bricks and mortar is worth dying for.' She patted Ro's hand. 'I'm just so grateful to have been given this chance to move on, Ro. I want to see my grandchildren grow up. There's still so much I want to do.'

'I see.' Ro stared unseeing out of the window, oblivious to the kaleidoscopic patterns of the clouds streaming across the sky. All she could see was Ted Connor. He was everywhere she looked, his all-American smile beaming through the camera as she spent long days in the studio whittling down his radiant family life – bright smiles and in-jokes, beachy weekends and good hair – to a bijoux chunk of perfect moments set to a soundtrack; his persistent stare following her at parties, trying to figure her out. It was no wonder his face was burned on her retina when she closed her eyes at night and in her yoga class. He was always there, standing by her side as the coffee burned, beside Florence's as the electricity coursed and the water rained down . . .

'Anyway, I've had some good news for a change: the doctors have said I can be discharged next week,' Florence said, watching the emotions running over Ro's face and briskly changing the subject.

'That soon?' Ro was astonished, even though physically there was little evidence in Florence's appearance now of her injuries and she was growing visibly stronger by the day.

'It'd be right this instant if I had my way. I can't wait to get out of here. From what I'm reading in *Dan's Papers*, the Town Board sounds like it's falling apart with all this in-fighting about the report.'

'Report?'

'The Montauk Beach Proposal?'

'Oh, that.' Ro felt distracted still.

'Yes, the sooner I get back there, the better.'

'You mustn't overdo it, Florence – you've been through so much.'

'The best thing that could happen to me is to get back to normality. I've told the doctors I'll do whatever they want – physical therapy, meds, diet, you name it – but they have to let me out in time for the Artwalk. It's one of the high-lights of my year.'

'What's that?'

'You'll love it – you must come. Your friend Melodie runs it, in fact – a prestigious post.' Ro picked up on the sharp edge to the words. The antipathy between the two women ran both ways, then? 'It's an organized evening walk through the town's art galleries. The artists are there to give talks; drinks and canapés are laid on. It's a perfect mix of culture and sociability, and there's always quite a crowd. I shall look forward to seeing some familiar faces again after this dratted confinement.'

'It sounds great. Where is it and when?'

'Next Friday, seven p.m., outside the bookstore. Bring your friends if you would like.'

'Thanks. I'll ask them. I think we could all do with something to look forward to.' That was putting it lightly! She slapped her hands on her thighs, staring into space without moving for a moment. Her head was so full of worries and anxieties and suspicions, sometimes it felt hard to move. 'Well, I suppose I'd better head off. You are *clearly* fine and don't need any bolstering at all, and I'm so behind on work. I need to throw a mattress on the floor and lock myself in the studio for next three weeks.'

It was the last thing she wanted to do. The thought of trawling through the rest of the Connor films and photos was actually depressing her, the perfect family they supposedly reflected nothing more than an empty hologram. She sighed wistfully and got up slowly, feeling older than her years.

Florence was standing now too. 'Rowena, you look like you have the weight of the world on your shoulders. All this trouble, it's behind you now.'

'I know.'

Florence shook her head. 'You are without question the worst liar I've ever known.' She smiled, kissing her on the cheek. 'But never change, mine heart, never change.'

**04/18/2011**                                                           **06h49**
Baby, swaddled, in a clear plastic hospital crib.

'World, welcome to the little boy who's going to rock you off your axis and make you a better place.' Ted. Whispering. 'Finlay Patrick Connor. Eight pounds six ounces. Born at eighteen minutes past three this morning, April 18 same date as his grandma. As if his mom wasn't already clever enough.'

Camera pans to Marina, washed out, sleeping, hospital gown. One white stocking visible. Caesarean?

Camera pans back to baby. Pauses on photograph of Ella on bedside table. 'Just wait till this little lady wakes up this morning and finds out she became a big sister overnight.'

Camera zooms in, then moves down to Finn. White jersey cap, no hair visible, fleshy cheeks already.

'My boy.'

Blackness.

**04/18/2011**                                            **14h27**

'Smile.' Ted.

Marina, sitting in bed, looks up. Finlay in her arms, breastfeeding. She moves her hand and detaches the baby. Turns him and holds him up to the camera, her hands under his armpits, his body stretched long like a rabbit's. Finn cries.

'No, Marina, I didn't mean—' Ted.

'What? Isn't he beautiful?' She smiles. Proud. Radiant but pale. Butterfly tube still in her hand.

'Nothing.' Ted. Quiet.

Blackness.

**04/23/2011**                                            **12h31**

'Home sweet home.' Ted. Walking ahead of Marina – she is stepping out of lift, pushing buggy with car-seat attachment. Bouquet of flowers in the tray.

Glossy wood floor. Metallic walls. Enormous blue heart-shaped helium balloon attached to basket of muffins. '*A Baby Boy.*' Her eyebrows arch.

'Nothing to do with me,' Ted says, as she stops to read attached tag.

'Your parents.'

Walks into sitting room. Multiple vases of long-stemmed white roses on every surface.

'Everything to do with me.' Ted.

Marina looks around the room.

Camera moves towards her. Ted appears just in shot as he kisses her cheek. 'Welcome home, honey.'

'Ta-da boo!' Ella springs up from behind coral sofa, holding her pink pig in one hand, a brand-new blue elephant in the other. Hair fair now, in plaits. Wearing red cord smock dress with red-piped white blouse.

She walks towards Marina, holding out the blue toy. Reaches up and places it in the buggy. It covers sleeping Finn's face.

'Oh my God!' Marina cries, grabbing it and throwing it across the room. 'How could you be so stupid, Ella?'

Blackness.

**05/02/2011**                                                  **11h27**

Darkened room. Pale grey silk walls. Pink bed.

Ted asleep, bare-chested, thin sheet covering him, one arm dangling over side of bed. Other arm holding Finn in place on his chest.

Finn sleeping, his cheek against Ted's chest.

Sound of deep, heavy breathing.

'My boys.' Marina. Whispers.

Ro sat slumped in her chair, her chin on her hands, earphones on, her eyes immobile on the screen. She wasn't sure how much of this she could take.

'So did *not*!'

The sudden sound made her start, automatically pressing 'pause' and sitting up like a naughty schoolgirl.

Hump and Melodie stopped at the sight of her.

'Hey!' Hump grinned from the doorway. 'And what's got you looking so guilty?'

'I do not look guilty,' she replied indignantly, watching as the two of them walked into the shaded studio. 'I have nothing to feel guilty about.'

'No? Then why are all the blinds down? You're not hiding a guy in here, are you?' He grinned devilishly.

'It was too hot in here. And it makes it easier to see the screens.'

'You missed class *again*,' Melodie said pointedly, leaning on the opposite side of Ro's tall counter as Hump wandered over to his desk and began bashing the keyboard.

'I know.' Ro's shoulders slumped. 'I'm sorry. Work.'

But that wasn't strictly true. Things hadn't quite returned to normal between them since her disastrous attempt to confide her fears about Ted had turned into an attack on Florence instead. And she had stopped looking to meditation as her way to connect with Matt; it was never Matt she found anymore.

'She's stalking some poor family,' Hump offered from behind his screen.

'Well, I guess too much work is a nice problem to have,' Melodie said knowingly, watching Ro as though detecting the tiny dip in temperature between them. She was wearing all white today – either in homage to the heat or Ghandi – cropped harem trousers teamed with a draped-neck vest and a diamond anklet.

Ro frowned as she looked across at Hump, something occurring to her. He was wearing jersey track pants cut off below the knee and a white wife-beater vest. 'Hump, don't tell me you did yoga too!'

Hump shrugged. 'Yeah. Why not?'

'Uh . . . because you said it was for pussy-whipped men who couldn't throw a ball!' she laughed, crossing her arms and tipping back in the chair.

'I knew he'd capitulate,' Melodie said, standing on one leg effortlessly and relaxing into the tree pose in the way other people dropped into a slouch. 'He couldn't bear that I can do more press-ups than him.'

'Yeah, but on an arm wrestle . . .' Hump replied, flexing his biceps.

'Hump, do I look like the kind of woman who *armwrestles*?'

Ro listened to her two friends' banter, feeling slightly like the dumped friend (even if she was the one ducking out). She had grown in lots of ways since living here – she could now order a flagel without laughing, she thought nothing of pouring almond milk in her tea, and it felt almost normal to wear her swimsuit as underwear, but she still couldn't move from stranger to bosom buddy in less than twenty stages.

Melodie turned back to Ro, her gaze steady and enquiring, as though trying to draw the truth from Ro without words, and Ro found she couldn't quite meet her eyes. The intensity of their friendship had passed; Ro had changed. She wasn't the depressed, slightly lost girl anymore that Melodie had found on the steps that summer morning, and Matt wasn't the only one struggling to adapt. Ro didn't need Melodie in the way that she once had, and she was almost beginning to resent Melodie's assumed authority over her – as though she knew Ro better than Ro knew herself, and always knew best.

'So what are you up to for the rest of the day?' Ro asked lightly.

Melodie checked her watch quickly and groaned. 'I've got my hairstylist coming over in an hour. Another night, another dinner.'

Hairstylist? Ro felt a stab of disappointment at the revelation. Crazy hair that came with its own ASBO was her and Melodie's link; it was what they had bonded over. That Melodie actually had her hair professionally styled seemed like . . . cheating, somehow.

'How about you?'

'Nothing so glamorous. Are we doing anything, Hump?'

'It's Mighty Meat Feast specials night at Pedro's Pizzas tonight,' he said, punching the air with both hands.

'I guess we're slobbing out doing that, then,' Ro sighed happily.

'I would do anything for a night in like that,' Melodie replied, making Ro frown – she knew full well that nothing that wasn't macrobiotic went near Melodie's mouth.

'Well, you could if you weren't so busy being one half of a power couple,' Hump teased, from across the room. 'But I guess someone's got to rule the world.'

Melodie looked unimpressed. 'My husband's job doesn't define *me*, Hump.'

'No? You always look pretty happy to be found at every A-list party, chairing every fancy-pants charity—'

'I hear you've got another big night tomorrow night,' Ro butted in, a sympathetic look on her face as she clocked Melodie's affronted expression. Sometimes Hump took his teasing just too far. 'The . . . Artwalk, is it?'

'Oh yes!' Melodie replied brightly. 'Can you make it? I'd love you to be there.'

'Thanks, I will be. Florence has already invited me.'

'Oh, that's such a shame. I thought we could go for dinner after.'

'Sorry.' Ro bit her lip. 'Isn't Brook going?'

'Yes, but he gets our driver to actually drive him between the galleries.' She rolled her eyes. 'Missing the point completely. Art*walk*, darling?'

'Oh dear,' Ro sympathized.

'Take my advice – never marry an older man,' Melodie stage-whispered wickedly, before straightening up and tapping the counter with her hand. 'Right, well, I'd better get going. Zen counts for nothing when your hair won't behave, am I right?' She blew a kiss to Ro, pointedly ignoring Hump as she walked across the room and out of the studio.

A moment later, she popped her head back in again. 'I forgot to ask – how's Bobbi doing?'

'Bobbi?' Ro echoed. 'She's good. Getting through it.'

'Send her my love, OK? Tell her to try to get down for some more classes. I could really help her with her grief, get her to find the light in this time of darkness.'

Ro nodded, not quite sure what to say to that, already quite sure of Bobbi's retort if she told her to 'find the light'. She listened to the sound of Melodie's bare feet padding back to the studio next door.

'You should apologize to her, Hump. She gets really sensitive about that stuff.'

'What stuff?'

'She hates being seen as just some socialite.'

'But she is! Every time I open *Dan's Papers*, there she is, arm in arm with Brook and some benefactor billionaire.'

'Just because she's rich doesn't mean that's all there is to her. She takes her spiritual life very seriously.'

'Yeah, don't I know it,' Hump grumbled.

Ro frowned. 'You're down in the dumps all of a sudden.'

Hump tutted but didn't say anything more.

'Well . . . I can't believe you did yoga,' Ro muttered after a few minutes' silence.

'I thought it wouldn't hurt to work on the mind as well as the body for a bit,' he mumbled. 'Just while all this crazy shit's going on.'

Ro looked up at him from her stool, but he was engrossed in reading an invoice on his desk. It was easy to forget that he bruised too. He seemed so indestructible with his puppyish grin and loping run, his boundless energy and good humour. But events had taken a toll on him too, and he was still playing doctor, putting one after another of his housemates back together again. Ro realized she hadn't seen a single woman emerging from his room for weeks now.

'Well, I wish you'd told me, that's all. I'd have loved to see you doing the monkey pose,' she drawled, trying to make him smile at least. 'I'd have paid good money for that.'

'Is that the one with the splits?'

'With your arms overhead, yeah.' She chuckled at the thought. Flexible he wasn't.

'Well, you can, next time you go along,' he shrugged, unusually flat.

'You mean you're going to go again?' Her eyes popped wide with surprise.

'Maybe,' he said after a moment. 'It was fun.'

'Fun,' Ro repeated, frowning and wondering whether he'd caught too much sun driving the Humper today.

'So how is Bobbi getting on really? You heard from her today?' he asked, changing the subject.

'No, not yet. I called on her mobile, but it went to voice-mail. She said yesterday she had a stack of meetings to get through. I'm worried about her, Hump. I think she's doing too much, trying to prove a point. Now it's all out in the open about her and Kevin, I think she thinks her position is precarious.'

'What do you mean?'

'Well, let's face it, it doesn't look good for the firm to have an associate who was having an affair with a murdered client.'

'Right.' Hump shook his head in silent dismay. He looked about twelve.

'How about Greg? How's he doing?' she asked.

'Same.' He pulled a face. 'Working harder than ever too – who knew it was even possible, right? Says he probably won't get down this weekend.' He tutted. 'Honestly, him and Erin, Bobbi and Kevin – life just got tangled in such a twisted mess that weekend. I don't think Greg wants it in his face.'

'You can understand that,' Ro said sadly, wondering if she actually would ever see Greg again. She wouldn't be surprised if he stayed in the city for the rest of the summer now. He'd only ever come out to see Erin anyway. 'It's such a shame. He looked so happy that night – you know, before.'

'Yeah . . .' Hump kicked back in his chair, newly focused, his eyes falling to the screen behind her. 'It was a night full of surprises, that was for sure.'

Ro looked across at him. Something in his tone . . . 'What?'

KAREN SWAN

'Well, when I came back to get you at the Southampton fundraiser, I was sure I'd walked in on something between you and Long Story too. The two of you looked guilty as hell.'

'Don't be daft,' Ro said quickly. 'And for the last time, stop calling him that.'

'He couldn't take his eyes off you when we were standing on the lawn. I thought I was going to have to challenge him to a duel or something, to uphold your honour.'

Ro swallowed back the words. If only he knew what was really going on, the thoughts that were really going round in her head about him. 'He's a client, Hump. A married/divorced/whatever father-of-two with a girlfriend. Hardly my type! And you *know* I'd never cheat on Matt.'

'I know you wouldn't.'

There was a silence.

'But?' she demanded. 'There's definitely a "but" coming.' Her cheeks were flaming, indignation building up inside her because anything he said after the 'but' was going to undermine her and Matt. She already knew that. That was what 'buts' did.

He looked at her for a long moment. 'Look, Big Foot, you need to wake up and smell the coffee. You know you love Matt. I know you love Matt. Bobbi does not know you love Matt, but she wouldn't know love if it punched her in the face, so . . .' He made a dismissive gesture with his hands. 'But you've lived with me long enough now to know I'm the freaking king of seduction. I *know* chemistry when I see it and there's something between you two.'

'Yes, and it's called suspicion!' she blurted out, unable to keep the words down any longer. She couldn't let him say those things. 'I'm not attracted to him, Hump. I'm almost frightened of him!' She was nearly shouting, her breath coming in shallow sips as the words tumbled out of her – all the fears and misapprehensions that she'd kept to herself finally breaking free.

'Frightened of him?' Hump echoed.

'Yes.'

'You're frightened of *him*?' His eyes moved pointedly to the frozen image on her computer screen of Ted sleeping with his baby son on his chest.

Her mouth dropped open. Admittedly, Ted Connor did not look remotely worrisome at that moment in time.

The phone rang on his desk and he shook his head, a small smile on his lips. 'Nuh, you're not frightened of him.' He picked up the phone, cupping his hand over the receiver. 'You're frightened of how he makes you feel.'

He winked, swivelling away from her in his chair as he began talking with his newest advertiser.

Ro glared at his back from across the room, mute with rage. Scared of an attraction? To Ted Connor?

She'd never heard of anything so bloody stupid.

# Chapter Twenty-Nine

'Knock, knock.' Ro poked her head round the door to find Bobbi sitting on the bed, staring at the wall. 'Hey.'

Bobbi turned at the sound, but her eyes were vacant.

Ro sat down softly on the bed beside her, squeezing her shoulder lightly. She was wearing a black suit that three weeks earlier had been vixen-tight on her, but now hung loosely on her hips, a string of pearls round her neck, flat shoes instead of her signature heels. Ro guessed she was going to find putting one foot in front of the other a struggle today.

A tiny, white scale model of the 'stepped' house she had designed for Kevin – the job on which they'd met – was on the dormer's deep windowsill. Ro studied it from the bed. Now that the plot was laid out for Ro to see, she realized how compromised it was and how ingenious Bobbi's solution had been. The house complied with regulations, looked beautiful and accommodated everything Kevin had wanted. The girl had talent. But had her ambition meant she'd overreached this time? In trying to secure the deal, she'd crossed lines she had no business dancing near. She'd gambled and lost, and everything she cared about was on the line.

'The car's here. Are you ready?' Hump had ordered a

black Chrysler to take them to the church. Turning up to a funeral in a bright yellow Defender didn't seem appropriate, even to a maverick like him.

'I just keep trying to figure out *why*,' Bobbi murmured, as though she hadn't heard Ro.

'Bobbi, that's something for the police to discover. You need to focus on looking after you.'

'But maybe he said something . . . maybe he tried to warn me. Do you think he might have? I could have missed it.'

Ro paused, knowing better than try to get Bobbi to do something she didn't want to do. And right now, she wanted to talk. 'Well, did you ever get the impression he was frightened or being threatened? Maybe he was nervous or agitated? Couldn't sleep, eat?'

Bobbi shook her head.

'There you go, then. And even if he had known he was in trouble, he probably went out of his way to act normal around you. He wouldn't have wanted you to worry, or to have become involved.'

'Unless he didn't know he was in trouble.'

'In which case, that would have been a blessing,' Ro murmured.

'He was just so . . . so relaxed that night. I've been over it, like, a million times in my head, wondering whether I forgot to tell the police one thing, one detail that might make all the difference.'

'They're trained in interview techniques, Bobbi. They know how to get all the information they possibly can out of people. Whatever you know, they now know.'

Bobbi dropped her head in her hands. 'I shouldn't have let him go that morning. I'd tried talking him out of it the night before. I wanted us to have a whole weekend together, but I was so sleepy when he got up. I hadn't slept well and . . . well, he said he'd come back. He wanted to meet you all.' She shook her head. 'I didn't even open my eyes when he kissed me goodbye.' Her voice – her strong, bossy, don't-mess Manhattan voice – was thin and reedy, climbing higher.

'Bobbi, you couldn't possibly have known. There was nothing you could have done. The police don't think it was either opportunistic or manslaughter. Whoever did this knew they were going to do it. They had planned it. And if it hadn't happened then, it would have happened elsewhere. He was a marked man, Bobbi.'

Bobbi was quiet for a few moments, her eyes fixed on a hairline crack at the top of the wall. 'The police still think it was someone he knew through his business.'

'I know.' The local papers were feeding off titbits, anything to keep the story on their front page every day. Murder simply didn't happen in the Hamptons.

'So then maybe I knew him. I'm in the same business. Kinda.'

'No! Now you listen to me. You'll only frighten yourself talking like that,' Ro said forcefully, remembering her own fear as Florence had asked her if she'd thought the murderer had seen *her* at the window. 'You're a creative. He was a wheeler-dealer realtor. There's very little overlap in what you do other than you're both trading in bricks and mortar. Besides, from what the papers are saying, I wouldn't be surprised if the police already have a good idea of possible suspects. Did you read the piece in the *Montauk Herald*?'

Bobbi shook her head, focusing intently on Ro's words.

'Oh.' Dammit. She didn't want to say too much, risk upsetting Bobbi now of all times.

'What did it say? Tell me.'

'Well . . . it's come out that Kevin upset a lot of people with his tactics when it came to getting commissions.'

'How?' A trace of irritation lined Bobbi's voice.

'It seems he didn't simply wait for people to come to him wanting to sell; he liked to be more proactive. Apparently he was known to the regulators for trying to "induce" people to sell. But after Sandy, he became a whole lot more productive than that: he spent the first weeks in the immediate aftermath in the area, convincing the worst hit in the Montauk Harbor wharves to sell to him. He told them he knew Senator McClusky and that the senator had told him, in confidence, he was reporting back to Congress that Montauk – under the terms of local policy for strategic retreat – *shouldn't* qualify for federal aid for redevelopment.'

'What? But he's all over the media saying the opposite.'

'I know, and the senator's madly disputing this conversation ever took place, but . . .' She shrugged. 'That was what Kevin told those people. It's how he got them to sell. He said their businesses and homes were worthless and were to be left to the ocean, but that he alone would help them – he'd buy them out as a philanthropic gesture.'

'*Why* would he do that? He didn't have that kind of money.'

Ro shrugged. 'Well, that's what everyone's asking, now that it's all coming out. You see, no one knew that he was going round saying the same thing to everyone. He made every vendor sign a confidentiality agreement: each one thought he was doing them – and them alone – a favour.'

She watched Bobbi's expression carefully, knowing that this wasn't painting her boyfriend in a flattering light. 'He bought up the entire area, paying peanuts for every premises, while they all thought he was the good Samaritan.'

'So? He was enterprising,' Bobbi said defiantly, her dark eyes shining. 'Even if he did stretch the truth, those business owners were probably all more than happy to take the money and run; they're on a hiding to nothing out there on that point. I don't see how that justifies his being *murdered*.'

'No. Of course not! There's never justification for murder. I'm just saying . . .' Ro sighed, trying to tread lightly. 'He was an unscrupulous businessman, a man with enemies. Those people in Montauk may just be the thin end of the wedge, the ones we know about. Who else did he swindle?'

They sat quietly together, Bobbi absorbing Kevin's underhand tactics that made her ambition – dating a client! – look positively bucolic.

Bobbi looked at her, a look of unbearable sadness written across her face. 'I just can't shake the feeling that I know.'

Ro put her arm around Bobbi's shoulder. 'You don't, sweetie. You're just very emotionally involved in a tragic situation. It's normal to feel like you could have prevented it or done more. But the die was cast long before you and Kevin hooked up.' Downstairs, she heard Hump coughing 'discreetly' in the hall. Ro squeezed her lightly. 'And we really have to go.'

Bobbi sighed, her shoulders rolled forward, her back humped, all her yoga poise and Pilates control and New

York fighting spirit gone. She stood up, wobbly on her coltish legs, pale beneath her tan, and Ro hooked her arm through Bobbi's and led her down to where Hump was waiting for them. Ro had never even said hello to the man, but it was time to say goodbye.

Florence was outside the bookstore the following evening, just as she'd said she'd be, at 7 p.m. sharp. She was talking animatedly with another couple, her short white hair swept back from her face, her grey eyes vibrant and dancing as she made her point with extravagant hand gestures, her anthracite linen tunic swaying with her movements. No one passing would believe that she'd been – just a few days earlier – recuperating in hospital from a near-fatal accident (although Ro still believed there'd been nothing accidental about it no matter what Ted had said).

Melodie was standing a short distance away, with a separate group, all hanging on to her every word. Ro quickly checked out her hair.

'Rowena!' Florence called her over, and as she approached, she overheard her saying to her companions, 'This is the girl I was telling you about.'

They all shook hands and made small talk, the group quickly swelling to almost twenty people, until Melodie checked her watch and clapped her hands quietly and they obediently followed her towards the first gallery: Robert Ingermann's, in a studio behind Starbucks, off Main Street, which specialized in graffitied collages. Ro walked slowly along with Florence at the back of the group, insisting Florence held on to her arm. She was feeling energetic and bullish in spirit, but several weeks of almost complete bed rest, Ro knew, would have taken more strength from her than she yet realized.

As forewarned, Brook was already in there, wearing cream trousers and a panama, drinking the first glass of vintage champagne and holding forth with Robert on prices for Pollock. Ro hoped he would give Florence a wide berth tonight and not corner her with town politics. Florence needed a night out and a night off.

Not that Brook stood much chance of getting anywhere near her. They had no sooner stopped walking than Florence was encircled by a group of mature-student women gardeners, all eager to hear more about her guerrilla seed-bombing of the dunes.

'I'll get us some drinks,' Ro said to Florence, who smiled back apologetically.

Ro wandered to the drinks table and took a couple of glasses of rosé, stopping in front of a giant canvas that had 'Ecstasy' spelled out in newspaper print and overlaid on a blue and white striped background. She wasn't quite sure what to make of it; personally, she preferred a pretty watercolour landscape that made her daydream.

Handing Florence her drink – over the heads of the faithful – Ro wandered around the room, one hand soothingly holding on to the straps of the camera round her neck. It seemed to her that everything was ludicrously overpriced, and she was sure she could have achieved the same results herself with a newspaper and a tube of Pritt stick. She walked around slowly, finishing her drink slightly too quickly – nerves – and getting a refill, reading every information card that had been positioned beside each piece and occasionally checking her brochure as though she was considering paying for one of them.

She stopped in front of a giant mural of a 1960s likeness of Audrey Hepburn, her back to the viewer, dressed only in neon-pink knickers, with the line 'The sexiest curve on a woman is her smile.'

'Isn't it wonderful?'

That voice. Ro didn't need to turn her head to know that Melodie had come to stand beside her. Thank God. She had been standing here on her own for almost twenty minutes – although, she was surprised to realize that it didn't bother her as it once would have done.

Ro laughed. 'Yeah, right!'

The laughter gurgled in her throat as she took in Melodie's expression.

'Oh God, you were being serious. I'm so sorry. I . . .' She swallowed, mortified. 'I . . . uh . . . It's just not really my thing, But I can see, maybe, how . . . uh . . .' Audrey Hepburn in pink knickers? That cheesy line? Was she *kidding*? First the hair, now this . . . Ro felt the foundations of her world begin to shake.

Until Melodie winked.

'Oh God! Melodie! You cow,' Ro hissed, slapping an arm over her body and folding over with laughter. 'I so thought you were serious. You totally had me.'

'I know. I'm good, right?'

'The best. Bloody hell, I was dying on my feet.'

Melodie leaned in, lowering her voice. 'We only stop by here because Robert's one of Brook's biggest cohorts. He's loaded and wants to put his money where Brook's mouth is. He keeps urging Brook to run for senator next term.' She rolled her eyes dramatically.

'How depressing that it has to hijack *your* night,' Ro said, remembering Melodie's own words that she wasn't defined by her husband's job. Wasn't this exactly a case in point?

'Tell me about it. But then, I feel like a bad wife for not supporting him and . . .' She shrugged. 'I figure, how much does it really hurt for me to try and oil the wheels? And at least the champagne's vintage.'

'You are too selfless, Melodie. Sometimes you need to be a little more selfish –' she nodded towards Audrey '– for all our sakes.'

Melodie laughed, but it wasn't her usual sound – it was high and hollow, drawing Ro's attention more closely. As ever, she looked exquisitely exotic, wearing a fluid teal silk-jersey harem all-in-one suit with gold mesh cuffs, her dark hair exploding in a riot of frizzy curls behind her headband, but her skin didn't have its usual just-buffed, gold-dipped lustre, and she seemed a little on edge, her eyes constantly flitting around the room, making sure everyone had a drink, the canapés were warm, cheque-books were being opened.

'You look tired,' Ro said quietly. 'Is everything all right?'

Melodie looked surprised. 'You're sweet to notice. I'm not sleeping well at the moment. Brook's all wound up about the federal-aid application and he's talking about it every waking minute. I'll just be so glad when the damned proposal gets voted through and we can get back to our own lives.'

'I bet.'

Melodie dipped her head lower to Ro's, her hand on Ro's arm. 'An amendment to my previous advice the other day: never marry an older man *or* a politician,' she said quietly. 'And definitely don't marry an older politician.' She laughed her exhausted laugh again.

A beep came from Melodie's watch and she smiled. 'Oh, thank God. We can get out of here and go see some real art. That's where the fun really begins. A lot of the regulars have learned to skip this stop and join us at the next one.'

Ro finished her drink in one go and they wandered outside, everyone joining them like sheep as they walked back onto Main Street and towards the old pharmacy, Melodie's arm looped proprietorially through Ro's this time. She looked around for Florence, but she was walking in a slow huddle with another group and seemingly in her element to be part of the wider world again.

The light was fading fast as night blew in and the street lamps were beginning to glow. There were plenty of people still milling in the streets. It was after eight now and some of the boutiques had only just closed; other people were enjoying window-shopping in the cooler temperatures, hands and noses pressed to plate glass as they eyed python-print dresses and fluoro bracelets, moss-stitch cotton sweaters and pressed shorts. The well-dressed, lightly lubricated group attracted plenty of stares from the kids in the queue at the cinema, even absorbing a few more passers-by along the way as they headed to the next gallery.

From the windows, Ro could see this one specialized in bronzes that didn't look bronze at all, but rather had been powder-coated in matt colours. Most of the forms were from the natural world and true to life – much to Ro's relief – such as a trio of baby owls on a branch, a leopard sleeping in a tree, a dolphin mid-dive, an antelope mid-skip . . .

'I'd better be a good hostess now,' Melodie said reluctantly, squeezing her arm.

'Of course. I can't hog you all night.'

Ro accepted another glass of wine – sauvignon, this time – and sipped it quickly as she looked at the sculptures thoughtfully. Now this was art. This she could do.

She walked slowly round a life-sized bronze of an antelope, its skittishness captured in the frisk of its legs, the angle of the head, eyes dark and unreadable and innocent. She held the camera up to her eye, not to take a picture, but to gaze at it through the lens.

'I don't think photographs are allowed,' a female voice said beside her.

'Oh, it's OK. I wasn't going to . . .' Ro looked up, startled to find Julianne beside her.

Julianne looked back at her with faint surprise too, dull recognition glimmering in her kohled eyes, although Ro looked a different breed from the girl she'd been when buying beers at the Maidstone on the night of Fourth of July, now she was groomed for the night in an olive-green miniskirt and a fluffy cream waffle jumper.

'It's beautiful, isn't it?' Ro said quickly, her eyes flitting like butterflies around the space. Where was he? Was he here?

'I love it. So . . . sculptural,' Julianne murmured, clearly trying to place her.

'Well, yes,' Ro answered, thinking how Marina would never have said anything so stupid. She smiled vacuously and tried to move off like a seasoned networker, but Julianne stopped her with a question.

'We've met before, haven't we?' Julianne asked, turning her body towards Ro and compelling her to stay put.

'Um . . . oh yes, yes, I think you're right. Was it the . . . ?' She put her finger to her chin and stared up at the ceiling, trying to convey an impression of an overloaded social diary. 'Oh, was it the Independence party at the Maidstone?'

'Yes. I think so.' Julianne nodded slowly, the expression in her eyes cooling. 'And the fundraiser in Southampton too. You wore the red dress.'

*The* red dress? 'That's right.' Ro nodded, looking around the room for Melodie, or Florence: rescue. She didn't find it – quite the opposite. Her eyes were stopped in their tracks by Ted Connor, who was watching their fledgling conversation from across the gallery with two full glasses of wine in his hands and was clearly oblivious to anything his companion was saying. She hadn't seen him since the Southampton fundraiser either and their conversation, everything they'd said – and more particularly, everything they *hadn't* – swam through her mind.

She watched as he abruptly held up the two full glasses by way of apology to his companion and began to wind his way through the crowd towards them. She turned back to Julianne quickly. Not even manners could keep her here. 'Well, it's just lovely to see you again, but if you'll excuse me, I was on my way to say goodbye to my friends. I'm not feeling too good.'

Julianne took a step back as though she'd said she had the plague. 'Of course.'

Ro turned and moved into the crowd, just moments before she saw – in the reflection of the window – Ted appear at Julianne's side, his eyes on Ro's retreating back. She felt chased by him, somehow. Tracked and hunted.

She darted over to Melodie, who was in full flow with the group of overeager women who had taken Florence hostage earlier.

'I'm sorry, but I've got to go,' she said, talking over them all.

'No,' Melodie cried, clasping her by the hand. 'But we're only just getting going.'

'I have a headache.'

Melodie nodded sympathetically. 'Poor you, Ro. Wine can affect some people like that.'

'Yes, I think I need to lie down and try to get a good night's sleep.'

'You need to come back to yoga properly. That would sort you out. You slept soundly when you came to my classes – I could see it in your aura. Everything about you relaxed. But now—' Frowning, she took both Ro's hands in hers and waggled them. She tutted. 'All your channels are blocked. I can't read you. No wonder your head hurts.'

The women all looked at Ro pityingly, as though they too could see her blocked channels.

'I'll try and get there on Monday, I promise.' Ro leaned forward and kissed her on each cheek. 'Enjoy. This is a brilliant evening. Brilliant. Yet another string to your already overloaded bow.'

'Well, Brook has his committees; I have mine,' she shrugged lightly.

'Have you seen Florence? I need to say goodbye to her too.'

'Yes. Actually, she was talking to Brook last time I saw her – surprise, surprise.' The flinty edge sounded in her voice again. 'He accompanied her outside for some fresh air. I think the heat in here was getting to her.'

'Oh, I hope she's not overdoing it.' Ro looked around, concerned. It was warm in here. 'Anyway, look, I'll see you tomorrow maybe?' Checking the coast was clear again, she moved silkily through a small channel that had opened up between bodies.

'Ro—' She heard a man behind her say, a hand managing only to brush her fingertips – the touch like an electric volt – as she slipped through the door.

*Way* too close!

'Florence!' she cried loudly, propelled by panic and striding towards Florence and Brook with exaggerated bonhomie.

'Oh, Ro, there you are.' Florence smiled, taking Ro's new vigour as a consequence of the free wine. 'Brook and I are just wildly disagreeing on my proposals to the Town Board at the next meeting.'

Brook lifted his hat lightly, bending down to kiss her on each cheek. 'And how are you, Ro?'

'Fine, thanks. Headache, though.' She put a hand to her forehead to make the point. She looked back at Florence. 'I just came to say I'm off.'

'What? No!' Florence cried. 'We haven't gotten to Terry Sanger yet, and he's always the most thrilling.'

'Headache,' Ro reiterated, placing her fingers to her temples for good measure.

'But dinner?'

'Still headache,' Ro cringed.

Florence sighed, disappointed. 'Oh dear. I really wanted to have a pleasant evening out with you, something to restore both our spirits.'

'And we will, I promise.'

Florence scowled. 'This is all Brook's fault, of course, cornering me on this dratted proposal when I'm off duty.'

'You're never off duty, Florence,' Brook replied, clearly

bemused by the thought. 'You're the least off-duty person I've ever met.'

'Well, now, how can I be when you insist on proposing such outlandish ideas? Someone has to stand up to you.'

'And it always has to be you, doesn't it, Florence?'

'Well, you agree with me, Ro, don't you?'

'To be honest, I don't really know what you're disagreeing about,' Ro said apologetically.

'Well,' Florence said, shifting into a more comfortable stance and settling into her rhetoric, 'if what the papers are saying is true, I'm firmly of the view that Senator McClusky should stand down from his post.'

'Oh, come on, Florence! How can it be proven? It's his word against a dead man's! He has said he will attest on oath that he *never* said anything about blocking Montauk's petition for federal aid. Hell, the man's been its biggest supporter. He ran his campaign on it. It doesn't make sense that he would then advise to the contrary in private. He's being set up – it's obvious! That murdered fellow, Kevin—' He tried to remember his surname.

'Kevin Bradley,' Ro said helpfully.

'Thank you. Kevin Bradley. Well, I'm sorry the man's dead, of course I am, but let's not rewrite history on account of the fact. He was a charlatan and a crook, and he had every reason to lie to those people about his so-called relationship with the senator. It was one man's words against his, and those people were desperate – desperate, I tell you. They thought they'd lost everything. Kevin Bradley saw an opportunity to exploit them and he took it. It's that simple. The senator's got nothing to do with any of this.'

'I agree we can't know for certain, Brook, but the waters

have been sullied. The fear is out there: is he blocking the region's access to federal aid? Whether he is or not, their trust in him has gone.'

'But, Florence,' Brook interrupted, 'do you not see that the very same could have been said of *you* after the deficit scandal? What if everyone had lost faith in you because of rumour and hearsay? The man deserves a second chance at least. There's no evidence to support he ever even met the dead man, much less shared confidential Congress information. You know what these journalists are like – they'll say anything for a story.'

'There was a photograph taken of them together at some party!' Florence refuted passionately. 'They had certainly met.'

Ro caught a movement out of the corner of her eye. Ted Connor was standing just inside the doorway. He had begun talking to someone, but Ro had no doubt the second she extricated herself from this conversation . . .

'Well, if you want my honest opinion,' Ro said, wading in with a passion she didn't feel, 'I think I probably have to agree with Brook. From everything I've read, Kevin Bradley sounded like the kind of person to say anything that suited his ends. He was a bit of a player by all accounts. I don't think it's outside the realms of possibility that he name-dropped Senator McClusky to strengthen his point and get those people to sell to him at rock-bottom prices.'

'Precisely.' Brook grinned at her, pleased to have her support. 'I think you're just going after McClusky to divert attention away from the *real* issue here. It's going to be September and the end of the season here before we know it and then – boom, the storms are coming and we're no better off than we were last year. We need to act, Florence. We need to start engineering the beaches in Montauk and that means some pretty big decisions have to be taken pretty damn quickly.'

'Engineered beaches aren't the only solution to this area's problems, Brook, and you know it.' Florence's eyes were glimmering darkly, but with relish. Her fire was back. Politics was in her blood.

'I do, but it's the Coastal Erosion Committee's recommendation. You know as well as I do that an engineered beach in Montauk is the interim measure required to make this area eligible for federal aid. Without the beach, there's no federal money, and without that, there's no hope. Homes and businesses will be lost – the economy and infrastructure there will collapse. And you know we can't keep raising levies and taxes against the locals here.'

'I still believe there are other measures we can adopt.'

'Building dunes, you mean?' Brook said, with a measure of disdain.

'Among other things. We need to look at the dredging problems too. They're exacerbating local erosion to a huge extent.'

'What dredging problems?' Brook frowned.

'The survey came in from the Army Corps of Engineers while I was resting up. I had nothing else to do but read the damn thing from cover to cover.'

'Which survey is this?' Ro asked, trying to remain in the debate, painfully aware of Ted Connor's stare sweeping over to her every few minutes. What did he *want*?

'It's examined the severe erosion on the Sound-side view of Montauk Harbor jetties. They say there's evidence the area has been over-dredged by at least eighty-six thousand cubic tons of sand.' Florence looked back at Brook. 'And that's just the surplus! No wonder the area's so vulnerable. I'm going to be calling for a review of the dredging companies operating in the East End area at the next meeting. The ten-year permits come up for renewal in October and I think it's the right time to really sit down and examine who we're giving the business to—'

Brook shook his head dismissively. 'This is precisely the kind of time-wasting delay I'm talking about. People need action, not surveys. Winter is on its way round to us and we're like sitting ducks.'

Ro put her hand up, feeling like she had to request permission to speak. 'Uh . . . so anyway, my headache.'

Florence laughed, drawn out of her debate at last. 'Oh, Rowena. You are *too* polite, standing there listening to us old warhorses battling it out while you're feeling so bad.' She gathered Ro in an embrace. 'Let's have breakfast and an early morning swim together soon.'

'How are you getting home?' Brook asked.

'I'll get a cab.' She eyed the street for a lit taxi sign. Oh, what she'd do to see the Humper right now, but she knew Hump was settled in for a quiet night with Bobbi. She was still subdued from the funeral yesterday, and only Ro's manners had propelled her out here tonight.

'Nonsense. Take my car. My driver can come back for me. No doubt Florence and I will still be here disagreeing violently.' He raised his arm before Ro could protest further and a driver stepped out of the silver Mercedes parked by the kerb.

'Well, if you're sure it's not too much trouble . . .' Ro said hesitantly.

'Just make sure he doesn't take the long way home. I do

enough walking on the fairways without adding more miles to these poor feet of mine.'

'Thanks. I really appreciate it.'

She kissed them both goodbye and walked quickly across the pavement, as the driver opened the door for her and she slid into the toffee-coloured leather seats and air-conditioned comfort. The windows were black-tinted and impossible to see into.

The driver was just getting into his seat when the passenger-side door opened.

'Oh, you did *not* just do that!' Ro exclaimed in alarm, as Ted turned to face her, like it was the most natural thing in the world that he should be sitting there.

'You *are* trying to escape me,' he said.

'N-no!' she protested, wild thoughts running through her head.

'So then why did you go running when you saw me coming over to talk to you?'

'Why did you come running over when you saw me talking to your girlfriend?' she shot back.

'Good question . . .' He looked quizzical. 'And I'm not sure.'

'Ma'am, is everything OK back there?' It was the driver, talking to her through the intercom system. The privacy panel was shut, but she could make out his silhouette.

Ted held up his hands. 'I'll get out if you want me to. I just thought we could talk.'

'About *what*?'

'. . . The children's photography session?' he said.

Yeah, right. The thought had clearly only just occurred to him. 'Now? What about Julianne?'

'She's haggling over Bambi. She won't notice if I'm gone for ten minutes.'

'Ma'am?' It was the driver again.

'Uh . . . God, fine. Yes. It's fine,' she grumbled, doing a thumbs-up sign for good measure, not sure she had pressed the correct button. 'Sea Spray Cottage, Egypt Lane, please.'

The car began to roll forward and she settled herself on the seat, legs away from him, while she fiddled with her seat belt.

'It's OK – you're pretty protected in a car like this,' Ted said, watching her fidget.

'I don't want to be an elephant.'

'An elephant?' he repeated.

'Yes. In a car accident, if you're not wearing a seat belt, the forward momentum of impact makes the person in the rear seat hit the seat of the person in front with the same weight as an elephant. It's one of the commonest causes of death in traffic accidents.'

'I didn't know that,' Ted grinned. 'Although I guess the driver's safe today at least. There's a wall between you and him.' Ro arched an eyebrow and he quickly turned and grabbed his seat belt. 'Principle, though, I agree,' he murmured, buckling up.

They sat in silence for a minute, Ted intermittently looking across as Ro clasped her hands between her knees, trying not to jiggle.

'So . . . you wanted to talk about shooting the kids,' she said finally.

'What?'

Ro laughed hard at his mistake. Too hard. Either her nerves were getting the better of her or the wine *had* gone to her head after all. 'I don't mean with bullets, you numpty. Shooting film. The photography session.'

'Did you just call me a "numpty"?'

'That's right,' she replied, trying to stop an unstoppable smile. Definitely the wine.

'That some British word for a jerk?'

'Something like that.' She recovered herself, clearing her throat. 'Sorry.'

'No,' he murmured, looking out of the window. 'I rather liked it.'

She caught his profile as though she was seeing it through the lens – the straight sweep of his nose, the deep swoop of his lashes, the soft curl of his hair that needed a cut soon . . .

'So . . . the children.' He looked over at her, but she found it almost impossible to hold his gaze. She couldn't lie like he could; she couldn't hide behind a smile. She couldn't pretend he was just a client when all the time she was trying to work out his hold over Florence, his motivation. He hid behind his manners all the while the facts stacked up against him in hers and Florence's recent misadventures. But which was right: fact or instinct? Which man was he: the man on the films or the man on the beach? How could he be both? She felt she couldn't trust her own judgement anymore. Everything was blurred, confused. 'I thought we could do it on Shelter Island.'

'Shelter Island?' She'd heard of it . . .

'It's just off Sag Harbor. Not far as the crow flies, but we have to sail over. Obviously – being an island.' He smiled. 'I've got a place we can use. It's pretty. There's woods, beaches . . .'

'OK,' she nodded. 'That sounds good.'

The car rolled to a gentle halt and she realized they were back at the house already. It was only a few blocks, after all. 'Oh. This is me.'

'I'll walk you to the door,' Ted said, quickly climbing out of the car before she could protest.

'Thanks,' she said reluctantly, as he opened the car door for her. They walked up the short path over the green, then through the gate and onto the porch steps. 'Um, so when were you thinking for that? How's Finn's hair?'

'Behaving itself finally.' He stared down at her, his gaze so steady, so unflinching, so undrunk. 'I don't suppose you can do next weekend?'

'I can't think of a reason why not.' She couldn't think of much, actually. The wine really had hit her.

'We'll come pick you up at ten o'clock Saturday?'

She nodded. 'OK.'

'Great.' And without warning, he leaned down and kissed her once on each cheek, his lips soft against her skin, his hands on her arms, their eyes locked in a momentary pause before he straightened up. 'Saturday, then.'

Ro watched him go, utterly unable not to, so completely paralyzed it was like her feet had taken root. She watched him get back into the car and the car pull away again. She couldn't see if he was looking back at her looking at him through the tinted windows. She carried on looking for at least a minute after the car had gone, trying to regulate her breathing, temper her erratic pulse, recover from the shock of his touch. It had been nothing, just a social kiss – no different to the ones she had so unthinkingly just given Brook and Florence.

No different. It was the wine, making everything feel . . . different.

Slowly, she turned – and stopped again. Hump was standing behind the screen door, frozen mid-step with a plate of pizza in his hand, watching her.

'What?'

'Still frightened of him, are you?' he asked, as he turned and continued into the kitchen.

No, not frightened, she thought, as she put one trembling hand to her cheek. It felt singed by his touch. Terrified was more like it.

# Chapter Thirty

At the park. Ella being pushed on a trike by Ted's mother. Finn sleeping in the buggy. Ted pushing Finn.

Overcast day. No shadows on the ground. Everyone in coats.

'Does he sleep this much all the time?' Man's voice behind camera. Ted's father?

'All the time. He's the easiest baby.' Ted.

'No wonder Marina's back on her feet so quickly.' Ted's mother.

'Quite literally.' Ted.

Finn jerks suddenly, his hands flying up beside his head. Begins to cry. Ted stops the buggy and quickly rearranges the blankets, tucking Finn's arms back down and securing the blankets firmly. 'His startle reflex. Boys get it worse than girls, apparently.'

Begins pushing the buggy again. Finn's cries drop to a whimper.

'You were always doing that. You had such bad colic as a baby, it'd take forever to get you settled, and just as I'd creep back to bed – wham! You'd jolt yourself awake and I'd have to do the whole routine again. Do you remember, Edward?'

'Do I ever,' Ted's father grumbled. 'I thought *we'd* never sleep through the night again.'

Finn silent now, sleeping. Ella sucking her thumb as she is pushed along. Drops her (no longer) pink pig.

'Oops. We don't want to lose Binky.' Ted's mother picks it up and hands it back. 'Oh look! Here comes Mommy!'

Ella waves excitedly, almost topples off tricycle.

Marina power-walks towards them. Navy running tights, fluoro-yellow trainers, water bottle in her hand, cheeks flushed.

'Hi!' Ted hooks arm around her waist, kisses her. 'So how was that?'

Camera angle drops down to path. Brown suede loafers. Forgotten it's on?

'Great!' Marina. Panting. 'Really great.'

'Not too much? You mustn't overdo it.' Ted.

'Not at all. In fact I'm feeling strong today. I thought I might do one more lap.' Marina.

'Marina, it's been three weeks. That's too much.' Ted.

'Ted, I know my own body. I've been craving this for nine months.' Pause. Unidentifiable movements. 'You all enjoying the walk?'

'Oh, absolutely.' Ted's father. Jocular. 'We've just been feeding the ducks.'

'I'm the park-keeper, Mommy.' Ella.

'*Are* you?' Marina. Smile in her voice.

'We thought we'd go to Inn on the Park for coffee. Why don't you join us?' Ted's mother.

'I may as well meet you back at the apartment. By the time I do my extra lap, you'll be ready to go.' Panting sound. 'And I'll take it easy. I promise.' Sound of fast-moving feet, retreating.

'She's like Superwoman.' Ted's father.

'She's saying she wants to go back to work when Finn's twelve weeks.'

'Really?' Ted's mother.

'Mmm.' Ted.

Camera swings up to buggy, focuses on Finn, sleeping, for split second.

Blackness.

**05/23/2011**                                             **15h37**

Ella seated in a high chair, a cake of a red hot-air balloon on the table in front of her, one candle flickering. Lots of helium-filled balloons tied to the backs of the chairs. The bottom of a birthday banner just in shot.

'Happy Birthday, Ella!' An older female voice behind the camera. 'How old are you today?'

Ella, in a Liberty-print needlecord dress, grins at the camera. Shouts excitedly. 'Grandma! I'm two!'

'Who's two?' incredulous voice.

'Me!' Ella jabs her chest with her thumb.

'Well, did you get any presents?'

'I got a scooter for the park.'

'A scooter? I'll bet you're really good, huh?'

Ella nods. Moves to pinch some of the red icing.

'Uh-uh, not yet. Wait for Mommy.'

Ted in the background. He comes to stand beside Ella, swaying slightly as he rubs Finn's back. A half-filled bottle of milk in his jeans pocket. Begins pacing. 'Where is Marina?'

'She went to get the cake slice from the kitchen.'

Male voice off camera – Ted's father? 'I heard her cell go. You want me to get her?'

Ted rolls his eyes and shakes his head. Ella tries to sneak more icing.

'Ella, sweetie, just wait one more minute.'

'Binky's hungry.' Pushes bottom lip out and scowls at Ted. Folds arms across her chest.

Marina walks back in, raking her hair back, smiling. Lithe in navy trousers and ribbed silky sweater. 'You haven't cut the cake yet, have you?'

'No, we were waiting for you.' Ted. Slight pause. 'The cake slice?'

Marina slaps her forehead. 'Oh, yes. Right! I forgot.'

Ted frowns. 'Who was that on the phone?'

'The locksmith. He called back.'

'The locksmith?'

'Yes, he's coming over now. I told him it was an emergency.'

'What? What is?'

Marina puts her hand up to stroke Finn's cheek. He's sleeping on Ted's shoulder. 'We discussed this, Ted, remember? The kids mustn't be getting out of their rooms in the night.'

'Marina, what are you talking about? They're both in cots.'

Marina smiles. Pats his arm. 'Listen, honey, you may sleep through it, but I don't. I hear them every night. It's for their own safety.' Marina frowns. 'Oh, yes. Right. Cake slice.'

She walks out.

Ted, frowning, looks to person behind the camera. *'What?'*

Blackness.


**07/15/2011**                                                    **14h43**

'Turn it off, Mom.' Ted, standing by baby Finn at changing unit. Ted holding both his ankles in one hand, lifting him up and sliding under new nappy.

'You'll thank me—'

Ted looks to camera. Stony stare. Cold eyes. Red-rimmed eyes.

Blackness.

**04/15/2012**                                              **12h20**

Beach. Ted lying down, Ella covering him in sand. He scrunches his eyes shut as sand goes flying off her yellow spade.

'Careful, Ella! Poor Daddy.' Older woman's voice behind the camera.

Ella looks up. Hair in pigtails. Pink heart-shaped sunglasses on, red gingham swimsuit with frilled skirt. Chubby legs. 'Daddy my pwisoner.'

'I'll never get out of here,' he groans, making face to suggest effort. No movement. 'It's no good. I'm trapped here forever.'

Ella squeals delightedly.

Camera swings to show Finn sitting with a rubber ring round his waist. A floppy blue sunhat on his head, wearing a swim nappy. Hitting an upturned bucket with a small spade.

'Right. Well, if Daddy's well and truly stuck in there, I guess there's no one to stop us going and getting an ice cream, is there, Ella?' Woman's voice.

'Ice cweam!' Ella shrieks, jumping up.

'Ice cream? Who – said – ice cream?' Ted. Putting on a deep voice. 'Nobody eats the Sand Monster's ice cream.'

'Da Sand Monsder!' Ella shrieks again, jumping up and down as Ted begins to wriggle side to side, cracks appearing in the sand 'tomb'.

'Quick, Ella, run! Run!' Older woman's voice.

Ella scampers down towards the shore. Ted breaks through sand and stands up, still covered. Beats his chest like King Kong, raises his arms out with a roar. Grins at camera. Starts chasing Ella down the beach.

Ella screams, half frightened, half delighted.

Ted scoops her up in his arm and runs with her into the waves.

Camera swings back to Finn, still beating the bucket. Oblivious. 'You know, Finn, I'm not sure boys ever really do grow up.'

Finn looks to camera. Tips his head. Smiles. Continues beating the bucket.

Blackness.

'I wish you'd stop looking at me like that. It's just a job,' Ro muttered, packing her camera into the protective soft case.

Hump, assuming his usual position of arms behind his head and ankles crossed on his desk, shook his head. 'Nup. It really isn't.'

'Are you prepared to forgo my last month's rent?' she said stroppily, wondering where she'd put the tripod.

'I wish I could, but you know I need every last cent—'

'In which case, I have no option but to do this shoot, so enough with the pointed stares.' She ducked under the counter, rifling through the cardboard boxes that she'd kept from when her equipment was air-freighted over.

Hump, taking in her pursed lips, changed tack. 'Isn't it weird when you see them? I mean, you know their lives pretty much inside out now. You've spent, like, *hundreds* of hours studying them. Doesn't it feel weird that there's so much imbalance?'

'It's a job, Hump. They're not my friends. Do you expect to share your life story with the people you take to the beach?'

'Yeah, but it's different. You've seen all their most private moments. It's like you've shared them with them.'

Ro shot him a look but didn't reply. The fact was, Hump couldn't have been further from the truth. The more she saw about the Connors, the less she understood. Where

was Marina? What had made the marriage fail? What
*hadn't* the camera shown?

'A part of you must be sad that you've finished the
movie.'

'Not really.'

'You've worked so hard on getting it finished. You were
almost as bad as Greg and Bobbi. Honestly, if I'd known I
was signing up a group of workaholics . . .'

'What, you'd have chosen a girl in a string bikini from
the foam pool?' Her hands closed round the telescopic
tripod.

Hump chortled and she shot him an amused look. 'It just
seems odd that you're suddenly so desperate to finish it
and be done with him.'

'*Them*. They're a family.'

'Nothing to do with the kiss, then.'

Ro sighed. He wouldn't let it go. All week she'd been
putting up with this. This was the downside of brothers.
Maybe it hadn't been so bad being an only child after all. 'I
needed to get those films edited and done because they've
been hanging over me almost all summer. At least now the
stills are pretty easy to sort, and once I've done this shoot –'
she rubbed her hands together '– I can finally get my
invoice in to him and get paid.'

'It's just all about the money with you, isn't it?'

'That's me. Money-digger.'

'You are *ruthless*.'

'Yes, I am,' she grinned.

'So what are you gonna wear?'

'Where to?'

'The island tomorrow.'

Ro straightened up. 'Why? Is there some flipping dress code to adhere to before you can set foot on it?'

'Nuh, I just thought you'd want to look nice for him, that's all.'

'Hump!' she shrieked, picking up her elastic-band ball and lobbing it at him. Perfect hit.

'Ow!' he laughed, rubbing his shoulder.

'You are a nightmare!'

'And you're in denial!'

Melodie appeared at the doorway, her arms resting high up on the doorframe. 'And what is going on in here?' she smiled. 'They can hear you two all the way in Bridgehampton.'

'My housemate has discovered his death wish,' Ro laughed, as Hump threw the ball back and she caught it with one hand. She put it next to her monitor and did a quick visual sweep of the various lenses and batteries before closing up her camera bag.

'Where are you off to now?' Hump asked, as she put the strap over her body and looked for the padlock key for her bike.

'Home – to get away from *you*. Bobbi'll be back soon and I'd like to spend some time with her given that I'll be working tomorrow.'

'I thought you might be going back to wash your hair,' Hump teased.

'Urgh!' she cried, throwing her hands in the air. She stopped in front of Melodie. 'He is maddening.'

'I know.' Melodie nodded sympathetically. 'I don't know how you put up with him. It must be like living with an ape.'

'A gibbon,' Ro shot back.

'Hey!' Hump shouted as the two women joined ranks. He jumped up from his chair and ran round the desk, but Ro was already leaping over the steps and racing across the grassy square towards her bike. 'Sorry, Melodie!' she laughed. 'He's all yours!'

It was just before 9.30 a.m. when she heard the car pull up outside the next morning. Ro ran to the window and crouched low at the sill, still only in her bra and knickers. Ted was pulling up the handbrake on a metallic pale blue vintage Mercedes convertible. Ro didn't know the vintage, but she recognized the gull wings as being iconic, and therefore expensive.

'Hey!' Ted waved, spotting her at the window and flashing a brilliant-white smile that lifestyle-matched the car.

'You're early,' she called down, visible only from the nose up.

'I know. Sorry. The kids were so excited.' He tipped his head back towards Ella and Finn, both in their car seats in the back.

'Hi!' she called – knowing she had to win their trust quickly if she was going to get the pictures she needed – instinctively standing up to wave at them and realizing only too late that the movement clearly flashed her bra to anyone on the street. How excellent. She pressed herself back down low again, her cheeks against the wood. 'I'll, uh . . . I'll just be a minute!' she shouted, hoping they could hear, and backing away from the window on her hands and knees.

'Take your time!' Ted called back. She could hear laughter in his voice, even twenty feet up.

Her bag was already packed with her equipment, and

she'd washed her hair last night – not for the reasons Hump had teased but in order not to be rushing this morning. She stepped into the white shorts and navy T-shirt she'd bought on sale in one of the boutiques off the backstreets in town and turned a circle in the room, wondering if there was anything else she was missing. Like her sanity.

She stepped out of the house two minutes later, her camera bag on her shoulder, her plimsolled feet making no sound on the path.

Ted, who was leaning against the car, jumped up as she approached.

'Hi,' he smiled, taking her bag from her and putting it in the boot.

'Hi,' she said, slightly clipped, wanting to establish a clear tone that this was work, business – not some jolly day trip.

'Hop in.'

She slid into the passenger seat, turning round immediately to make eye contact with the children. 'Hi,' she smiled. 'You must be Ella and Finn.'

The children nodded at her – not so much shyly as warily.

'And these fellows here,' she said, in a slightly lower voice, her eyes on the grubby, too-loved pink and blue toys. 'They must be Binky and Boo.'

Both children's eyes widened with surprise.

'How did you know that?' Ella asked in a forthright voice that seemed should belong to a child older than four.

'Oh, they're famous where I live,' she said, knowing her foreign accent would be discernible even to children as young as them. 'Where I come from, everybody knows Binky and Boo.'

Eyes wider still. 'Why?'

'Because they're the most loved toys in the world – everybody knows that. And I live a really, really long way away from here.'

Wonder filled their faces as they each held their toys to their noses and inhaled, closing their eyes at the familiar, comforting smell.

Ro turned to face the front, to find Ted sitting beside her, the ignition still off, an expression on his face that she couldn't interpret. She looked at the keys hanging idle. 'Ready when you are,' she shrugged.

'Yes. Right,' he said, jumping into action and starting the car. It made a lovely sound and Ro turned to look at the cottage as they pulled away.

Hump was standing on the drive, holding his kayak paddle in one hand, wearing his brown and pink leaf Hawaiian baggies, yellow flip-flops and a bemused grin. Ro stuck her tongue out at him as she passed.

A small gasp came from the back. 'I saw that!' Ella said.

'What?' Ted asked, peering at her in the rear-view mirror.

Ro turned and put her finger to her lips, her eyes gleaming.

'Nothing,' Ella giggled, putting her finger to her lips too.

They were in Sag Harbor within half an hour, everyone enjoying the feeling of the breeze and sunshine against their skin as the Mercedes glided gracefully along the streets, the grey, ice-blue and charcoal clapboarded houses becoming more densely packed together as they approached the town centre.

They passed the old movie house, which had the name

of the latest film spelled out in retro red letters, cruised past the smartly clipped hedges of the American Hotel and pulled up in the car park opposite a small marina.

'Can you carry Finn for me and hold Ella's hand while I get the bags out?' Ted asked, pulling on the handbrake as she'd seen him do earlier.

'Sure.'

Ro unclipped the kids from their seats, hoisting Finn onto her hip and taking Ella's hand with a wink. They were already allies, it seemed, Ella repeatedly trying to catch her eye in the mirror on the way over. Ro smiled down at her as they walked, her usual reserve banished. Going through the home videos was proving useful here – it was like a crash course in understanding the two children; she had studied them like a student and already she knew their histories, not just their names. But if she had mugged up on their pasts, she knew nothing about their present.

'Oh dear, where should we go?' she asked, looking at the rows and rows of jetties, all with dozens of moored boats.

'I know where the boat is,' Ella said proudly, tugging her along.

'Maybe we should wait for your da—'

'Lead on, Ella,' Ted called behind them. Ro turned and saw him struggling with the bags, grinning away.

Ella led the way down one of the boardwalks. Ro could see the water through the gaps, and she looked from side to side at the mix of boats. Most of them were small-use fishers, along with one or two smarter cruisers for buzzing in the bays.

Ella stopped at a medium-sized sailing boat with a wooden cabin and a cheery yellow hull. What was it with yellow over here? she wondered, as Ted caught them up, bags stuffed under his arms, and one particularly heavy one hanging round his neck.

'Here, let me help,' she said, reaching up and unhooking it, making very sure she didn't brush against him.

'Thanks,' he replied, as he dropped the bags gently at his feet.

'Nice boat.'

'Do you sail?' he asked, rifling in his red and navy sailing jacket for a set of keys, his eyes on her all the while.

'Not unless you count a one-week course when I was twelve.'

'Oh, I think we *will* count that,' Ted smiled, crouching down to pull the boat in with the ropes, before springing on board himself. 'Given that otherwise my crew has a combined age of seven.'

Ro couldn't help but laugh, passing him the bags one by one, and he passed her back the lifejackets. She put them on the children, while Ted put the engine blowers on and disappeared below deck to run through his checks.

There was a breeze and she shivered, wishing she'd thought to pack a jumper. She had become quickly accustomed to always feeling warm and never needing a cover-up.

'Do you like sailing?' she asked Ella, who was sucking her thumb and watching her as she fiddled with getting the straps between Finn's wriggly legs. Finn was more interested in trying to watch the ducks swimming between the boats.

'I'm Daddy's first mate.'

'*Are* you?' Ro asked, eyes wide. 'Well, then you'd better keep me straight on this, OK? I don't have a clue about boats. I hardly know which end is the front and which end is the back.'

Ella giggled, putting her finger to her lips again.

'Exactly,' Ro grinned, copying her. She straightened up.

'You're da lady who played in da sea wiv Daddy.'

Ro looked in astonishment at Finn, who was pointing up at her lest she should be in any doubt he was talking to her.

'Yes. Yes, I am,' she nodded. 'How clever you are to remember, Finn.'

'It looked fun,' he said, putting his thumb in his mouth like his sister.

'Oh, it was! It really was,' she nodded, hands on hips, noticing that Ted had stopped halfway up the steps. She kept her eyes away from his. It was in no one's interest to dredge up that particular incident again.

'Are you ready for us?' she asked, batting away the topic.

He jumped up the steps and handed her a navy jumper. 'For you. You may need it when we get further out. It won't be a great fit, I'm afraid. It's one of mine, but it's all that's on here.'

'Oh. Thanks,' she murmured, the tumble of cashmere sitting like a cloud in her hands. She couldn't possibly put this on; after the sentimentality of wearing Matt's clothes for the first month here, how could she possibly just shrug on another man's clothes as though it would mean nothing?

She draped it casually over one shoulder as Ted hauled on the ropes again, pulling the boat in towards the jetty. He reached out his arms for her to pass Finn and then Ella, holding out his hand for her to grasp as she jumped on last.

'Thanks,' she murmured, steadying herself and keeping

her eyes safely down, determined not to acknowledge the tingle that came with his touch.

They agreed it would be best if she sat on the bench behind the captain's wheel, with Finn on her lap and Ella to her right so she could hold on to the side and 'be the lookout' for flying fish. They motored gently out of the marina, Ted handling the boat with refined ease, looking back intermittently to check they were all OK. When they were in open water, he cut the engine and moved over to wind power, unravelling the mainsail and jib, and letting them fill and billow, propelling the boat in leisurely tacks across the Sound.

For the second time that morning, Ro tipped her head back and enjoyed the feeling of sun and wind on her skin, vowing to take up sailing the second she got home. Quite where, in the London suburbs, she wasn't sure, but somewhere. Definitely.

As Ted had predicted, the wind whipped up as they moved further from land, knitting her hair and making her skin goosebump. Several times Ted turned, a quizzical look crossing his face as he saw the jumper lying on the bench beside her. Only after her skin started to take on a blue tint did she reluctantly admit defeat and slip the jumper on, holding her breath as it slid over her head.

'Are you wearing sunscreen?' she asked Ella after a while, aware of the heat behind the breeze.

Ella shook her head.

'Can I put this on them?' she called out to Ted, who turned to find her holding up a small tube of Nivea sun lotion. She always carried some in her bag. 'It's for sensitive skin.'

'Sure. Thanks. They wouldn't sit still enough for Julianne this morning.'

The mention of Julianne's name was like a bucket of cold water and she fiddled with the cap, unable to understand its shock value. She knew he was divorced; she knew he was with Julianne. She had spoken to the woman herself just days ago. And – *and* more than anything else – she was with Matt. And he was a client. And she didn't trust him. Not a word. Not until she discovered why he was really inveigling his way into Florence's life.

But even in spite of all that, she still felt like she'd been kicked.

She rubbed the cream into the children's podgy pink limbs, smiling as they tipped up their faces for her, all snub noses and rosebud mouths and baby hair sticking to their cheeks. Afterwards, she watched the white sails of the other boats flickering like tissues in the distance, letting Finn fiddle with her bracelets – cheap leather things she'd picked up at the till in Waldbaum's – as Ella pointed out a pod of dolphins off starboard, Ro more excited than any of them to see them out in the wild. They played 'I Spy' and 'What Am I?', told their best jokes and tried to guess everyone's ages. (Ella guessed that she was fifty-four, which was depressing; although she fared better than Ted, whom she guessed at sixty-seven, and who turned out to be thirty-four.)

Ro spent the passage looking left, right, behind and up – anywhere other than directly ahead, determined not to notice the way Ted turned the huge wheel so easily, the way his hair looked as the wind rippled it back off his face, how his back narrowed as his jacket flapped against him. Nope, she didn't see any of it.

They rounded a point where, according to Ella, 'the Injuns used to live' and entered a vast but narrowing inlet with various points, bays and coves. Houses became visible through the trees, a smattering of people on the sparse beaches. There were a few boats moored at small private jetties, masts down, engines cut.

Ted got busy, rolling up the sails again, cutting their speed and switching back to engine power for the final stretch, so that they drew alongside a short ramshackle jetty, almost inch perfect with no bumping at all.

Ro stayed seated with the kids as he jumped off and secured the mooring ropes, Ro's gaze determinedly out to sea, and then on the water as he held her hand to help her out.

Ella led the charge again now that they were on dry land, her little feet pounding heavily on the wooden slatted planks that had weathered grey long ago. To the right of the jetty was a tiny sandy cove that sloped gently into shallow waters and was fringed with tall birch trees that flanked a wood.

Ro reached for the camera round her neck, automatically positioning herself to take photos of the children as they ran onto the little beach, crouching over something – a crab, Ro thought she heard Ella say – their hands on their short thighs, their heads touching.

But she stopped. She'd done this once before.

'Is it OK—' she began, turning to find Ted immediately behind her, carrying the bags again.

'Yes.' He was so close, his head tipped down like he was studying her, and as their eyes locked, she felt a gasp of air pulled from her and knew that somewhere, somehow – even though every part of her screamed, 'No' – they had crossed a line, a line she had tried to deny but that was as real and invisible as the breeze in the trees. There was a charge between them that made the air crackle and her blood rush. She'd been determined not to acknowledge it – it seemed almost wilfully perverse to admit to an attraction when there was so much about him that repelled her – but for hers and Matt's sake, she had to now. Hump had been right. This spark, chemistry, whatever it was, was bigger, badder, stronger than even the terrible suspicions she carried in her head about him. And her head wasn't winning this fight; every moment she spent with him, she felt like she was hurtling inevitably downhill on a luge. She had to get these shots done and go and never turn back.

'So how do you want to do this?' she asked. 'As in, do you have anything particular in mind, or are you happy just for me to observe and gently direct?' Her words came out in a rush. A panic.

His eyes scanned her face slowly, too slowly, so that it felt almost like a touch. 'I'm going to let you lead.'

She swallowed, nodding briskly. 'OK, then. Well, I'll let them just play and I'll take my opportunities where I can.'

A hint of a smile sprang to his eyes. 'That sounds like a plan.'

She nodded, watching as he walked ahead with the bags. Remembered to breathe.

In spite of various such moments, the day passed quickly. Ted built a small log fire on the beach, cooking up sausages and heating baked beans in the tin, as Ro scampered, lunged and crawled around the children as they played. More often than not, she got drawn into the games too – unable to pass up on making a tunnel for the hermit crab to make its way back to the ocean and pretending to be a donkey for Finn to ride on her back. She even showed them her big foot, Ella waggling her own pudgy toes next to her, which were barely a third of the size of Ro's. Sporadically she would sit on the sand, scrolling back through the images, her head tilted to one side as she examined the mix of images – close-ups, atmospheric shots, details like sandy toes or a blonde tendril against the blue sky, panoramas of the siblings . . . It was all going well, but then how could it not? They were beautiful children.

She liked the setting here. The cove was tiny, but it was more characterful than the enormous, broad, uniformly white-sand ocean beaches of Long Island's South Fork. Even the water had that dappled green, lapping lake quality, instead of the anonymous thundering navy-blue surf that had travelled hundreds of thousands of miles to crash upon the shore.

Eventually, though, the children began to flag, worn out from a day of playing in the sun and wind, delighted by their new friend who 'spoke funny' and got sand in her swimsuit and had weird tan lines and kept secrets from Daddy. The sun had dropped behind the trees and the first cool of the evening was outstripping the tide.

'I think maybe we've had the best out of them,' Ro said, as Finn burst into tears because Ella was using his hat as a bucket and filling it with sand.

'I agree. Come on, kids. Time to go.'

Finn ran into his father's arms, jubilant to be saved from himself. Ella walked calmly over to Ro, her arm outstretched, confident that Ro, her ally, would take her hand.

Ro smiled, touched by the compliment, marvelling at how tiny Ella's hand felt in hers.

KAREN SWAN

'Uh . . . the boat's this way,' she said, pointing towards the conspicuously yellow boat that was moored not fifteen feet away as Ted and Finn walked in the opposite direction into the trees.

'So it is.' Ted grinned, amused by her pointing out the obvious. 'But they don't want to bathe in there, trust me. It gets way too hot in that cabin.'

'So where are we going, then?' Nerves were beginning to rise in her like flames.

'To our house in the woods,' Ella said, looking up at her as they stepped over broken branches and a deep leaf layer even this late in the summer. 'I get to sleep in a cupboard. And the bath is orange.'

Panic joined the cocktail of hormones rushing through her: they had a house here? They were bathing the children here? She remembered the bags. Too many . . .

She closed her eyes and inadvertently squeezed Ella's hand for comfort. Ella squeezed back. She opened her eyes and looked down to find Ella gazing up at her. 'Are you feeling sad?'

'Ummm, maybe a little bit.'

'I'll look after you,' Ella said, ever the big sister.

Ro smiled as they walked through the trees to a clearing where a tiny wooden cabin stood with shutters that had hearts notched out in the middle and a perfectly crooked metal stove pipe poking through the roof.

'This is yours?' she asked, as they caught up with the boys.

'Not technically,' Ted smiled, Finn in his arms, watching her reaction. 'Although it's been promised to us – we spend so much time here. Do you like it?'

'It's absolutely darling,' she murmured, her spare hand wandering up to her camera again. 'May I?'

'Of course,' he said, taking Ella by the hand too now and walking her with him up to the cabin.

Ro began to click as the little family walked away from her in the early evening light, Ella turning back with big eyes to check she was coming too, Finn's head resting on Ted's shoulder, his thumb in, his eyes already closed and Boo hanging down his father's back.

For once, she didn't need to check the playback screen to confirm the moment. The image was timeless, nostalgic, bucolic – their little family, happy, tired, peaceful . . . But it was bittersweet too, the family incomplete and lopsided. Broken, even. Where was Marina? Why wasn't she here? What had gone so catastrophically wrong between her and Ted that she was away from her own family? Had she gone back to work after twelve weeks? Was that it? Had she chosen the big career over them? Had she found someone else too? First?

Ro followed after them, instinct telling her she shouldn't follow them into the gladed shadows. But the sun was setting and the day was done. And what other choice did she have?

She opened the cabin door to find the children already stripped down and running around all but naked, Ted lighting a pre-stacked stove, a pan already filled with milk. In another room, she could hear water running.

The room was reasonably sized, dark (on account of the shutters being closed) and sparsely furnished. To her left, a long Aztec-patterned sofa was positioned with its back to her, and a round table with chairs was set to its right at the back of the cottage, the stove on the right near a small hall and seemingly the only source of heat.

'Come see my bed. It was my mommy's when she was little,' Ella cried, grabbing her by the hand and pulling her into a tiny room, just a box room at the end of the short, stubby corridor. There was only a fitted wardrobe and a cot in there. Nothing else.

Ella ran to the far wall and opened the stable-style wooden wardrobe doors. Sure enough, halfway up was a bed atop fitted drawers whose handles doubled as footholds. Ella demonstrated how the bed worked by scampering up and climbing in, pulling the sheets up to her chin and closing her eyes, pretending to sleep. Ro burst out laughing, immediately capturing it all on film.

'You are such a funny little imp,' she smiled, stroking Ella's cheek.

At the touch, Ella opened one eye and stared at her, her childish eyes filled with a deep aching sorrow that didn't belong anywhere near a four-year-old. They brimmed with tears that began sliding down her velvet cheeks.

'I miss Mommy.'

Tears immediately sprang to Ro's eyes. 'Oh, of course you do, darling,' Ro whispered back, feeling her heart break at the sight of this small child's despair, a rush of anger pulsing through her that she was the one who suffered. 'It's only normal to have these feelings.' She brushed her hand gently down Ella's hair, smoothing it away from the tear tracks that plastered it to her cheeks.

Ella's eyes moved suddenly from Ro's face to something behind her. Ro turned and saw Ted standing beside them, his own face stricken – a look she had seen before. She instinctively stepped back and he reached down, lifting Ella from the bed and wrapping her in his arms.

Ro discreetly left the room, hearing Ella's sobs grow faster and Ted murmuring to her softly, trying to paper over the fatal crack at the heart of this family.

Out in the hallway, she saw Finn running about, ready for his bath, and she carried him into the copper bath, pushing a small wooden boat for him that looked like it was supposed to be for ornamental use only, her cheek resting on the warm roll-top as he chattered away to her in a half-language she could just about keep up with. The soft hum of voices on the other side of the wall told her Ted and Ella were talking, or reading a story at least, and after twenty minutes or so, she took him out and dressed him in the fresh pyjamas that had been laid out on the floor.

She was pouring the warmed milk from the pan into his beaker when Ted walked back in, looking depleted and harrowed. Finn staggered over to him, overtired now and crying for his milk. Ted sighed wearily, shooting her an apologetic look as he lifted Finn and carried him down to the bedroom too.

Ro watched them disappear, feeling just short of hysterical herself. The cabin was quiet now and growing dark. There didn't appear to be electricity, so she couldn't turn the lights on, and after a few moments of standing forlornly in someone else's sitting room, she stepped outside and sat down on the steps.

With the children already in bed, it was now abundantly clear the family was sleeping here tonight. But what about her? The cabin was tiny, with only two bedrooms, and she didn't think for one minute Ted would be stupid – or ungallant – enough to assume *they'd* share. There must be a ferry back to Sag Harbor. But when and where?

She was rifling through her bag for cash – $6.47 in loose change so far – when Ted came out to join her, a bottle of red and two glasses in his hands.

'I'm sorry about that,' he said quietly. 'It's an ongoing process. Ella is starting to notice that other little girls have mothers, and that hers has gone.'

'Of course. Anyone would. And she's only four.' Not to mention she's got a glamazon like Julianne as stepmother-in-waiting to contend with, she thought to herself.

'Would you like a drink?'

'Actually,' she said, standing up quickly before he could sit down. 'I'd better start heading back to catch the ferry.'

Ted looked alarmed and checked his watch. 'But the last one's already gone,' he said, frowning as the misunderstanding became clear. 'I'm sorry, I thought you realized we were staying for the weekend. It's a bit too far for a day trip with young kids.'

'Uh, no, I-I've never been here before, so . . .' she said quietly, wondering what the hell to do now. An overnight stay? Was he *kidding*?

'Oh.' He placed the bottle and glasses on the deck between them. 'The children are sleeping or I'd sail us all back—'

'It's fine. There must be a B&B or something where I can stay, though, right?'

'Well, I imagine so, but . . .' He put his hands in his pockets, looking at her with his usual still demeanour. 'Listen, Ro, everything's set up here. I assumed you were staying, so I've given you the bedroom. I'm more than happy on the couch.'

'No, definitely not. I couldn't possibly.'

'Honestly, I've slept on the couch before.' He gave a rueful smile, but she didn't find it charming that he should make light of the problems in his failed marriage, especially when the effects of it had clearly been so devastating to his daughter.

'No, I mean . . . I haven't packed or—' She wrapped her arms around her. It was cool in the dusk now and she wished she still had his jumper to put on, but it was packed in the bags in the house somewhere, probably the kids' room.

'I've got a spare T-shirt and toiletries you can use.' He took in her closed body language and evasive eye contact. 'Listen, we'll be back tomorrow afternoon. It really isn't a big deal. And we'd all like you to stay.'

She swallowed hard, looking around at the woods surrounding the cabin. She had no idea where the nearest road was – if there even was one – or where the ferry point was, much less finding somewhere else to sleep for the night. She had to face it – she was pretty much stranded. 'Well, thank you,' she said reluctantly, 'but I'll take the couch.'

'No, there's no question of it.' His tone was firm and it felt ridiculous to argue. And without saying another word, he pulled off the jumper he was wearing and held it out to her. 'I don't feel the cold either.'

She smiled, feeling embarrassed and grateful all at once. 'Thanks . . . again.'

'So then . . .' He picked up the bottle and unpeeled the foil, as she pulled the jumper on. It was still warm from his heat, as fresh with his scent as though he'd bathed in it and instinctively her eyes closed as it covered her.

He poured them each a glass. 'For you.'

'Thanks.' She sat back down on the steps, resting her elbows on her knees as she curled herself into a small ball.

He joined her, stretching his legs out in front of him and leaning back on his elbows. They were quiet for a beat.

'So, how did you feel today went? Professionally speaking?'

She glanced across at him. 'Excellent,' she said, her voice quiet. 'I think I've got some really great material. Although, it would be hard to take a duff shot of either of them. They're such gorgeous children.'

'Well, they're smitten with *you*. They'll be asking if we can file adoption papers for you all the way back to the city tomorrow.' His tone was light, but she kept her gaze on the trees regardless.

'Is that where you live, then? New York?'

'For now.' He looked past his toes. 'It's not a long-term prospect, though. Manhattan's no place to bring up kids.'

'I don't know. You seem to make good use of Central Park.'

He looked baffled, then remembered she had seen all their private videos and was intimately acquainted with their home life. 'Yes. I suppose we . . . Oh God, you saw the clip with the pug,' he groaned.

'Kite-gate?' she smiled. 'Oh yes.'

'Not my finest hour.'

'Oh, I don't know. The Sand Monster was pretty special too,' she grinned.

He took a deep gulp of his wine. 'I'm going to drink faster if all my greatest hits are going to be dredged up tonight.'

Dredged. The word had become fixed in her mind with

the first video she'd seen of the Connors – her first glimpse of Marina, so beautiful and witty and driven, the two of them on the cusp of change, only hours away from becoming a family . . . She fell silent.

Ted was quiet too, though she sensed their not talking didn't bother him. She sensed his eyes on her again too, and she stared determinedly at her own feet. It was all she could do.

'So do you have to stay in New York for your job?' she mumbled, aware of how pedestrian her conversation seemed. Her social skills weren't as polished as his – or Julianne's, or Erin's, or Marina's no doubt.

'Not necessarily. I'm a finance director at an investment bank. I guess I could work anywhere – Zurich, Paris, Singapore, London.'

'Oh.'

They lapsed into another small silence that felt big, and Ro felt her heart begin to hammer from the strain of trying to hit an easy note. There was no one to defer to, no one who could interrupt, no Hump or Florence or Melodie for her to hide behind like a little girl behind her mother's skirts. There wasn't even a soundtrack of traffic or surf to sink back into, only the resounding silence that pulsed around them like a heat haze, pointing out that they were here and they were alone.

She exhaled nervously, biting her lip as she peered through the trees.

'You know, it's strange to think you probably know so much about us – me . . . and yet I know practically nothing about you. It hardly seems fair.'

'It is a bit weird, I guess. But I've had clients say that to me before,' she said quickly, hoping he'd pick up on her reinforcement of their professional status and take the point. 'So you're not alone.'

'Oh no, I am.'

She glanced at him quizzically.

He recrossed his ankles, angling his body very slightly towards her. 'For example, I bet none of your other clients has asked you who Matt is.'

The mention of Matt's name had the same effect on her as Julianne's earlier – shocking, like a slap – and she recoiled. 'Matt?'

'You were calling for him the day you were attacked.' Images from that afternoon – how he'd picked her up from the floor, stroked her hand as she drifted to sleep – flashed through her mind like memory cards.

He waited a moment, before laughing shortly. 'You're determined not to tell me, aren't you?'

She didn't reply. She couldn't. She didn't think this conversation – or where it might be heading – was funny.

'You just won't let me know what I'm up against.' His voice was quiet, but he could have hollered, such was the fright he gave her.

'Matt's my boyfriend,' she said quickly, knowing that would close the conversation down.

His eyes covered her face, though she wouldn't look at him. She just wouldn't. 'Is it serious?' he asked.

'Exceptionally.' She nodded earnestly, making him laugh. And her too. *Exceptionally?*

'Oh. Well . . .' His eyes stayed on her. 'So then I guess that answers my other question about you and Hump. Whenever I see you together, you're always laughing and . . . well, he seems to take every opportunity he can to touch you.'

Jealous? He was jealous of Hump? Her heart accelerated at the realization. She looked away, her fingers playing with the stem of the glass. She couldn't stay here. 'He's my friend. Nothing more.'

She took a deep glug of wine. Maybe she could swim back. It would certainly be safer.

They fell quiet again.

'What about you and Julianne?' she blurted out, as surprised as he was by her question. 'Is that serious?'

'Exceptionally not.'

She smiled, taking the tease on the chin, using it to hide the relief that his words unlocked. 'Oh.'

Silence.

'So when you say "exceptionally serious", you mean . . .'

'Imminently engaged. Next month, in fact.'

'Oh. That serious.' He nodded, looking away finally.

More silence.

Awkward.

He shifted position suddenly. 'So then . . . where the hell is he? Why is he never around?' He sounded exasperated, his light tone of moments earlier gone now.

'He's travelling for six months in Asia. Back in September. That's when I return home.'

'To the UK.'

'Right.'

Another minute passed, both of them locked in their thoughts, the late summer breeze rippling over them in the dying day.

'So you're in a serious relationship, about to get engaged and leaving for home in a few weeks,' he murmured, his eyes on the pale stretch of water that could be glimpsed

KAREN SWAN

through the trees. 'I think I preferred it when I knew nothing about you.'

He was aiming for levity, but the subtext – that he cared about her, that he wanted her . . . She put her glass down on the deck. They couldn't keep the conversation neutral after this. It was beginning to come out; he was making them acknowledge what couldn't be – and shouldn't ever be – recognized. One of them had to do the decent thing and go, while they still could.

'Look, I think I'll head off to bed. I'm really tired.'

He sat up. 'But what about dinner? Aren't you hungry?'

'No, I think sleep's what my body's calling for right now.' Lie. Lie. Lie. It was not calling for that.

'Really?' He sounded disappointed, but she kept her eyes well away from his, as usual. 'OK, well, let me show you to your room.'

'It's fine, really. You stay here and enjoy the sunset. I'm sure I'll find it. How hard can it be, right?' she joked, looking at the tiny cabin.

'Still, I'll turn the lights on for you. They're oil-fired, so there's a knack to them.'

Dammit. He curled up his long legs and stood up beside her. For just a moment she felt his nearness, the hairs on her arms standing on end as though trying to reach out to him, but she kept on staring into the bottom of her wine glass until he moved away.

They wandered inside, Ted opening the door onto a small room, maybe only twice the size of the box room, with a double bed in the middle dressed with old lace sheets and painted wooden pegs for hanging up clothes all the way round the walls.

'It's so lovely,' she said quietly, sure she could hear the

sound of her own heart pounding and trying to stand as far away from him as she could in the small room.

He walked round to light the wall lamps, and as he came back towards her, she could have sworn the walls were moving inwards, making the small space smaller, pushing them together . . .

And then she remembered something suddenly – the perfect diversion! 'I've got something for you,' she said, rifling in her camera bag, almost weeping with relief that she had pulled all those crazy hours working over the past week.

'It's your film,' she said, handing over a DVD, scrawled with 'CONNORS' in black marker pen. 'I finished editing it this week. I thought maybe you'd like to look it over sometime and just check it's what you were after before . . . well, before I get the shoot printed up. Because then we're pretty much done, so . . .'

'Oh.' He took it from her, almost warily, swallowing as he held it in his hands. 'I'll get you something to wear,' he murmured finally, the atmosphere between them different now, as she'd predicted it would be after bringing Marina into the room with them.

'Thanks.' She waited. There was just 'goodnight' to get through and she'd be home and dry. She took the camera off her neck and kneaded her muscles, which were tired from supporting its weight all day long. She put it on the bedside cabinet, then for good measure decided it would be safer in the drawer – a habit from childhood ever since she'd once knocked her water glass in her sleep and ruined the Kodak she'd bought with her pocket money. She slid open the drawer.

A small oval-framed photograph – sepia-tinted – was

lying in there. It was of a young woman and, judging by the clothes she was wearing, had been taken at least forty years ago. The paper had begun to crack with age, but even with the slight overexposure, Ro knew instantly who it was.

'Here you are,' Ted said, coming back in with a folded T-shirt and a still-boxed toothbrush. 'I always keep a spare in the bag in case the—'

'This is Florence,' Ro said, cutting him off and holding up the photograph.

Ted stepped forward and looked at it. 'Yes.'

'Why . . . ?' Ro's eyes scanned the room, but it gave away nothing. 'Is this *Florence's* house?'

Ted nodded. 'Yes. Why? What's wrong?'

'What's wrong? What's wrong?' she demanded. 'Why are we here?'

'Why wouldn't we be? She said we could use it.'

'Oh, I bet she did!' Ro crossed her arms across her chest. She remembered his confidence earlier: *It's been promised to us.*

Ted looked at her, seemingly confused, and for the first time in the course of the day, she felt the distance between them grow, not contract.

'What do you mean?'

'Well, she doesn't refuse anything you suggest, does she? You've got her twisted round your little finger. Is this all part of the plan? You want to get your hands on this as well as Grey Mists?'

'Ro!' Ted said firmly. 'What the hell are you talking about?'

'I'm talking about *you* trying to swindle Florence out of her estate,' she said, the words bursting out of her with a force that came from transposing one high emotion into another. She watched the new expression bloom in his eyes and felt the distance between them grow further still. 'I know all about it. I figured it out – you, always there at just the right moment to "help out", play the good Samaritan in her times of distress.'

'I don't know what you're talking a—'

'No? Was it just supposed to be coincidence that you happened to be at the Golden Pear seconds after the attack, or that you just happened to be at the house when she turned on the shower?' she asked, her voice dripping with a sarcasm that took no account of the horror on his face. 'And then you use the threat of something happening to her grandchildren to finally force her to sell? What kind of person does that? Who draws children into something like that? You're a father! Where's your sense of decency? Of compassion? Does money really matter that much to you?'

He didn't answer. Ro thought he looked too shocked to reply, but she wasn't going to fall for his denials. She had resisted the charm offensive; this she could handle with ease.

'She might be taken in by you, but I'm not. I'm going to the police and to hell with proof. They can investigate you and find out what I already know, because I've seen the other side of you, remember? You put on the charm to keep people off the scent – and you're bloody good at it, I'll give you that – but I've seen your temper and how it makes you behave to people you think have crossed you—'

'Just stop right there!' he said sharply, grabbing her by the wrists, the same anger in his eyes that she had seen once before, that day on the beach. A moment passed as he saw the truth of what she really thought about him for the first time and an expression of something closing down crossed his features. He looked down and saw he was holding her and he let go – almost violently – shaking with anger. When he spoke, she almost had to strain to hear.

'I was at the cafe that day because I had arranged to meet Florence there for lunch; and I was at the house because I was dropping off the children for her; and the reason I cared about what happened to her grandchildren is because they are *my* children!'

'Your . . . ?' Ro echoed, as she suddenly felt a niggle that had lodged in the back of her mind wrest free like an air bubble and rise to the surface. *Mine heart . . . Mommy's bed . . .*

'She's their grandmother! And she will always be their grandmother. That doesn't stop just because her daughter's dead!'

'Marina's . . . ?' Ro felt like she'd been double-punched, a quick one-two manoeuvre, the blood pooling to her feet as shock after shock assailed her. 'But she never—'

'What? Talked about it? No! Because she can't! She can't make sense of it. None of us can.' His voice broke and he turned away, his head dropped, his shoulders pinched up to his ears.

'I thought you . . . you divor . . .'

He turned back to her, his eyes cold. 'You've clearly thought a lot of things about me.'

'Ted, I—'

'She killed herself. Five weeks after Finn was born. Puerperal psychosis, it's called, a severe form of postnatal depression. Walked out in front of a truck.'

Ro's hands slapped across her mouth, tears streaming instantly down her cheeks at the true, unthinkable horror of what had really happened to his family, so much worse than she could ever have imagined. The despair in Ella's eyes mirrored in the husband's now standing before her.

'I don't know what to say,' she wept, her voice cracked and hoarse. 'I'm so, so sorry. I thought—'

'Save it.' He stared back at her with a contempt she found devastating. 'I'm really not interested in what you think. Not anymore . . . I want you out of here first thing.'

And he walked out of the room, closing the door softly behind him – so as not to wake the kids.


Ro clutched the pillow, burrowing her face in it as another sob hiccupped through her. How could she have been so wrong? How could she have thrown those conspiracies and slanders at him when he'd already been through so much?

She had been in bed for hours now and she wasn't even close to sleeping. She had lain on top of the sheets, listening to him moving about in the living room, too ashamed to try to apologize, to try to explain that she'd had Florence's best interests at heart, to let him know that she'd thrown all those words at him wanting to push him away, terrified by the feelings he aroused in her. Even when she'd thought the very, very worst of him, she'd still wanted him. It had been easier to believe the worst in him than confront the worst in her.

She pushed the T-shirt back up to her face, smelling it, smelling him, a scent she remembered from that first day on the beach when he'd held her in the ocean and she'd twisted into him, trying to protect her camera – something in her, then, had known, had understood the chemistry and told her to keep back, keep away from him, keep pushing back. Don't let him close. Don't let him in. He's dangerous and to be seen as such . . .

She sat up suddenly, something else dislodging in her mind from that first day on the beach. The photos. She scrunched her eyes shut . . . The children – they'd been throwing something in the water. What was it? What was it?

The truth drifted up like a cold hand in black water . . . A white rose.

Her thoughts slowed down, clarity shining on her like a sunbeam. She had arrived at the end of May. Finn had been born on 18 April. Five weeks earlier.

Oh no. No. It had been the third anniversary of Marina's death and . . . and she'd just casually photographed them, 'a pretty scene', intruded in the most private of all ceremonies.

She threw off the covers. She had to tell him. Before she left for the last time, she had to tell him how sorry she was, that she understood now, everything. He was the man she'd feared most after all, the man she'd seen in the home videos and in her dreams and in her subconscious when she'd tried to find Matt. He was the man she'd hoped he wouldn't be – because then she'd risk everything.

He would freeze her out, she already knew that, but she had to say the words anyway. Because she had to live with this night – the things she'd said and what they'd have done.

She opened the door, peering out into the small, dark hall. The children's door was shut. Holding her breath, she tiptoed through to the main room. It was dark, but she could hear voices, see a dim glow coming from the other side of the sofa.

She advanced slowly, scared even to breathe, trying to find the words to put this right when she knew there were none. It was done.

A portable DVD player was sitting on a small stool; Ro saw the footage of Marina breastfeeding Ella, knew it would splice into the segment with her with the cabbage leaf and her joke about gratitude to goulash . . . She looked at Marina moving, laughing – so beautiful, so witty, so independent. A woman Ro could never hope to be. How could she be gone?

Ted was lying on his side, his body rigid, one hand pinched over his face as he paused the footage with the other, unable to keep watching. Hesitantly, she took a step closer, a floorboard creaking beneath her weight, and he sat upright in a sudden, fierce movement, his face turned up to hers. Before she could stop herself, though words wouldn't come, her hand was on his cheek, trying to wipe away the tears that had fallen tonight and so many others before. His eyes took her in – her regret, her sadness, her longing, her here in his T-shirt – and in the next moment, he had pulled her down to him, his mouth on hers finally. *Finally.*

She gasped for air, for a moment's clarity, pushing herself up so that she straddled him. Their eyes locked and she knew this was it – the final moment, the one before no return, the one she had been both dreading and waiting for since her first ten minutes here. And then she pulled his T-shirt over her head and tipped her head back, groaning as she felt his mouth on her breasts. She closed her eyes, knowing she was walking off the cliff, but she let go anyway . . . and realized she could fly.

# Chapter Thirty-One

They sailed back through the Sound, drove slowly through the streets, and Ro wondered how everything continued to look the same when the world had changed overnight. She kept waiting for reality to bite back. All night, as she'd looked into his eyes, explored him, listened to the sound of his heart beating and she knew it would catch her up sooner or later – the magnitude of what she'd done would bear down upon her like a fury, for she had stolen this night, stepped off her own path and into someone else's life, and it was a perfect fit. Lying in his arms had felt like home.

They turned left off Newton Lane and right into Egypt Lane. She had only a few minutes more with them now, minutes that insisted upon racing past her, though she tried to catch them with desperate fingers.

She turned back to look at Ella and Finn, both dozing in their seats in the back, worn out from another day that had started at 6 a.m. – before Ted and she had even *tried* to sleep. They'd gone for a walk through the woods (Ted pinning her behind trees every time the children briefly ran ahead), had lunch at a farm and spent the afternoon on the boat, sailing round the coastline and showing Ro their favourite bays. She'd photographed it all, but for once, she didn't need the camera to make it real. Every memory had made an impression in her heart.

They rolled up outside the house, so slowly the engine could scarcely turn over, and she knew he didn't want to be here yet either. She looked down at their hands, intertwined since the children had fallen asleep. She felt his eyes on her again and she looked up at him, her heart contracting with pain that he was leaving her, leaving here and driving ninety miles away for another week . . . when she only had three left.

He kissed her, crushing her lips against his with the same desperation she felt, making the tears fall from her eyes till the saltiness touched his tongue. He pulled back, gazing at her, and she didn't care if Hump could see them from the window, or Bobbi, or anyone.

'I should go,' she whispered, her hands over his on her cheek, her eyes refilling with the words she couldn't quite say.

He nodded reluctantly, Ella stirring lightly in the back as the car's new stillness lightened her sleep. She got out, retrieving her camera bag from the boot as quietly as she could.

'Ro,' Ted said, jumping out without even opening the door, pushing a piece of paper into her hand. 'My number. Look, I'm talking to Julianne as soon as I get back. There's no turning back, not for me.' He squeezed her hand in his. 'But I know it's not as straightforward for you.' He swallowed as he looked at her. 'It's your decision.'

She nodded, knowing what he was saying. She had to decide this, choose their future.

He dropped her hand from his gently, and she watched as he walked back round the car. He turned to her. 'Ro? For what it's worth, we're serious about you too . . . Exceptionally so.'

'Hello, stranger!' Hump called, leaping up the studio steps in one bound and landing like a gymnast – arms outstretched – just inside the doorway.

'Morning, Hump.' Ro raised an unimpressed eyebrow, her hands wrapped round her favourite red KitKat mug, trying (and failing) to get her day started. 'Why are you here so early?'

'Thought I'd better just check you actually were alive, given that none of us saw you all weekend. Figured if you weren't here, I'd better call the authorities.' He winked.

'I got my facts wrong. It was a weekend trip.'

'You don't say,' Hump drawled, eyes shining delightedly.

Ro gave nothing back. After Ted had driven away, she had walked through the door, through the empty house (everyone still clearly at the beach) and had fallen straight into bed, where she had slept solidly for fourteen hours.

'Bobbi's pissed she hardly saw you.'

'Yeah?' She sighed. 'I'll make it up to her next weekend.'

Would she, though? When Ted had said he was serious, what had he meant? Did he expect her to break up with Matt? How could they make such massive life decisions on the strength of one night?

Hump stared at her for a moment, taking in her lacklustre demeanour and lack of eye contact. She wasn't in the mood for teasing. He walked over, putting a hand on her shoulder. 'You OK, Ro?'

'Yup.' She slurped her tea noisily, trying to make him back off. She couldn't cope with kindness right now –

didn't deserve it. 'Tell me about your weekend. What did you and Bobbi get up to?'

He jumped up on the counter, resting his feet on the wall behind her. 'Just the usual – bumming on the beach, drinks at the Surf Lodge.'

'Anyone good playing?'

He shrugged. 'Don't really remember.'

'How did Bobbi seem?'

'Bit better. Brighter.'

'I don't suppose Greg showed?'

'No, although he's down next weekend apparently. Competing in the Classic – why am I not surprised?'

'The classic what?' Ro noticed one of the portraits on the wall was hanging at a slight angle. She got up and slapped his legs down so that she could walk round the counter to straighten it.

'It's a showjumping thing in Bridgehampton. Very smart. About as Gatsby as it gets.'

'Oh.' She tilted the portrait and stepped back to appraise it.

'Up a bit on the bottom left,' Hump said, squinting.

'Any idea how Greg's been doing – apart from working himself to death?'

'Nup.'

'It worries me that he's just holding it all in like this. He was *wrecked* that night. He seemed so self-destructive.'

'I know. The old Greg.'

The Skype on her laptop began ringing and she turned, frowning. It couldn't be Matt – he never called at this time. He was usually on the road by 7 a.m., as the group did most of their trekking early morning and late in the evening to avoid the high temperatures and humidity.

'Who is it?' she asked, wandering over.

Hump grinned back at her. 'Luvvaboy! You know we've never met?' he said, reaching over and pressing 'connect'.

'Wai—'

'Yo, Matt! Good to meet you at last. I'm Hump.'

'Hey, Hump. Ro's told me lots about you.' Matt grinned in surprise. 'How's it going over there?'

'Well, I'll be honest, I may never give your girlfriend back. That marmalade she makes? I'm hooked! We all are.'

'It's the only reason we're together,' Matt quipped.

'And she's got us all drinking tea with *tea* in it. Go figure,' Hump guffawed. 'So how's your trip, dude? It sounds pretty rad.'

'We're trekking to Angkor Wat now, which is, like, the highlight of the entire expedition. Seriously, you ever been to the Far East? Everyone should come here once in their lives. The things I've seen, the people I've met . . .' He gave a whistle. 'So pleased I did it.'

'So lucky Ro *let* you do it! Most chicks I know . . .' Hump shook his head.

Matt laughed again. 'Yeah, I know!'

The screen flickered between them. 'Hey, the connection's not too hot. You wanna speak to Ro? She's right h—' Hump stalled, looking around the empty studio. 'Oh shit, yeah,' he said slowly, turning back to the screen. 'She ran out the door just before you rang. Doing another shoot.'

'Oh. Right . . . So it sounds like work's taken off for her there.'

'Oh, man, yeah.' Hump nodded. 'She's, like . . . swamped.'

'Well, would you tell her I called?'

'Sure! Course I will.'

502

'Great. Well, listen . . .' Matt's voice sounded strained. 'Good to meet you, Hump.'

'Yeah, you too, buddy.'

'And, uh . . . thanks for looking after her for me.'

'Hey, it's easy to, man. We all love her.'

'See ya.'

Hump nodded, smiling inanely until the screen went black, then throwing himself out along the counter and looking down on the other side.

Ro was curled up in a ball on the floor, sobbing.

'Hey, hey, baby, what's wrong?' Hump hushed, jumping down beside her, his arm pulling her into him.

'You were r-right – about everything,' she hiccupped. 'I-I've messed up, Hump. Really, really badly.'

His eyes tracked her face slowly, concern written all over his. 'Ted, right?'

She nodded, grateful he hadn't called him Long Story – even though it was. The longest.

'You really didn't see it coming, huh?'

She blinked up at him, hiccupping wildly, her brown eyes splashy and wide. 'What am I going to do?'

'It seems to me the doing is already done. Looks like now you've got a decision to make.'

'But how can I possibly choose? I mean, Matt was the only man I'd ever been with. I hardly remember a time when I wasn't with him. It never crossed my mind he wouldn't be the one I'd grow old with.'

'Life throws curve balls all the time, Ro, and it's pitched a corker straight at you. You need to look at who you are now – not who you were when you met him. You've got to be honest with yourself – is Matt still what you need? Do you make each other happy?'

'Yes! I mean, I . . . I thought we did! I thought we had everything until this . . . this fucking *pause* happened.' She gripped her fingers in her hair, her face scrunched up with pain. 'Oh God! We're supposed to be getting engaged within the month. How could I have done this? How could I have endangered everything I know for one . . . one . . .' Her voice trailed off, the sobs stopping in her throat. Because it hadn't been just one night, any night. Even if it had all been lies and she never saw him again, it had been the night that changed her life. And it had been worth risking everything.

Hump gave her a squeeze as he felt her fall still, truth gradually dawning like a sunrise.

She dropped her head slowly on his shoulder. 'I don't understand how you . . . *you* can be so wise. I must be mad to listen to you. It's like getting knitting advice from Bobbi.'

'Huh?' He looked baffled by her usual confused analogy.

'Oh, you know what I mean! You're such a dreadful tart, Hump. I mean, really, what do you know about committing to a relationship and the sacrifices you have to make?'

'More than you might think,' he said quietly, pulling his knees up and resting his arms on them.

'Hump, I'm sorry – that was a shitty thing to say.' She pulled away to look at him. 'I didn't mean—'

'Hey, yeah. I know, I know – you said it with love.'

They both managed a smile, one of the mantras of the summer.

'We've all been living with Bobbi too long,' she mumbled.

He jogged her body with his and they sat together in silence, both lost in their own heads, something beginning to swirl around in hers, a red petal in white confetti drawing the mind's eye.

'Hump,' she said after a while, her voice quiet and thoughtful.

'Mmm?'

'You said "curve balls".'

He looked down at her. 'What about 'em?'

She stared back at him, thinking of his enormous capacity to love and heal others. It didn't make sense, his behaviour – not just the jacking in of medicine but the carousel of women in and out of his bed. He *liked* women; he didn't treat them badly or break their hearts. 'What was your curve ball?'

He blinked and she saw a flash of it then, the sorrow streaking across his eyes like a firework in the November sky, leaving nothing but a sense of the splendour and beauty that had existed there for a few short moments. She shifted position to get a better look at him. She saw the denial rise in his features, but she shook her head, stopping it right there.

'Greg and I were talking about you quitting medicine and he said to me, "You never can tell how people are going to react to a curve ball like that." What's "that", Hump?'

Hump looked away, his jaw pushed forward like a brake, stopping him from pitching forward. He didn't say anything for the longest time. And when he did . . .

'My wife dying.'

Air rushed out of the room, stripping everything of pigment and tone, substance and weight, as she watched his head drop and his face collapse, the words making the fact true all over again.

Ro didn't try to speak. Silence is the greatest kindness; she knew that herself. How often she'd longed for silence instead of sympathy in the weeks after her parents' deaths, willing the kind-hearted to let compassion suffice. His were the words that mattered and her silence drew them to her.

'Her name was Mei, and I knew she was supposed to be mine the second I laid eyes on her. She was teeny, half my size and –' he rubbed his thumb over the pads of his fingers '– like velvet, her skin.'

Ro watched a fleck of dust whirling in a sunbeam past the doorway, gravity pulling it down before a thermal current tossed it high again.

'We met at med school. She was the high flyer in the year, the one to beat, but I just knew she was the one to catch. God knows how I did it. I don't know what made her notice me, but we got married at the end of our first-year rotations.' He stared at the knuckles of his hands. 'Everyone said we were too young, of course. Her family was freaking, but we just knew. It was no biggie. We knew.'

He was quiet for a long time again and she took his hand and clasped it in hers, warming it as he spoke.

'And then, one day, she got this bite on the back of her hip. She didn't notice when it happened, but she just kept rubbing it, and by the time she showed it to me, it was bad. She'd had an anaphylactic reaction to a spider bite. It was nasty but not . . . not dangerous. She was prescribed antibiotics, antihistamines and anti-inflammatories to deal with it. The usual.'

He rested his head in one palm, taking a breather.

'Thing was, we'd got married just before our exams. We'd been pretty stressed and hadn't taken a honeymoon, so we decided to go away for a long weekend and do it then. She was taking the contraceptive pill, but . . . you probably know that antibiotics can reduce its efficacy, right? I mean, everyone knows that.'

Ro nodded mutely, hoping this story wasn't going where she thought it was.

His voice had become flat and strained. He shrugged at the bald truth of it. 'She was worried about getting pregnant, so she stopped taking the antibiotics. There were three days left of a seven-day course, but she figured it had cleared up. It was only a spider bite.'

'And she didn't tell you she'd stopped the course?'

Hump shook his head. 'First I knew of it was when she got a fever on the Sunday evening. She collapsed an hour later, went into a coma the next morning. And just never woke up.' The last words were a rasp, only the husk of his voice left like an emptied honeycomb.

'Oh, Hump,' Ro whispered, her arm over his shoulder and holding him close.

'And the simple fact is, it wouldn't have happened if I'd just checked. That was all I had to do – check the bottle, check her hip.'

'Hump, it wasn't your fault. She was a doctor too. She knew the risks. She wouldn't have wanted you to give up medicine because of it.'

He shook his head slowly, batting away her absolution. 'Her death was absolutely preventable. A hundred per cent. She shouldn't have died – it's a travesty.' He almost spat out the words. 'Doctors hold beating hearts in the palms of their hands every day, but someone can still die from a spider bite?' His hand clenched into a fist in front of him, his arms stretched out over his bent knees. 'She was dying in front of me the whole time and I never even knew it.'

Ro remembered his excessive care of her burns a few weeks earlier, how over the top it had seemed at the time. 'Hump, no,' she whispered, horrified by the blame he bore. 'It was not your fault.'

He looked across at her. 'You know you remind me of her a bit. Not . . . not to look at. Her hair was darker and straight. But your manner, you know, kind of crazy sense of humour, kooky laugh.'

Ro had a kooky laugh? 'Was she always falling over too?'

'No, but she was always losing things.' He rolled his eyes. 'Like, all the time. And, for all her cleverness, she could be totally ditzy. One time she bought this magnet thing that you stuck to the fridge and put your keys on it, so they didn't get lost.'

'Yes?'

He shrugged. 'We had an integrated fridge, so it wasn't magnetic. She still lost her keys.'

Ro laughed. 'My kind of girl.'

'Yeah. Yeah, she was a "once in a lifetime".'

His head dropped again and Ro squeezed the back of his neck. 'Hump, you'll never forget her, obviously you won't, but one day you will meet someone.'

He shook his head quickly. 'Uh-uh, not me. I had the real deal. The best I'm going to hope for now is fun. Just fun.'

Ro thought she'd never heard 'fun' sound so bad. 'But you're seeing someone now, aren't you? You don't have to tell me about her, but she must be . . . different. You've not had any hook-ups for weeks.'

Hump glanced at her, deliberating. He took in her puffy eyes and mottled cheeks, the sadness in her own eyes. 'Agh, it's a whole load of crazy. Besides, there's nothing to say.' He stared at a knot in the floor. 'Even if she was different, it can't go anywhere.'

Still he wouldn't confide. Ro bit her lip, not wanting to push. 'I wish you'd told me about Mei sooner.'

'I thought about it,' he nodded. 'Several times. But . . . how do you bring something like that up?' He shrugged. 'And anyway, you've had your own thing going on.'

Ro cringed. Compared to his, her problems seemed utterly trivial. In fact, compared to everyone, her problems seemed trivial. A pause? That was *it*? When she thought about what Florence and Greg and Bobbi had been through. And Hump now. And Ted – him most of all, the children . . .

'He's a widower too, Hump,' she said quietly. 'Marina died.'

Hump whipped round to face her, shocked.

She blinked back at him, her eyes instantly refilling with tears. 'It's the . . . it's the saddest story I ever heard. And those poor babies . . . I couldn't ever be enough. *I* couldn't match up.'

'That's obviously not what Ted thinks. It's plain as day on his face. I saw it the first time I clocked him watching you.'

'But . . . all of it . . . it's . . . it's another woman's life, *her* family, *her* husband. I can't just step into her shoes and pick it up, like a second-hand dress.' A fresh sob hiccupped out of her.

'Yeah, you can. That's the curve ball right there. It's not the path you thought you were going to take, but suddenly . . . you're at the crossroads and you've got to choose.'

'But what if I don't want it to be like that? What if I want to do it all fresh with someone who's learning along the way, like me? I didn't come out here looking for this – a grieving husband, a ready-made family. It's everything I don't want.'

Hump put his hand on her forearm. 'I know, baby. But did you ever think that it might just be everything you need?'

# Chapter Thirty-Two

Time was playing games with her – rushing through her hands like running water last weekend when she'd wanted it to stop, freeze into ice and become something she could hold, play with at will. Now it was dragging its feet.

She'd had to leave the studio early, even shaking her head and pretending she was just a part-timer when a couple had come up, enquiring for her, as she'd locked up. She had no appetite for work. Or food. Even when she remembered to fix a meal, she forgot to chew, her eyes trained on the middle distance, somewhere between here and there, trying to find an answer, find the will to call.

Now she was sitting on the porch, a beer in her hand, waiting for Hump to come back with Bobbi from the Jitney stop on Main Street – just like he had their first weekend, the day after she'd arrived, the day after she'd first met Ted.

How much had changed since that day. How much *she* had changed since that day. She had survived for one thing – arriving out here, dressed in Matt's clothes, a bewilderment clouding around her like perfume as she tried to navigate her way in this strange new world, feeling like a pilgrim, out on her own now. She'd made new friends, set up her career, established a strangely healthy lifestyle of walking on the beach, yoga and cycling (with sprinklings of kayaking, tennis and early morning swims thrown in sporadically). She had done all that, one day at a time. But she'd lost her heart on day one. It had been the very first thing she'd done here, before she'd even unpacked.

The Humper rumbled down the road and Ro inhaled, bracing herself for the assault that always was Bobbi in the house. She smiled as the big yellow nose turned round the hedge and jiggled up the drive, amazed to see not just Bobbi in the car, but Greg too – Bobbi had bagged the front seat, of course – before remembering he was riding in the showjumping competition this weekend.

She held up her beer bottle in greeting as they jumped out, reaching inside herself for a smile. Her housemates didn't need to add her misery to theirs.

'I am so fricking glad to hear you jumped his bones at long last!' Bobbi greeted her back, bellowing for good measure as she ran across the small lawn and up the porch steps. 'It took you long enough. Hump and I noticed it at the freakin' vineyard. We had a bet goin'.'

Ro's jaw dropped open as Bobbi reached down and grabbed a beer from the cold box beside Ro's chair.

'You told them?' she screeched at Hump, as he – sheepishly – followed after.

'I told you to be discreet,' Hump scowled at Bobbi, as she perched on the veranda. He looked back at Ro. 'And I only told them so that they would know to treat you delicately. And with care.' He glowered at Bobbi. 'Del-i-cat-ely. She's not been herself this week.'

Ro pouted and Greg came over, pulling off his tie and planting a kiss on her forehead. She looked up at him in astonishment. He winked as he got a beer. 'Lucky chap.'

'"Chap"? You say "chap" now?' Bobbi scorned, swinging her legs. 'You really do think this is Fitzgerald's era, don't you?'

Greg stared at her for a moment as he rolled his tie slowly in a ball round his fist before pocketing it. Then he walked over to her and took her face in his hands.

Everybody stopped breathing – Bobbi, Ro, even Hump – as he stared down at her, before slowly planting a kiss squarely on Bobbi's forehead too. 'Don't be so jealous. You only had to ask.'

Ro burst out laughing, Hump too, at Greg's new handling of Bobbi's tantrums. Three minutes home and already they were lifting her mood.

'You seem chipper,' Ro said, watching as Greg settled himself on the veranda on the other side of the steps to Bobbi.

'"Chipper"? Now there's a word, Greg,' Hump interjected.

Greg smiled, seemingly enjoying their teasing. 'Chipper is exactly how I feel.'

'Care to share?' Ro asked, sensing something coming.

'I just handed in my notice.'

'You did *what*?' Hump spluttered, coughing up beer. 'But you were just about to get MD!'

'I've had enough of pedalling the corporate wheel. It's time to get my life in order. Do like Ro's done and make some changes.'

'But . . . you're, like, the only grown-up here! You can't just jack it all in.' Panic danced across Hump's face. 'Oh God, it's like my father just dyed his hair blue and came downstairs in a dress.'

'Greg,' Ro protested, as distressed as Hump, 'I am no one's role model.'

'On the contrary, you're inspiring, Ro. Someone you loved let you down too, but you've built a life up from scratch this summer.'

They thought Matt had let her down? 'It was only ever meant to be a pause. Nothing permanent. If I'd thought that was what I was doing, I wouldn't have left the house, much less the country,' she said. 'Greg, look, I know that Erin's hurt you terribly, but our circumstances are very different. Please don't throw your career away.'

He shook his head. 'It doesn't feel like that. Not this time. It feels like freedom.' He looked at the floor momentarily. 'I've spent a lot of time thinking about what happened that weekend – and how close I came to making the biggest mistake of my life.' He looked back up at her. 'And I never thanked you properly for what you did for me that night. I'm sorry if it frightened you.'

'We just want you to be happy, Greg.'

'And I'm going to be.' He grinned at her. 'Everything suddenly seems incredibly clear. I've drawn up plans for my own practice. There's another VP who's resigning with me and we're setting up together.'

'Plus there's a woman, right?' Hump added, pointing a finger at him. Greg looked at him in surprise. 'My bro said you'd met someone. Dude!' Hump cheered, handing him another bottle as his mobile beeped in his pocket. 'You're on the up again. This deserves a celebration.'

'Why does it?' Bobbi stormed, jumping off the railing in temper. 'Why are we cheering to the high heavens that Gatsby here's got himself another Daisy? So your girlfriend got engaged? Well, boo-fucking-hoo! My boyfriend died! Bite me, why don't you?'

And before anyone could utter one word, she had stomped upstairs like a grounded teenager, their collective Friday feeling suddenly as flat as week-old champagne.

Greg went to follow, but Ro held up one hand. 'No! Leave it to me. I've had enough of this.'

She ran up the stairs two at a time, tripping over her own feet at the top and falling headlong into Bobbi's room.

Bobbi, who was lying on the bed, looked up in alarm at the clatter.

Ro straightened up, pulling down her T-shirt and smoothing her hair from her eyes. 'That's it! I'm up to here with you sniping and bitching at Greg. It's been going on all bloody summer and neither Hump nor I know where to look when you two are in a room together. It's ridiculous. We don't know what the hell's going on with you two, and frankly, we don't want to! It's your problem. Just sort it out and stop making *our* home feel like a war zone. Don't you think we've all been through enough?'

Bobbi blinked back at her, momentarily stunned into silence. She had never heard Ro raise her voice before and she didn't know that the rash on her neck that looked like meningitis was actually just temper. Her mouth kept opening and closing, but nothing would come out – only one tear sliding slowly down her cheek. Ro swallowed at the sight of it and sank onto the edge of the bed. Seeing Bobbi cry was like snaring an eagle – something majestically fierce and strong and free now humbled and broken.

'Oh bugger,' she mumbled, her resolve crumbling. 'What happened, Bobs?' she asked quietly.

Bobbi was silent for a long time, struggling to say the

words her pride wanted to silence. 'You know how you said with Matt you just knew?'

Ro blinked, not wanting to hear her words – proven now to be empty and meaningless – quoted back at her like some authority on love. What did she know? What had she ever known? Greg thought she was brave and pioneering; Bobbi thought she was loyal, steadfast and all-knowing. But she was none of those things – she was as lost and uncertain as she'd ever been, the foundations of her world, her life, her self, crumbling away beneath her feet like chalk cliffs.

'I got what you meant, finally, with him. He felt like the fit for me.' Her voice was small and unnaturally quiet. If Bobbi had never heard Ro loud before, Ro had never heard Bobbi quiet. It was odd, like they were wearing each other's clothes. She looked up at Ro. 'I never had that.'

'Does he know?'

Bobbi shook her head quickly. 'No. There's nothing to . . . explain. Nothing actually happened between us. We . . .' She swallowed hard, pride intruding again. 'We got back here and he stopped . . . Said he was involved with someone and it was only fair to tell me, that he was trying to do the right thing.' She raised a small smile. 'His manners, right?'

'Oh, Bobbi.'

'I thought I could be grown-up about it – said we could still be friends. But I just kind of froze every time I saw him. I . . . I didn't know how to be, how to hide it, you know? I felt like it was written all over my face the whole time, making me look like a schmuck and making him feel guilty. Because I respected him for doing the right thing.' She was quiet for a moment. 'Or at least, I did till *she* strutted into the kitchen.'

'Who? Erin? You mean you knew about them?'

'I knew it was her he was in love with. I just knew it. I could . . .' She held her hands up in the air like she was compressing something. 'I could just feel it between them. Like it was Erin's private joke.' She looked across at Ro, eyes flashing dangerously. 'She always was a bitch.'

Ro frowned. 'You knew her before, you mean?'

Bobbi shot her a look. 'Penn. She was the queen of the campus. *Everyone* knew her.'

'Well, she obviously remembered you too. She asked whether you'd met.'

'Ha! If she thought I was going to give her the satisfaction of placing me . . .' Bobbi sneered.

'Why not?'

Bobbi stared into the middle distance, a look of cold rage on her face. 'She took my boyfriend off me. For a *bet*.'

Ro gasped. 'Oh, Bobs, you poor thing.'

'Hey, he was a loser anyway. It was going Nowheresville.' She shook her head, eyes glazed with reluctant tears. 'But to be dumped for that bitch twice? I don't think so – moving on!' She sailed her arm through the air defiantly.

'Except that you didn't. Or rather, you haven't,' Ro said quietly. 'You wouldn't get this upset around him if you really had moved on.'

'*I* will be fine,' Bobbi said determinedly. 'I'm all about making partner this year anyway.'

Ro looked at her sadly.

She remembered Bobbi's venom the day of the tennis tournament – how desperate she'd been for Ro not just to beat Erin, but smash her. 'Bobbi, I wish you'd at least told me. It must have been awful for you keeping this all bottled up.'

She looked at Ro, a desperate look on her fierce face suddenly. 'Listen, you don't repeat a word of this, Ro. Not one word.'

Ro shook her head. 'Of course not. Not a word, to anyone.'

A creak on the landing floor made them both jump. 'Shit,' Bobbi whispered, her eyes wide.

Ro jumped up to look, but Bobbi pulled her back. 'No, I'll go.'

She crawled off the bed and tiptoed to the door. Ro noticed the window was open and crossed the room quickly to shut it.

'Who's that?' Bobbi demanded, flinging open the door. She peered out into the hallway. 'Oh, it's you. Where are you going?'

'Popping out.' Hump's voice sounded small and distant from where Ro was standing.

'What? But we're supposed to be going out!' Bobbi whined.

'And we will. I'll only be an hour—'

'Bobbi,' Ro said from inside the room.

'Won't be long, I promise,' Hump replied, his voice growing ever more distant and the stairs creaking. 'I just need to get something from the studio. Greg's still here—'

'Bobbi!'

'Tch, what is it?' Bobbi frowned, looking back in.

Ro was standing beside her chest of drawers, holding up a necklace. 'Who gave you this?'

Bobbi stepped into the room, her eyes pinned on Ro's expression. 'Kevin did. Why? What's the matter?'

Ro looked down at the pearls, her thumb rubbing lightly

over the gold oval clasp studded with a ruby. 'I think this changes everything.'

The girls ran down the stairs. Greg looked up from the swing seat, a beer in one hand, *Dan's Papers* in the other.

'Have you read this? There's rumours that the people behind Wild Waters in Miami have been spotted sniffing around a development lot in Montauk. Can you imagine? A waterpark in the Hamptons?' he scoffed. 'Two hundred million, they're quoting.'

Bobbi put her hands on her hips. 'You're reading that upside down.' She glared at him.

Greg frowned as he saw she was right. 'Oh.'

But Ro didn't care about upside-down newspapers. 'Where's Hump?' she asked, her eyes wild.

'He got a call and he's just gone out. Why?'

'Dammit, I need the car!'

Greg stood up, taking in their intense expressions. 'Well, he took the bike – the car's still here. Why? What's going on? What's the necklace for?' he asked, noticing the string of pearls in Ro's hand.

'Kevin gave this to Bobbi the night before he died.'

Greg's eyes flicked over to Bobbi, an unreadable expression in them. 'So?'

'So, I know for a fact that this same necklace was given to Florence. I was in her kitchen when she received it.'

There was a short pause. 'Personally, I find one pearl necklace tends to look very much like the next,' he said diplomatically.

'No, it's the same one. I remember admiring the clasp.' She showed him the ruby-studded oval clasp.

Greg planted his hands on his hips. 'So then Florence returned it.'

'Yes, because it was a *bribe*. I saw the look on her face when she read the card with it – I thought it was odd at the time, but didn't know why. Then she told me in the hospital that someone had been trying to force her to sell the house. They'd started off as nice bribes and then, when she didn't bite, they changed to threats.' She caught sight of his expression. Bobbi's too. 'Look, I know how this probably sounds right now. I'd be sceptical too, but she's convinced that what happened at the Golden Pear was intended for her, not me.'

'Why would anyone do that to Florence?' Greg asked, reasonably, doubtfully.

'Her drive cuts along the bottom of the plot for the neighbouring property, meaning they have neither beach frontage, access or a view. She told me it knocks five million dollars off the value of the estate at a stroke.'

Greg's eyes narrowed at that. 'Go on.'

'She tried telling the police, but they just thought she was a paranoid old woman. They said what happened to me was unrelated: no case. She'd done her own investigations and discovered that the house next door had been sold last Christmas to a property development company. She couldn't find any names of the directors on the board because it's registered offshore. That was as far as she could get. When I got hurt, she tried telling the police but they just thought she was a paranoid old woman: that her accident was just that – a civil matter, not their problem. And that what happened to me was unrelated. No case . . .'

'And because of this necklace, you think it was Kevin

trying to blackmail her?' His eyes slid again to Bobbi, who was wearing a face like thunder.

'Well, after everything that's come out in the press about him, it makes sense. People have gone on record as saying he tried to bribe them with flights, meals, designer clothes, jewellery . . .'

'Actually, he never used the words "bribe" or "blackmail",' Bobbi said defensively. 'We talked about it once at dinner. He told me he saw them as bonuses for the vendor. It often happens the other way round at the levels he worked at – people commonly throw in a Ferrari from the garage or a boat with a big-money lot. And the market's been so bad – there aren't enough sellers out there. He just thought he was approaching it creatively. He was proud of it, if anything.' She narrowed her eyes. 'And he certainly never got heavy on anyone. He would never have threatened Florence. He may have been a bit fluid with rules and regulations, but he was a pussycat. I can tell you that for sure.'

Ro turned to her. 'But all the evidence points to him, Bobbi! I'm sorry, I know you were fond of him, but Florence nearly died.'

'And Kevin *did* die,' Bobbi retorted. 'Did he beat *himself* to death with the golf club?' Both Ro and Greg winced at the brutality in her words.

'Maybe you're both right and both wrong,' Greg said, cutting in, and breaking their deadlock.

'Huh?'

'From what's been reported in the papers and what Ro's saying about this necklace, it sounds like maybe Kevin did try to induce Florence to sell the house. But if what you're saying is true too, then he probably wasn't behind the other incidents. Throwing boiling coffee over someone? Cutting earth wires? Those are *big* escalations from a pearl necklace being returned.'

Bobbi planted her hands on her hips, looking so fierce she could have been standing on a chariot with flames shooting out behind her. 'So then, what are you saying?'

Greg inhaled slowly. 'I'm not sure. Maybe that someone else is behind the other attacks?'

'Someone *else*?' Ro whispered, feeling a cold shiver tiptoe through her bones. 'You mean, if the person who hurt Florence wasn't Kevin, and Kevin is now dead, then they were *both* attacked by the same person?'

'I'd say there's a chance all the events are related,' Greg said quietly, putting a soothing hand on her arm.

'But how could Florence possibly be linked with Kevin?' Ro asked, her voice tremulous. This was getting worse and worse. 'And if they've killed him ... what ... ?' She couldn't finish the sentence, couldn't bear to articulate the danger her friend must be in still. 'But what do they want from *her*? She's said she'll put the house up for sale,' she added quickly.

Greg was quiet for a long while, his eyes moving along the ground as he tried to join the dots. 'It may not be about the house at all. It was for Kevin, clearly, but for these others – whoever they are – it could be something else entirely. You said that Florence found out that the house next door was sold to an offshore company. Did she say where? Caymans, the British Virgin Islands?'

'Bermuda.'

'Bermuda?' he echoed thoughtfully. He looked back at Bobbi. 'Did Kevin ever talk to you about going out to Bermuda? Any trips he took there?'

Bobbi shook her head slowly. 'Not that I recall. He said he'd had a holiday at Easter in Antigua.'

He chewed his lower lip, deep in thought.

'What?' Ro pushed. 'What's so interesting about Bermuda?'

'Just let me make some calls. My resignation isn't being announced till Monday, so I've still got the company resources at my disposal till then.' He disappeared inside quickly, leaving Bobbi and Ro alone again.

Ro glanced at Bobbi, trying to gauge her housemate's mood. The discovery of the necklace put them on opposing sides of both incidents – Bobbi on Kevin's, her on Florence's, as they struggled to find the link between one's friend and the other's lover.

They sank in silence onto the porch swing.

'Listen, I'm sorry about what I said about Kevin,' Ro said. 'I'm not trying to make him out to be a monster. I just have to protect Florence. She's been through so much – you couldn't begin to imagine.' She thought about Marina and the sadness in Florence's eyes whenever she'd talked about her family. She'd lost her daughter in the most terrible of circumstances, and now all this . . .

'Hey, listen – I don't know why I'm defending the guy, like I'm Girlfriend of the Year or something,' Bobbi murmured. 'The truth is, we went out a few times. I wanted his contacts and a promotion; he wanted . . .' She shrugged, pointing to the obvious. 'It was never a love thing. And if I'm honest, I was using him to get back at you-know-who.' She fell quiet. 'I guess I just feel like . . . 'cos of the way he died, he deserves a little loyalty. He's had a bad enough deal.'

'I understand,' Ro nodded, her mind trawling back to

the morning he had died. *She* had been the last person to see him alive. If Matt hadn't picked up, she'd have seen it all – every terrifying, soul-destroying moment of it. In all likelihood, she had seen the murderer. She remembered his companion, in the red trousers and panama, drawing his clubs from the bag . . .

She stiffened.

'What is it?' Bobbi's voice sounded far away.

'I'm not sure.' Fragments of memories were drifting up, her mind having settled momentarily into the free-flow state she sank into so easily in Melodie's classes, making associations that ordinarily she wouldn't think to connect . . .

Greg stepped out onto the porch and leaned on the railing opposite. 'So, I just asked for a search to see what came up on Kevin's assets. Turns out he sold his entire portfolio to a firm called SB Holdings Ltd, registered in Bermuda, three weeks before his death.'

Ro looked up at him, the tenuous connections fading again like footprints in snow. 'Yes, that's the name. Florence told me that.'

'SB Holdings? That's the name of the company he was non-exec for. I saw it on LinkedIn. Remember I told you, Ro?' Bobbi said, her eyes keen and intense.

'But hang on a minute, how could he be both?'

'Both what?' Bobbi asked her.

'How could he sell them their stock and also be a director on their board? A friend of mine from uni was asked to be one last year and she was telling me all about it – independence is mandatory; she said she couldn't be involved in the running of the company or have a key relationship with them, like being a customer or a supplier. And surely Kevin would be counted as a supplier?'

'You're right,' Greg agreed. 'It's not an ethical way of running a board.'

'That business sounds dodgy to me,' Bobbi offered, crossing her arms over her chest. 'We should take this to the police.'

Ro stared into space, trying not to make snap judgements, trying to make sense of the half-clues they had. 'Hang on, let's just take a minute and go over what we know for sure. We know Kevin tried to bribe Florence. We know he sold his entire portfolio to a company that operates outside board regulations, and that this same company owns the house next door to Florence. We know Kevin's been killed, obviously, and that Florence has been the victim of a supposed freak accident that nearly killed *her*.'

'Right. But one thing's niggling me,' Greg frowned. 'Why list the company in *Bermuda*? Bermuda is an offshore hub for insurance and re-insurance and the banking sector. Not property investment.'

'Insur—' Ro's voice trailed away. *Ninety-eight per cent of my business is conducted on the golf course* . . . 'The police think Kevin was killed by a business associate,' she murmured.

'That's their angle,' Bobbi agreed, watching her.

Oh no. No. Ro paced the porch, her head in her hands, pushing down on her temples, trying to fit the pieces together and in the same breath trying to push away the answer that kept forming.

'Ro? Talk to us,' Greg said, following after her, touching her elbow. 'What is it?'

She looked up at him. 'I think I know who killed Kevin.'

# Chapter Thirty-Three

They rang the bell three times, but the solid-wood gates remained closed.

'They don't have dogs, right?' Greg asked her, clearly deliberating scaling them.

'No, I'm pretty su—'

'Hello?' a woman's voice crackled through the intercom.

'Hey! It's me – Ro!' Ro called out, leaning across Greg in the front of the Humper.

'Ro? . . . Just a second.'

There was a minute's pause and then the mechanism sounded up and the gates began to swing back. They rumbled noisily into the drive, not that they had ever thought there was a chance of entering the property unheard. This wasn't a stealth attack. They weren't expecting him to run. As Greg had impressed upon them at home, 'We're simply there to ask questions – the necklace alone isn't enough to link Kevin and Florence: she's got no proof she ever received it. We just have to get him to talk about Bermuda, trip himself up.' Greg had his phone set to Siri in his pocket.

'Hey,' Melodie smiled, greeting them on the doorstep, wrapping a towelling robe round her. Her hair was wet. 'Is anything wrong?'

'No, no.' Ro shook her head, greeting her warmly as usual. 'We were just passing on our way back from the beach and wondered if you were in.'

Melodie took in Bobbi's navy suit and heels, Greg's work clothes too. The beach?

'But please do say if it's a bad time.' Ro shifted weight nervously, worried her friend could see through her act. Oh, why couldn't she have a poker face, just once?

'Not at all. I was just having a swim. Come through.'

The small troupe wandered through into the enormous living space, the water trickling down the far wall like a fairy wonderland, Bobbi taking care to 'mind the gap' this time in her heels.

The lights were on in the pool, the water still disturbed from her recent swim. Ro looked out, remembering the dinner they'd had there over two months earlier – how Brook had dominated with his political and ecological posturings.

'Can I fix you some drinks?' Melodie asked, wandering over to a butler's tray and holding up a bottle of gin.

'I'm driving, thanks,' Greg said.

'So I see. You've got the Humper . . . but no Hump?'

'No, he's out.'

She handed a gin and tonic with a twist of lime to the girls, a sparkling water to Greg.

'Is Brook out too?' Bobbi asked.

'Of course.' She rolled her eyes. 'The Town Board is meeting tomorrow to vote on the recommendations put forward by the Coastal Erosion Committee. He's still lobbying for the beach project, even with just hours to go. *Some* people still need persuading, apparently.'

So then he wasn't even here? Ro's eyes slid over to Greg

and she could see the same sense of disappointment on his face too. Ro took tiny sips of her drink, feeling bad that they had barged in here and were using Melodie's hospitality to investigate her husband.

'It sounds to me like Senator McClusky might have competition,' Greg said lightly, lapsing into social chit-chat, a smile on his handsome face. 'Pressure's growing on him to stand down. Has Brook ever thought about setting his sights higher than local politics?'

'You joke, but you're not the first to say it. He's so passionate about these issues.' She smiled. 'Of course, he says passionate; I say obsessive.'

'What drives him, do you think? Philanthropy?' Greg asked, raising his hands slightly to indicate the lavish house they were standing in. 'Giving something back?'

'Oh, definitely. I think he's seen enough hardship over the years, through his work, that he feels a sense of civic responsibility.'

'You mean through running the National Flood Insurance Program?' Greg confirmed, strengthening his theory.

'I don't know what that is,' Ro said, shrugging apologetically.

'It's the insurer of last resort for those poor souls who can't otherwise get mortgages along the coast; theirs are the properties most at risk and the other banks won't touch them.' Melodie shook her head. 'But even the NFIP can't help everyone, and Brook's seen too many people left ruined and homeless. He wants to be the good guy, but more and more he finds he's got to say "no". There are entire swathes of areas that have been effectively ghettoized now by legal small print.'

And therefore going for stony-broke selling prices, Ro

thought – remembering what she'd read in the paper about how Kevin had bought up the entirety of the Montauk Harbor wharves in the immediate weeks following Sandy. Everything made sense now: Brook knew what was uninsurable; Kevin swooped in with a smile, an inducement and a better-than-nothing offer. They had been in this together. But still she didn't understand one thing: if the properties were uninsurable, why buy them at all? Without insurance, the buildings were effectively worthless, and even the plots themselves held no value when the town policy was to leave them to the ocean . . .

*Some* people still need persuading.

The glass fell from Ro's hand, shattering on the concrete floor and making them all jump, as she made the connection at last.

'Ro? What's the matter?' Bobbi asked, running over in her heels, crunching glass beneath her leather soles.

'She's gone as white as a sheet!' Melodie cried. 'Quick, hold her, Greg – in case she faints.'

Greg ran over to her too as Melodie, who was barefoot, slid her feet into a pair of flip-flops and ran over to a cupboard to get a dustpan and brush.

'Good diversion,' Greg whispered, as he threw her arm around his shoulder.

'The vote's tomorrow,' Ro mumbled. 'It's all for nothing if he doesn't get the vote for the beach. Don't you see? It secures the funding for the area's long-term protection and regeneration. With that, he can redevelop and sell on at a massive profit – say to a waterpark?'

'Jesus,' Greg whispered.

'Is she OK?' Melodie asked, running back and beginning to sweep up the broken glass.

'She doesn't look well. We'd better get her home. I'm so sorry – we didn't mean to barge in and then run out again,' Greg said to Melodie as they led Ro out towards the front door.

'Don't worry. Just look after her. She's been overdoing it recently. I'll come by in the morning,' Melodie said, crouched down and watching after them with concern.

Ro let herself be led away, feigning light-headedness but her mind running over the same two things.

One person was standing in the way of that vote.

And Melodie's flip-flops were yellow.

'No, don't park there – we could be seen on the CCTV,' Ro said two minutes later, stopping Greg from turning right into the driveway. 'Just go straight ahead. We'll park in the general car park.'

'But how will we get in?' Bobbi asked from the back seat. 'These places are all like fortresses.'

'Not the older ones. Follow me,' Ro said, throwing open the car door.

Greg stopped her, his hand on her arm. 'You're sure about this, Ro?'

'Absolutely certain. Florence is opposing the measures he's trying to push through and he needs to win that vote tomorrow. That development deal is worthless without the new beach. He'll be here, I can promise you.'

Greg nodded. 'OK. Come on, then.'

They all jumped down from the Humper, Greg having to help Bobbi in her tight suit. For once, she didn't fight him. They had bigger concerns than each other right now.

'We'll have to take our shoes off. You especially, Bobs,' Ro said, stopping at the sand line and walking onto the dimly lit beach. It was dark now and only the brightness of the white sand created any kind of glow, although Bobbi quickly helped out with the mega-wattage of the torch on her phone.

The three of them followed the cone of light as they stumbled through the cool, dry sand, none of them speaking, none of them quite sure what they were going to do, all of them safe in the knowledge at least that Greg – if needed – could overpower the older man. But were they in time?

'It's up here,' Ro said, finding the small chain across the bottom of the boardwalk and the polite notice: 'Private property. Please no trespassers.'

'You'd better turn the torch off now,' Greg said to Bobbi, and she obeyed for once, without argument.

They ducked under the chain and walked along the boardwalk that protected Florence's beloved dunes. As they crested the top, the pretty, beleaguered shingled house reared up ahead of them. The lights were on.

'Keep to the shadows,' Greg whispered, leading them to the left-hand side of the lawn, furthest from the drive. 'We don't want to announce our arrival too soon.'

They walked barefoot in the grass, Ro feeling like her heart had quadrupled in size, blown up like a balloon, and was pressing against her ribs, trying to break free.

It wasn't about the house. It wasn't over yet . . .

She stared at the pool house as they passed; a lilo shaped like a dolphin was propped against it, an innocuous distraction to the dangers that had been hidden therein, the lights off in the pool tonight.

They reached the back door. Greg put his finger to his

lips and softly pushed down on the handle. It yielded with a faint creak. They all froze.

Nothing.

After another pause, he pulled the door wide and they stepped through into the utility area at the back – past the washing machine where foam boogie boards and water pistols were sticking out of a wicker basket – Freddie and Jude's? She saw a smaller, frilled gingham swimsuit and some UV vests still hanging from a drying rack, a half-inflated rubber ring sitting on top of the tumble dryer.

Ella and Finn. Ro wanted to double over at the thought of them: Ella's hopeful eyes, conspiratorial smile and the feeling of her small hand in Ro's as they'd walked through the trees in the early evening light; Finn's precocious chatter and staggering walk, his unabating love of a spade and a bucket and a tatty blue elephant . . .

They stopped by the doorway into the kitchen. No voices. No sounds.

Greg looked through, motioning for them to follow him.

They walked into the kitchen, towards the island and the table set along the right-hand wall.

There were papers scattered all across the table, a black ballpoint pen with the lid off, two glasses of wine with the dregs still in, lipstick marks on one, and a three-quarters-finished bottle of wine with the cork pushed back in.

Whoever Florence had been here with, she had invited her guest in, felt comfortable with them. And – her eyes scanned the papers on the table – they had been doing business together.

It was obvious Brook had been here with her. But where were they now?

They walked over, sifting quickly through the piles scattered across the tabletop: complicated spreadsheets for budgets, stapled legal clauses, a survey stamped with the logo of the Army Corps of Engineers, an application form – filled in but unsigned – addressed to the State Office of Emergency Management.

'What's that for?' Ro whispered, showing it to Greg.

His eyes flicked over it. 'That's the office that manages grant applications for federal funding,' he whispered back. 'Only the town officer is qualified to submit it. In the event of a "yes" vote, of course.'

Ro felt her stomach lurch. 'She hasn't signed it.' She pointed to the blank signature box.

'Yet,' Greg said, looking at her, both their eyes falling to the pen, its lid off. Had she refused to?

Oh God. Ro looked around the empty kitchen. There wasn't a sound in the rest of the dark house. Where were they?

'Guys . . .' Bobbi said, picking up some papers. 'Army Corps of Engineers' was stamped across the top, a paragraph seemingly angrily encircled with red pen.

They all peered over her shoulder.

Greg, expert in legalese, was quicker than the girls at skimming the report. 'No, it's nothing – just a report on the erosion issue in the Block Island Sound area of Montauk,' he murmured, pulling away disinterestedly. 'It's saying the erosion and flooding problems in the area have been amplified by over-dredging at the harbour inlet.'

'Oh yes, Florence mentioned that on the Artwalk,' Ro said. 'She's talking about not renewing their permits. Brook thought she was just trying to pen-push and waste time. He was pretty angry about it.'

Greg thought for a moment, then shook his head. 'It's got nothing to do with the new beach. That's what we need to find.'

A sudden sound made them all start – but not in fright. Someone was laughing.

They looked on, frozen to the spot as Florence came through the French doors, a tartan blanket wrapped around her shoulders, her seed-bomb basket over her arm, her hair windswept, her cheeks pink – and followed closely after by Brook.

It was hard to say who was the more astonished, although Florence recovered first.

'Ro?'

'F-Florence . . .' she stammered, not sure where to start. 'We came over to see that you were all right.'

'Why on earth wouldn't I be?' Florence asked, shaking her head and putting down the basket. She frowned quizzically. 'And how did you all get in?'

Greg, Bobbi and Ro's eyes slid over to Brook. He was standing by Florence, growing wary as he picked up on the suspicious stares being directed at him.

Greg stepped forward, his eyes darting back and forth between the older couple. 'Florence, I'm sorry to say we came over because we believed you were in danger.'

At Greg's words, Brook put a hand on her arm, but Greg stepped further towards her. 'From Brook.'

'*Brook?*' Florence laughed.

'What?' Brook uttered in disbelief. 'Why on earth would you think Florence is in danger from me?'

'Because she's the last person standing in the way of Montauk building an emergency engineered beach and therefore qualifying for federal funding,' Ro said, her eyes sparkling, her cheeks flushed as anger spurred through her at the thought of what he'd done – to Florence, to her, the threat he'd raised against Ella and Finn. 'And you need that approval to come through. You've bought up the Montauk Harbor wharves using your privileged access to uninsurable properties in the area, and getting Kevin Bradley to negotiate the rest. As soon as the area's protected again, those values will skyrocket and you'll be a very rich man – especially if you pull off the deal for the waterpark.' She looked at Florence. 'It's about hundreds of millions of dollars, Florence, not five. It isn't about the house. It's about the vote.'

'I don't know what you're talking about!' Brook cried. 'I don't own any property in Montauk.'

'Granted, you've certainly made it difficult for anyone to attach your name to it,' Greg said. 'Registering the company offshore makes it all but impossible to get names. But we do have one.'

'*What* company? Whose name?'

'SB Holdings Ltd,' Greg replied. 'And we have proof that Kevin Bradley was a director.'

'Well, maybe he was, but how does that link to *me*?'

'It's registered in Bermuda – an odd choice for anyone in property, but for someone in the insurance trade who travels there numerous times a year . . .' Greg paused, his voice calm and steady, letting the cool logic of his words settle over Brook's bluster. 'You told us yourself you conduct most of your business on the golf course, the exact place where Kevin Bradley was murdered.'

'I never murdered Kevin Bradley. I never murdered anyone,' Brook protested angrily.

'I saw you, Brook,' Ro snapped. 'I was watching from

the window. You were wearing a panama, the same hat you wore to the Artwalk two weeks ago.'

'Anyone can wear a hat.' Brook's mouth fell slack. 'I would never kill anyone.'

'Not even for two hundred million dollars?' Greg asked.

'Give it up, Brook,' Ro said. 'Now that we can link Kevin to SB Holdings, it's only a matter of time before the police get the names of the rest of the board. I mean, you even named the company after your own wife. Songbird? I've heard you call her that myself!'

'Uh, guys . . .' Bobbi murmured, holding up a finger.

'What is it?' Greg asked, alerted by her tone.

'The dredging company – the one that's had the permit for works in Montauk.' She pointed her finger to some print that, upside down and too far away, Ro couldn't read.

'What's wrong?' Ro repeated as Greg fell silent too.

Greg looked up at her slowly, a look on his face that made her blood suspend its race through her veins.

'It's owned by SB Holdings Ltd. The permit was signed ten years ago by someone called . . .' He squinted, unable to decipher the photocopied scrawl. 'S-something Barrington.'

Brook's eyes met Ro's – real fear in them now.

But Ro already knew. She remembered that very first conversation, eating breakfast in the sun, how badly her parents had chosen her name. SB, not for Songbird at all, but Samantha.

Brook was right. Anyone can wear a hat.

# Chapter Thirty-Four

Ro stayed with Florence after Greg called the police and he and Brook drove back to the house to meet them. Bobbi went home. Hump would need someone to talk to when he got back. Out of all of them tonight, he was the one in for the nastiest shock.

She slept – or rather, didn't – in the room that had been Marina's when she'd been a child, and which Florence had kept almost the same for her grandchildren – a pink pony print on the wall, the view over the dunes and out to the ocean unchanging but for the daily vagaries of clouds, wind and tide.

Ro sat on the single bed all night, her eyes tracking the moon's silver march over the black ocean as she thought about the girl who turned into the woman who would always be the one before her. She thought about Florence and the children, and how she'd fallen for them all in such tiny spaces of time, their lives flung together from across an ocean and enmeshed with the deep, abiding trust that comes from surviving tragedy.

And Ted. He was back again. She could almost feel his closeness, knowing he was sleeping somewhere – maybe within a mile of here – knowing he had moved through this house, sat on this bed, swam in that pool . . . She looked down at the phone in her hands, the brief text flashing as a draft.

He had said she had the decision to make. She had to be the one to do it because she wasn't free. He was, in the most terrible of ways, and he was waiting for her; had been – he'd said – since almost the beginning, when she'd stood laughing across the Wölffer party in a too-small dress, flip-flops and wild hair. She had spent the summer running from him, hiding from him even as she'd been propelled towards him, drawn into the folds of his family as she watched their past with a fast-beating heart. But how could she be their future? How could they be hers? Nearly half her life had been devoted to another man, another dream . . . How could she put her trust in another future when last night's revelations had shown the flaws in her judgement? Her thumb tapped the 'send' button and she watched the icon spin on the screen, closing off the door to another life. No matter what her heart told her, the bonds of history felt like a chain she just couldn't break.

Ro walked slowly home, her feet dragging and her head full as she tried yet again to recast Melodie in the light of her actions: she had been provocative, Ro saw that now – flirting with Hump like it was a combat sport and dazzling him with a spirituality and flexibility that threw a shadow over all the pretty party girls wanting his eye. And what about the odd chip on her shoulder about the smart society scene she helped to lead, despising it on the one hand, craving its approval and acceptance on the other? She remembered Melodie warning her off Florence too – some sort of misguided show of friendship, perhaps? Trying to protect her? Painting Florence as erratic and unpredictable—

Wait . . .

Ro stopped walking, a frown on her face – the money, the missing $3 million. That would count as pocket change to Melodie surely, with an offshore bank account and a loaded husband?

Her feet began moving again, the thoughts non-stop, whirling around in her head like spells in a cauldron: she remembered Hump's petulance that day in the studio as Melodie left to get ready for another party. He had been jealous, pulling her down with envious spite as she went back to the husband whose status and financial clout she needed – and would never surrender. Put together, everything painted a brightly coloured picture, clear to see. Why, why hadn't she seen Melodie for what she was?

God, what a mess. She had sat down to a breakfast with Florence that neither of them ate; she had looked for catharsis in the pool and found nothing but exhaustion. Everyone had been undone, and she knew Melodie couldn't even begin to understand that Kevin wasn't her only victim in this – Florence fretting almost constantly about Brook, Ro almost constantly about Hump.

A trio of sun-kissed girls in Lilly Pulitzer dresses cycled past, their beach bags slung across their shoulders as they chattered about last night's party, and she suddenly felt old, like she wasn't part of their carefree world anymore. Last night, she hadn't been looking pretty and flirting with a stranger; she'd been confronting an ugly truth about a new friend. The golden shimmer of her all-American summer had been tarnished and she felt sullied by the truths she had confronted. To have been so deceived . . . how could she know, anymore, what was real? Her shoulders slumped again as she tried to imagine Melodie in a windowless interview room, lying, justifying . . . 'Ambition in a bikini,' Hump had said once, but it had turned out to be more like a pair of harem pants and a diamond toe ring – materialism disguised by spirituality, ruthlessness hidden by a smile. At least in a bikini there was nowhere to hide.

She walked up the porch steps and opened the screen door. 'I'm home,' she called, hearing voices in the kitchen.

They fell quiet, only the sound of her feet to be heard on the wooden floor. 'What?' she asked, leaning against the doorframe and looking in.

Hump (looking dreadful) and Bobbi stared back at her.

And—

'Matt!' she gasped, running over to him, her arms around him before he'd even risen from the chair. He laughed as she buried her face in his neck, tears spilling helplessly from her as his presence marked the sudden end of the dream, the nightmare, the pause. He was her safety – always had been – and finding him sitting in this kitchen pressed 'play' in her again, releasing her from the freeze-frame she'd been stuck in since that windy March day in the park.

He said nothing as she sat on his lap, sobbing, his tanned hands rubbing her back slowly as everyone else discreetly scarpered – Hump, no doubt, to bed. He looked like he'd been up all night.

'W-what are you doing here?' she hiccupped, finally drawing back and looking at him, her hands running tentatively over the dark fuzz that was still too short to flop but could only bristle beneath her palm.

'We got to Phnom Penh on Thursday and I visited an internet cafe to pick up emails. There was one from my father saying he'd read an article in the papers about a murder in the Hamptons – and citing *you* as a witness.'

Ro blinked as she saw the hurt in his eyes, picked up on the glint of bitterness in his words. He had been worried; now he was angry – she had specifically told him everything was fine.

'It wasn't as bad as that makes it sound. I didn't see it happen,' she said quickly. 'And I didn't lie to you, Matt. It happened after we last talked.' During, actually, but she shrugged the thought away. It was academic now.

'But a *murder*, Ro.' His voice cracked, hoarse, as he shook his head sadly. 'What the hell have you got yourself into out here?'

There it was again – the suggestion that she'd floundered in his absence, got it wrong, made poor decisions . . . The decision that had felt most true, most right, swam into focus again and she rose quickly from his lap, walking over to the sink to wash her face, trying to hide the truth he would surely see in her eyes.

'Would you have told me about last night, or would I have had to find that out on the internet too?' he asked, watching her back.

She turned off the tap, shaking the droplets off her hands slowly. He knew about Melodie already?

'Hump was dropped back in a police car,' he elaborated. 'I was sitting outside on the steps wondering where the hell you all were. He explained everything.'

'Oh.' She turned back to him, stubbing the floor with her toes. She couldn't find her voice, couldn't meet his eyes.

Matt waited as she said nothing, his thighs beginning to jig from the frustration that she'd hidden so much, cut him out . . . 'Well? You find out your friend killed a man, but that doesn't warrant letting me know?'

'Look, we found out *last night* – what did you expect me

to do? And what could you have done?' She saw his expression. 'What? Don't look at me like that. I'm not as helpless as you think. I've got my friends. We've been getting through it all together, OK?'

'Oh, they were scalded in a random attack too, were they?' he asked, the sarcasm out and proud now.

'Trust me, everyone's had something going on. Bobbi, Greg, Hump . . .' Understatement of the century.

They fell quiet, neither of them wanting to argue, both aware it was supposed to be a happy moment. She realized she hadn't kissed him yet and she looked away again. It wasn't the right time now. Or was it that it wasn't . . . right?

Matt rubbed his face in his hands. 'Sorry, I . . . I'm shattered; I've barely slept in thirty-six hours.'

'No,' she sighed, relenting just as quickly. 'So much has happened and I'm just thrown that you're here, that's all.' She gave a small, dry laugh. 'After all those weeks counting down the days and suddenly – bam! – here you are, before schedule. Didn't see *that* coming.' She shrugged. 'I just can't quite get my head round it yet. Shock. I guess.'

Matt looked around the tatty old 1950s kitchen. 'It's nice here,' he said after a while.

'Thanks. I love it.' She nodded, trying to see it through fresh eyes again, but it was impossible. It had become home now, as familiar as a favourite jumper. She watched him taking it in, trying to imagine the conversations she'd had in here, the hung-over breakfasts, the clamour in the mornings for the last of the marmalade . . .

A thought occurred to her suddenly – she still had two weeks to run on her rental agreement. What happened now? Did Matt expect her to pack up and go home with him? Was he going to stay on here with her? She knew Hump wouldn't refuse her request if she asked, but she couldn't see it – life here with him. It was hers, sweet and precious to her, like a flame she'd kindled from a spark and that was finally giving out some heat. No, it didn't fit. His return meant her summer was over. It was time to go back to real life.

She thought of what she was leaving behind, who . . . and a shiver of tears caught her off guard. She turned quickly and filled the kettle, keeping her back to him as she imagined Ted waking to her text this morning. The very thought of it made her crumple and she knew that alone was proof that it was better this way. She had to go, and the sooner the better.

She blinked the tears out of her eyes and turned. 'Tea?'

Matt was watching her. 'I can't believe how blonde you've gone. It suits you. And that haircut . . . How have I never noticed your neck before? I thought I knew all of you, every last bit.'

She felt herself blush and tried to smile, tucking her hair self-consciously behind one ear.

'You've lost weight too.'

'Have I?' She looked down at herself, still in yesterday's clothes, her feet tanned and bare on the lino floor. She didn't want his compliments or attentions. She was scared of the scrutiny, worried he could see . . . sense the betrayal, the real reason she was different.

He got up and walked over to her, lacing his hands behind her back. 'God, I missed you more than I thought humanly possible.' He kissed her lightly on the lips, his eyes beginning to dance. 'Want to show me your room?'

'But . . .' She looked up at him, startled, feeling actual panic trammel through her. 'I mean . . . what about your tea? You've had a long journey.'

'*Tea?*' he laughed softly. 'Trust me, it's not tea that's going to make me feel better.' His hands began skimming up her and she gave a nervous laugh, wriggling out of his grip and almost running over to the tea caddy.

'Well, I really need one. Badly,' she said in the lightest tone she could muster, plunging her hand into the tin of teabags and hiding her face from view. 'I think . . . I think last night's revelations . . .' She turned back to him, trying to smile. 'You know?'

Matt stood in the middle of the kitchen, his eyes watching her closely like he was examining her, pinpointing all the microscopic changes in her since they'd last met – not just the hair and tan and weight loss, the clothes and new muscle tone and good posture that came from a summer of yoga. There was more besides. 'Ro?'

Something was ringing out like a bell to him, soundless to her. He was guessing it, beginning to suspect, the questions he could feel in his heart starting to spread, like iodine in the blood, to his head.

'Let's go out!' she blurted.

'Huh?'

'Yes, I . . . I want to show you around. We'll go to the beach and then we can have brunch at Colette's.' They could not. She knew she couldn't stomach a thing, but she had to get him out of here, stop the questions in their tracks. 'They do amazing flagels.'

He laughed. 'What the hell is a flagel?'

'Trust me,' she said, grabbing her handbag from the

table and pulling him along by the hand, anything to stop the scrutiny. 'You're going to love them.'

She sat on the handlebars as Matt pedalled the bright yellow bike, Ro indicating for him when to turn left and right with her arms. She shrieked when he wobbled the bike deliberately on the lane, laughed when he rang the bell so that it vibrated against her bottom, but she felt like an actress playing a part in a film.

They stopped by Florence's gates as they passed, picking up the last of the seed bombs sitting in brown paper bags in the barrow. It hadn't been refreshed today and some of them had dried out and cracked in the sun, beginning to crumble.

'They look like truffles,' Matt said.

'I know, right?' Ro smiled as she watched him sniffing one.

He wrinkled his nose, unimpressed. 'And you're seriously telling me this little nugget's going to protect the town from the next hurricane?' Scepticism hung off his words like cobwebs.

'Indirectly. From small acorns . . .'

He heard the piquant note in her voice and relented. 'Well, if you believe it, so do I.' And he kissed her on the forehead as they pulled off their shoes and walked onto the sand. 'So what do we do?'

'Just throw them into the dunes and wherever they fall, they'll sprout.'

'Well, we should probably go along a bit, don't you think? I bet most people chuck theirs for the first fifty metres and then nothing at all for the rest of the stretch.'

'OK.'

545

'Bloody hell, this beach is long,' he said after a while, squinting into the sunlight, his feet unsteady in the deep, dry sand.

'I know.' She looked out over the water as they walked. The water was meek today, turning onto the beach in gentle roly-polies instead of the usual pounding that smashed the water like broken glass. The memory of the day Ted had waded into the surf with her – their first touch – swam in front of her eyes, making them fill with tears in an instant, and she looked away again quickly.

'D'you want some?' Matt asked, holding out the bag for her to take a handful of bombs.

'No, you do it. I've thrown plenty of bombs this summer.'

His eyes met hers briefly – quizzically – before he started throwing them, succumbing immediately to the usual male prerogative to throw it like a cricket ball as far as he could. 'Gotta get them along the back too.'

'Of course.'

They walked haltingly along, making up for the long, slightly awkward silences with reassuring smiles. They were both tired and overtaken by events. But they were going to have to go back to the house – and her bedroom – sooner or later.

'He's not a pudding, by the way,' Matt said, reaching for her hand and trying to draw her back into his orbit.

'Who's not?'

'Hump. You called him a pudding.'

'Did I?' Ro frowned, unable to remember.

Matt grinned, squeezing her hand in his. 'I'd have been home a lot sooner if I'd set eyes on him before. You know we spoke on Skype, right? You'd gone out.'

Ro smiled weakly at his light-hearted assumption that it

was Hump who was his greatest threat. 'Uh, yes. He mentioned it.'

She heard the flimsy link chain that kept strangers out of Florence's garden rattling gently in the breeze just ahead. It was more an appeal to their manners than a strict enforcement of her rights to privacy, but everyone obliged. Well, apart from one . . . Was it really only last night she'd been standing here by torchlight with Greg and Bobbi, preparing to confront Brook?

'It's just like in the films, isn't it?' Matt said, looking at the rickety wooden bridge and platform that protected the dunes from the residents' historic rights to access. It lay stretched above the sand like dinosaur claws. 'Tch, how the other half live, right?' Matt mused, stopping and staring at the gabled rooftop of Grey Mists. The roof was pretty much all that could be seen of the house from here.

'Yeah,' she nodded. He had no way of knowing it was Florence's house, and she had no intention of telling him. The name brought too many associations for him – different ones for her – and she didn't want the questions to start up again.

He looked up and down the beach. It hadn't yet filled up for the day, and most people were walking down by the shore.

'D'you know what? Fuck it, I'm going to be nosy,' he grinned, scrunching the paper bag tightly in one hand and ducking quickly under the chain.

'What? No, Matt! You can't!'

'Relax – I'm just having a look. No one's around.'

'Matt, stop it. Come back here!' she said, ducking under the chain herself and running after him. But he was already bounding up the spindly wooden steps, two at a time, and cresting the top of the dunes, the house and garden already now on a level with him. 'It's private, Matt, for God's s—' She fell silent.

'Shit, that's embarrassing,' Matt said, dipping his chin and turning away as he scratched his head. 'What are the chances of someone being in the bloody garden?'

On a Saturday morning in late August? Pretty damn high, actually! She'd have told him that if he'd given her the chance. But she didn't say a word. She couldn't. All she could do was stare back at Ted standing stock-still on the lawn, wearing his trunks and holding a beach ball under his arm. She could guess where the children were from the splashes in the pool behind him.

'Come on.' Matt grabbed her limp hand, pulling her away. 'Let's just go.'

But her feet wouldn't move, she felt as planted as an oak, and she almost tripped as Matt's strength overrode hers, lurching her onwards suddenly. She turned back as Matt led her towards the steps, her hand in his. Ted was still watching, the ball bouncing to a stop by his feet now, Ella and Finn running across the grass with orange water pistols as water droplets flew off them like shaking Labradors – their family of three just as she'd found it and like she'd never been there at all.

# Chapter Thirty-Five

The coffees were a hit, the flagels rather less so, and window-shopping was a complete misnomer for the brisk walk past the designer boutiques that Matt could ill afford after a six-month sabbatical (well, five and a half) from work.

They were home again within the hour, and on the way back she didn't laugh at all as he pinged the bell against her bottom, her knuckles white as she gripped the handle-bars tightly. When Greg walked into the kitchen, fifteen minutes after they got home, he found them sitting at the kitchen table, steaming cups of tea beside them in the ninety-degree heat.

'Hey,' Ro said, her head jerking up as she heard the screen door close in the hall.

Greg walked in, his jacket slung tiredly over one shoulder. He looked startled as he saw Matt sitting with her, but seemed to guess his identity quickly, from their intimate body language.

Ro withdrew her hands from Matt's grasp and sat straighter at the table. 'Greg, this is Matt. Matt, my house-mate Greg. Otherwise known as Gatsby . . .'

'Gatsby, right . . . Pleased to meet you, mate,' Matt nodded, as the two of them shook hands. Ro thought

Matt looked faintly ridiculous in his pumpkin-coloured, three-quarter-length linen trousers, compared to Greg's – albeit crumpled – Ralph Lauren Black Label suit. They smiled briefly, but Matt could see now wasn't the time for small talk. Greg looked like hell.

'You look terrible,' Ro said quietly, as Greg threw his suit jacket over the chair. 'Have you slept?'

'I've been at the police station all night,' he shrugged. 'I figured Brook needed some support. He's not taking it well.'

'I'm not surprised. Neither's Hump from the looks of him.'

'Poor guy.' Greg shook his head. 'He looked as sick as Brook when we walked back into the house. I think he'd really fallen for her. The only once since Mei.'

Ro bit her lip, knowing that for the moment at least, Hump's heartbreak would have to fade into the background – as Greg's had – in the face of Melodie's darker desires. 'So what's she saying?' Ro wasn't sure she wanted to know.

Greg slumped back in the chair, one arm slung out along the table. He shook his head, a depressed look on his face. 'I think it's going to come down to plain old greed. She said she was trying to get back what her family had lost.'

Matt coughed lightly. 'What *had* they lost?'

Greg looked back at him. As Ro's boyfriend, he was unspokenly, automatically, on honorary housemate status and entitled to full disclosure. 'They're one of the old families around here, but they lost their money in quite spectacular style. Everyone knows the stories and their name was mud for a long time.' He looked back at Ro. 'Erin's family knew them and she said it was only when

Melodie inherited what little was left and got Barrington Dredging turning a profit again that attitudes towards the family softened. She was an only child and always seemed the black sheep in her family . . . capable, driven. Ambitious in every sense, I think they said.'

Ro frowned. 'But if everyone knew her family, then they must have known too that her name wasn't really Melodie? Didn't people think it was odd that she'd changed it from Samantha?'

'No. It was just a nickname that stuck. There was never any reason to suppose there was more to it than that.'

Ro sighed.

'What about Brook? Was he in on it?'

'From the looks of him, I don't think so. You can't fake that kind of shock.' Greg stared at his hands. 'Personally, I think Melo—' He stopped himself. 'I think Samantha saw an opportunity in him and took it – secretly accessing his confidential material to identify which properties were uninsurable, while publicly encouraging his political ambitions to benefit her investments. Poor guy never suspected a thing, it seems. To be honest, I wouldn't be surprised if that was why she married him in the first place.'

'Maybe,' Ro nodded. 'She certainly never seemed to like him much. Florence, on the other hand – she was really worried about him after you left.'

Greg looked at her, weighing up the light insinuation – it made surprising sense – before shrugging. 'Well, he's going to need all the friends he can get in the next few months. It's not going to be pretty. Samantha seems to have had it all worked out. When you take into account the over-dredging by the family company too: she was exacerbating local erosion on the one hand and slowly buying up the depreciated lots on the other – she played a long game. She was prepared to wait.' He was quiet for a second and he rubbed a hand over his tired eyes as more facts fell into place. 'Jeez, Sandy must have seemed heaven-sent to her. It delivered everything to her in one neat chunk.'

'Thanks to Kevin.'

'Yes,' he murmured. 'Bobbi . . .' His voice trailed off, but Ro knew what he was thinking – how close Bobbi had come to real danger herself. His face darkened and he pushed himself away from the table and stretched his legs out, staring at his feet. 'Did she say why she . . . y'know . . . Kevin?' Ro asked, watching him brood.

'Well, not in front of me, although obviously the police have been questioning her all night, so . . .' He groaned. 'Christ, who knows how she justified it in her head? Maybe he'd outlived his usefulness to her once she'd secured her ownership of the wharves? She didn't want any witnesses? Or maybe because of his boasting on LinkedIn? That created a link to a company she'd gone to great lengths to keep hidden.' He shrugged.

Ro fell still, remembering Melodie's expression change as she'd described Kevin to her before the yoga class. She'd thought Melodie had disapproved of Bobbi's overt materialism, caring about his car and job title over his distinctive gait, but . . . She went cold. Had Melodie been alerted to Kevin's boastful indiscretions because of what *she'd* said?

Greg suppressed a yawn. 'Mmgh, sorry.'

Ro winced, her attention drawn back to him. 'Oh, Greg, what are you doing here talking to us? Go to bed.'

'If only I could,' he sighed, checking his watch. 'But I'm competing this afternoon. I've only come back to get changed.'

'Changed?' she frowned. 'Why? Where on earth are you going?'

'The Classic. I'm in the showjumping class.'

'The thing at Bridgehampton? You can't be serious!' she exclaimed. 'You can't possibly sit on the back of a horse and jump—'

'Two-metre jumps on two hours' sleep? I agree. But I have very little choice. I'm already committed.' He rose wearily, patting her hand. 'You'll have to sleep for me.'

'Oh, *you're* back,' Bobbi said loudly to Greg with her usual dismissive tone – normal service resumed – as she wandered downstairs towards the kitchen. 'I was coming to check on Ro.' She saw Matt as she rounded the door and gave him a dazzlingly friendly smile. 'Oh, hey, Matt.' The snub to Greg was all the more pointed by contrast.

'It's just as well you're so damned loud,' Greg said, talking over her so that Bobbi looked over at him in astonishment. 'At least now I know you hate me because you're crazy about me.'

Silence exploded around them all in a sonic boom. Ro dimly remembered the open window in Bobbi's room yesterday – it was when she was closing it that she'd seen the necklace and everything had unravelled. Matt looked on nervously as he sensed the sudden tension.

'I'm not crazy about *you*!' Bobbi stormed.

Greg stared back at her, his hands stuffed in his pockets and his eyes absolutely and intently upon her, not fooled. He looked as calm as Bobbi looked shaken, and he walked over to her, stopping only inches away, his head bent to hers. 'Well, then that's a shame,' he said quietly, his eyes scanning her beautiful, proud, frightened face. 'Because you're all I'm able to think about.'

No one in the room – Matt included – dared move as he carried on looking down at her, before he walked out of the kitchen and up the stairs. Bobbi stared open-mouthed after him.

'Did he . . . did he . . . ?' she whispered, her eyes locked and hopeful on Ro's.

Ro grinned. 'He did.'

Bobbi rushed over to the table and sat down where Greg had been sitting moments earlier, her hands clasped on Ro's, seemingly oblivious to the fact that Matt was still there.

'So then what should I do? I mean, what should I . . . ? Should I *follow* him?'

Ro was silent for a moment. 'Yeah, you have to tell him how you feel, Bobs.'

Bobbi beamed, her eyes alive with delight. "Cos when you know, you know, righ—' She stopped mid-flow, a shaft of sunlight winkled into her eye by the pretty diamond sitting unobtrusively on the table between them.

'That's right,' Ro smiled, looking back at Matt. 'When you know, you know.'

Ro walked slowly through the crowd, pushing her hair back from her face with one hand and keeping down the hem of her dress with the other. There was a gusty wind making a mockery of silk wrappings today and half the women were scaring the horses.

It was hot, though, the breeze but momentary relief, and Ro stopped to watch as the horses in the exercise ring were hosed down, their blue veins bulging beneath velvety hides. She could see Bobbi sitting up in the stands, almost hyperventilating with excitement as she waited for Greg's round and trying to hide it by being particularly fussy about the size of the woman's hat in front of her. There was no question of *her* getting the coffees – her hands were almost continuously shaking with nerves. Ro looked down at her own hands, instinctively cupping the left in the right, as she continued putting one foot in front of the other. That was all she had to keep doing. She had done the right thing.

'Ro!' a voice shrieked, carrying over the rumbles of the crowd and snorting horses, and she turned just in time to see Ella – almost dropping her ice cream on the ground – breaking free from her grandmother's grasp and running towards her.

'Ro!' she shrieked again, launching herself so that Ro had to scoop to catch her mid-air, catching a shoulderful of vanilla ice cream in the process.

'Whoopsie!' Ro laughed, squeezing her tightly as Florence approached with Finn, sleeping in his buggy with Boo.

'You didn't say you were coming to this,' Florence smiled, putting on the footbrake. She looked exhausted. She had been through too much recently. 'We could have come together.'

'I-I didn't know I was coming, to be honest.' She swallowed, thinking how much had happened even in the time since she'd left Florence at breakfast. 'But I thought it would be better to stay busy ... My housemate Greg's competing.'

'So's Daddy! Daddy's winning!' Ella said, kicking her legs alternately with excitement.

Ro stiffened. Ted was *here*? He rode?

'Ella, Daddy hasn't ridden yet – don't tell fibs,' Florence

said, leaning over and affectionately kissing the top of her head. 'His team's next.'

Ted and Greg rode on the same showjumping team? She remembered Greg's quiet approval after Hump had spilt the beans about her and Ted last weekend, Ted's attendance at the Southampton fundraiser – so then he wasn't one of that crew's ghastly social climbers? He and Greg were friends. Somehow that fact seemed like a further – albeit unneeded – character reference for them both.

'Where are you sitting? Would you like to join us?' Florence asked, intruding upon her thoughts.

'Oh . . . uh, I'd have loved to, but we're already seated. I'm just on a coffee run. But why don't you sit with us? Bobbi's just over there in the East Stand, behind the woman in the straw hat.'

'We'd love to . . . Is Hump with you?' Florence asked, concern clouding her face.

'No. He said he wanted to be alone today.'

'Yes, Brook's the same, understandably.'

Ro fell quiet for a moment – knowing the emotional clean-up had begun for them all – before realizing Florence was looking at her. As they looked at one another, she instinctively sensed there was something unsaid between them. After everything they'd been through, there was only one secret remaining between them. But how could Ro tell it, to Florence of all people?

'Uh, would you like a coffee? I'll bring it over.'

Florence hesitated a second, before smiling. 'That would be lovely.'

'Daddy!' Ella's legs began waggling again as Ro held her, and she looked round to see Ted on the far side of the exercise ring, coming out of one of the horseboxes.

'Oh, look, Finn! There's Daddy,' Florence said, pointing to his father.

They watched Ted fasten the box door behind him, his hat under one arm, his head bent to the ground as he checked his phone.

Was he reading her text again? Did he hate her? Ro didn't realize she was holding her breath as she watched him put his phone to his ear.

Julianne. He was calling Julianne.

Her phone rang in her bag, making her jump, and Florence look over at her – and then back to Ted again. He began pacing, his riding hat still tucked under one arm, as the phone rang like a buzzing wasp determined to make her move.

But Ro couldn't move. How could she possibly pick up in front of Florence? The conversation they would have . . .

'Daddy!' Ella yelled again, and this time he heard, looking up and spotting them. He fell still as he saw all of them together – Ro standing with Florence and the children, Ella on her hip – his arm holding the phone dropping away from his ear.

Ro felt her mouth dry up and her heart take on an ad-lib rhythm as he pocketed the phone and slowly walked towards them, looking so good it was wrong in cream jodhpurs, black boots and navy hacking jacket. She couldn't move, couldn't blink, couldn't breathe. She certainly didn't notice that Florence was watching her.

'Ted came over this morning actually. You just missed him.'

Ro looked back at her, feeling every sinew in her body tighten. 'Really?' It was supposed to be a deflection, a polite social move during the course of a casual conversation, but instead the word was like an arrow, pointing out her heartache as her voice trembled, barely able to carry the lie she had to carry, for Florence's sake.

'Yes, he looked dreadful.'

'Oh.' Oh God. Oh God.

'As you do now, in fact,' Florence said, taking a step closer to her and gently placing a hand on Ro's arm. 'He told me everything, Ro. I know you know about Marina –'

Ro's eyes filled instantly with tears as she heard the break in the mother's voice on speaking her daughter's name. She nodded.

'And I'm sorry I didn't share it with you myself. It's just that the words are . . . they're too . . .' Florence cleared her throat, shaking her head as her grey eyes clouded with tears that wouldn't fall – not in front of the children. 'I just can't say them, you see. Not yet. Even after three years.'

Ro nodded, desperation in her eyes, wanting to say that she understood, but knowing that there could be no further elaboration than that here. Ella was watching.

'The day-to-day, that's what I focus on – issues that are bigger than me. And my grandchildren, of course – always them,' Florence said, a smile growing in her desolate eyes as she reached over and took Ella from Ro's arms. 'But I do know one thing, Ro. Marina would never have wanted Ted to be unhappy.' Ro looked at her and she saw tears in the mother's eyes. 'And I know she would have just adored you. As we all do.'

'M-me?' Ro blinked.

'She couldn't lie either,' Florence nodded, smiling even as a single teardrop fell, kissing her on the cheek. 'Come on, Ella, let's go find our seats.'

Ro watched them go, unaware of the wind's mischief with her skirt or the way Ted caught his breath as he approached.

He stopped as she turned, and her eyes met his. He opened his mouth as if to speak, but no sound came, and he just nodded instead. They were quiet for a long time, neither one knowing where to start, after her text.

'So, that was him earlier?'

'Yes.' Her voice was tiny. 'I'm so sorry about that. He didn't know it was . . . y'know, Florence's house.' She coughed, trying to clear her throat, make herself heard. 'Your house. He was being nosy and got carried away.'

'I didn't care about that.'

That? Meaning the breach of privacy? She swallowed. 'He didn't know about . . .' Her voice trailed off.

'Us?'

Us. Collective pronoun. An embrace in a word. A family in a sound. An entire world encapsulated in just two letters: him and her. Them and the children. Them all and Florence.

'No.'

They stared at each other. Had it really been just seven days ago that they'd been sailing over the Sound, running towards each other at warp speed? Only seven days ago that she was lying in his arms as the simple truth that had been in his eyes at every awkward, confused, kind and hostile encounter between them finally tackled her to the ground?

'But he knows now.'

She blinked and nodded. Matt had known it before she'd put voice to the words in the kitchen, his eyes reading her like scans as she tried to hide her feelings behind blood and bone. But he knew her too well, he had loved her too long, and the secret in her heart was a black mass that he could read. He hadn't even been angry; his blue eyes had shone as despair mingled with the will to fight. He understood how it could happen – she'd set up a life here, made friends, good ones; he could see that himself.

'He knows, but he thinks it isn't real.'

The tannoy boomed suddenly and they heard Ted's named called up. He was on.

'Well . . . maybe it wasn't,' he said quietly, even as he stared at her with hungry eyes, soaking her up as if for the last time. He turned, his head down as he unclasped the chinstrap of his riding hat and put it on.

Ro watched him go, her heart drumming like horse's hooves, her body bruising already from the words that what was between them was imagined, ephemeral, an illusion.

She watched as he ducked under the bars of the exercise ring and took the reins with a nod from the groom who'd been walking the horse. He put a foot in one stirrup and swiftly, easily, swung his other leg over the horse's back. He sat up straight, looking so strong and magnificent, everyone's eyes on him, and she didn't understand, didn't believe he could ever have been serious about her. Maybe he was right. Maybe Matt was right. It had been a dream.

He pulled back on the reins and the horse whinnied, taking three steps backwards. Ted turned, looking over at her still standing where he'd left her – unable to move, to turn her back on them – his eyes almost shaded from her by the peak of the hat. Almost, but not quite – and the desolation she saw there . . . One dream had already died today.

'You're wrong!' she blurted out, running over to the bars of the ring. 'It *is* real. I told him that.' He looked back at her in astonishment, the horse pulling him forward a little as it tugged on the reins, dipping its head. 'Can . . . can I . . . ?' she asked everyone and no one, ducking under anyway and running up to him before the steward could catch her.

'I said "no"! It was he and I who were dreaming thinking that the solution to being together lay in being apart. There's no rewind in real life! There's no pause in real love! It either grows or dies. And we died the day he left, though neither of us knew it at the time,' she said, almost panting from the effort of articulating the burden she'd been living under. 'I feel like I've spent these six months grieving for him, trying to hold myself back in one life all the while a new one built up around me.' She swallowed. 'But you're what's real for me. You and Ella and Finn and Florence. You're my family.' The last word came out as a sob and she couldn't see him as the tears blinded her eyes, leaving her wretched and shaking in the exercise ring. She didn't see him jump down, just felt the grip of his hands on her arms as he pulled her in to him, his kiss the only answer she needed.

Somewhere, far away, she was aware of cheers and some applause. Maybe it was for the other rider? Maybe not. She didn't care, for once, if people were staring.

He pulled away, eyes dancing. 'Just stay there – don't move,' he murmured, grinning. 'I'll be right back.'

She nodded and laughed as he jumped on the horse and cantered into the show ring, her hands flying to her mouth in delight as he punched the air victoriously before the judges and the crowd, as though he'd already won. But then, they both had.

As she watched him steady the horse for the bell, she remembered how six months ago, all she'd wanted was a happy ending, but she'd come out here and found, instead, a bright new beginning. She could never have known they were one and the same thing.

Her eyes shone as she watched him set off – *hers* at last. It had been a complicated love story to get here, a long story. And it was only going to get longer.

# Acknowledgements

I travelled to the Hamptons to research this book, and most of Ro's teething troubles were my own – driving badly from JFK airport, coming to terms with flagels and complicated coffees . . . Much of what you read about the setting is technically accurate – the square in Amagansett, for example, where Ro and Hump's studio is, Mary's Marvellous, their local coffee shop, the Maidstone Club and, of course, East Hampton itself with its three Ralph Lauren stores (still gobsmacked by that), the hardware store, bookstore . . . But it should be said that plot-wise, what you read is completely fictitious. There is indeed a Coastal Erosion Committee, there is indeed a LWRP and Strategic Retreat is a real policy, but I have manipulated reports/recommendations entirely for the purposes of the story and to my knowledge there has never been a murder at the Maidstone Club!

This book owes a huge debt to my editor, Caroline Hogg, who was endlessly patient as I wrote, then re-wrote, and then re-wrote it again. Also, my copy-editor, Laura Collins, who unpicked and realigned the all-important timeline for the story, thus giving it its emotional power. If this book succeeds at all, it is because of the transformative powers of editing, and I thank everyone who has collaborated on it with me.

Amanda Preston, you are now up there with my husband and children as I say to you: Never leave me!

To my parents and my parents-in-law, thank you for enabling me to have it all – the career and the kids. I couldn't meet my deadlines without you, knowing that the children are adored, safe . . . and being plied with sweets. And to Anders and our babes, you are my hub, my heart, my home.

# *Prima Donna*

by

# KAREN SWAN

**Breaking the rules was what she liked best.
That was her sport. Renegade, rebel, bad girl.
Getting away with it.**

Pia Soto is the sexy and glamorous prima ballerina, the Brazilian bombshell, who's shaking up the ballet world with her outrageous behaviour. She's wild and precocious, and she's a survivor. She's determined that no man will ever control her destiny. But ruthless financier Will Silk has Pia in his sights, and has other ideas . . .

Sophie O'Farrell is Pia's hapless, gawky assistant, the girl-next-door to Pia's prima donna, always either falling in love with the wrong man or just falling over. Sophie sets her own dreams aside to pick up the debris in Pia's wake, but she's no angel, and when a devastating accident threatens to cut short Pia's illustrious career, Sophie has to step out of the shadows and face up to the demons in her own life.

ISBN: 978-1-4472-2374-0

# Players

by

# KAREN SWAN

**Friendships are strong. Lust is stronger . . .**

*Harry Hunter was everywhere you looked – bearing down
from bus billboards, beaming out from the society pages,
falling out of nightclubs in the gossip columns, and
flirting up a storm on the telly chat show circuit.*

Harry Hunter is the new golden boy of the literary scene.
With his books selling by the millions, the paparazzi on his
tail, and a supermodel on each arm, he seems to have the
world at his feet. Women all over the globe adore him but
few suspect that his angelic looks hide a darker side, a side
that conceals a lifetime of lies and deceit.

Tor, Cress and Kate have been best friends for as long as they
can remember. Through all the challenges of marriage, raising children and maintaining their high-flying careers, they
have stuck together as a powerful and loyal force to be reckoned with – living proof that twenty-first-century women
can have it all, and do. It is only when the captivating Harry
comes into their lives that things begin to get complicated, as
Tor, Cress and Kate are drawn into Harry's dangerous games.

ISBN: 978-1-4472-2373-3

# *Christmas at Tiffany's*

by

# KAREN SWAN

**Three cities, three seasons,
one chance to find the life that fits**

Cassie settled down too young, marrying her first serious boyfriend. Now, ten years later, she is betrayed and broken. With her marriage in tatters and no career or home of her own, she needs to work out where she belongs in the world and who she really is.

So begins a year-long trial as Cassie leaves her sheltered life in rural Scotland to stay with each of her best friends in the most glamorous cities in the world: New York, Paris and London. Exchanging the grouse moor and mousy hair for low-carb diets and high-end highlights, Cassie tries on each city for size as she attempts to track down the life she was supposed to have been leading, and with it, the man who was supposed to love her all along.

ISBN: 978-0-330-53272-3

# The Perfect Present

by

# KAREN SWAN

**Memories are a gift . . .**

Haunted by a past she can't escape, Laura Cunningham desires nothing more than to keep her world small and precise – her quiet relationship and growing jewellery business are all she needs to get by. Until the day when Rob Blake walks into her studio and commissions a necklace that will tell his enigmatic wife Cat's life in charms.

As Laura interviews Cat's family, friends and former lovers, she steps out of her world and into theirs – a charmed world where weekends are spent in Verbier and the air is lavender-scented, where friends are wild, extravagant and jealous, and a big love has to compete with grand passions.

Hearts are opened, secrets revealed and as the necklace begins to fill up with trinkets, Cat's intoxicating life envelops Laura's own. By the time she has to identify the final charm, Laura's metamorphosis is almost complete. But the last story left to tell has the power to change all of their lives forever, and Laura is forced to choose between who she really is and who it is she wants to be.

ISBN: 978-0-330-53273-0

# *Christmas at Claridge's*

by

# KAREN SWAN

**The best presents can't be wrapped**

Portobello – home to the world-famous street market, Notting Hill Carnival . . . and Clem Alderton. She's the queen of the scene, the girl everyone wants to be or be with. But beneath the morning-after make-up, Clem is keeping a secret, and when she goes too far one reckless night she endangers everything – her home, her job and even her adored brother's love.

Portofino – a place of wild beauty and old-school glamour. Clem has been here once before and vowed never to return. But when a handsome stranger asks Clem to restore a neglected villa, it seems like the answer to her problems – if she can just face up to her past.

Claridge's – at Christmas, Clem is back in London working on a special commission for London's grandest hotel. But is this where her heart really lies?

ISBN: 978-1-4472-1969-9

extracts reading groups
competitions books new
discounts extracts extracts discounts
competitions extracts
books new extracts
events books
new books extracts
new titles reading groups
interviews
events extracts extracts
discounts books
new books events events
events new books extracts
discounts extracts discounts
www.panmacmillan.com
extracts events reading groups
competitions books extracts new